TO MARRY
AND TO
MEDDLE

Also by Martha Waters

To Love and to Loathe

To Have and to Hoax

TO MARRY AND TO MEDDLE

A Novel

MARTHA WATERS

ATRIA PAPERBACK

New York   London   Toronto   Sydney   New Delhi

ATRIA
PAPERBACK

An Imprint of Simon & Schuster, Inc.
1230 Avenue of the Americas
New York, NY 10020

First Atria Paperback edition April 2022

ATRIA PAPERBACK and colophon are trademarks of Simon & Schuster, Inc.

For information about special discounts for bulk purchases, please contact Simon & Schuster Special Sales at 1-866-506-1949 or business@simonandschuster.com.

The Simon & Schuster Speakers Bureau can bring authors to your live event. For more information or to book an event, contact the Simon & Schuster Speakers Bureau at 1-866-248-3049 or visit our website at www.simonspeakers.com.

Interior design by Kathryn A. Kenney-Peterson

Manufactured in the United States of America

1   3   5   7   9   10   8   6   4   2

Library of Congress Cataloging-in-Publication Data

Names: Waters, Martha, 1988– author. | Olson, Kaitlin, editor.
Title: To marry and to meddle / Martha Waters ; [Kaitlin Olson, editor].
Description: First Atria Paperback edition. | New York : Atria Paperback, 2022. | Series: The Regency Vows Series; 3
Identifiers: LCCN 2021044272 | ISBN 9781982190484 (paperback) | ISBN 9781982190491 (ebook)
Classification: LCC PS3623.A8689 T615 2022 | DDC 813/.6—dc23
LC record available at https://lccn.loc.gov/2021044272

ISBN 978-1-9821-9048-4
ISBN 978-1-9821-9049-1 (ebook)

This one is for me.

Prologue

London, 1813

In retrospect, things might have gone better if Julian hadn't been drunk.

Oh, he wasn't well and truly foxed; it was, after all, midmorning, and he'd been able to catch at least a few hours of sleep in the wake of a round of energetic if ultimately uninspiring bedsport, so he was reasonably coherent. But he was quite certain that there was still a fair amount of brandy sloshing around in his head, which might explain why it took him several repetitions to understand his father's demand.

"I want you to sell the Belfry."

An incredulous laugh escaped Julian, causing the lines on his father's face to deepen. They were in the study of Julian's recently purchased home on Duke Street—one of the only rooms in the house, in fact, that was fully furnished and decorated. There was an empty drawing room, and a dining room with only half the chairs that the table required, but at least this room offered him a quiet, peaceful place to retreat, to read, to attend to his correspondence.

At the moment, however, it was not feeling terribly quiet or peaceful—not with his father seated on the opposite side of his desk, frowning at him in that way he had done since Julian was a boy. The frown indicated severe displeasure with whatever happened to be Julian's latest indiscretion (these had ranged from being sent down from Eton for distributing lewd pamphlets—twice—to attempting to elope with the stablemaster's daughter, to name a couple).

Today, though, Julian wasn't even certain he *knew* what specific indiscretion had prompted this rather extraordinary demand, so he merely said, "You cannot be serious."

"I assure you, I am." His father, the Marquess of Eastvale, was a handsome man in his mid-fifties, his dark hair liberally streaked with gray, his blue eyes an identical shade to those of all three of his children. Those blue eyes currently regarded his youngest son with displeasure. "You've had your fun—and, in truth, you've turned the Belfry into a more profitable establishment than I would have thought possible when you purchased it. But enough is enough."

The Belfry was Julian's theater, purchased in a fit of youthful impetuousness (fueled by more than one bottle of brandy) five years earlier, when he'd finished at Oxford. At the time, it had been a derelict building with an appalling reputation, employing a company of actors whose enthusiasm vastly outstripped their talent. Julian—being a second son, and therefore mercifully free of the responsibilities that plagued his elder brother Robert—had hired a manager, invested a sizable portion of his inheritance in restoring the building, and then sat back and watched the gentlemen of the *ton* flood through the doors. Occasionally, when the fancy struck him, he went so far as to appear onstage himself, which had the added benefit of scandalizing the mamas of the *ton* sufficiently to prevent them from flinging their eligible daughters at him.

The venture had, in other words, overall proved to Julian to be entirely satisfactory. The tic in his father's jaw at the moment, however, indicated that *he* might feel otherwise.

"Your sister is about to make her debut into society," his father continued, leaning forward to rest an arm on the desk, tapping the wood with an index finger for emphasis. "The Belfry has been subject to more and more gossip of late—as has your ridiculous insistence on appearing onstage from time to time—and whilst your mother and I have been more than tolerant of this little lark of yours, we're not prepared to allow any gossip surrounding you to ruin your sister's chances."

Julian stiffened at those words: *this little lark*. He had always known, on some level, that this was how his parents viewed the Belfry—indeed, he'd initially had cause to be grateful for this fact, since it prevented them from getting too worked up when informed of its purchase. But now he bristled to hear it described so dismissively.

"The Belfry is my business, Father," he said, taking care to enunciate, as he always did when he was a bit the worse for drink. He spared a moment to cast a dark thought at the Julian of twelve hours earlier, who had cheerfully consumed "just one more glass" for several hours running. Had he realized he'd be meeting with his father—and therefore needing all of his wits about him—he certainly would have gone to bed sometime before dawn.

"The Belfry is turning into little more than a brothel, Julian," his father shot back.

"That's hardly a fair—"

"The Duke of Wildermere cavorting with an Italian opera singer in plain sight—not even in the privacy of a box," his father interrupted. "Lord Henry Cavendish reportedly appearing with a set of *triplets*—"

"They were twins," Julian said wearily. "The third lady was their cousin, I believe—they all evidently found it amusing that she resembles the other two so strongly."

"Oh, of course," the marquess said politely. "Then in that case, there was nothing at all untoward about the fact that he was seen kissing all three of them at various intervals throughout the evening."

Julian sighed. "I'll grant you, we've attracted our fair share of rowdy behavior—but that's why the gentlemen like it, don't you see? A place they can come with their mistresses, where there's no danger of running into friends of their wives?"

"I understand that it's a profitable venture," his father continued, and Julian momentarily brightened—perhaps this entire conversation could be wrapped up neatly, and he could see himself back to bed—"which is why I've no qualms about asking you to sell it."

"Father—"

"You've made a tidy profit already—more than recouped your initial investment, I should think. So there's no reason not to sell it now, and find some way to occupy your time that doesn't threaten your sister's matrimonial prospects."

"Frannie is going to be the most beautiful debutante of her year," Julian said quite truthfully. Eight years his junior, and now eighteen, his sister Frances was about to make her curtsey before the queen. Given her beauty—and the size of her dowry—he was not losing much sleep about any harm to her reputation a slightly scandalous brother might cause. "And furthermore, she's the daughter of a marquess who also happens to be one of the most respected men in England. I hardly think she'll be lacking in suitors."

"Julian, you seem to misunderstand the conversation we are having," his father said pleasantly. "I am not making a request—I am *telling* you that you will sell the Belfry."

"And what occupation do you have in mind for me, then?" Julian asked. "I'm a second son, in case you've forgotten—I'll need one." This was not entirely true—he had a sizable inheritance from a great-aunt who'd had an inexplicable fondness for her scapegrace of a nephew; furthermore, any profit he saw from selling the theater would likely have been sufficient to support him for years.

But Julian didn't want to become an idle gentleman of the *ton*, spending his days reading newspapers at White's and discussing horse-flesh at Tattersall's. While he'd had enough good sense to immediately hire a manager upon acquiring the Belfry, he still enjoyed maintaining an active role at the theater, giving his days some shape, lending himself some sense of purpose.

His father, however, was unmoved. "The clergy. The army."

Julian snorted. "The clergy would sooner have Lucifer himself in their service."

"And who can blame them?" the marquess muttered. "But I'd imagine His Majesty's army would be more than grateful for another officer in the fight against the French."

Julian stared at his father in disbelief. "You can't possibly think I'd make a suitable soldier. I've never willingly woken before noon."

"There's a first time for everything," the marquess said icily. "And if it kept you respectable enough to allow your sister to be married someday—and you as well, for that matter—I'd say it would be a sacrifice well worth making."

"Who said anything about *my* marriage?" Julian sputtered; this conversation, with its suggestions of the military—and matrimony!—was taking a decidedly dark turn.

"I'm not suggesting you book St. George's for next week," his father said calmly, "but it's something worth considering."

"This is absurd," Julian said. "I've no intention of marrying for another decade, and in the meantime, I don't see why I can't follow my own pursuits, if I've the funds to do so." While some small part of him, easily ignored, whispered that his father *did* have a point—that the Belfry's reputation, which Julian had always found somewhat entertaining, was truly becoming quite sordid indeed—this quiet voice was drowned out by the irritation coursing through him.

After all, why *shouldn't* he enjoy himself, with his own money, doing as he wished? If this conversation were anything to judge by, his father's plans for his future were nothing that Julian wanted any part of.

"Because your behavior reflects not just on yourself, but on this entire family," his father said coldly, his voice gone quiet—always a dangerous sign. "And I will not have you disgracing us."

Julian had to resist the urge to flinch. *Disgrace.* He didn't know why the word should land so sharply, but he felt it deep in his chest. He'd spent much of his adolescence and university years being something of a trial to his parents, and particularly to his father, who always seemed to require a great deal of patience when it came to accepting the fact that his youngest son was not at all like his father or brother. His purchase of the Belfry had merely been the latest in a yearslong series of antics that made his parents sigh and shake their heads.

But he realized, in that moment, that his father, while certainly disapproving of plenty of the trouble he'd gotten into over the years, had never once made Julian feel as though he were truly ashamed or embarrassed by him.

Until now.

"Is that what I am to you, then?" he asked, leaning forward in his seat, his eyes locked onto his father's. "A disgrace? An embarrassment?"

As he spoke, Julian felt as though he were unleashing a torrent of pent-up feeling, long unspoken. Had he not for years always wondered in the back of his mind if his father loved him as much as he loved Robert—if he truly loved his roguish second son, unable to resist the opportunity to cause trouble whenever it arose?

"You are my son," his father said, his own gaze unwavering. "And as your father, I am informing you that you'll sell the Belfry—or you won't see another penny from me."

"Fine," Julian said, his head beginning to pound, anger and brandy proving to be an unpleasant combination. "I don't need your money, Father—I've plenty of my own." He rose, and crossed the room to open the door. "Bramble can see you out."

"Julian," his father said, rising to his feet, then pausing, surveying his son. "I've humored you in your antics for years," he continued, his voice even. "A boy has to sow a few wild oats, after all. But I refuse to allow you to drag this family into scandal, and if you disobey me now, you'll not set foot through the doors of my house again until you've made things right."

This threat should have stopped Julian, or at least given him a moment's pause; the marquess was not a man to make threats of any sort lightly, and particularly not toward one of his own children.

But Julian was past such concerns. At the moment, he was consumed by a reckless, overpowering urge to show his father that he was his own man, someone to be treated as an equal, taken seriously, no matter what the cost of his actions.

"If you think I'm disgracing the family, then perhaps that's for the best. But I promise you that I can do much worse," he said, his voice soft.

"You'll know where to find me when you change your mind," his father said, his voice tight, as he passed through the doorway to the corridor where Julian's butler was waiting to show him out.

"I could say the same to you, Father," Julian replied. "The doors of the Belfry are always open to you, of course."

But it would prove to be quite some time before his father took him up on that offer.

One

The English countryside in early September was a glorious place. The sun shone. The bees buzzed. The heady scent of wildflowers lingered in the air.

Emily Turner could not think of a more romantic setting for the world's least romantic marriage proposal.

The trap had been sprung after breakfast—if *trap* could really be used to describe what had occurred. Namely: she had exited the breakfast room to find Lord Julian Belfry lurking just outside the doorway. *Lurking*, too, might not be an entirely fair choice of words, considering the gentleman in question made the action look far more appealing than implied.

But then, he made most things look appealing; he was tall and dark-haired and almost unfairly handsome, with icy blue eyes that had the unnerving knack of pinning one to the spot with the strength of their gaze. Or, at least, they certainly had that effect on Emily—she couldn't speak for the other ladies of the species, she supposed.

Mustering her sangfroid as best she could, however, she merely lifted her chin and said, "Lord Julian. Have you forgotten the way back to your room?"

"Entirely possible, given the size of this house," he responded lazily, one shoulder braced against the wall. The house in question was Elderwild, the country seat of the Marquess of Willingham, where she and Lord Julian were both currently guests at Lord Willingham's annual late-summer house party. "But in fact, I was waiting for you. Would you care to take a walk?"

She surveyed him for a long moment, weighing her response. "I should ask permission from Lady Willingham," she said demurely, naming the grandmother of the current marquess, who was—theoretically—Emily's chaperone, though she had not proved to be terribly attentive thus far.

"Of course," he agreed readily, and she was immediately suspicious, having expected some form of protest at these stipulations. After all, Julian Belfry—the black sheep of an aristocratic family, disinherited by his father, the owner of a *theater*, of all things—was not the sort of man to look fondly upon chaperones.

"In fact," he continued, "I've taken the liberty of asking Lady Willingham herself to accompany us, so that your virtue will be in no danger."

Emily opened her mouth to reply, but before she could speak, the unmistakable voice of the dowager marchioness rang down the corridor.

"Ah! There you are!"

Emily and Lord Julian turned. The dowager marchioness was in her seventies—Emily guessed; she was too fond of her own life and limbs to risk making any inquiries regarding specifics—and barely five feet tall, but she moved with surprising swiftness when she wished to.

"I understand we are to go for a walk in this charming weather?" the dowager marchioness asked as she joined them. She was wearing a gown of yellow muslin and had already donned a jaunty hat that involved an improbable amount of lace and feathers, and she looked eager to partake in a morning of sunshine and exercise. Emily had no objection to Lady Willingham's company; her friend Diana had arranged for Lord Willingham's grandmother to serve as her chaperone, and Emily had so far found the experience to be a marked improvement over her usual lot, which involved trying to convince her mother to leave her in the company of her friends for more than ten seconds, so that she might discuss anything of interest. Lady Willingham, by contrast, seemed to adopt the philosophy that so long as Emily was in possession of all her limbs and not in imminent danger of being deflowered in a linen cupboard, she could be left well enough alone.

"I . . . need to fetch my bonnet and wrap," Emily said, faltering a bit, taken aback by the speed with which this plan was progressing.

"I sent your abigail to do so," Lady Willingham said smugly. "She should be reappearing any—oh! Here she is!"

Emily turned in time to have her wrap and bonnet pressed into her hands by Hollyhock, her lady's maid and—she suspected—a spy on behalf of her mother, who would no doubt be waiting in London for a full accounting of Emily's behavior while away. Turning away from Hollyhock with a murmur of thanks, Emily looked from Lord Julian to the dowager marchioness and back again.

"This has all been very . . . smoothly arranged," she said blandly, trying to keep her voice absent of any trace of suspicion; despite her best efforts, she still thought she sounded a bit like someone noting that an execution had been efficiently planned.

"Hasn't it?" Lord Julian asked, pushing himself off the wall and giving her that lethal smile of his. He offered her his arm. "Shall we?"

They had scarcely made it through the front doors before the dowager marchioness began her performance.

"Oh!" she exclaimed, and Emily and Lord Julian turned to see the lady clutching at her chest in dramatic fashion.

"Are you quite all right, my lady?" Lord Julian asked.

"Nothing but a flutter, I assure you," Lady Willingham replied, waving a hand. "I shall be right as rain in a moment."

Lord Julian released Emily's arm to offer it to Lady Willingham instead.

"Oh, that is *most* kind of you, my lord," the dowager marchioness said fawningly; Emily, who had spent a fair amount of time with the lady over the past week and had never before heard her employ such a tone, suppressed an uncharacteristic desire to roll her eyes. Perhaps she unwittingly showed some sign that she found this display less than convincing, however, because Lord Julian shot her an amused look.

Ignoring him, she instead cast an appreciative glance around at their surroundings. Elderwild, in rural Wiltshire, was set amid rolling hills and woodland; the party had already explored the woods some days earlier, and today Lord Julian had instead set their course for the lake that stretched out at the base of the sloping lawns at the front of the house. There was a gravel path that led from the front door down a gentle incline to the lake's edge, and they continued down it now, conversing idly about the beautiful late summer weather and the agreeable nature of the house party thus far.

Lord Willingham's shooting party was an annual affair, but this was the first year that Emily herself had been in attendance; she was always invited as a matter of courtesy, given the fact that her two closest friends were Violet, Lady James Audley, the wife of one of Lord Willingham's best friends, and Diana, Lady Templeton, a widowed viscountess who was the sister of Lord Willingham's other closest friend, but her parents had never allowed her to attend. Emily's mother liked to keep a watchful eye on her only daughter, and generally adhered to the philosophy that one's offspring (particularly when female) should be kept in sight as much of the time as possible—particularly when one was rather dependent on said offspring's beauty and pristine reputation to prevent the family's precarious finances from slipping entirely into ruin.

This year, however, thanks to Diana's intervention, Emily was mercifully free—for an entire fortnight!—from both her mother's hovering and the suitor she'd been entertaining for years now.

Which, in turn, left her free to entertain other suitors.

Not that she would have characterized Lord Julian precisely as a suitor—he had a dreadful reputation and had never given much of an impression that he was interested in matrimony. Their meeting that summer had come about when Lord Julian—a university acquaintance of Diana's brother, Penvale—had been convinced to put his acting skills to unconventional use, playing the role of a physician as part of a rather half-baked scheme in which Violet had feigned a deadly case of consumption to get her estranged husband's attention. Somehow, the plan had worked—though Emily remained privately unconvinced that the drama involved had been strictly necessary to bring about the reconciliation between Violet and Lord James—and, in exchange for his assistance, Lord Julian had extracted a promise from Violet to attend a show at his somewhat disreputable theater.

Violet, never one to shirk a promise—and, truthfully, never one to miss a chance to get to visit a place that she really wasn't supposed to go—had attended a show with Diana and Emily in tow. Emily and Julian had struck up an odd sort of friendship in the month that followed—he waltzed with her at society balls and had escorted her to the odd musicale or Venetian breakfast; their arrangement was unspoken, but there had always been an understanding between them that they were of use to each other.

Emily had no complaints about this state of affairs; she knew that Lord Julian liked being seen with her on his arm to improve the reputation of his theater, and thought that the theater's owner giving the appearance of courting a respectable lady would help in this aim. Given that any time spent with him meant less time spent in the company of a certain Mr. Cartham, the odious man her parents had insisted she allow to court her for three Seasons now, Emily wasn't terribly bothered by Lord Julian's motives.

Until the past week. Because ever since they'd arrived at Elderwild, he'd given less an impression of a man feigning a courtship than an impression of a man conducting one in earnest. There had been long, lingering glances—ones that, were Emily in her first Season rather than her sixth, she might have mistaken for the glances of a lovestruck, enamored swain—and constant offers of his escort—around the grounds, to meals, even between the drawing room and the library to fetch a missing glove. There had even been rather bold allusions on Lord Julian's part to her family's financial woes and their entanglement with Mr. Cartham, and an implication that he could somehow make these troubles go away, were she his wife.

He had, in short, done everything shy of proposing outright.

Emily still wasn't entirely certain why. But she suspected she was about to find out.

Matters could not proceed in that direction, however, while they were in the presence of Lady Willingham—but then, right on schedule, that estimable lady once again brought their progress to an abrupt halt.

"I think . . ." She trailed off dramatically, reaching her hand up in the general vicinity of her heart. "I think I felt *another flutter!*"

"Lady Willingham, you must allow me to escort you back to the house," Lord Julian said—Emily would have found his offer gallant, were it not for the fact that he, despite being a rather skilled actor, seemed barely able to muster the appropriate note of concern. "You are clearly unwell," he added, in the tone of someone observing that it looked like rain.

"No, no, my dear boy," the dowager marchioness said tremulously. "I simply moved too quickly. I shall find my own way back, at my own pace. Please allow me this moment with my own thoughts. . . ." She turned and began to make her way back toward the house; for about five steps, she moved at a convincingly feeble pace, before breaking into what Emily could only characterize as a trot.

"She's not even trying," she said, uncertain whether to be amused or offended. "How stupid does she think I am?"

Lord Julian grinned down at her, the quick, fleeting flash of amusement across his face making him look younger than usual. "I think you should take it as a compliment. She clearly thinks you're too intelligent to fall for her tricks, so she's not wasting the effort of a convincing performance on you."

"My goodness," Emily murmured, her gaze flickering to the

retreating back of the dowager marchioness. "Whatever am I to do with such an honor?"

"Walk with me instead?" he suggested.

"All exactly as you planned it, no doubt," she muttered, but she took his arm once again as they resumed walking toward the lake.

"I should note," Lord Julian said, "that I never once asked the dowager marchioness to abandon her chaperonage of us."

"Mmm," Emily said skeptically, thinking that this had all worked out rather too conveniently for Lord Julian's purposes to be the workings of fate.

"I cannot help it if she is incredibly skilled at reading my thoughts," he added, sounding smugly amused.

Emily gave a huff of quiet laughter, despite knowing she shouldn't reward a gentleman for this sort of conspiring. "You have me alone, Lord Julian," she said briskly, feeling that she ought to turn matters to whatever his aim was. "What is it you wish to discuss with me?"

Lord Julian drew to a halt; they had reached the lake's edge, and Emily gazed out over its still surface, marred by the occasional ripple. On the opposite side of the lake, a pair of ducks paddled about in lazy circles, and the early September sunshine was warm overhead. Lord Julian loosened his cravat, making his only concession to the weather; the rest of him was as impeccably attired as ever in the height of fashion, a blue waistcoat making the blue of those arresting eyes stand out even more brilliantly.

He squinted in the bright afternoon light, the expression causing faint lines to appear at the corners of his eyes, and then he dropped his hand from his cravat and turned to face her, his height shielding Emily from the direct glare of the sun. She tilted her head back slightly to gaze up at him from under the brim of her bonnet.

"Lady Emily, I brought you out here because I'm very much hoping to convince you to marry me."

It was not, Julian would freely admit, the most romantic of proposals. He'd never given much thought to how he would ask a lady to marry him, if it ever came to that—that appalling prospect had always seemed comfortably distant, and so not something that he expended mental energy on. More recently, when he had begun to consider it in earnest, his deliberations had been so calculated that thoughts of how he'd actually ask the question hadn't even entered his mind.

However, if he ever *had* taken the time to ponder this prospect, he was fairly certain he would have envisioned himself coming up with something a bit more impressive than standing by a lake in the blinding sunshine, sweat already beginning to dampen the back of his neck, stating the prospect of marriage as though he were proposing a business arrangement. He'd heard complaints that romance died as soon as the wedding vows were spoken, but he hadn't realized this could happen before the lady's hand had even been secured.

But then, this wasn't about romance—that was rather the point.

He cast his gaze about and spotted a large oak tree twenty feet or so away and, without thinking, reached down to seize Emily's hand. She followed without complaint, and when they reached the shade of the tree, he—in a complete breach of etiquette—flung himself down onto the grass and squinted up at her while she stood, framed by dappled sunlight, staring down at him suspiciously.

"Sit," he ordered, not at all gallantly, patting the patch of lawn directly to his right. "It's quite dry, you needn't worry about your dress."

"I doubt my maid will agree when I come back covered in grass stains," she said, but nonetheless lowered herself—with considerably more grace than he had displayed—to the space next to him. Once seated, she loosened the ribbons securing her bonnet beneath her chin, and, with a furtive glance toward the house, tilted the bonnet back slightly, allowing the light to hit her face.

"My mother would be appalled if she could see me right now," she said, bracing her hands behind her and leaning back on them. She inclined her face up toward the sun. Even in profile, he could see the expression on her face easing.

It was odd, he reflected—until that very moment, he hadn't thought she seemed particularly tense ordinarily, and yet something had softened in her expression the moment she lifted her face.

She looked almost absurdly lovely as she did so, of course; everything about her was lovely, from the smooth golden hair, carefully curled around her face, to the rosy, unblemished cheeks, to the clear blue eyes that were currently shut against the bright sunshine.

But he was not marrying her because she was beautiful. That was merely an added advantage.

"Why?" he asked in response to her comment. "Alone with a gentleman of unsavory reputation?"

"No," she said serenely, not bothering to open her eyes. "Freckles."

Julian let out a chuckle at that, and saw the corners of her mouth curve up slightly, the only sign that she was pleased with herself.

"I like freckles," he said.

"According to my mother," she replied, "the sight of a single freckle upon a lady's nose is sufficient to send a gentleman racing in the opposite direction, dooming the lady in question to a life of spinsterdom." She cracked an eye open, frowning a bit, wrinkling her smooth brow in a way that should not have been as appealing as he found it. "Is that a word?"

"Spinsterhood?" he suggested helpfully.

"Spinstery."

"Spinstering."

"Whatever the word, it did not sound pleasant," she said primly. "Though," she added, in a confessional tone of voice, "Diana has at least two dozen freckles on her nose, and it does not appear to have hurt her matrimonial prospects. Lord Willingham seems to find her suitably enticing."

"To say the least," Julian said, thinking of the gazes Willingham had been giving Emily's friend Diana, Lady Templeton, of late, which were barely suitable for polite company. Julian did not consider himself a prude, but apparently even he had his limits. Fortunately, the two had announced their engagement a couple of days earlier, which offered the hope that this phase of lustful mooning would soon be ended by the dreary reality of marriage.

"Emily," he said, addressing her for the first time without using her courtesy title, and she turned to look at him. Her bonnet slid farther back from her face, exposing more of her skin to the sunlight filtering through the oak tree's leaves.

"I was not jesting a moment ago. I want to marry you."

Want, he supposed, might be a bit of an exaggeration—he could not, in all honesty, confess to wanting to marry anyone. But he'd recently come to realize that matrimony was his best chance at rehabilitating his rather blackened reputation and, having decided upon Emily as the most suitable candidate, he certainly didn't want to have to start over again with someone else.

She gazed at him for a long moment, a slight frown forming a faint line between her eyebrows. "Why?" she asked.

If Julian was as much of a cad as some portions of society believed him to be, he would lie to her now—convince her that he'd fallen in love, overcome by her beauty; he could recite poetry, fling himself at her feet, and give an all-around convincing portrayal of a man who'd turned over a new leaf, changed by love.

But while he did hope to convince the rest of society that he had done just that, he couldn't bring himself to enter into marriage with a bride who believed it, too.

"I need a wife," he said bluntly. "And, furthermore, I need a wife who can withstand the scandal of marriage to a man who owns a theater with a reputation as unsavory as the Belfry's—whose reputation can elevate my own, rather than being muddied by it." He wasn't certain whether she'd be offended by his implicit reference to her family's various scandals, but he wanted to be honest with her. This was not, after all, a typical courtship, when a man might seduce a lady with sweet words and promises he had no intention of keeping. What he proposed was a mutually agreeable arrangement absent of any deep sentiment. He had no intention of luring her into marriage under false pretenses.

"But *why?*" she asked again, a faint note of frustration in her voice. "Until the past fortnight, I didn't think you actually meant anything by your courtship—I thought it was all for show."

He did not pretend not to take her meaning, because she was entirely correct—or at least, she *had* been. They'd met in July when she'd attended a show at the Belfry in the company of her friends, an outing that, as he understood it, they'd had to coordinate with the precision of a general planning an attack on the battlefield in order to ensure that her mother didn't understand where her daughter was that evening.

He'd taken notice of her, of course, because she was beautiful. It had to be the first thing about her that anyone noticed, and Julian was certainly not a man to disregard a pretty face. But then, almost as quickly, he had realized that this was the only daughter of the Marquess of Rowanbridge, who, if rumor was to be believed, was in horrendous debt to Oswald Cartham, a man who had used his distant aristocratic connections (he was the second son of a second son of a second son, whose family had emigrated to the colonies a generation earlier) to draw gentlemen of the *ton* to the notorious gaming hell he'd founded a decade earlier.

And, Julian had recalled, if he'd heard correctly, the daughter was being used as some sort of pawn—rumor had it Rowanbridge was allowing Cartham to escort her to society events in exchange for keeping his debts at bay. Julian had also heard faint whisperings that Cartham might be blackmailing Rowanbridge—that the marquess's debt was not merely monetary. It was all quite . . . unsavory. And so Julian had gazed with some curiosity that evening at this unspeakably lovely, doe-eyed creature, who seemed far too innocent to have gotten caught up in her father's sordid affairs.

And he'd found himself strangely . . . intrigued.

So he'd gone to a ball—not specifically to see her, if anyone had asked, and yet, by the evening's end, he had realized how any appearance of interest on his part could perhaps allow him to bask in the respectable glow that surrounded her. And so, the following week, he'd escorted her to a Venetian breakfast—an event that, under ordinary circumstances, he would have rather flung himself from a roof than attend. He'd gone riding with her in Hyde Park. He'd called on her at home—even braved the horrifying experience that was taking tea with her mother.

And yet, all the while, he hadn't been terribly serious—his reputation preceded him, after all. But there had been advantages to them both nonetheless: Julian found himself being gazed at with curious speculation by ladies of the *ton*—a breed that even a month earlier would have discussed him in shocked whispers, their daughters tucked safely behind them. And Emily—well, she got to dance with someone other than that bounder Cartham, which Julian supposed was nothing short of a blessed relief for her.

There'd been nothing more in it than that.

Until he'd begun to wonder if perhaps there should be.

It had been an offhand conversation with his friend Bridgeworth that had first lodged the thought in his mind. Bridgeworth was a chum from his Oxford days and they'd lingered over a bottle of claret late one evening about a week before Willingham's house party had begun.

"You've turned respectable now, Bridgeworth," Julian had said lazily, turning the wineglass in his hand, watching the candlelight reflected in its surface. It was a warm evening, the grate empty, and Julian had long since discarded his cravat, his collar open to allow a bit of breeze wafting into the room to cool his skin.

"No more late nights carousing with a bottle of brandy and a willing woman—or two," Julian added, pausing to spare a thought for that particularly fond memory. "Instead, you'll be spending your evenings tucked up beside the fire, warming your slippers, a book in hand." He was speaking largely in jest; Julian was fond of Jemma, who was a young widow Bridgeworth had met at a ball earlier that summer. What had started as a heated affair had turned into a marriage within a matter of weeks—so quickly that Julian found himself blinking at the realization that he'd lost one of his best friends to matrimony, before he'd even had the chance to fully consider the changes this would bring to his own life.

Bridgeworth, for his part, regarded Julian with a tolerant smile. "You've been acting fairly respectable yourself these days, old chap. I can't recall the last time you met me for a ride still in your cups from the night before—and, from what I hear, you've been sniffing around the skirts of an eligible lady." He gave Julian a pointed look. "If you're so desperate for the approval of the *ton* then why don't you just get married?"

Why don't you just get married?

Julian had laughed the comment off at the time, and the conversation had soon turned to other matters, but Bridgeworth's words had stuck with him. Was marriage the key, then? Was it his path to respectability—to convincing polite society that he had changed, that his theater was worthy of notice?

The thought, at first, was wildly unappealing—despite his parents' and sister's (eventual) happy marriages, the institution had never seemed terribly enticing to him. He liked answering only to himself, and found it hard to imagine coming home to a wife each evening, inquiring after her day, feigning interest in whatever news she had to share with him. And yet, the more he considered it, the more he thought Bridgeworth might be correct. Julian had recently turned thirty, and while he was not precisely in his dotage, it was undeniably true that his exploits had gotten less raucous of late. Was marriage really such a sacrifice? He could still keep a mistress, he supposed, if he grew bored with whomever he married. Would it truly be so difficult to smile charmingly across the breakfast table at the same woman for the rest of his life? It wasn't as though their lives need be linked in other ways—there were certainly numerous married couples of the *ton* who rarely saw one another, aside from across the dinner table from time to time.

The more he thought about it, in fact, the more convinced he became—and the more certain, too, he was that Lady Emily Turner would make the perfect wife for him. After all, he'd already given the impression that he was courting her—why waste all that work? So he'd followed her here, to Elderwild, to Willingham's house party, determined to convince her of the wisdom of his new plan.

"I will not pretend to have fallen in love with you," he said bluntly to her now, barely managing to refrain from a wince as the words left his mouth. It was in his nature to be charming, to smooth the uttering of any difficult truths with the rakish smile that never failed to set female hearts fluttering, but he did not want to win her hand by nefarious means. He was determined to do this honestly. "But I do like you quite a bit, which is certainly more than many men can say."

"This is not very romantic," Emily said mildly.

Julian refrained from uttering the first reply that leapt to mind—that as far as he was concerned there was absolutely nothing romantic about the entire ghastly institution of marriage—and instead lifted an eyebrow at her. "And would you trust anything I said if I came to you and made a pretty speech and compared your eyes to pools of starlight and your cheeks to rosy apples and your nose to—to—that of a baby bunny?" he asked, feeling that perhaps he had lost his way a bit at the end there.

"I like bunnies," she said, smiling at him.

"That's hardly the point. And in any case, rabbits have no business in close proximity to marriage proposals."

"Is that still what this is?" she asked cheekily. "You've wandered a bit from the point, I can't help but notice."

"Emily," he said, exasperated. "Let me ask you a single question: do you want your life in a year—in two years, in five—to look like it does now?"

She frowned again. "No," she said, quietly but firmly, with no more than a moment's hesitation. "I do not."

"I'm offering you escape. I know your father is indebted to Cartham—whatever the figure is, I promise you I can pay it."

Emily opened her mouth to object. "But—"

"I promise you," he repeated, leaning forward and clearly enunciating each word as he held her gaze with his own, "I can pay it."

She shut her mouth again, looking faintly impressed. Good.

"Furthermore," he added, "if my suspicions are correct, and Cartham is keeping your father in line with threats that go beyond merely a financial debt, I promise you that I can avert any scandal."

Her frown returned and deepened; perversely, it made her more attractive to him, rather than less so. "How?"

"Let's just say that Cartham and I have a number of mutual acquaintances, and I've heard all sorts of whispers. Should he be blackmailing your father, I'll see that he regrets it," Julian said grimly. He wondered for a brief moment if he had shocked her—after all, he couldn't imagine that she was accustomed to anyone speaking to her like this, or about matters like this.

When she spoke, however, she didn't sound shocked—merely, perhaps, a bit confused. "You are willing to go so far as to marry me—to pay my father's debts, to make a lifetime commitment—just so that society will think you are respectable?"

"Courting you clearly wasn't enough," he said bluntly. "There's a pile of regrets from half the *ton* sitting in my house in London—I'd invited them all to the opening night of our staging of *Macbeth*, and encouraged them to bring their wives. Old acquaintances, friends of my family, you know the sort. Not a single one accepted. But you—" He paused, momentarily uncertain how to phrase this, not wishing to offend.

"I've proven I can weather a scandal?" Emily suggested, taking the words right out of his mouth.

"Yes," he agreed, thinking of her elder brother's disastrous, deadly duel over the honor of a married lady he'd insulted, and of his later death on the Continent, just as Emily was making her debut into society; thinking also of three Seasons spent on the arm of a man like Cartham. And still, he'd never heard anyone accuse her of anything remotely scandalous. It was impressive.

"If I marry you, people will be forced to look at me differently. To look at my theater differently. And you—you'll be free to live a life of your own choosing."

He reached out to take her hand, the first time he had touched her since dropping her arm, so determined had he been not to allow seduction to play any role in this proposal.

"Marry me," he said, "and I'll do my best to see that you are . . . content." He hesitated over the word for a moment, not wishing to promise anything he could not deliver. He did not know if he could make her happy—indeed, he wasn't sure he knew *how* to make a creature like Emily, all innocence and light and kindness, happy. But he could certainly see that she was content.

"I know this is not the marriage proposal many ladies dream of," he continued, very aware as he spoke that both of her closest friends had made love matches, and that he was offering her something entirely different. "But I think you and I deal rather well together because we speak frankly with one another. I don't intend to promise you anything I can't give you, nor do I expect that of you."

She held his gaze for a long moment, then turned, looking out over the lake. The slight breeze pulled at a loose, uncurled strand of hair at her temple. Everything about her was so utterly, perfectly composed—from the simple blue-and-white morning gown to the careful knot of golden hair at her neck—that he was somehow heartened by this loose strand, this slight crack in her perfect facade. Without thinking, he reached out and tucked the strand behind her ear, his fingers lingering for a moment longer than necessary. She didn't turn to him, which gave him an excuse to continue gazing at the softness of her cheek, the smooth curve of her lips and chin, the length of her throat.

"I will marry you," she said, turning to look at him without blinking. "On three conditions."

"Name them," he said simply.

"The first is that you must not lie to me." She hesitated, searching his gaze—for what, he wasn't quite sure. "I will not . . . If there comes a time in our marriage when you wish to seek company elsewhere, I will not pry. But I would ask you not to lie to me, not to a direct question."

"Let's not worry about other company for now," he said, attempting to sound soothing.

Her eyes flashed briefly with something that he thought might have been annoyance. "That's precisely what I mean, my lord," she objected. "I don't wish you to say comforting things to me to shelter my delicate female sensibilities. Let us deal honestly with each other, as you said."

"I'm sorry," he said, feeling faintly abashed. Some distant part of his mind noted that prim virgins were not as flattering to one's self-esteem as he might have expected; she had an unmatched ability—or, at least, unmatched by anyone not related to him—to make him feel like a bit of an ass at times. "And you're right, of course. What is your next condition?"

"I would like to be married as quickly as possible," she said. "My parents—I'm not certain how they will react to this news, and I don't wish to give them time to put a stop to it. If we could call the banns as soon as we returned to London—"

"I can do even better," he said. "What if I procured a special license and we wed right here, in the country?"

She blinked at him. "You—you would do that?"

"If it means you say yes, and it spares me the horrifying prospect of having to stand up at St. George's in Hanover Square—"

"But aren't you worried it will make our marriage seem . . . hasty?" she asked.

He shrugged. "There's bound to be a bit of gossip, no matter what. And I think the advantages of not allowing your parents—or Cartham, for that matter—to have any warning outweigh any whispers we might cause. Besides," he added, a bit smugly, "the Archbishop of Canterbury was a school friend of my father's, and he's always been rather fond of me. What a perfect opportunity to take advantage of that fact."

"Are gentlemen always this pleased with themselves when they propose?" she wondered aloud, and he resisted a sudden desire to grin.

"Was there another condition?" he asked instead.

Emily, he was interested to note, suddenly blushed. This in and of itself was not noteworthy—she was more prone to blushes than any woman he'd ever met, a fact that he actually found rather charming—but it *did* make him curious as to what request she wished to make of him that would provoke such a reaction.

"I would like you to kiss me," she said before he had time to contemplate further.

It took his mind a moment to catch up to his ears, and by the time he'd worked out what she'd said, she was already looking like she regretted her bold words. She did not, however, take them back, nor did she break eye contact with him; in fact, she gazed steadily at him all the while, as though determined not to be cowed, or to be ashamed of what she'd said.

And Julian—not being a man known to hesitate when a beautiful woman made a bold invitation—proceeded to acquiesce.

"Wait!" she said hastily, leaning back as he ducked his head toward her, a lock of hair falling forward onto his forehead in a way that he knew ladies found appealing.

Emily, however, seemed unmoved by the lock of seduction, and instead held up a hand, letting it hover awkwardly between them. He had the distinct impression that she wished to reach out and place it on his shoulder or chest, to prevent any movement on his part, but that she didn't quite dare make any sort of physical contact.

Which, of course, begged the question of how she thought he was going to kiss her without touching her. Except that, at the moment, it did not seem that she wished him to kiss her at all.

It had been a few months since Julian had parted from his most recent mistress, but he didn't recall her behavior being quite so confusing.

"Did you not, just a moment ago, ask me to kiss you?" he asked mildly.

"Well, yes," Emily hedged. "But I didn't expect you to spring into action so quickly."

"Did you think I'd send it to a committee to debate?"

"No," she said slowly, drawing the word out. "I'm not actually sure what I thought. I don't have any experience to draw upon here, you understand."

Julian nodded absently, then paused, her words belatedly registering.

No experience.

No experience with kissing.

He was somehow both unsurprised and entirely shocked. He should have expected it from her guileless and innocent demeanor. But on the other hand, she was three-and-twenty, had been out for several London Seasons, and was beautiful enough to attract more than her fair share of notice. Had no man ever tried to steal a kiss on an isolated terrace? Had she never been . . . curious?

"I've wondered what it would be like," she said softly, as if reading his thoughts, "but . . . well, no one has ever taken any liberties." She sounded both embarrassed and, if he was not mistaken, a trifle disgruntled. "Not that I would wish to be seduced by a lecher," she added hastily. "But well . . . you hear so many dire warnings about balconies and unscrupulous gentlemen. And yet I have spent entire evenings inside well-lit ballrooms without a single attempt to lure me to a darkened corner, or out a set of French doors. It has been most perplexing."

"I would be happy to remedy this oversight on the part of the other gentlemen of the *ton*," he drawled, taking care not to lean in too quickly and startle her—he felt like he was approaching a shy deer. "And, in fact, it would only be proper to seal our betrothal with a kiss."

Her lips pressed together as if she were suppressing a smile. "I don't think the word *proper* is one that is often associated with you, Lord Julian."

He frowned. "None of this 'Lord Julian' business, please. We are going to be married, and you just asked me to kiss you—I think we can dispense with formality and call one another by our first names, don't you?"

"Julian," she said slowly, as though testing out the sound of the word. Julian realized with a start that no one outside of his immediate family addressed him by simply his given name; in formal situations, his courtesy title was always used, and to his friends—and even his lovers—he had always simply been Belfry.

"I feel rather brazen," she confessed, and he bit back a grin at that. If the mere act of using his first name felt bold, he was curious to see how she'd feel about some of the other activities that marriage entailed.

"Would you like to feel a bit more brazen?" he asked, lifting his hand to cup her cheek. It felt impossibly soft and warm against his hand.

She gazed at him for a moment, and gave him a slow nod. That was all the encouragement he needed, and he leaned in and touched his lips to hers.

It was a soft kiss, not at all like the kiss he would have given one of his previous lovers. His hand still cupped her cheek, and he felt her tense slightly at the first press of his mouth. After a moment, however, she let out a little sigh and relaxed into the kiss, allowing her head to rest more fully against his hand. Hesitantly, she lifted her hand to his shoulder, her thumb pressing softly at the side of his neck, and all at once he was tempted to deepen the kiss, pull her against him, feel the heat and softness of her body pressed against his own.

Instead, reluctantly, he pulled back, relishing the second before she opened her eyes, taking in the sight of her, cheeks flushed, lips still slightly parted. She blinked slowly, and met his eyes with her own. He half expected her to blush—if ever there had been a moment for it, this seemed to be it—but instead her mouth curved into a small smile.

"I can see why Violet and Diana have been acting so foolishly this summer, if they've been doing lots of that."

Julian felt his mouth curve upward into a smile before he could stop himself. "You never do say what I expect you to."

Emily gave him a cheeky smile in return. "Once we are wed, I'm certain you'll become more skilled at expecting the correct thing," she said consolingly, as a governess might reassure a pupil who'd received a bad mark. "You mustn't trouble yourself about it now."

"I was hardly—" he began, but broke off, seeing her smile widen, realizing she was deliberately provoking him. And all at once the strangest thought flitted across his mind: marriage to Lady Emily Turner might be rather fun.

Two

Emily had spent her entire life not making a stir. She had been a well-behaved child—one who spoke softly, who smiled prettily, who curtseyed gracefully. She'd been an agreeable debutante, parading around ballrooms in her gowns of white and pale pink and pastel yellow. She did not argue. She did not pout. She did not cause scandals.

But she was rather looking forward to dinner that evening.

"You don't wish to tell your friends first, privately?" Julian had asked as they'd walked back up to the house after their interlude by the lake.

"No," she said cheerfully. "Let's just tell everyone at once, at dinner."

He had given her a long, considering look, but had not protested further. She now sat before her vanity, allowing her maid, Hollyhock, to dress her hair. The room was silent; she and Hollyhock had never particularly gotten along, as Emily suspected her of reporting all of Emily's activities back to her mother. Though, given the alternative— Diana's lady's maid was openly hostile toward her—Emily supposed that a bit of eavesdropping was not the worst quality in a servant. But it did not lead to idle chatter at the dressing table.

At last, however, she was ready, and Hollyhock was dismissed.

Emily surveyed herself in the mirror. She was wearing one of her favorite evening gowns, a pink silk concoction that she always thought made her skin glow. It was not particularly daring—none of her gowns were—but the bodice was cut a smidge lower, and Emily felt quite adult as she stared at her reflection.

She *was* an adult, she reminded herself sternly. She was twenty-three years old, had just that afternoon accepted an offer of marriage, and had kissed her handsome betrothed. Outdoors! In daylight!

Her mother would not have been pleased, but Emily felt quite satisfied with the afternoon's developments.

There was a soft tap at the door, and Emily crossed the room to open it. Julian stood in the hall, wearing a black coat and an emerald-green waistcoat embroidered with a pattern of leaves and vines, looking so handsome that for a moment Emily could not believe that the man standing before her was actually going to marry her. Somehow, despite her beauty—and her beauty was something that Emily was very much aware of; she tried her hardest not to be vain, but her mother had long ago made it clear that Emily's face was her most valuable asset, so it was impossible to be unaware of it entirely—Emily had never imagined herself marrying someone like Julian Belfry. He was too dark and dashing and rakish and dangerous. She had imagined a future for herself as the wife of some dull, wealthy viscount or other gentleman—and even this had been much better than the years she'd spent with a growing fear that she'd become the wife of a scandalous gaming hell owner instead. Even if, in her imagination, she longed for something more exciting.

Well, it seemed she was going to get that, at least. She wasn't quite certain what to expect from marriage to Julian Belfry, but she somehow knew that it wouldn't be boring.

"Are you ready to cause a stir?" he asked, smiling at her and offering his arm.

She reached out and took it, smiling back at him. "Absolutely."

It was after the fish course that Julian took the plunge.

Dinner was a long, leisurely, lively affair—they were nearing the end of the house party and, after close to a fortnight in one another's company, had grown used to sharing meals. Emily was seated between the dowager marchioness and Lady Fitzwilliam Bridewell (or Sophie, as she had invited Emily to call her; she was a new friend of Violet's and an old flame of Lord James's elder brother, the Marquess of Weston, known as West). Emily had spent the better part of the past quarter hour being lectured by Lady Willingham on the importance of a gentleman's calves. Emily, initially thinking she was discussing a gentleman's wealth and property holdings, found this a touch mercenary but not unreasonable, but it eventually transpired that she was not discussing baby cows at all but, in fact, gentlemen's legs.

"Finely muscled calves tell you everything you need to know about a man," Lady Willingham said wisely, sipping from her wineglass with all the solemnity of a trusted counselor of the king imparting valuable wisdom.

"I . . . see," Emily said, making a point of not glancing farther down the table at Julian, seated next to Violet, with whom he was deep in conversation. She had never paid much attention to his calves—or his legs in general—which, if Lady Willingham were to be believed, had been a grave error in judgment.

"Your grandson has very nice calves," Sophie said boldly, leaning around Emily in a breach of etiquette to speak directly to the dowager marchioness. She seemed to be attempting to shock the lady into propriety, but—as would become evident a moment later—was merely an amateur attempting to outwit a master.

"You would know far better than I, my girl," the dowager marchioness said serenely, and Sophie dropped her fork on her plate with such a loud clatter that half the table fell momentarily silent.

Julian seized the opportunity. "Thank you, Lady Fitzwilliam, for sparing me the trouble of doing that," he said with a grin, raising a glass in the direction of Sophie, who was visibly pale, clearly traumatized by the realization that the dowager marchioness was aware of her short-lived affair with Lord Willingham. "But if I could ask you all to spare me a moment of your attention, I have an announcement to make."

The rest of the table fell silent, everyone's gaze directed at Julian—everyone, that is, except Violet and Diana, whose eyes were flicking back and forth between Emily and Julian so quickly that Emily worried they would grow cross-eyed.

"I am pleased to announce," he continued, "that I have asked Lady Emily for her hand in marriage, and she has accepted."

In a single, uniform movement, every head at the table turned to look at Emily, who blushed to find herself so suddenly the object of scrutiny. She kept her gaze fixed on Julian, trying to ignore the others, and allowed a small smile to curve across her face—the sort of expression she imagined a besotted bride-to-be would make.

"Is there something in the water here?" Viscount Penvale asked, breaking the silence. "First Jeremy and Diana, now you two—"

"Shall we find a bride for you next, dearest?" Diana asked her brother sweetly. "Feeling left out?"

"Hardly," Penvale said, casting a dark look down the table at her;

they looked remarkably alike under ordinary circumstances, and even more so when they were glowering at each other. "It's more that I'm wondering if I should stop eating or drinking anything served at this table, if this is the result."

"What I *believe* Penvale is trying to say is congratulations," Diana said, giving him a death glare.

"Quite right, quite right," Penvale agreed hastily, and it was as though the floodgates had opened, with a chorus of best wishes ringing up and down the table.

"You *are* a clever one," the dowager marchioness said in an undertone to Emily. "Excellent calves, that one."

"Of course," Emily replied, before she was remotely aware of what she was saying. "Why do you think I said yes?"

Sophie—who had just taken a sip of wine—choked upon hearing this, leading to Lady Helen Courtenay, who was sitting opposite her, shrieking and dissolving into hysterics at the prospect of Sophie's untimely demise. By the time Lady Helen had finally slumped into a dead faint in her chair, been revived with smelling salts by West, and fallen into watery-eyed paroxysms of gratitude, several minutes had elapsed. At last, however, general order was restored, and Julian was able to once again attract the attention of the party at large.

"Lady Emily and I are so eager to begin our married life together that we cannot bear to wait even a moment longer than necessary to be wed," Julian said, modulating his tone so that he managed to convey the impression that each day that stretched between himself and his wedding day was an unbearable agony. He really was quite talented, Emily reflected. "Which is why I will be leaving tomorrow morning, and returning as quickly as possible with a special license, so that we may be wed right here at Elderwild."

This statement provoked a greater reaction even than his announcement of their engagement.

"Here! But we return to London in three days!" Violet said.

"Getting the job done quickly—you're a wise man, Belfry," said Lord Willingham.

"I hope *you* don't get any ideas in your head," Diana said with a narrow-eyed look at her betrothed. "I will have you up before all of society in St. George's so that I might revel in my triumph."

"In snaring the most eligible bachelor in London?" Lord Willingham asked, grinning cheekily at her.

"No," she said smugly. "At winning our wager. I've decided to spend part of my winnings on a truly horrendous waistcoat for you to wear to the wedding." Diana had bet Lord Willingham that summer that he would be married within the year, and seemed to find the fact that she herself had been the cause of his losing the bet to be particularly satisfying.

"I, for one, think a speedy wedding is precisely the thing," Lord James interrupted, nodding encouragingly at Julian.

"You would, James," West called down the table. "How long were you and Violet engaged? A fortnight?"

"And just *look* how well that worked out," Penvale said, taking what Emily thought was a bit of a cheap shot. "Nothing but unsullied bliss for the past five years, is that it?" Violet and Lord James had married young in an impetuous love match, and had promptly become estranged for four years following a heated argument; their estrangement had recently been happily, if somewhat laboriously, resolved.

"And when are *you* planning on marrying, Penvale?" Violet asked waspishly. "It does rather seem that everyone is pairing up. Are you not concerned about returning to your lonely bachelor lodgings, eating a stale crust of bread before the fire?"

This *also* seemed somewhat unfair—to begin with, Penvale lived in Bourne House in St. James's Square, the London home of the viscounts Penvale for seven generations, which was hardly a cold bedsit.

"How could I not be, given how calmly and undramatically you have all gone about your love affairs of late?" Penvale asked, deadpan.

"Excuse me," Emily objected mildly, "but I don't believe Lord Julian and I deserve to be jumbled together with Violet and Lord James and Diana and Lord Willingham." Considering that Violet and Lord James had spent the better part of a month this summer in an escalating battle of wits involving a nonexistent deadly illness (which had been an entirely convoluted and roundabout way of leading both parties to admit that they were, in fact, still in love), and that Diana and Lord Willingham had entered a rather ridiculous wager regarding Lord Willingham's matrimonial prospects while also attempting to conduct a clandestine affair, she really felt that she and Julian were behaving quite sensibly by comparison.

"Hear, hear," Julian murmured, taking a sip of wine.

"But Emily," Diana said, returning to the matter at hand, "how are we possibly supposed to plan a suitable wedding with such little notice?"

"There is nothing to plan," Emily said. "We will have a quiet ceremony—anyone present who wishes to extend their stay a bit longer so that they might attend is more than welcome, of course—and then, perhaps, a wedding breakfast afterward. If it's not too much trouble for your cook, on short notice?" she added, this last query directed at Lord Willingham.

"Not at all," he assured her. "Anything at all that you need, my household staff is at your disposal—as am I, of course." For all his rakish ways, Lord Willingham could really be quite gallant when he wished to be, Emily noted. Not that this should be entirely surprising to anyone who had witnessed his almost absurdly romantic proposal to Diana a couple of days earlier. Emily felt a slight pang at the thought; Diana and Lord Willingham, for all their bickering, were clearly in love. So, too, were Violet and Lord James—and despite the bumpy road their marriage had traveled over the past few years, they had also been deeply in love on their wedding day. Emily knew that in accepting Julian's proposal she had ruled out once and for all the possibility of a love match of her own.

Still, a pleasant marriage of convenience to Julian Belfry was a far sight better than any of the other options currently open to her. This was her life, and her marriage, and she was choosing it for herself— and that act alone, that choice, was far more than she had dared to hope for.

"I don't think there's any need to make a fuss," she said determinedly.

"But it's your wedding day!" Violet wailed. "That's the entire point!"

"I am quite set on Lady Emily having exactly the wedding day she wants," Julian said quietly, "and not the one that anyone else wants for her." There was nothing in his tone that implied anger, but something about the determination in his voice made one sit up and take notice. Emily caught his eye, and he winked at her.

Winked!

She had always thought that any gentleman who winked at a lady must be an incorrigible rogue—at best—and yet here she was, unable to stop herself from smiling back at him in return.

"I think," Sophie said, speaking for the first time since murmuring her quiet congratulations, "that this is going to be rather a nice wedding."

And, as it turned out, it was.

One week later, at eleven o'clock in the morning, Emily, dressed in her favorite gown of sky blue silk, clutching a bouquet of fragrant lilies that Violet had picked from the garden for her that very morning, descended into the drawing room where her friends were gathered, and spoke her wedding vows to Lord Julian Belfry.

Lord James, Lord Willingham, and Penvale had all separately offered to escort her down the aisle, but she had declined, having decided that she was going to walk herself into her marriage.

"I've spent far too much of my life being moved about like a chess piece," she explained to Diana and Violet that morning as they gathered in her room, watching with critical eyes as Hollyhock dressed her hair. "I'll be taking this step for myself, I think."

"It's unconventional," Diana said, "but I personally could not be more pleased that you're finally telling your parents to shove their plans for you up—"

"Diana!" Violet laughed. "Not on her wedding day, please."

"She *is* about to become more familiar with certain portions of the human anatomy," Diana said, a hint of laughter in her voice. "She won't be half as easy to shock anymore."

"I wonder that I'm easy to shock at all, after all these years with you," Emily said, gazing at her own reflection in the mirror. She'd asked Hollyhock for a coiffure that was simple but flattering, with none of the curls bobbing about her face that were so fashionable these days. Some ladies—like Violet—could carry off the style quite well, but Emily always felt like a particularly fluffy sheep, and the scent of singed hair from the curling iron was one that she would not like to associate with her wedding day.

And, besides: her mother wasn't here to make her.

So instead her hair was twisted into an elaborate braided knot at the back of her head, her face unobstructed by curls or fringe. Since they were marrying in the drawing room, she didn't even need a bonnet. She thought she looked quite nice—the blue of her dress matched the color of her eyes, and as she pulled on her gloves, she could not suppress a shiver of excitement.

In less than an hour, she was going to be someone's wife. Lady Julian Belfry. She found she liked the sound of it.

She could scarcely believe she was marrying a man she'd met barely over a month before—though, given the amount of time unmarried ladies were permitted to spend with gentlemen, she thought she still might know Lord Julian better than she would have known any gentleman her parents would have chosen for her.

"Speaking of being shocked," Diana said, watching Emily rise from her dressing table and dismiss Hollyhock with a nod, "this is your last chance to ask any questions you might have about the wedding night. I'm certain Belfry will be more than happy to instruct you, but if you've any last-minute concerns, voice them now."

"Should I be concerned?" Emily asked a touch anxiously. Her friends were not the shy and reticent sorts, and as a result she felt that she already knew more about the marital act than any proper young lady of good breeding should—and yet, the fact remained that hearing about it and actually *doing* it were two vastly different things.

"Of course not," Violet said. "Surely Belfry knows what he's doing. Look at his reputation!"

Diana frowned. "But has he ever been to bed with someone as sweet and innocent as Emily? His experience likely runs more in the vein of trysts with opera dancers against the wall of a dressing room."

"Diana," Violet said, fixing her friend with a sunny smile, "is that *really* the most helpful commentary you can offer just now?"

"I just don't want her to be unprepared!" Diana exclaimed.

"*Now* I am becoming concerned," Emily interjected, and Diana and Violet immediately plastered identically horrifying smiles of deranged glee upon their faces. "That is not making me less anxious," Emily added.

Violet's smile softened into something more natural and less nightmare-inducing. "I feel that we're bungling this a bit," she said, reaching out to place a hand on Emily's shoulder. "It's just . . . for so long, I worried we'd be helping you prepare to marry that *odious* man"—she did not name Mr. Cartham, refusing to pollute Emily's wedding day with even a whisper of his name—"and I just can't tell you how pleased I am you're marrying Belfry instead. There's nothing to worry about in the bedroom—I have the utmost confidence that you two will be able to work out whatever issues may arise. And," she added, her voice growing uncharacteristically tender, "I think you two will be very happy together."

Emily realized with alarm that Violet was near tears, and felt her own lip quiver a bit in response. Emily, Violet, and Diana had been best friends for the better part of a decade, and they were not overly sentimental, as a rule, but it seemed there were exceptions.

"Oh, no," Diana said warningly. "None of this, if you please. I will truly never forgive you if I am brought to tears for the second time in as many weeks. The first was bad enough!"

"But you were crying over Jeremy!" Violet protested waterily. "It was love, Diana! It was romantic!"

"It was horrifying," Diana retorted, "and now I'm dangerously close to tears once more." This being Diana, "dangerously close" indicated that she was entirely dry-eyed and stiff of lip, an occasional rapid blink the only detectable sign of an excess of feeling. Emily nonetheless felt rather touched by this display.

"Diana, I do love you," she said, utterly sincerely. "And you, Violet," she added, reaching up to squeeze Violet's hand where it still rested on her shoulder.

"I am leaving this room in ten seconds," Diana said, watching in resigned fashion as Violet dabbed at her eyes and Emily sniffled nobly. "Correct me if I'm wrong, but do we not have a wedding to attend?"

They did indeed. And an hour later, Emily was married. She was not certain she'd ever be able to recall the events of that hour with any degree of clarity; the drawing room had been full of fresh flowers and looked bright and cheerful in the morning sunlight streaming through the windows. In addition to Violet, Diana, Lord Willingham, Lord James, and Penvale, only West, Sophie, and the dowager marchioness were in attendance, the other houseguests having departed as planned.

They had been married by the vicar from the small church on the outskirts of Elderwild's grounds, and Emily recalled not a single word of the entire ceremony, so distracted had she been by the warm, solid presence of Julian at her side. She had noticed before how sometimes Violet would sink against Lord James's side when standing next to him, seemingly without realizing it, and how her shoulders would ever so slightly lower, as though releasing some faint but constant tension. All at once, Emily entirely understood the impulse, because she somehow felt just a small bit braver and more sure merely from the warmth of Julian's body a foot away.

The rest of the afternoon was a blur—there was a long, chatty wedding breakfast, full of toasts and laughter and free-flowing champagne. And then there was a last round of hugs and well-wishes as they made their way to Lord Julian's carriage, and with a fair amount of laughter and some undignified waving, they were off. Julian, it transpired, was rather eager to return to London—he had not intended to remain at the house party so long. They were to begin the journey this afternoon; there was a coaching inn a couple of hours down the road that Julian was familiar with, and which he had assured her would be a perfectly respectable place to pass the night. Emily had readily agreed; in truth, the idea of spending their wedding night at Elderwild, under the same roof as all of their friends, had been causing her no small amount of anxiety, and she vastly preferred the idea of being in an inn full of strangers instead.

"Is something wrong?" Julian asked as they rattled along a country lane, the late-afternoon sunlight giving a golden, hazy glow to the rolling hills outside the carriage window. Julian's valet and Emily's abigail were to follow them in another carriage with their luggage, so that the newlyweds might have some privacy. She gave him a questioning look, and he added, "You looked a bit concerned."

"Oh, no, I—I was woolgathering," she said, because she certainly wasn't going to tell him the direction her thoughts had taken. It was one thing to engage in whatever acts made up a wedding night, but quite another thing to *talk* about them. With a *man*. "I apologize—it was frightfully rude."

"No, it wasn't," he said, frowning a bit. "You're not here to entertain me. You're allowed to be lost in your thoughts."

You're not here to entertain me.

Emily wasn't certain why it was these words, more than anything else that had transpired that day, up to and including the moment that Julian had slid a wedding band onto her finger, that drove home the reality of her current situation, but they did, with great force.

She wasn't in this carriage to entertain him. Her family's fortunes no longer depended on her entertaining a man, keeping his interest, projecting sweetness and light and charm. She was married to a man who knew precisely why she had married him—and who had his own, equally practical reasons for marrying her. He didn't expect her—at least in private, when it was just the two of them—to be anything other than herself.

She wasn't a source of entertainment. She was merely his wife.

"Now you look as if you might weep," he said, beginning to sound truly alarmed, as men so often did at the prospect of female tears—one of the many reasons that, as Diana was fond of noting, it was absurd that ladies were considered the weaker sex.

"No, no," she said hastily, covering her mouth before any sort of alarming sound, be it a sob or a fit of hysterical laughter, could come out. "I'm merely thinking how . . . relieved I am. To be married to you."

"You don't look relieved," he said skeptically. "You look . . . er."

"Yes?" she asked, fighting harder than ever to resist the impulse to laugh.

"I don't know," he said frankly, leaning forward as if to get a better look at her face.

This was the last straw; Emily let out a peal of unladylike laughter, so loud that it made Julian start slightly in his seat, and dissolved into helpless giggles.

"If this is the effect marriage has on a lady, I'm not sure I recommend the institution," he said, looking utterly perplexed.

"I don't know what's wrong with me," she managed to say before collapsing into further giggles. "I never behave like this."

"I'd noticed," he said, still regarding her as if she'd recently escaped from Bedlam. "Are you going to spend the entire journey back to London doing this?"

"I hope not," she said, reaching up to wipe her eyes—at some point, a few tears had joined the laughter. An instant later, Julian was pressing a handkerchief into her hand; for a man with such a scandalous reputation, he had a surprisingly proper handkerchief, a carefully pressed, white linen affair, with the initials *JAB* stitched in one corner.

"What's your middle name?" she asked as she wiped her eyes and he continued to regard her uneasily.

"My middle name?" he repeated, confused, and she waved the scrap of linen in his face. "Oh—well." He looked a bit cagey all of a sudden. "I don't think it really signifies."

Emily raised both eyebrows. "Oh, now you absolutely *must* tell me—and if you will recall, I did make you promise me honesty, so do not attempt to wave me off with *Alexander* or *Arthur* or anything else similarly mundane."

Julian sighed heavily.

"If you must know," he said in aggrieved tones, "it's Albinus."

"*Albinus?*" Emily asked incredulously, and dissolved into laughter once again. "Why on earth were you given that middle name?" she asked several moments later, once she'd gotten herself somewhat under control.

"It was a difficult birth, and my parents wished to acknowledge the doctor who saved my mother's life," he said with a long-suffering sigh. "It would be too much to ask that their doctor be named John, apparently."

"We'll certainly exercise more caution in our own choice of physician," Emily agreed solemnly, managing to keep a straight face for approximately five seconds before being overcome by laughter yet again.

She felt . . . giddy. It was as though some sort of heavy weight had been lifted from her shoulders; she had felt this way to some extent for the entire duration of the house party, so liberating was it to be out from under her mother's watchful eye, free from Mr. Cartham's company for evening after evening. But now, with wedding vows having been spoken, there truly was no going back. She did not belong to anyone anymore.

Or, rather, she belonged to Julian. Legally so. But they had an understanding—they weren't going to make any sort of unreasonable demands on one another. They would simply be husband and wife.

It was going to be *wonderful*.

And as she sat there happily, grinning across the carriage at him, delighted to see a reluctant smile appearing on his own face, seemingly against his will, she thought that so far being married seemed very nice indeed.

And then, just as that thought flitted across her mind, there was a loud cracking sound, followed by an alarming swaying, and the carriage, without any further warning, proceeded to topple onto its side, sending Emily and Julian crashing into each other as it fell.

Three

"*This is not, you understand, how I envisioned this afternoon pro-*gressing," Julian said for at least the third time.

Before him in the saddle, Emily nodded, the motion causing her bonnet to rub uncomfortably at the underside of his chin. It was a rather elaborate straw concoction which was no doubt quite successful at shielding her fair skin from the threat of a freckle, but it did not make for entirely comfortable riding.

"This is really quite pleasant, though," Emily said, looking around and causing the damned bonnet to do some more uncomfortable chafing. They were riding on horseback through a meadow—a proper, green, flower-filled meadow, with the summer sunshine beating down upon them and the sound of bees buzzing nearby. Just a bridegroom and his golden-haired, ambitiously bonneted bride.

It was all very . . . wholesome.

Julian found this disturbing.

"It would be significantly more pleasant viewed through the window of a carriage," he said, lifting his chin to spare it from a straw-chafed fate.

"That was quite bad luck, breaking an axle," Emily agreed, her head still turned to the side, no doubt in search of a frolicking lamb or an entire family of rabbits or something else similarly horrifying. "I do hope Reeve is able to find someone willing to make the repair."

Reeve, Julian's coachman, had ridden ahead as soon as he'd ascertained that Julian and Emily were unharmed—they weren't far from a small village, according to Reeve's map, and he was hoping to enlist aid in making the repair. Julian and Emily had followed Reeve more slowly on the other horse, and were just now coming within view of a sign announcing their location to be the village of Butcher's Green.

"I hope this place is big enough to have some sort of inn," Julian said, eyeing their surroundings skeptically as they descended at a gentle incline down a tree-lined lane, the road flanked by several cottages in varying states of charming dilapidation. It was with some relief that he noted the presence of a somewhat ramshackle inn as they made their way into the village—it wasn't quite what he'd had in mind for his wedding night, but at this point, so long as there was a bed and a kitchen serving food, he didn't think he would complain about much of anything.

Fifteen minutes later, however, standing in the small room on the top floor, having to duck his head so that it didn't collide with the sloped ceiling, he was revising that assessment. The innkeeper had been most apologetic as he'd shown them upstairs, explaining that there had been another unexpected arrival that afternoon, and this was the only room remaining. The lumpy bed appeared to have been made for a family of elves.

"How . . . cozy," Emily said brightly, giving the innkeeper a warm smile. "This will do very nicely, sir, thank you."

"Of course, my lady," the innkeeper replied, appearing a bit dumbfounded by the sight of Lady Emily Turner—Lady Julian Belfry, now—in all her beautiful aristocratic glory, looking around as if she'd just been shown to a suite at a royal palace. "Will you be wanting supper? I can have something sent up, if you'd prefer not to dine downstairs."

"That would be lovely," Emily agreed. "And perhaps a bath, too, if it's not too much bother?"

"Of course," the innkeeper said eagerly; Julian had the distinct impression that Emily could, by this point, have asked him if he would be so kind as to flatten himself into an axle-like configuration and attach himself to their carriage to hasten their speedy departure, and he'd have happily complied. To be fair to the poor man, it was difficult to resist her when she was directing that dazzling smile of hers in one's direction, as she was currently doing to the innkeeper.

Within moments—and with a few more simpering compliments— he was gone, and Emily and Julian were alone together. In a bedroom. On their wedding night—or, he supposed, wedding late afternoon. But did he really want to split hairs at the moment?

He decided that he in fact did not.

"So," he said slowly, turning to his wife—wife!—and reaching out to take her gloved hand in his. "Here we are."

"Indeed," she said, giving him her best look of wide-eyed innocence. He wondered idly if she practiced it in the mirror.

"On our wedding night," he continued.

"Late afternoon, I should think," she said with a frown.

"Details." He waved a dismissive hand, and tugged her closer to him. She came quite willingly, and he bent his head to focus on the business of unbuttoning every one of the damned buttons on these gloves. Who in God's name had come up with this design? Was it intended to deter lecherous seducers—leave them so frustrated by the glove removal attempt that they gave up in disgust before even trying to remove any more interesting articles of clothing?

"What—what are you doing?" she asked, her voice a bit uncertain.

He glanced up. "Taking off your gloves." He bent his head to the cursed buttons once more.

"For what purpose?"

"Ha!" he said in triumph, having mastered one of the squadrons of buttons, and proceeded to slide the first glove from her hand. "I thought you might like to be a bit more comfortable," he said, looking up at her as he lifted her hand to his mouth, pressing a soft kiss there. "After all, if we don't intend to leave the room again—"

"We don't?" she asked, her eyes widening.

"We just asked for dinner to be sent up," he pointed out. "If we're not going downstairs, I see no reason not to make ourselves at home."

"But I have to bathe!" she said as he lowered her bare hand and directed his focus to his one remaining glove nemesis.

"I'll retreat into the hallway for that," he said chivalrously before adding, with somewhat less chivalry and a lazy grin, "though if you should like some assistance in the endeavor, I'd also be happy to stay."

"But what about . . . when *you* bathe?" she asked, her voice hushed, as if the mere discussion of the act of bathing was too scandalous to even consider.

"You are welcome to remain," he said, his grin widening, discarding her second glove and taking both of her hands in his own. "In fact, if you should like to offer any aid—"

"I don't think that will be necessary," she said with great dignity, and Julian couldn't help but laugh. She scowled. "You're doing this on purpose, aren't you?"

"Getting those bloody gloves off? I fail to see how one could possibly do it accidentally, given the amount of labor involved."

"Trying to embarrass me," she clarified, her scowl deepening as he pulled her close once more.

"Somewhat," he confessed, unrepentant. "It's hard to resist the temptation, when you make it so easy."

"I'm *supposed* to be embarrassed," she pointed out, even as she turned her hands so that she could lace her fingers properly through his. She tilted her head back to look straight into his eyes with that direct gaze of hers. She didn't employ it very often—she was very skilled at regarding gentlemen coyly from beneath her lashes, or keeping her eyes shyly downcast—but when she did, it was hard to look away. "I've spent my entire life being coddled and cosseted and protected, told to guard my virtue at all costs, that no one will want me otherwise. I had to work particularly hard at this, once Mr. Cartham appeared—merely associating with him was enough to damage my reputation, and I had to make sure my behavior was above rebuke.

"And now, when I'm only reacting as all of society has taught me to react, you're teasing me." Her tone was irritated rather than hurt, but that didn't stop Julian from feeling like a bit of an ass all the same. She sniffed indignantly. "I'm starting to think that Mary Wollstonecraft knew what she was talking about."

"What do *you* know of Mary Wollstonecraft?" he asked, astonished.

"Violet," she replied primly, "is a voracious reader, and is very fond of sharing what she learns with her nearest friends. It was all most enlightening."

"I should imagine it was," he said. He shook his head. "I must confess, marriage to you is not what I expected."

"And we're only half a day in!" she said brightly. "Think what other surprises await us."

"I'm not certain I dare to imagine," he said, both to make her smile—at which he succeeded—and because, in fact, it was not entirely untrue. "Did you wish to take me up on my offer, then?" He lifted an eyebrow at her.

"Which offer was that?" she asked, her smile faltering uncertainly.

"To help you bathe," he said slowly, using their interlaced fingers to tug her a bit closer. He leaned down so that he could murmur in her ear. "I feel quite certain it would involve all sorts of surprises."

He could practically feel her cheeks heating. "Be that as it may," she said, attempting to tug loose from his grasp—he promptly dropped her hands once he realized what she was doing—"I think I can manage nicely on my own, thank you."

He sighed dramatically. "All I can tell you, wife, is that it is entirely your loss." The word *wife* felt strange on his tongue, as if it was a foreign language he didn't know how to speak—which was not, come to think of it, an entirely inaccurate way to describe his feelings about marriage in general.

Somehow, though, as he gazed down at his lovely, blushing bride, he thought he would be a rather quick study.

Four

The words **wedding night** *had always conjured up a confusingly* nonspecific litany of images in Emily's mind. Her mother, of course, had always been quite close-lipped on the subject of the activities involved, merely offering dark reminders regarding the importance of doing one's duty and not complaining, which did not make one terribly thrilled by the prospect of engaging in the marital act. Friendship with Violet and Diana had fortunately taught her far more—including the fact that she might expect to enjoy said act very much indeed.

But still, the prospect of doing it for the very first time, with a man whom, when it came right down to it, she still didn't know terribly well, was undeniably daunting.

He had, after a last bit of teasing, left her alone to bathe, which she had done with some haste. Hollyhock and Humphreys, Julian's valet, had yet to arrive with their luggage, so she had no choice but to put her chemise back on, having no other garments to wear, wrapping a blanket around herself for good measure. Shortly thereafter, there had been a tap at the door, and a couple of maids had appeared with trays bearing their dinner, which Emily and Julian had consumed before the empty grate, making idle conversation.

And then the maids had reappeared to clear it all away, bobbing curtseys on the way out, and Emily and Julian were alone once more—and alone in a way that felt entirely different somehow, without the barrier and distraction of their meal and the table that had separated them.

Emily was very conscious, for some reason, of the fact that it was not yet dark—it was early September, and the days were still long; it would not be fully dark for a couple of hours yet, and it felt rather indecent, somehow, to stand here dressed for bed even as sunlight peeked around the edges of the curtains that shaded the windows.

Julian stood watching her, his expression unreadable, his face made even more handsome by the glow of evening sunlight, and she hugged her blanket more tightly to her chest. She opened her mouth to speak, but there was a tap at the door, and Julian went to answer it, vanishing into the hall for a moment, leaving her alone with her thoughts.

Calm down, she told herself. It was not that she'd expected to face her wedding night with complete sangfroid—she'd known she would be nervous. But she hadn't been prepared for the way her body would feel attuned to every move Julian made in the small, quiet room. At one point during dinner, she'd become so distracted by watching him holding his wineglass, his index finger tracing up the stem to tap at the bowl of the glass, that she'd paused with her fork halfway to her mouth, causing him to quirk an inquisitive brow at her after a moment.

Now, with him temporarily absent from the room, she could take a moment to gather her thoughts. Settle herself.

Try not to act like a lovesick fool.

Which she wasn't, of course—she was merely a newly married lady with a healthy appreciation for her husband's aesthetic appeal.

Husband.

It seemed so strange a word to be able to use—to be able to

claim someone as her own. It was a word that, in the past few years, she'd come to worry she would never be able to use. She had felt herself suspended in a strange state of limbo, squired about on Mr. Cartham's arm, her presence apparently more valuable to him than whatever amount of money her father owed him and could not pay. And yet, in all that time, there had never been any indication that a proposal was imminent. She had not wanted one from him, of course—had been grateful that whatever specific arrangement her father had come to with Mr. Cartham had not involved marriage, merely her company at this ball or that musicale.

But keeping constant company with him had more or less ensured that she did not receive a marriage proposal from anyone else, either.

And yet here she was, with a husband.

How on earth were her mother and father going to react?

Hopefully she would beat the news home—she'd like to break it herself, rather than face the reaction of two very irate parents.

The door opened again, and she glanced up—Julian walked in, followed by a couple of boys bearing their luggage, and maids who hastily set about refilling the copper tub before departing.

"I take it Humphreys and Hollyhock made it safely?" she asked, watching Julian hand a coin to each boy once they'd set the trunks at the foot of the bed and departed.

"They did," Julian agreed. "I've also heard from Reeve that we'll be able to have the axle repaired tomorrow morning, but it will delay us by at least half a day, if not more."

"Oh," she said, thinking a bit anxiously of the aforementioned irate parents that she would have to face sooner or later. She had a feeling that *sooner* would likely be less painful than *later*.

Julian sighed, running a hand through his dark hair. "I was hoping to make good time back to London," he said with some frustration. "I don't like being away for too long, and I've already lingered in the countryside considerably longer than I planned to."

"Because of me?" Emily asked hesitantly, feeling a wave of utterly illogical guilt wash through her as she recalled him mentioning soon after his arrival at Elderwild that he did not intend to stay for the full duration of the house party. It was ridiculous to feel guilty, she told herself sternly—she had hardly forced Julian to remain at Elderwild. But the fact was, he had lingered solely for the purpose of courting her, and she'd therefore prevented him from returning to his regular life sooner. She could feel something within her shrinking in horror at the thought of inconveniencing someone, especially someone who had already done her a rather large favor.

One involving wedding vows, in fact.

"Don't worry about it," he said, waving a lazy hand.

"But if I held you up—"

"You didn't," he said simply. "Or, rather, it was me holding myself up—I didn't have to propose to you, after all. You hardly held a gun to my head."

"Quite the opposite, I should think," she said, resisting the temptation to cross her arms over her chest defensively.

"I know," he agreed. "It was part of the fun."

"Oh," she said, not knowing what else to say. She was very conscious of the fact that she owed an enormous amount to this man, who had . . . rescued her.

It sounded silly even to think it, and yet was it not true? Hadn't he rescued her—from her parents, from Mr. Cartham, from the life she'd resigned herself to?

"You look guilty," he said, sounding confused. It was somewhat entertaining to hear him sound confused—the suave, rakish Julian Belfry always seemed in command of every room he entered. Confusion didn't suit him.

But Emily liked it all the same.

"I don't like to inconvenience people," she said by way of explanation, which was something of an understatement. She had spent years of her life twisting herself into knots to ensure that she was doing exactly what was expected of her, precisely what other people needed her to do.

"We're married," he said, the confusion in his voice slipping into amusement in the space of a moment. "I think it inevitable that at some point over the next fifty years, we'll inconvenience each other."

Fifty years.

Emily could not imagine being married for fifty years—though such an outcome was, of course, vastly preferable to any of the other possibilities (namely, scandal or widowhood or death).

"I suppose you're right," she said ruefully. "I just don't wish to be a bother—not when you've done me such a favor."

Something darkened in his gaze at that, even though on the surface his calm expression did not alter in the slightest. But there was a certain look in his eyes, a shifting of mood, that she'd never seen before. And before she could fully register it, he was in motion, eliminating the space between them with long strides, drawing to a halt with only inches left between them.

"A favor," he repeated, his voice low and dangerous. "Is that what you think I've done?"

"Well," she faltered.

"Because I view it a bit differently," he continued before she even had a chance to reply. He reached out a hand and trailed a single finger down her cheek, her skin prickling everywhere he touched. His hand came to rest on the curve of her neck, the weight of it somehow both comforting and electrifying at the same time.

"We both stood to gain something from this marriage," he said softly, his eyes locked on hers. "And now that it's done, I think we both stand to enjoy ourselves quite a bit."

She looked up at him, her mouth gone dry. There was something intoxicating about standing this close to him, breathing in his scent, feeling the weight of his undivided attention. She wondered idly what it must be like to share a stage with him, whether an actress playing opposite him felt this same fizzing in her veins, but she buried the thought just as quickly as it had arisen, all at once not having any wish to think of him with any woman but her.

And—in part to banish those thoughts, and in part to do *something* with that fizzing feeling that consumed her, and in part because it seemed the only thing *to* do in that instant—she reached up, cupped his face in her hands, and kissed him.

The benefit to being married to a notorious rake, Emily reflected, with what small portion of her brain was capable of intelligent thought at the moment, was that he certainly responded quickly to such overtures. It was the matter of a moment, somehow, for control of the kiss to entirely change hands, for it to no longer be Emily kissing Julian, but him kissing her. His arm slid around her waist, his free hand gliding up to the nape of her neck, his fingers cradling her head, tangling in the braided knot that still rested there, the remnants of her wedding coiffure.

He broke the kiss with a half laugh, half curse, disentangling his hand from her hair and turning her away from him so that he could attack it in earnest. "How the devil do you take this down?" he asked, hands working quickly; Emily could hear the *plink* of hairpins hitting the floor.

"I would think you had some experience in the matter," she said primly, and felt the warmth of his laugh against her neck a moment later. She was inordinately pleased with herself—Diana was the one known for her wit among their set; no one ever used the word *amusing* to describe Emily. But she *liked* being amusing—she'd simply been scolded one too many times by her mother for making what was deemed an unseemly joke, and so had learned at a young age to keep such observations to herself.

But no longer, she thought with an almost giddy sense of glee. Because what her mother found appropriate, or inappropriate, was no longer Emily's concern.

What *was* Emily's concern was the feeling of Julian's fingers in her hair, the loosening of the heavy knot of hair at her nape, the slight tug as he began to unwind it. She was acutely conscious of the sound of her own breathing in the room, a bit quicker than usual and just the slightest bit unsteady, and she turned to face him once more, suddenly unable to bear the tension, the feeling of his hands on her without her being able to see him, a moment longer.

No sooner had she turned than his mouth was on hers again, his hands at her waist, one of them beginning a steady journey downward. At some point she dimly realized they were moving, Julian backing her steadily toward the bed, and a moment later the backs of her knees made contact with the mattress and she sank down upon it, Julian following, twisting at the last minute so that he landed next to her rather than burdening her with his weight.

He reached over to cup her cheek in his hand, already moving in for his next kiss—

And that was when, with only the briefest, angriest *meow* in warning, the bloodshed commenced.

Julian had been warned more than once about wedding nights being painful, bloody affairs, but he had been determined that his should be otherwise. And, at the very least, he had not expected to be the bloodied party.

"This is romantic," he said darkly, three-quarters of an hour later, as Emily checked the tightness of the bandages covering his arms. The dangerous creature who had inflicted such injuries was sitting happily on the floor about ten feet away, attacking a plate of food with great gusto. Emily had previously attempted to soothe it with a dish of milk, which it had lapped up with enthusiasm before promptly vomiting all over the floor, necessitating yet another visit from the inn's beleaguered maids, who were no doubt beginning to wish that Julian and Emily's carriage had broken an axle in any village in England other than theirs. They had already been summoned when, once Julian had managed to extract his flesh from the creature's claws, he and Emily had retreated far enough from the bed to realize that the hissing, spitting, fluffy demon was, in fact, a rather hungry kitten.

The maids and the innkeeper all professed their ignorance of the creature's origins, claiming that they did not recognize it as the offspring of any of the resident barn cats. At this, predictably, Emily's eyes had widened, and she had seized Julian's recently mangled arm in a grip that, had he had even slightly less dignity, would have prompted a howl of pain. Sighing in resignation—and feeling all at once Extremely Married—he had watched as a blanket was lovingly crafted into a bed for the monster, and numerous dishes were prepared to tempt his lordship's fancy. (A furtive peek in an indelicate location had confirmed that he was, indeed, a he.)

Julian, resigning himself to the reality that there would be no further amorous activities this evening— which might be for the best; he would hate for one of his gaping wounds to bleed all over his sweet, blushing bride—had taken a bath in water that, by that point, could only be charitably described as lukewarm, hissing as every single one of the scratches on his arms came into contact with the liquid.

Emily, who had once been filled with such maidenly horror at the idea of them bathing in the same room, was too occupied with cooing at the murderous ball of fur to even note Julian's state of dishabille; he had the distinct impression that he could have paraded before her in his smalls—or quite possibly *out* of them—and she would not have taken a moment's notice.

Once he had washed off the dust from their unexpected horseback ride, and ensured that none of his scratches were actively bleeding, he'd pulled on a shirt and breeches and she'd bestirred herself enough to see to the bandaging of his wounds.

"Marmalade," she said, checking his final bandage and then perching on the edge of his armchair.

"I beg your pardon?"

"For a name," she clarified, looking down at him. "For the kitten."

"Ah. I was thinking Beelzebub."

"Julian!" She swatted at his arm, though she did so gently enough that it was really more of a pat than anything else.

"Lucifer?" he suggested.

She crossed her arms over her chest and frowned at him; across the room, the hell-beast sneezed directly into his dinner, which apparently startled him so much that he jumped approximately a foot in the air, managing to upset a good portion of the remaining food onto the floor in the process.

"How is it possible to be surprised by one's own sneeze?" Julian wondered aloud as Emily rushed over to mop up the mess, cooing platitudes at Beelzebub-Lucifer all the while. "Are you certain he didn't sustain some sort of mental damage during our tussle on the sheets?"

Which was decidedly *not* the sort of tussle on the sheets he had envisioned for this evening.

"Shh!" she said, then whispered to the demon, "You're perfectly intelligent, aren't you, Marmalade?"

"You can't call him Marmalade," Julian objected. "Even if you won't agree to my perfectly brilliant names, you've got to come up with something else. He's not orange!"

"Fine," Emily conceded, staring down at the kitten. He had seemingly completed his dinner at last, and was now arching his back in an exaggerated stretch. Emily reached out a finger to gently scratch him behind the ears, and a sound began to emerge from the creature that after a moment Julian identified as a purr.

"Look! He likes me already!" Emily said, giving Julian a watery-eyed smile.

"*I* like you," Julian grumbled. "And yet I've never seen you get quite so excited about it."

"*You* are not this adorable," Emily said. She looked back down at the kitten, stroking a finger down the length of his spine, smiling as he arched his back under her touch, the purring growing louder. "Cecil," she said definitively.

"Excuse me?"

"His name is Cecil."

"Why Cecil?" Julian asked.

"Because he looks like a Cecil," Emily said simply, and Julian knew there would be no arguing with her.

"Cecil Lucifer Beelzebub," he said thoughtfully. "It has a nice ring to it."

Emily glared at him. "Cecil Turner-Belfry," she said firmly.

"Well, you may certainly call him that if you wish. I'll just rest easy in the knowledge of his *true* name."

Emily opened her mouth to reply, but before another word could be uttered, Cecil Lucifer Beelzebub Turner-Belfry climbed into her lap, turned around three times, and sat down contentedly.

"Oh!" Emily said rapturously. "Julian, look at him. He just wants someone to take care of him."

"He has that," Julian said, not liking the pleading look she was beginning to direct at him. "You're going to keep him. There's no need to turn into a watering pot over this yet again."

"But," Emily said, widening her eyes at him, "he needs someone to cuddle with tonight—he's *scared*."

Julian gazed skeptically at Cecil Lucifer Beelzebub, who looked— was it possible for a kitten to appear *smug*?

"He is not scared," he pronounced with great certainty.

"I think he'd be comforted if he could sleep somewhere he felt safe."

"How fortunate, then, that you spent a quarter of an hour arranging a pile of blankets to just the precise degree of softness for his lordship's delicate bones," Julian said, giving a pointed look at the makeshift cat bed near the fireplace.

"Julian."

"Emily."

Emily's eyes widened, if possible, even further—how on earth did she do it? She looked exceedingly innocent and lamblike and nothing at all like the woman who, an hour earlier, had been sighing in his ear as he pushed her back onto a bed, a whole banquet of possible wedding-night activities laid out before him.

Then, the coup de grace: the faintest tremble of her bottom lip.

Julian sighed, a pragmatic enough man to know when he was beaten. "Fine," he said shortly. "But if he murders me in my sleep, I expect you to observe a proper mourning period for a husband, even though our marriage hasn't been consummated."

"Julian!"

He bit back a grin as he turned back the sheets, thinking that really, for all its troubles so far, this marriage business might not be half-bad.

Five

It was midway through a rasher of bacon that Emily first sensed something was amiss.

She and Julian had slept until midmorning, and had not bothered to make much haste in their morning ablutions; Julian had vanished while Emily was dressing, and had returned a quarter of an hour later to report that, with any luck, they would be back on the road by midafternoon. Since that left several hours to be filled, Emily had taken her time dressing, with Hollyhock's assistance.

At last, they had made their way down to breakfast, while Cecil had been left upstairs with another plate of scraps and a dish of water. She was in the process of wondering if Julian would notice if she slipped a piece of bacon into her napkin and smuggled it upstairs for Cecil when a sudden change came over her husband. He, like her, had been idly gazing around the room as he ate, not seeming terribly interested in any of the activity surrounding them. He had a way of doing that, she reflected—of looking around him like a prince surveying his subjects, always seeming just ever so slightly *bored*. She wondered if he was aware of this—if he was doing it on purpose, even. It was certainly effective, as it immediately made one conscious of all the ways that one might be personally responsible for his boredom. It was . . . intimidating.

In the blink of an eye, however, his demeanor changed; the shift was subtle enough that Emily did not think anyone who had not been watching him closely would have noticed, but she *had* been watching him closely, she realized with faint embarrassment. And she did notice.

All at once, the air of lazy, bored contentment was gone; slouched slightly in his chair in a way that implied that he sat up straight for no one (Emily, by contrast, had a spine as straight as a measuring stick), he did not alter his posture, but his gaze sharpened, and Emily became aware that he was intently focused on something outside the window they were seated next to—or, as it happened, some*one*.

Two someones, in fact.

The lady caught her eye first, because she was undeniably striking—hair of a burnished copper color, green eyes, tall and waifish. Her face was lovely, but not so lovely as to be uninteresting in its perfection—there was a slight hook to her nose, and when she spoke, Emily noticed that her smile was a bit crooked. There was something about her that drew the eye, some magnetic aspect to her demeanor that made it almost impossible to look away once one had noticed her.

She was also, Emily thought, very young—her own age, perhaps, or even younger. Her skin was smooth and unlined, her complexion luminous. Her green eyes were knowing, however, and there was assurance in the angle at which she cocked her head, and even in the way she held herself, as though aware of the male eyes sure to be resting upon her. Emily, despite being recently married, suddenly felt rather naive by comparison to this creature.

And then, belatedly, she noticed the man who stood next to her beside their carriage, deep in discussion with the innkeeper, who seemed to have accompanied them out the door.

She sucked in a breath. "Is that—" she began in a murmured

undertone to her husband, and he cut his eyes toward her for a moment, faint surprise registering in his expression, as if he had forgotten that she was even there.

Following the line of her gaze, he gave a sharp nod. "Delacre." He uttered the name rather as one would utter that of Lucifer—in fact, Emily had heard him utter Lucifer's name just the evening before, regarding dear Cecil, and she thought he spoke Delacre's with an even darker tone.

To be fair, however, everything she had ever heard of Viscount Delacre indicated that he thoroughly deserved it. The man was infamous among the *ton*—enormously wealthy and powerful, but an absolute blackguard. She knew plenty of gentlemen who had reputations as rakehells—both her new husband and Diana's fiancé, to start—but Lord Delacre was something different entirely. Julian and Lord Willingham were the sorts of men who wouldn't be caught dead near an eligible debutante, for fear of being trapped into marriage; Lord Delacre was a man who would ruin a young lady and still refuse to wed her. Emily distinctly remembered her own mama warning her away from him during her first Season—and, she recalled with a start, she had encountered him once at a ball, while she'd been on Mr. Cartham's arm.

It had been her fourth Season, the first that Mr. Cartham had been courting her, and they'd been in some crowded ballroom or other, taking a turn about the room, when they'd run into Lord Delacre.

"*Cartham,*" *Lord Delacre said, stepping directly in their path so that avoiding him was impossible.* "*I wouldn't have thought to see you here.*" *There was a note of arrogant condescension in his voice that caused Emily to cut a quick glance to her companion, who had been interrupted in the middle of a lengthy monologue on the subject of his favorite haberdasher.*

Despite the rather seedy nature of his profession, she had found conversation with Mr. Cartham to be surprisingly monotonous over the past two months. He was an odd, fussy man when he was not conducting his business matters, fixated on the visible signs of status—the right hat, the most impressive cravat knot—that he seemed to think were the key to earning the ton's approval.

"Delacre," Mr. Cartham said curtly. Her gaze flicked back and forth between the two men with interest. "If you'll excuse us—"

He made to step past Lord Delacre, but the other man blocked his path, taking a step sideways so that Mr. Cartham was once more forced to draw to a halt. "You're not still angry about that matter with that—er, lady—from the Adelphi, are you?"

"Consider the company you're in, Delacre," Cartham had said sharply, glancing at Emily for the first time during this encounter. This drew Lord Delacre's dark, considering eyes to her as well, and Emily found that she didn't like being the object of this man's attention. She had grown used to men's admiring glances, to the way Mr. Cartham paraded her around ballrooms like some sort of prize to be displayed—but that suddenly seemed vastly preferable to the way she felt under Lord Delacre's gaze.

She felt . . . naked.

"Lady Emily Turner, is it," Lord Delacre said slowly, not really asking, and Emily gave a cool nod.

"I don't believe we've been introduced, my lord," she said.

"No," he said, giving her a slow smile that made her feel as though she needed to take a bath, "I don't imagine we would have been." His gaze flicked away from her back to Mr. Cartham. "Attempting to buff yourself up to a shine, Cartham? It's a worthy effort, but I don't think even an accessory as lovely as this one will get the scent of the colonies off of you."

"*And yet I don't think you'd find a single debutante in London willing to be seen on your arm, Delacre,*" Cartham retorted, leaning closer to the other man.

He tightened his grip on Emily's arm at this juncture and led her past Lord Delacre, who made no further move to impede their progress. And later that evening, alone in her bedroom, long after her parents had gone to bed, Emily had shed half a dozen tears, then quickly wiped her eyes and climbed in bed—because never, before or since, had she ever felt so much like a trophy, and so little like a person.

So little like herself.

And so it was perhaps unsurprising, this jolt of visceral dislike that she experienced now, watching Lord Delacre through the window. His presence here, in the company of a young lady, did not bode well.

Before she could contemplate this further, however, Lord Delacre was shaking hands with the innkeeper and the couple were vanishing into their carriage.

"I wish I could go warn off that young lady," Emily said, watching the coachman leap up to his perch and gather the reins in his hand. "Though I suppose, not knowing her situation, she might not have any options other than being Lord Delacre's mistress." She uttered the last word in something close to a whisper; she was perfectly aware of such arrangements, of course, but it was not considered polite for ladies to acknowledge them.

"She has other options," Julian said grimly, his eyes still fixed out the window on the now-departing carriage.

Emily looked at him in surprise. "How can you possibly be certain of that?" she asked.

"Because," he said, tossing his napkin onto the table and pushing his chair back as he rose, "that's Susannah Simmons—the leading lady in my next production."

"I don't wish to complain," Emily said several hours later, "but things do not seem to be going entirely well at the moment."

Opposite her in the carriage—now with a fully operational axle once more, rattling merrily down a country lane—her husband gave her a dark look. "Things are fine," he said shortly. "A spot of rain won't stop Reeve—he's a very skilled driver."

Emily cast a skeptical look out the window, where black clouds had gathered, entirely blotting out the bright sunshine that just half an hour earlier had dappled the surrounding countryside in a summery glow. As if on cue, a clap of thunder sounded; Cecil started slightly from his spot in his cozy nest. He was currently reclining in great comfort in the basket that she had designated his carrying case, which she had padded with a couple of her chemises. She had noticed Julian leveling more than one malevolent look in Cecil's direction, as he happened to be doing now.

"Don't look at him like that," she said protectively, her hands fluttering around the kitten as if to shield him from Julian's glares.

"I cannot help but think," Julian said, "that it seems terribly unfair that that mangy bundle of fur has been in closer proximity to your undergarments than I have."

"I think you are determined to hate him."

"When he has mauled a significant portion of *your* upper body, then I will be happy to debate the matter with you," Julian said with exaggerated gallantry.

"In the meantime," Emily said, casting a pointed look out the window, where the rain was beginning to fall in earnest, "perhaps you would care to debate the wisdom of haring off through the countryside in search of a disreputable viscount and an actress who, whilst not perhaps making the most intelligent of decisions, is certainly old enough to know her own mind?"

Julian's scowl deepened. The morning had taken a rather dramatic turn after they had witnessed Lord Delacre and Miss Simmons depart—Julian had interrogated the innkeeper for every last scrap of information (Emily strongly suspected money had changed hands at some point), then moved heaven and earth to see their carriage repaired in record time (Emily knew for a fact that money had changed hands that time).

She was a bit befuddled by the speed with which matters had progressed—she had gone from calmly eating her breakfast, expecting to pass her day traveling toward London and her exciting new life as a married woman, to being bundled into Julian's carriage in hot pursuit of the fleeing couple, for reasons she didn't entirely understand.

"Perhaps," Emily continued, "we should not have taken the word of that gentleman in Butcher's Green who suggested a quicker route west?"

"I can think of any number of words I would like to use to describe that man," Julian said, running an exasperated hand through his hair, "and *gentleman* is not one of them." He sighed, then leaned forward to get a better look out the window, no doubt taking in the same ominous sight as Emily. The carriage had begun swaying alarmingly in the wind. "It's my own fault, though—I shouldn't have listened to him, and should have agreed to the route Reeve suggested instead."

They were attempting to move in a general northwesterly direction—Julian's inquiries among the staff at the inn had suggested that the fleeing couple were making for Lord Delacre's estate in Cheshire. Emily did not particularly relish the thought of traveling all the way to Cheshire on what she privately thought was a bit of a wild-goose chase, so she was not entirely unsympathetic to Julian's desire for haste—though she would have been even *more* sympathetic to a desire to abandon this half-baked plan and return to London instead.

"I must say, this is not how I thought I would be ending the day when I woke up this morning," she said brightly. Julian, she could tell, was growing more frustrated by their slow progress and by the weather conditions, which were deteriorating by the moment, and she instinctively adopted her most cheerful tone of voice, as she had done so often in the past, when her parents had quarreled, or something was troubling them.

This, she knew how to do.

"I promise you, I am entirely in agreement with you," Julian said, still craning his neck to look out the window.

"Would it be so terrible if we were not able to catch them?" Emily asked a bit hesitantly—she had the distinct impression that Julian wouldn't respond well to having his plans questioned at the moment.

"Yes," came his curt reply. "Aside from the fact that Miss Simmons is my leading lady—and considerably more suited to the role than her understudy—I can hardly afford any sort of scandal, not when I've just gone to the trouble—" He broke off abruptly, seeming to realize what he'd been about to say—and whom he'd been about to say it to. He gave a bit of an awkward cough. "I don't wish to further damage the theater's reputation," he concluded, but Emily heard the unspoken words, too: what would the point have been of marrying her, if the Belfry found itself mired in further scandal? Avoiding disgrace was the entire point of her marriage.

Julian reached his hand up to rap on the roof of the carriage, which promptly came to a halt and, lifting his coat up to shield himself from the elements, he hopped out the door, leaving Emily alone with a purring cat in a basket and the uneasy feeling that she had not managed to ease Julian's temper one bit.

Within a minute, he was back, his dark hair gleaming with raindrops, his expression grim. His mouth was set in a thin line, his brow low. No sooner had he reentered the carriage than a loud clap of thunder sounded. Emily peered into the basket, concerned.

"Are you frightened, Cecil?"

"I can't think why he should be," Julian said. "He probably summoned the lightning himself."

Emily shot him a severe look as she traced a finger down the small patch of white fur around Cecil's nose.

"Are we going to stop and take shelter somewhere, then?" she asked her husband. "I can't think we'll make much progress if the storm grows any worse."

"We are," Julian said, and there was an odd, resigned note to his voice that Emily did not understand.

"I know you must be lamenting lost time," she said, hoping she sounded soothing, "but surely Lord Delacre and Miss Simmons will have to stop too."

"Oh, I've no doubt you're correct—the storm appears to be moving in from the north, in fact, so they've likely already been delayed." He said all of this extremely gloomily.

"Why are you so bothered, then?" she asked, confused.

"Because," he said with a heavy sigh, "I've realized where we are—and who the most logical person to take shelter with would be."

"Oh?" Emily asked; by her calculation, they were somewhere in Oxfordshire.

"We're distressingly close," Julian pronounced, in the tone of a man announcing his own death sentence, "to the country seat of the Earl of Risedale."

"Risedale," Emily repeated, frowning slightly. "But isn't he married to—"

"Yes," Julian said darkly. "My sister."

Six

"I just cannot tell you how delightful this is," the Countess of Risedale said for at least the third time. Emily supposed it *was* delightful, in the sense that she was no longer in a carriage that seemed in imminent danger of toppling over—really, the past twenty-four hours had given her grave doubts about the advisability of carriages as a mode of transportation—but it would also undeniably be a good deal *more* delightful if she were wearing dry clothing.

"We greatly appreciate your hospitality, Lady Risedale," she said, scampering to keep up with her tall husband and his nearly-as-tall sister as they traipsed along one of the corridors in Dovecote Manor, the Earl of Risedale's country seat. The countess had appeared downright overjoyed when a very soggy brother and sister-in-law had presented themselves at her door, especially considering that she had not, until that moment, been aware that she *had* a sister-in-law.

"Frances, please," the countess said merrily. "After all, we are sisters now!"

"Then you must call me Emily," Emily said warmly, trying to ignore the faint squelching sounds that her shoes were making. There was truly no reason she should be this wet, when great pains had been taken to ensure that she stayed dry, but she had had the misfortune to step down from the carriage directly into an enormous puddle, and so squelch she did. Julian, noticing her struggle, paused to reach out and twine her arm through his.

The countess—Frances—was about Emily's own age, or perhaps a bit younger, and she was tall and slender, her hair a dark auburn and her eyes the exact same dazzling blue as those of her brother. Emily recalled that she had been a great success over the course of a couple of Seasons, turning down several offers of marriage from exceedingly eligible gentlemen before becoming engaged to the Earl of Risedale in what was rumored to be a passionate love match. Emily's impression, based on the past five minutes, was of a sister who was extremely fond of her elder brother—and positively burning with curiosity about the wife he had shown up with.

To the countess's credit, however, she was doing an admirable job of hiding that curiosity.

So far.

"We never get to see Julian as often as we wish," Frances continued, tossing a fond look over her shoulder at her brother. "I should have known all along that the key was simply to get him married, and then he'd immediately appear on our doorstep."

"I don't believe I can take any credit," Emily said. "It is a rather curious series of events that led us here this afternoon."

"Which I'd love to hear all about, once you've had a chance to dry off," Frances said. "Ah, here we are—this is our very best guest room. You should be quite comfortable in here." She opened the door before them as she spoke, revealing not just a single room but a suite, with a small sitting room leading into a bedchamber; through the open interior door, Emily could just glimpse the sight of a large bed.

From the basket in her hand came an inquisitive *meow*, and Emily glanced down, startled, having almost forgotten she was holding it. Cecil gazed up at her from his cocoon of chemises. He alone among them seemed to have emerged from the storm entirely warm, dry, and unscathed, and Emily, despite her great affection for the kitten, could not help but wonder if she herself would be a bit warmer and drier if she had not expended so much energy in seeing to his well-being during the brief journey from carriage to front door.

Frances, predictably, dissolved into paroxysms of delight at the sight of his fluffy little black-and-white face, and Emily gazed fondly upon the tableau of her new beloved companion basking in the glory and affection his hostess so eagerly bestowed upon him. It really was enough to bring a tear to one's eye.

"Jesus Christ," Julian muttered in an undertone.

Emily scowled at him.

Cecil started purring.

After a few more minutes of this, Frances at last departed, with promises to have a lavish feast from the kitchens sent up for his lordship.

"Thank you, Frannie, I really am quite famished," Julian said.

"I meant the cat, Julian, don't be absurd," his sister said severely. "You go change into some dry clothes. I do not believe that you are so traumatized by a bit of rain that you can't make it downstairs to eat and socialize like a normal human being."

"I hate that cat," Julian observed to the room, and Emily felt rather gratified when, this time, Frances joined her in her scowling.

Three-quarters of an hour later, Emily and Julian were warm and dry and happily munching on some rather excellent ginger biscuits in the cozy comfort of what Frances had called the green drawing room—it was, indeed, quite green, from the green silk sofa to the green-and-gold-papered walls—as the rain continued in a torrential downpour that was visible through the mullioned windows that lined one wall.

"Cream? Sugar?" Frances asked Emily as she poured her tea.

"Neither, thank you," Emily said, accepting her cup and watching with interest as Frances added a generous dollop of milk and two sugar cubes to her brother's cup. Catching sight of Emily's amused face, Frances grinned.

"Yes, he still drinks tea as if he were a small boy in the nursery," she said, handing the cup to her brother, who did not look remotely embarrassed.

"I don't see why I should drink the stuff if it doesn't taste good," he said unrepentantly.

"You drink your coffee black in the mornings," Emily pointed out, then paused, registering that she had noticed this. It seemed awfully . . . wifely.

"That is because I have no choice but to drink coffee, as it's the only thing that makes me feel remotely human in the morning hours," he said, taking another sip of tea. "Tea, however, is a choice, and I don't see why I should choose to drink it if I don't enjoy it."

Emily took a sip of her own tea, relishing the sensation of it scalding the roof of her mouth. "I think it tastes lovely," she said serenely.

"You are unnatural," he replied, but the look in his eyes as he teased her told her that he found her anything but.

Frances, meanwhile, had prepared her own cup and was regarding this exchange with great interest.

"So," she said, seeming to have decided that she'd been patient and polite quite long enough. "You're married."

"I believe we established that already," Julian confirmed.

"By special license," Frances said.

"As we told you," replied her brother.

"Yesterday."

"Do you merely intend to repeat everything we told you upon our arrival, or was there some sort of question you wished to ask us?" Julian asked lazily, leaning back in his chair. Emily could tell that he was being deliberately provoking, adopting the air of rakish disinterest that had served him quite well in the past decade. But, she realized, if she knew this, then Frances surely knew it too.

"You are the most infuriating man," Frances said, taking a sip of tea that was more irritated than Emily would have thought it possible for a sip of tea to be. "But since you mention it, yes, I would dearly *love* to know how it is that my brother, the most avowed bachelor I've ever met in my life, suddenly came to be married by special license in a cow pasture."

This, Emily thought, was a trifle unfair to Elderwild, which was, after all, one of the grandest estates in England, but she didn't think now was necessarily the wisest moment to voice an objection. She and her own brother had not been close—he'd been a decade her senior, and had always seemed to view her as more of an irritation—but careful observation over the years of Diana and Penvale had taught her that, even with siblings who *did* share a close bond, it was wise to remain uninvolved once they devolved into petty bickering.

"Yes, a cow pasture," Julian drawled, pretending to check his shoes. "I think I even stepped in a bit of—"

"Julian Belfry, so help me God, if you do not explain yourself to me right now—"

"Please recall that Mother used to allow me to hold your leading strings, so you must forgive me if I don't take threats from this quarter particularly seriously."

"Speaking of Mama," Frances said, brightening, "have you informed her and Papa of your nuptials?"

"I have not," Julian replied.

"Julian, you must tell them!" Frances protested.

"Frannie, it's been all of a day-and-a-half since the wedding—please excuse me if dashing off a note to them wasn't at the top of my list of priorities, as I was surviving traumatizing carriage accidents and a near mauling in my own marriage bed." He paused, grinning. "And *not* in the way I was hoping."

"Julian!" Frances and Emily both cried in unison.

His grin widened.

"I apologize," he said, not sounding terribly repentant.

"Does this mean *I* can tell Mama and Papa, then?" Frances asked a touch gleefully.

"It does not."

"But if *you* don't intend to tell them—"

"I didn't say that," he interrupted. "Merely that I thought to perhaps wait until I'd returned to London and all of my wounds stopped bleeding before I made my way to my desk."

"Julian," Frances said severely, "it's most unbecoming of you to blame all of your troubles on that darling kitten."

"Thank you, Frances," Emily said gratefully. "I agree on that count."

"But," Frances continued, her gaze on her brother sharp, "if I were merely to *mention* it to Mama and Papa—or perhaps just to imply that you might have exciting news for them—"

"Shall I *imply* the next time I'm able to see Mother that you were the one, not I, who broke the vase in the drawing room at Everly

Priory?" Julian asked pleasantly. "The one that was a gift from the queen?"

"Julian Belfry!" Frances exclaimed, outraged. "That was *fifteen years ago—*"

"And yet, I'm still sure Mother would be quite interested to hear the true sequence of events involved."

"Er," Emily said, observing that Frances seemed to have been rendered momentarily speechless with outrage at this threatened betrayal. "What is the age difference between you two?" This seemed a safe, innocuous question for approximately two seconds, before both sets of eyes narrowed.

"Seven years," Frances said quickly.

"Oh," Emily said, "the same as—"

"*Eight* years," Julian interrupted.

Emily looked at him, raising inquiring eyebrows.

"I was born in June. Frances was born in December. It's seven and a half years, so we round up, to eight."

"*We* don't do anything of the sort," Frances said indignantly. "It could just as easily be rounded down, to seven, which is of course the sensible way to approach it. Don't you agree, Emily?"

Emily was unprepared to be called on to arbitrate this dispute, which she suspected was long-running. "I really couldn't say," she murmured, which was always the safest reply a lady could make in any sort of situation—and, truly, the only one that seemed to be desired of her half the time, anyway.

"I believe Emily's birthday is in May, so our ages work out quite neatly," Julian said with a dash of smugness that Emily personally felt was a bit unreasonable; none of them had the slightest bit of control over their birthdays, after all.

"This does not seem like a very productive line of debate," she said diplomatically, then paused, his words belatedly registering. "How do you know when my birthday is?" she asked her husband. She was quite certain it had never come up in any of their conversations.

Julian suddenly seemed exceptionally interested in the contents of his teacup. "I asked Lady Templeton." He glanced up briefly to meet her eyes, his expression inscrutable.

Emily frowned. "But why would you ask Diana?"

"I was concerned that it was coming up soon, and you wouldn't tell me, and I didn't want to miss it. But I didn't wish to ask you, because if it was next week and you admitted to that, I thought you'd feel as though I only bought you a gift because you'd told me, and—" He broke off with an awkward sort of cough, and Emily thought it was easily the most uncomfortable she had ever seen him look. She quickly raised her teacup to her lips, to hide whatever expression was on her face at that moment.

They were interrupted by the sudden appearance of the earl, a tall, lanky man. She had met him before but had never exchanged more than a few words with him, perhaps a dance here or there. He was handsome, Emily thought, in a rather unprepossessing way—he had hair of a middling brown and eyes of a similar shade, but he was nowhere near as striking as Julian, or Frances herself, for that matter. Emily had no doubt, watching Frances's gaze soften the minute it landed on his face, that theirs was a love match; the earl crossed the room with long strides to stand behind her, resting a hand on her shoulder, as she tipped her head up to look at him.

"Is your interrogation complete, my love?" he asked, his voice mock-stern and full of affection.

"I've not the faintest idea what you're talking about." His wife feigned ignorance, lowering her face to look at her guests once more. "Julian's here!"

"I gathered," the earl said, crossing to shake Julian's hand; Julian rose to meet him, using his free hand to clap the earl on the shoulder. He seemed at ease around his sister and brother-in-law in a way that Emily had not expected, given what she knew of his family history—clearly, his supposed estrangement from his parents did not extend to his sister.

"And I knew," the earl continued, "that when Graves told me that Belfry was here with a mysterious new wife in tow, I must come at once to save them from whatever torture you were subjecting them to."

"Risedale, my wife," Julian said, his hand at the small of Emily's back.

"Lady Emily," the earl said, bowing over her hand. "Or Lady Julian now, I suppose."

"Emily will do fine," she said, smiling at him, her attention distracted by the feeling of the faint, gentle pressure of Julian's hand at her back. "As I suppose we are family of a sort, now." As she spoke the words, she felt Julian's hand sliding down to the slight curve of her waist, resting lightly there. She felt a strange pang as she uttered the word *family*; for so long—as long as she could remember, really—hers had not been a terribly great comfort to her. Her brother had scorned her company when he was alive, and her parents had been more concerned with the depth of her curtsey and the rosiness of her cheeks than with anything that actually made her herself—a daughter was a burden, in their eyes, someone to make use of as best as possible, to make up for the bother and expense of raising her. She loved her parents, in her own fashion—but, as she sometimes admitted to herself in the darkest part of the night, the occasions on which she *liked* them were fleeting.

Marrying Julian, knowing of his distance from his own family in the years following his decision not just to purchase a theater but to take an active role in its operation—to appear onstage, to spend his days in an office at the Belfry rubbing elbows with actors rather than at his club among his peers—she had not expected much to change in regard to her familial ties, and yet this afternoon had presented a picture of a vastly different relationship than she had expected. Here were a sister-in-law, a brother-in-law, both of whom seemed like the sort of people Julian liked. The idea of having a family that was not the one she had carved out for herself—for Violet and Diana were sisters to her at this point, and dearer than any of her blood relatives—was startling, and unexpectedly comforting.

"I expect Frannie has been weaseling all the details out of you about the circumstances that led to such a sudden union?" the earl asked, his eyebrow quirked, and Emily felt her cheeks warm slightly as she considered the thoroughly scandalous reason that many marriages took place with great speed—and the fact that Risedale and Frances might well assume that that was the reason for her hasty marriage, too.

"She has been . . . very enthusiastic about our marriage," Emily said diplomatically. Next to her, Julian let out a snort of laughter, and the earl's mouth twitched.

"She's been hoping Belfry would marry for years now—she and I first met because she wished to introduce my younger sister to Belfry, which of course I wouldn't—" He broke off abruptly, seeming to suddenly recall that he was speaking to the woman who had, in fact, married his brother-in-law. Emily felt Julian's hand tighten at her waist for the merest instant before loosening again, and she cast a quick glance sideways, seeing the faint lines that had formed at the sides of his mouth, though these soon eased.

"You wouldn't allow it?" she guessed, smiling at the earl to show that she hadn't taken offense. "I can't say I blame you, my lord—as I understand it, Julian had never given any indication that he was the marrying sort."

"I always knew he was merely waiting for the right woman," Frances insisted, with a self-satisfied tone that Emily did not feel was entirely deserved, considering she had not been aware of the union in question until approximately an hour earlier. "You know." She waved a hand vaguely. "Cupid's arrow, with its unerring aim—"

"What are you quoting?" her husband asked, amused.

"Myself," she replied, with great dignity. "Why quote a dead man when I can make up my own poetic sayings?"

"Fair enough," he concurred, and Emily had the distinct impression that he had long since learned caution when sparring with his wife. Violet and Diana, she thought, would like Frances immensely— perhaps in London, they could all come to dinner. . . .

"In any case, I have indeed succumbed to the parson's mousetrap at last," Julian said, and Emily shot him an irritated look. She had always disliked that expression, since the implication was that the lady in question was conspiring with the parson to catch the mouse.

"I believe that *you* were the one who was particularly eager for our marriage, my lord," she said sweetly, giving him her best wide-eyed stare. "Perhaps it is I who should claim to have been caught."

"How did he convince you, then?" Frances asked, looking fascinated. "I've never heard so much as a whiff of scandal about you—"

"Merely about my family?" Emily interrupted, the words out of her mouth before she entirely realized she was speaking them. She sometimes formulated replies like this in her mind, rejoinders that were sharp or witty (or, ideally, both). It was a habit she had adopted the year she made her debut, when she was subject to a never-ending litany of reminders about appropriate behavior at home, and a never-ending series of tiresome conversations with potential suitors each evening. Coming up with these replies was a way to pass the time—a way to keep herself from going mad. She never said them *aloud*, however.

Until now, apparently.

Frances was gazing at her with an eyebrow arched—she seemed to share that particular mannerism with her brother—and an expression on her face that clearly indicated that she was revising whatever her previous opinion of the former Lady Emily Turner had been.

"Let us say," Frances said, a bit more carefully, "that your reputation has always seemed remarkably pristine to me, despite whatever scandal swirled around you."

And wasn't that a pithy way of summarizing why, precisely, Julian had wished to marry her? Lady Emily, whose reputation could withstand a brother's scandalous duel, a father's sordid debts, the constant attentions of a man like Mr. Cartham. Who better to drag the notorious Julian Belfry to respectability?

It was an arrangement that Emily had agreed to with her eyes wide open—she had not been misled as to the nature of her marriage, or what her new husband hoped to gain from their union. She had considered it a fair trade, given the freedom, the control over her own life that he offered her. But it was a slightly unpleasant reminder that, as weary as she might be of perfection, that was clearly what Julian expected of her—indeed, it was the entire reason he had married her.

"You can see how wise I was, then, in selecting her as my wife," Julian said, sounding pleased with himself. Emily's heart sank ever so slightly at the dismissive words, though she felt oddly comforted to see Frances's eyes narrow in disapproval on her behalf.

"That's not very romantic, Julian," Frances said.

"I apologize," Julian said with exaggerated gallantry. "Should I instead have mentioned the way Emily's eyes are like radiant stars, her cheeks the color of a perfect summer rose?"

"Not if you don't wish me to be ill," Frances said sweetly. "I was merely hoping to hear you describe your marriage in terms that don't make it sound like a business transaction."

But that would be rather difficult, Emily thought, considering the fact that a business transaction was exactly what it was.

Seven

"*Tomorrow,*" Julian said determinedly, two days later, "we are going to leave at first light."

Emily and Frances lowered their teacups in unison, casting glances out the window. After two days of rain—two days during which Julian had, in fits of wild optimism, repeatedly proclaimed that they'd be on the road at first light—the weather at last seemed to have improved.

"It hasn't rained at all today," Emily admitted, taking a sip of tea as she continued to gaze out the window. "I suppose we really might be able to leave tomorrow."

"Please tell me you don't think you can still catch Delacre, Julian," Frances said, setting her own teacup down and picking up a pen to continue scribbling at a letter she'd been working on for much of the afternoon. She had been briefed on their aborted chase, and remained skeptical that they would be able to catch the fleeing couple. "You've an understudy for Miss Simmons, don't you? Isn't this precisely what understudies are for?"

"I do," Julian said as patiently as he could manage, "but I don't want the understudy. I want my lead actress to be onstage in London where she belongs, not fleeing to the love nest of a bounder like Delacre. Besides," he added, "she's *better* than the understudy. That's why I cast *her*. And this show is a departure for us, and I want to make it a success."

"Is it not a comedy?" Frances inquired; this was generally what the Belfry was known for.

"It's what I'm calling an *intellectual* comedy," Julian said. "It's a reimagining of *Much Ado About Nothing* in which Beatrice and Benedick's dislike for each other stems from theological differences. It's by a young playwright named Fustian, and it's really something—still funny, but with jokes and banter and music of a more elevated nature."

Opposite him, Emily and Frances both blinked.

"That sounds . . ." Emily began, then trailed off, clearly searching for the correct adjective.

"Groundbreaking?" Julian suggested.

"Insufferable," Frances supplied.

He shot her an irritated look and she busied herself with her teacup once more.

"Is there a reason a normal sort of comedy wouldn't suffice?" Emily asked carefully.

"There are plenty of comedies of 'the usual sort' already," Julian explained. This was all part of his plan for the Belfry, a step toward fulfilling the vision he had of turning what had once been a bawdy, wholly improper establishment into one lauded for its theatrical achievement. "Fustian has something to say about our idea of faith and the limitations of the human mind."

Frances grimaced at this. "But people *like* comedies," she said. "No one wants to go to the theater and feel like they're sitting through a sermon."

"I assure you, they'll feel nothing of the sort," Julian said firmly. "They'll feel . . . enlightened."

"Julian," Frances said patiently, "if people wanted to feel enlightened, they'd go to a lecture, not the Belfry."

"That is precisely what I'm trying to change," Julian said, striving to prevent irritation from creeping into his voice. "The Belfry won't be the sort of theater people attend when they're half-foxed, looking for a skirt to chase for an evening. They'll attend the Belfry for its artistic merits. It will become a place to see and be seen among the fashionable set—God knows they're all desperate to seem more intelligent than they actually are."

"And that's why you're so hell-bent on catching this actress of yours?" Frannie said, still sounding rather skeptical.

"Precisely." He sighed and raked a hand through his hair. "The last thing I need is bloody Delacre's name mentioned in the same sentence as the Belfry—the man soils everything he touches. So we need to catch Miss Simmons quickly, before word makes it back to London that Delacre has absconded with one of my best actresses." He voiced this plan with a bit more confidence than he actually felt; he had a sneaking suspicion that they'd lost a fair amount of ground on the fleeing couple, and with each day that passed, he was increasingly aware of the people in London expecting his return, not least his manager and business partner, Laverre.

"But Julian—" Frances protested, before halting abruptly and returning her attention to the letter before her. Julian blinked; he was nearly certain that his sister had ceased talking because of the quick glance Emily had shot at her, but he couldn't quite believe it—no one had ever successfully managed to shut up Frances that quickly. Had he married a witch?

"Julian," Emily said quietly, "my parents do not yet know we are wed, and every day that we are gone increases the likelihood that word will reach them—and Mr. Cartham." Her voice dropped slightly when she uttered Cartham's name, and that small sign of discomfort on her part bothered him, he realized. He didn't like to think of her spending years in the company of a man whose name she uttered in an unhappy murmur.

"I should very much like to be the person to deliver the news to them myself," she added, and he noticed, faintly impressed, that she had managed to say something in a fairly pointed fashion without *sounding* pointed at all.

And then she didn't say anything else.

Julian looked at her.

She lifted her teacup to her lips.

He sighed.

She glanced at him inquisitively.

"Fine," he said shortly, not so much of a fool as to not know when he was fighting a losing battle. "We'll return to London, then." He raked another agitated hand through his hair. "Probably best to sort out this mess as quickly as possible, anyway." Seeing her brow wrinkle slightly at his words, he added hastily, "With the theater, I meant. Not our marriage." He shook his head slightly, ruminating darkly on the fact that he was fairly certain he'd been significantly less likely to put his foot in his own mouth before he'd been wed.

Frances, he realized, was watching them with great interest. "Can I help you?" he asked her, somewhat grumpily.

"You getting married," his sister said, quite decisively, "is the best thing that has happened in *years*."

Despite the action-packed nature of their first two days of carriage travel, their journey from Dovecote Manor to London was largely uneventful.

Distressingly uneventful in one respect, Julian thought, as he gazed across the carriage at Emily, whose attention was fixed entirely on Cecil Lucifer Beelzebub, who was curled up in her lap and staring at Julian from his cozy perch with an expression of self-satisfaction. It had transpired that Emily was entirely certain that the small demon could not possibly be expected to sleep anywhere other than tucked in her warm embrace—at least not until they returned to London, where she could see him fitted out with a proper bed to call his own.

"He was probably born in a barn," Julian had pointed out on their first night at Dovecote Manor, when he'd realized which way the wind was blowing. "Surrounded by rats. I hardly think an armchair before the fireplace will be an overly traumatizing spot for him to spend the night."

"But don't you see," Emily had said, wide-eyed, clutching the wretched creature to her chest, "that's precisely why I want to keep him close. We can only imagine what sort of horrible circumstances he was born into—I want him to know that he has a real home with us, one filled with love and affection."

"*I* could do with a bit of love and affection," Julian muttered in an undertone, casting an evil look at the kitten, who had naturally commenced purring, thus sending Emily into a fit of rapturous cooing. He had not pressed the matter, however—he had no desire to lure a reluctant woman to his bed, although given how she had responded to his kisses thus far, he didn't think she was unwilling.

Merely not willing enough to overcome her deranged fixation on a creature that looked like a fluffy, oversize rat.

But now they were back in London at last, the late-afternoon sun casting long shadows along the streets of Mayfair as they rattled along in the carriage. They drew to a halt before an imposing town house in Portland Square, and Emily blinked out the window, seeming to register where they were.

"But . . . but this is my parents' house," she said, turning from the window to look at him in confusion. Julian, who had given the direction to Reeve upon their last stop, gazed at her with a bit of trepidation, hoping he'd judged correctly.

"I thought you might wish to tell them immediately," he explained, reaching forward to lift Cecil Lucifer Beelzebub off her lap and place him in his bed of unmentionables. "I know you were concerned that someone else would break the news, and if we wish to avoid a scandal, we need to give the impression to society that your parents support the match. Surely they're more likely to do so if they hear of it directly from us."

"Oh, yes," she said, and he noticed a slight tension in the way she held herself, a certain tautness in the line of her neck. She was nervous, he realized.

"Would you rather wait?" he asked, not wishing to force her into anything she was uncomfortable with.

"No," she said, straightening in her seat. Whatever traces of nerves he had seen seemed to vanish in an instant, and he was once again faced with the Lady Emily who had walked into his theater in July—golden-haired, impossibly lovely, her spine straight, no sign of discomfort detectable.

"No," she repeated, "let's tell them. On one condition," she added, raising a hand as he reached to open the carriage door. He raised a brow inquisitively. "I wish to be the one to do the talking."

He sketched his best imitation of a courtly bow, to the extent that it was possible in the close confines of the carriage. "Be my guest," he said, and had the creeping expectation that he just might enjoy this.

Emily was not certain what reaction she'd expected from her parents upon informing them of her precipitous marriage, but she didn't think it was silence. Silence, however, was what greeted her after a rather rambling and circuitous explanation of her recent nuptials.

They had been ushered into the morning room in Rowanbridge House with some confusion by Cloves, the butler, who was understandably perplexed to find the daughter of the house who had departed a month earlier returning, more than a week late and unannounced, with a husband in tow. Emily had seated herself in one of the uncomfortable, spindly yellow silk Louis XIV chairs her mother so favored, while Julian stood beside her, his arm resting on the back of her chair, his proximity oddly comforting. When her parents had entered the room, wearing identical frowns, Julian had offered a short bow and a murmur of greeting, but otherwise had deferred entirely to Emily.

She had wondered if she might find some satisfaction in the telling—in the moment she was able to inform her parents that she was no longer a puppet to dance on their strings.

But now, said parents sat before her, gaping in silence, and she was beginning to feel, primarily, a bit concerned.

"Mama?" she ventured. "Papa? Have you nothing to say?"

Across from her, her mother regained enough of her composure to shut her mouth, and immediately reached into her sleeve for a handkerchief, which she pressed to her suddenly trembling lips. Her father, by contrast, displayed no emotion whatsoever, barring a certain lowering of the brow that never boded well.

It struck Emily suddenly that her parents had aged in the past few years. Her mother was still a handsome woman, but her blond hair had lost some of its luster, and she was beginning to look careworn, lines bracketing her mouth and a crease permanently visible between her eyes. Her father, too, showed a considerable amount of gray in his hair and whiskers, his eyes less bright than they had once been. The sight caused Emily a small pang of grief.

Before she could linger on maudlin thoughts, however, her mother spoke. She reached a trembling hand out to grip her husband's arm as she did so, despite the fact that, in Emily's experience, her parents liked to spend as little time in each other's company as possible.

"How could you?" she asked, lowering her handkerchief long enough to get the words out before pressing it to her mouth again, as though overcome by emotion. "What are we to do, if Mr. Cartham should . . ." She trailed off, her eyes skittering to Julian before landing squarely on her daughter once more, obviously hesitant to sink to discussing something so vulgar as money before someone outside the family.

Julian cleared his throat, then glanced down quickly at Emily before speaking, clearly reading permission in her gaze.

"Your daughter was very concerned with any impact our marriage might have on your own well-being, my lady, so I was able to reassure her that I am perfectly capable of paying Lord Rowanbridge's debts, whatever they might be. You may consider it a wedding gift to Emily."

His voice was not terribly warm, but Emily could tell he was trying his best not to allow any distaste to show in his tone.

"It's not merely a matter of blunt," her father said, speaking for the first time. "Mr. Cartham—" He broke off, glancing between his wife and daughter. "Perhaps you and I might speak privately, Belfry? Away from the ladies? There's no cause to trouble them with these sorts of matters."

"Papa," Emily said, trying to curb her frustration, "if Mama is already aware of the details, which I think she must be, then I do not see why you cannot speak freely before me—not when I have arranged such a neat solution to our financial troubles." She kept her tone mild; of course it would be too much to expect that maybe, just maybe, her parents might be grateful.

"Emily, this topic is not suitable for your ears," her father said sharply.

Her mother, meanwhile, sniffled conspicuously.

"To think I should live to hear my daughter discuss such matters!" she complained.

Emily bit back a sigh, feeling suddenly, uncharacteristically impatient.

"But this is ridiculous," she said. "I understand that my marriage has come as something of a shock to you, but you must see that it will put you in a better position than you were before."

"If you are concerned, Rowanbridge, about any . . . other leverage Cartham might possess," Julian said to her father, his tone even and deadly serious, "I think you should know that Cartham and I have several mutual acquaintances, and I've a bit of knowledge of him, myself."

"I don't know what you are implying, Belfry," the marquess said stiffly, "but—"

"I'm not implying anything," Julian interrupted. "Merely suggesting that if you have at some point involved yourself in some sordid business matters with Cartham that you'd prefer remain a secret, I can assure you that I've ways to ensure Cartham's silence."

Emily's father and husband exchanged a long look, and Emily positively wished to scream in frustration at the fact that they would not speak openly before her. Instead of screaming, however, she simply said in her most cheerful tones, "Well, there you have it, Papa, Mama. All will be well!"

"But at what cost?" wailed her mother. "To think that my daughter, the daughter of a marquess, of a title dating back ten generations, should marry—"

"The son of a marquess?" Emily interrupted. "Whose title is also, I believe, quite ancient?"

"Who *owns a theater*," her mother said in a dramatic whisper, as if Julian were not standing five feet away.

"And how, precisely, is that worse than my marrying a man who owns a gaming house?" Emily demanded. "A man I could scarcely bear to spend ten minutes in conversation with?"

She realized, with a feeling of faint astonishment, that this was the first time she'd ever admitted this to her parents. She had felt so keenly, for so long, the burden of Mr. Cartham's company, and yet she had never voiced her distress to her parents. What would have been the point? Complaining would only have served to convince them that she was mulish, ungrateful, and unreasonable.

"Don't be hysterical, Emily," her mother said, nearly making Emily laugh in incredulity—she'd never been hysterical in her life. "Mr. Cartham was just a temporary suitor. We would never have dreamed of allowing you to settle for him."

Out of the corner of her eye, Emily saw her father, who looked furtive, and Emily realized: her mother had never fully understood how dire their situation was. She didn't know if her father had refused to tell her, or if her mother had refused to listen, but somehow, the marchioness had convinced herself that she was still going to make a spectacular match for her dowry-less daughter, who'd spent years surrounded by scandal.

"I apologize, my lady, if you feel that your daughter is *settling*," Julian said, casting a glance in her mother's direction and speaking as though the last word were something distasteful. "But I can assure you that I'm more than capable of seeing to your husband's debts—and any other difficulties that might arise—as well as of providing for your daughter." Julian's voice was cold and firm, almost unrecognizable to Emily's ears, and all at once she thought she understood why he had managed to turn his theater into such a successful business operation, despite his aristocratic upbringing. No one would want to argue with that voice.

"As *if* I should ever be concerned with anything so vulgar!" the marchioness said, adopting the tones of the grievously insulted, and Emily, all at once, had had quite enough.

"Wouldn't you, Mama?" she asked coolly, and—so quickly that she half wondered if she'd imagined it—she felt Julian's hand tighten briefly on her shoulder in a comforting squeeze. "When Papa's debts have dictated my behavior for *years* now? When perfectly eligible gentlemen have been scared away because we mustn't offend Mr. Cartham, the holder of those debts?" She rose from her seat, feeling somehow that this degree of indignation could not be borne while seated. "And was I ever consulted about any of this? Of course not. I was merely expected to behave exactly as you dictated, be the meek, obedient daughter you demanded—"

"You were expected to be a lady," her mother said sharply. "And behave as a lady should."

"Of course," Emily said, nodding. "And I was expected to be so perfect a lady that my reputation could emerge unscathed from close association with an unsavory character like Mr. Cartham. Do you *know* how difficult that was? How exhausting? To have to be *that* perfect, every day, for years?"

"You did what any daughter would be expected to do," her mother said thunderously. "You supported your family."

"My family," Emily repeated, feeling a wild desire to laugh. She controlled the impulse with some difficulty, but could not quite suppress the ironic twist to her lips, so unlike her usual careful smiles. "My family, who thought only of themselves. My family, who never once thought of what *I* might wish, of *my* future—"

"Your future was to make a brilliant match for the sake of this family," her mother said shortly. "As you knew perfectly well, from the moment you made your curtsey before the queen."

"Who, precisely, do you think would have married me, with no dowry, with Father's debts unpaid?" Emily asked her mother incredulously. "I was going to spend my entire life squired around on Mr. Cartham's arm, until perhaps he decided I was worth marrying after all, and Father would have agreed to it, just to solve all of our money troubles! Is that what you'd have preferred?"

"It never would have come to that," her mother insisted, and Emily gaped at her, unable to comprehend how her mother so wholly failed to understand the situation as it had truly stood. She glanced at her father, who continued to look furtive—all the confirmation Emily required to be certain that this was, in fact, precisely what would have happened. Her mother, however, did not notice this, and added, "This business with Mr. Cartham would have been sorted eventually, and then you could have gone on to marry a viscount or an earl—done your duty to us! And instead you've—"

"Instead, she married me," Julian said, quietly but quite firmly, his gaze fixed upon her parents with an expression of unmistakable distaste upon his face. "And I'd suggest you not speak to my wife in such a manner again—not if you wish me to help you, as I've promised."

Something within Emily warmed to hear Julian refer to her as his wife in such a proprietary, protective way. She had not fully realized how alone, how unprotected she had felt for so many years, that the sound of someone speaking up on her behalf should be such a novelty.

"I do not think we need discuss this further, at the moment," she said carefully, something within her already weakening at the sight of her mother's still-trembling lip. "Papa, I believe you and Julian can see to any financial arrangements at a later date; it has been a long day, and I should like to return home. I will send someone round tomorrow to collect my things."

"Surely Hollyhock—" her mother began.

"Hollyhock will not be accompanying me to my new household," Emily said shortly. "I will be hiring new help of my own." She turned to look at Julian, who was watching her with an expression she could not quite identify. "Shall we?"

"After you," he said, stepping back to allow her to pass him, and it was with some satisfaction that Emily swept from the room, her husband at her heels, leaving her still-stupefied parents in her wake.

Eight

Speaking one's mind to one's parents was most invigorating, Emily was discovering.

"I think I shall cherish the memory of their expressions for the rest of my life," she said cheerfully that evening as she and Julian lingered over glasses of wine before the fireplace in his bedroom, a small table between them. They'd dined *à deux* on braised ham and an assortment of vegetable dishes, with a platter piled high with pastries for dessert; this had been presented to them by a footman who vanished as quickly as he'd appeared. He, like the rest of the staff, had fought to keep any visible sign of surprise from his face when the master of the house had returned home that evening with a new wife in tow, but Emily had not been fooled—out of the corner of her eye, she had seen Julian's butler offer an infinitesimal raising of his brow, which, coming from an English butler, was the equivalent of garment-rending and hysterics from anyone else. For her part, Emily was grateful that they had skipped a formal dinner downstairs tonight; the knowledge that she was now mistress of a home was unexpectedly overwhelming, considering that she'd been preparing for this role for years. Now that it was a reality, however, she was finding the prospect a trifle daunting—particularly once she had laid eyes on the home in question.

"But this is so . . . respectable," she had said as she'd stepped down from the carriage in front of Julian's house on Duke Street.

"What were you expecting?" he'd asked, tucking her arm against his side as they ascended the steps to the elegant town house before them. "A den of iniquity? Tucked away down a seedy alley, scarlet curtains on the window, the odd scantily clad woman waiting nearby, ready to be of service?"

"Well," Emily had said, blinking, "yes."

Julian had laughed at that, and Emily, in turn, had laughed, too, and then there had been the rush of introductions to the staff, a brief tour of the house—which, while clearly lacking a female touch in terms of its decor, was undoubtedly the house of a gentleman, rather than that of a dissolute rake.

As dinner came to an end, however, Emily was increasingly aware of her own nerves—which were entirely centered on the fact that she and Julian had been married the better part of a week, and had yet to consummate their marriage.

Emily frowned as soon as the thought flitted across her mind. What a ghastly phrase. Diana and Violet had led her to believe that the marital act was quite enjoyable, but it didn't sound like it when the word *consummation* came into play. That word instead conjured the impression of the act that her mother had given her— in short, that it was an unpleasant but necessary experience to be borne without complaint, but ideally undertaken as infrequently as possible.

"Why are you frowning?" Julian asked from across the table, where he was reclining slightly in his seat, wineglass in hand, still chuckling over the memory of her parents' astonished faces.

"I was thinking about the word *consummate*," Emily said idly, and relished the moment that followed, in which Julian nearly tipped his chair over backward.

"Excuse me?" he asked.

"It's not a very romantic word," she continued. "It doesn't precisely make one wish to fling their clothes off and fall down on the Aubusson rug in a passionate interlude."

"What, precisely," Julian asked, setting down his wineglass, "do you know about passionate interludes on Aubusson rugs?"

"Nothing firsthand, of course," Emily said cheerfully, "but Violet has always been very fond of hers in the library in their house. She says it brings back happy memories."

Julian let out a sputter of laughter as he leaned forward, bracing his elbows on the table, and Emily grinned at him.

"I'm not sure I'll ever be able to stand upon that rug without contemplating what horrors it's witnessed, if we are ever invited to dinner with them," he said, rising to his feet and rounding the table toward her, the telltale lines at the corners of his eyes indicating his amusement. "Though, considering the fact that the last time I was inside Violet and Audley's home was when I was pretending to be a doctor giving Violet a dire prognosis, I'm still not certain Audley wants me under his roof."

Emily had a sudden, lovely mental image of dinners with Violet and Lord James, Diana and Lord Willingham—of finally getting to experience London the way her friends did, out from beneath the protective, suffocating wing of her mother. What did it matter if hers was not a love match? If it made scenes such as long, lingering dinners with friends possible, she would never for one moment regret her decision to marry Julian Belfry.

"You shouldn't complain about that scheme," she said to him lightly. "If Violet hadn't convinced—"

"Practically coerced," he said darkly.

"If Violet hadn't *convinced* you to put your acting skills to use in her attempts to reconcile with Lord James," she continued, ignoring his interjection, "she and I never would have attended a show at the Belfry, and you and I wouldn't have met."

He reached out and took one of her hands, tugging her out of her chair and toward him. "And what a shame that would have been." The words landed with more weight than she thought he intended, his voice lacking the sardonic note that was often present, the sentence uttered with complete sincerity. A pause stretched between them for a moment as they stood facing one another, her hand still clasped by his, and then he spoke again, his voice an octave lower this time. "Was there a reason you were contemplating that particular word?"

Of course Emily blushed. "Well," she said. "We did get married just a few days ago."

"I recall," Julian murmured, pulling her closer again, the space between them slowly being eliminated with each step she took. "An elderly man with a horrid collar rambled on about God, I believe."

Emily let out a startled laugh. "I don't think God looks very kindly upon husbands who mock vicars."

Julian reached out to rest his free hand gently on her waist. "I personally hope God doesn't pay overmuch attention to what a husband and wife do or say within the confines of their bedroom, to be quite honest."

"And what, precisely, is it that they do?" she asked, her voice falling to a whisper as she spoke.

In reply, Julian kissed her.

It was a slow, languorous kiss, one that implied that there was no rush, nowhere else to be, nothing else that mattered except for the feeling of his mouth on hers, his lips parting hers, the sweep of his tongue against her own. Emily kissed him back fiercely, the hesitation and uncertainty that had gripped her just moments before having vanished in a rush of sensation. She reached up to slide an arm around his neck, rising up on her toes to press herself against him, relishing the feeling of her body molding itself to his. His arm slid around her waist and his other hand gently cupped her cheek and the curve of her jaw, angling her face so that he could kiss her more thoroughly.

Thorough, Emily thought, with what limited mental capacity she possessed at the moment, was a good way to describe his kisses. He kissed her as if he were putting every part of himself into that kiss, as if there were nothing more important to him, in that moment, than kissing her.

Emily, without fully realizing what she was doing, lifted her hands to his cravat, fumbling a bit with the knot. Julian broke their kiss with a laugh, taking a small step back to create enough space between them so that he could assist her. His face was slightly flushed, and Emily felt a strange surge of power course through her with the knowledge that she had caused that. In all their warnings and advice about the marital act—and there had been many—Violet and Diana had not prepared her for the giddy rush that came from the knowledge that one had a man at one's mercy and within one's power. The knowledge that the man was, of all people, Julian Belfry somehow made it all the better. Emily had always been skeptical of the adage that reformed rakes made the best husbands, but—while it was too early yet to say what sort of husband Julian would prove to be—it certainly seemed to be true that they made exciting ones, at the very least.

Though, truth be told, Julian didn't look like quite his usual rakish self at the moment, as he stood before her, struggling with his cravat.

"I think Humphreys might have gotten a bit overly excited at the notion that we'd be back in town among polite society at last," he said, letting out a muffled curse, followed by a "ha!" of triumph when he finally tore it off. "He tied my cravat so elaborately that you'd think we were engaged to have tea with the queen."

"Does this knot have a name?" Emily asked, trying and failing to tear her eyes away from the patch of bare skin now visible at his throat.

"I believe it is one of his own dastardly invention," Julian said darkly, tossing the cravat aside and shrugging off his jacket as well. As he stood in just his shirtsleeves and waistcoat, Emily could not help appreciating the broadness of his shoulders. She reached a hand out to his waistcoat, undoing one of the buttons there. She cast a quick glance up at him, wondering if she was being overly bold, but he was regarding her with such warmth and heat in his gaze that she felt a blush creeping up her chest and into her face, and she decided that she couldn't possibly be doing anything wrong, not if he was looking at her like that.

She made quick work of the rest of the buttons, her fingers nimble from the long hours she had spent in the drawing room at Rowan-bridge House bent over her embroidery, though she didn't think this was precisely the activity her mother had had in mind when she'd encouraged her to hone those skills.

At the moment, she was particularly grateful for those hours spent doing delicate handiwork, because it meant that Julian's waistcoat was cast aside in a matter of moments and he was standing before her in his shirtsleeves, and even that was only for another brief moment before he tugged his shirt over his head and stood before her bare chested.

Emily wasn't certain what she'd been expecting, but it was not the sight before her. He reminded her of a statue she'd seen in a museum once, one that her mother had hurried her past, declaring it inappropriate for the eyes of a young lady. But Emily didn't find anything remotely inappropriate about the sight of Julian, all bare skin and muscle, his blue eyes intent on her face, his breath coming slightly more quickly.

She reached for him even as he reached for her and they met in a bruising kiss, her hands skimming across his shoulders and down his chest, and she thrilled at the feeling of her skin against his, the heat and smoothness of him. His hands went to her hair, the *clink* of hairpins hitting the floor a moment later. Then came the feeling of his fingers in her hair, loosening the braid and tangling at the base of her neck to cup her head, tilting it back to grant him access to the long line of her throat, upon which he placed a series of lingering kisses.

She gasped, then moaned, the noise sounding strange to her own ears, and she felt self-conscious all of a sudden, some of the lovely warmth vanishing. She could feel the curve of his mouth against her skin and knew he was smiling, but she could not stop herself from growing slightly stiff in his arms. He drew back and straightened.

"What's wrong?" he asked, and she noticed that there was the faintest ragged edge to his breathing. Could *she* have caused that?

"Nothing," she said quickly, giving him her most reassuring smile, but for once this smile failed her, because he frowned slightly, a crease appearing between his brows.

"Did I do something you didn't like?" he asked, sliding his hand down her arm to take her hand. "You should tell me at once if I do."

"No," she said hastily, a blush suffusing her face. "Quite the opposite. I just . . ." She trailed off, growing more embarrassed by the moment, and feeling so terribly *young* compared to him. He was seven years older than her, but in that moment it felt like more—all his years of experience as a gentleman out on the town stretching out between them.

"I worried I was—well, being too *noisy*," she said, the words barely above a whisper, feeling the heat spread from her cheeks down her neck and chest.

A slow grin appeared on his face at her words, but it didn't look like he was laughing at her—instead, it was a grin of satisfaction.

"What if I told you," he said, taking a step closer to her again, "that you can be as noisy as you like, and I won't mind it?" He reached his free hand up to brush his fingers against her burning cheek. "Indeed, what if I told you that I'd *like* it?"

"You'd . . . like it if I were noisy?" she asked hesitantly, meeting his eyes quickly before her gaze flicked away.

"Quite a bit," he said, his grin spreading, and his fingers slid from her cheek down to her chin, cupping it lightly, tipping her face up so that their gazes locked. "Anything you wish to do when we are alone together is what you should do. And if you're noisy—which I *do* like—it will just tell me when I do something particularly well. It's . . . helpful." He leaned in closer to brush a kiss to one corner of her mouth.

"Helpful?" Emily repeated breathlessly. "I—I like to be helpful."

"I've noticed," he murmured, kissing the opposite corner.

"In that case," she said, and with a sudden rush of boldness she slid her hands into the short hair at the nape of his neck, tugging his mouth back to hers, and she kissed him—and she was the one doing the kissing this time, not the other way around. It was she who snaked her free hand around his waist, keeping him pressed tightly to her, and she who darted her tongue out to trace at the seam of his lips. She felt daring and wanton and not at all like herself—but perhaps like a new version of herself, a new Emily whom she could come to recognize just as well, with time.

She drew back after a moment, and he leaned down, pressing his forehead against hers, the blue of his eyes all that she could see.

"Your eyes," she said idiotically, "are so blue."

The eyes in question crinkled at the corners as he smiled. She liked those crinkles—she'd noticed them several times over the past couple of days, and wondered that she had never noticed them before that.

"So are yours," he said.

"No." She shook her head vehemently, feeling more of her hair escape from what was left of her braid. "Not like yours."

"If you say so." He sounded skeptical and amused, and as though this were not, perhaps, the most interesting conversation they could be having at that particular moment.

"Surely some other lady has told you that," Emily said, huffing in indignation.

"I'm not terribly interested in discussing other ladies at the moment," he murmured, leaning forward to give her a long, lingering kiss.

A moment later, she broke away, laughing. "I thought we agreed not to lie to each other."

There was a flash of something in his eyes, gone as quickly as it had appeared. "I'm not lying," he said, and there was something almost . . . *annoyed* in his voice. "I'm not trying to flatter you when I say that I don't have any interest in talking about, or thinking about, anyone other than you right now."

Emily looked at him, her arm still locked around his neck, and in that moment . . . she believed him.

Truth be told, she didn't want to think about anyone else, either. All she wanted to do was cast herself into the heat building between them, and see where it took her.

So, very deliberately, she stepped back, locked her eyes directly on his, and began to wriggle out of her dress.

And then, just as quickly, realized that she had never undressed herself before.

She paused, befuddled. This was ridiculous. She was twenty-three years old—surely she could take a dress off! And yet—

Apparently, no.

Julian watched her, heat and amusement mingling in his gaze. "Having trouble?" he asked.

Emily flushed. "I just realized that I've never done this alone before," she admitted. "I didn't realize quite how reliant on my maid I was." She began to tug at her bodice, attempting to lift it over her head. "This is absurd," she said, blowing an errant strand of hair out of her face.

"Some assistance?" he asked, and really, she had no choice but to accept, given her current circumstances. It took him a matter of moments to extricate her from her gown and toss it aside—with a man's typical disregard for any of the wrinkles that might have caused, she thought—and then he stepped back, eyeing the sight of her in her corset and chemise with frank appreciation.

"I know I'll need help with this bit," she said, and turned her back to him. There was a moment of silence, and then a rustle of fabric as Julian stepped forward, then the feeling of his fingers at her back, loosening her corset. She almost, in her nervousness, made some joke about his past experience with this task, but she recalled that unidentifiable look in his eye a minute earlier, and this recollection stilled her tongue. Instead, she was achingly conscious of the sound of her own breaths, coming more quickly now, as his hands moved whisper-soft down her spine. In a few moments more the garment was loose, and she instinctively clasped her hands to her chest, keeping the corset clutched close to her, before a moment later realizing how absurd this was and letting it fall to the floor.

She turned in Julian's arms and he was there, meeting her, his mouth hungry on hers, his hand moving up to cup her breast through the fine fabric of her chemise, the other sliding down to her hip. She could feel him hard against her stomach, and—thanks to more than one educational conversation with her friends—knew what this meant.

He began walking her backward in the direction of the bed, until she felt the back of her knees hit the edge of the mattress and she sank down onto it, pulling him down next to her without breaking their kiss. A moment later, however, he leaned back and reached a hand up to cup her cheek.

"I think you should know that I've never done this before," he informed her solemnly.

And Emily, with all the poise and tact that came so naturally to her, said, "*What?*"

Seeing her incredulous expression, he quickly added, "Not—not the *act*, I didn't mean that. Obviously, I've gone to bed with someone before."

"I should hope so!" she said, relief washing over her, though she was still not certain she'd entirely recovered from her momentary shock. "Your reputation would have been quite appallingly inflated otherwise. Besides," she added, "I rather think at least one of us should know what they're doing."

"That's the problem, though," Julian said, looking the slightest bit uneasy. "I've never—what I meant was, I've never done this with a virgin before."

"Oh," she said, and paused for a moment, considering. "I—I suppose I assumed as much. You don't seem the type to seduce eligible ladies and then refuse to marry them."

"A touching vote of confidence in my character," he said dryly. "But my point is, I don't want this to be unpleasant for you."

She frowned. "Why should it be unpleasant?"

"Because it's your first time."

"Does one have to practice it an awful lot to come to like it?" This was mystifying, and certainly not at all the impression she'd gotten from Violet and Diana—indeed, Diana and Lord Willingham had not seemed to require much time at all to begin enjoying one another's company quite enthusiastically, despite the fact that Emily knew it had been several years since Diana had last engaged in marital relations.

"Well, no," he said. "Or, at least, men don't."

"But women do?"

"I don't know. I believe so. That's why I'm mentioning it."

"Well, what is the issue? Do you not know how to ensure that I enjoy myself?" This was disappointing—while Diana and Violet had at times been a trifle confusing in terms of the wisdom they had imparted, her overall impression from them had been that bedsport was something to look forward to.

"I certainly do!" Julian said, all outraged pride. "But I just want to warn you that since you're a virgin, it might . . . hurt."

"Hurt!" Emily crossed her arms over her chest, suddenly feeling very, very unclothed, and wishing that Julian had thought to start this conversation when she was still wearing her gown. "Why should it hurt?"

This was not at all in keeping with what her friends had told her.

"Because it sometimes does, the first time," he said. "Or so I've been told."

"Sometimes, but not always?" she asked.

"Er," he said. "I believe so?"

"You are not inspiring much confidence at the moment, I must say," she said a bit huffily.

"Jesus Christ," he muttered, rubbing his hand over his face in frustration. "Would it have been better to say nothing at all? I didn't want to hurt you unexpectedly—I brought up the possibility so that you'd know to tell me if you wanted me to stop."

"Well *now* I'm just going to be waiting for it to start hurting!" she said. "How am I possibly supposed to enjoy myself?"

He sighed a long-suffering sort of sigh, which Emily did not think was at all fair, considering that he was currently offering an impression of marital relations that implied that *she* was the one who was about to be suffering. "I suppose I should merely be grateful you're expecting to enjoy it at all, and not weeping and cowering in the corner, as I feared you might."

"I have very informative friends," she said primly. "I'm not as innocent as I look."

His mouth quirked in a crooked smile. "You'll be a lot less innocent in a few minutes, if you ever stop interrogating me."

"I'll stop interrogating you once you offer me some sort of assurance—"

"I am usually considered rather good at this, you know," he said.

"Do you always start off with warnings of pain and suffering?" she asked, eyeing him suspiciously.

"No," he said, looking offended. "Because I've never—"

"Gone to bed with a virgin, yes, I know," she said impatiently. It was astonishing, really, what wonders righteous indignation could work. She didn't feel remotely nervous anymore. "Is this some sort of attempt to set my expectations low?"

"Good God in heaven," he murmured. "No!"

"You seem to be referencing our heavenly father an awful lot for a man who told me not ten minutes ago that God had no place in the bedchamber," she reminded him.

"I don't think I've mentioned God as much in the past ten years as I have in the past ten minutes," he said, sounding exasperated.

"You have only yourself to blame for that," she said. "On both counts."

"If this is the punishment being visited upon me for a somewhat lackadaisical attendance record at church, I'd like to note that I am appropriately cowed."

"I believe we have wandered rather far from the point," she said.

"I'm sorry, do you even recall what the point was?" he asked her, incredulous.

Emily drew herself up straight—difficult to do in a terribly commanding fashion when one was sitting on a bed wearing only a chemise, but she gave it her best effort—and fixed him with a glare. "We are discussing the—the—the consummation of our union."

His mouth quirked. "I thought you didn't like that word. 'Not romantic,' wasn't that your complaint?"

"Well, it's certainly more polite than some of the alternatives," she admitted.

"Oh?" he asked, and there was a wealth of illicit promise in that single syllable. "I must confess, I'm suddenly desperate for you to tell me some of the *impolite* phrases you've heard to describe this particular activity."

"I'd much prefer that you *showed* me some of the impolite aspects of this activity instead," she said, and despite the fact that this was easily the boldest thing she had ever said in her entire life, for once she did not blush. This was her husband, and they had been robbed of their wedding night, and she, for one, did not intend to be distracted again.

Right on schedule, a plaintive *meow* came from the basket before the fireplace.

"Not now," Emily and Julian commanded in unison, never breaking eye contact with each other, and Cecil subsided with a sleepy, yawned *meow*.

"Emily Turner," Julian said, a slow, seductive smile curving at his mouth.

"Belfry," she corrected, and he paused—she thought, for a moment, that he thought she was addressing him, so she added, "Emily Belfry, if you please."

He gazed at her for a long moment, then reached out and picked up her hand, bringing it to his lips for a soft kiss that caused warmth to rush over her like a wave.

"Emily Belfry," he repeated, "I can't think of anything I'd like more than to be very, very impolite with you."

And without any further ado, he proceeded to do just that.

Emily's recollections of the evening became less clear from that point forward—her focus seemed to narrow, so that her entire world became their room and the soft firelight and the snowy expanse of the bed, and the spectacular sight of Julian Belfry, in all his naked glory, before her. He dispensed with his trousers and smalls in such a hurry that she didn't even have the chance to reach out to attempt to assist with their removal, and then he was kissing her again, and he was warm and close and she could do nothing but close her eyes and wrap her arms around his neck and not worry even the slightest bit about any noises she might be making.

He pressed her down into the mattress, and she never would have imagined that the feeling of his body, the weight of him bearing down on her, could be so strangely comforting. Soon enough, however, he was sliding a hand beneath her chemise, up the bare skin of her leg and thigh, reaching the juncture between her legs, and she could not manage more than a moment's embarrassment about the slickness he encountered there, because *oh God* was it normal for every single nerve ending in her entire body to take up temporary residence in that particular location? This was her last coherent thought for quite a while, because his fingers quite quickly got to work, and she could feel herself climbing some sort of unknown peak, moving higher and higher, but before she could reach the top his fingers were gone and she came quite close to uttering some frightfully unladylike words, but all at once fingers were replaced with lips and tongue and—

Oh.

And *oh*.

And then she didn't think anything else for quite a while.

When next she became aware of herself and her surroundings, she was lying in the cradle of his arms, blinking in confusion, and saying the first words that came to mind: "I don't understand why you were worried about hurting me."

He laughed at that, but she was too blissfully dazed to be much bothered by this, and instead leaned her head back on the comforting firmness of his shoulder, turning her face to the side so that she could press a kiss to his skin.

"This wasn't the part that I was worried about," he said, sliding a lazy hand up her arm. "There's more to it, you see."

"I know that," she said, still too rapturous to take issue with his knowing tone. "I do have two married friends, you know."

His hand stilled. "I still can't believe ladies talk about such things."

Emily snorted—she was not certain such a sound had ever passed her lips before, but *honestly*. "I don't know that ladies in general do, but I assure you that Violet and Diana, specifically, do."

"I suppose I shouldn't be surprised, knowing the ladies in question," he said with a resigned sigh.

"They're very useful friends," she said, a shiver coursing through her as his hand resumed its lazy path up and down her arm. "If I had to rely on what my mother had told me—well, I'd not even understand that clothing had to be removed."

"Technically, not much clothing *does* have to be removed," he said, casting a significant look down at the rumpled chemise that Emily still wore, though it was, at the moment, bunched up near her waist.

"Speaking of which," he added, and Emily let out a giggle as he sat up slightly—resulting in a very impressive display of abdominal muscles in the process; good heavens, did all men look like that under their waistcoats? Surely not—and reached down to tug at the hem of her chemise. Emily obligingly wriggled out of it, resisting the temptation to cross her arms over her chest as he cast the chemise aside and gazed down at her appreciatively. She was glad, in that moment, that she overcame her modesty—it was undeniably gratifying to have a man like Julian, with a reputation like his, gazing down at her naked body with such undisguised admiration. His blue eyes, which she normally considered icy, were full of heat as he regarded her with frank appreciation, and even as she felt a blush crawl across her chest, up her throat and into her cheeks, she felt another warmth, too, deep in her belly and between her legs.

She *liked* being looked at like this, she realized.

And, if his own physical reaction to the sight of her naked body was any indication—and, indeed, this reaction was impossible to ignore, given how closely they were pressed together—he liked doing the looking.

"Hello," she said softly, gazing up at him and reaching a hand up to touch the lock of black hair that insistently fell onto his forehead.

"Hello," he replied, his low murmur rich with promise.

And then he leaned down and kissed her.

It was a kiss that Emily felt with her entire body—her arms, seemingly of their own accord, reached up once more to twine around his neck, then begin a steady downward path along his back, feeling the muscles there, the warmth of his skin and the gooseflesh that arose in the wake of her trailing fingers.

His hands were busy, too, at her breasts, in her hair, and his mouth was on her neck and her legs were falling open seemingly of their own accord and all at once he was *there*, stiff and insistent, and his voice was in her ear murmuring, "Is this all right?" and her only reply was a breathless gasp of assent, and then he was pressing into her, and it didn't hurt, it was just a sudden, overwhelming pressure, a tightness, and then he began to move, and the only coherent thoughts she was capable of mustering were *yes* and *more* and *please*.

At some point in the proceedings, Julian rolled onto his back, pulling Emily with him, and she found herself straddling him, gazing down at him with sudden uncertainty. His hands moved to her waist, pulling her back down onto him, and she gasped at the sudden friction of this new angle, her eyes fluttering shut. Her body began to move of its own accord—there were a couple of moments where it wasn't quite right, but they soon found a rhythm, and she opened her eyes at one point to find him staring at her so intently that she felt herself blush once more.

He leaned forward to brush her hair back over her shoulder, exposing her more fully to his hungry gaze.

"God, I love looking at you," he said, his voice low and rough-edged, his breathing uneven, and somehow, despite the fact that she'd spent her life entirely aware of the weight of men's gazes on her, she'd never before felt so *glad* to be looked at—so powerful with the knowledge of a man's attention.

She began to lose all track of time, and it was perhaps a minute or an hour later that his hand was between her legs again and he was murmuring, "Tell me where to touch you," and she—who an hour earlier could never have imagined herself uttering these words—gasped, "There—now faster—" and she was climbing that peak once more and his thrusts, too, were becoming more erratic—

In the aftermath, collapsed atop him, trying to catch her breath, his own breath coming fast and heavy against her neck, the only thing she could think to say was:

"I still believe we could have dispensed with the unnecessary five-minute discussion about it hurting."

At which—of course—he laughed.

Nine

Going to bed with a virgin was vastly more entertaining than advertised, Julian thought.

It was early the next morning; the sunlight peeking around the curtains had a soft rosy glow to it, and beside him Emily still slept. She was a remarkably heavy sleeper, he'd discovered; he, admittedly, was an unusually fitful one, but every time he'd awakened in the night, she'd been just as she was now: curled up on her side, all that glorious golden hair cascading over the bare shoulder visible above the sheets, one hand resting on the bedspread between them. She looked peaceful in slumber, her face relaxed into an expression of ease that made him realize how carefully she held herself during all of her waking hours.

Or, at least, all of her waking hours except her last one, last night.

He could not help a smile from creeping over his face at the memory, and he tucked an arm behind his head, reminiscing. He'd never, of course, believed all the rubbish men of his station liked to toss around, about wives not enjoying bedsport and thus necessitating the procurement of a mistress. As far as Julian was concerned, if a woman did not enjoy going to bed with her husband, that said more about her husband than it did about her.

However, he had approached the task before him with a slight amount of apprehension. He'd not the faintest clue what to expect from a gently bred virgin—it was, after all, a species that he had avoided like the plague from the time he was old enough to understand what went on between a man and a woman, and the fact that he'd very much like to enjoy said activities without getting leg-shackled himself—and he'd been terrified of somehow ruining the experience for her. As it turned out, he might have spared himself all that angst and simply gotten on with it.

He realized, for an absurd moment, that what he really wanted to do in that instant was wrap his arm around her, tug her close to him. It was such a strange impulse, so affectionate, so domestic, so . . . *tender*, that he nearly started with surprise. What on earth had possessed him?

As if summoned by his thoughts of her, she stirred beside him, and he glanced down, watching her face lose a fraction of its relaxed elasticity, even before she opened her eyes. He was surprised by the pang of sadness this caused him, and he sternly reminded himself that her ability to exert such forceful control over her facial expressions, and everything else about her behavior, was, in large part, the reason he'd married her. There was no room for sadness.

He could tell the moment she came fully awake, because she suddenly grew very still, and then reached with her hand to tug the blankets more firmly toward her neck, tragically hiding the enticing view Julian had been enjoying of the hollow above her clavicle.

She peeked one eye open, and Julian took great pleasure in the fact that *he*, by contrast, had left the sheets draped around his waist—he always slept hot—and therefore was offering quite a fair bit of bare skin for her perusal.

Predictably, she blushed.

Perversely, he was delighted. He was growing concerned that he was becoming bizarrely fixated on those blushes—especially now that he knew precisely how far down her neck and chest they extended.

"Good morning," he said slowly, trying not to sound too pleased with himself.

She cleared her throat. "Um." It came out as a squeak. She tried again. "Good morning."

"Sleep well?" he asked, all polite inquisitiveness.

She nodded, managing as she did so to tug the sheet even higher—it was approaching her chin now.

"This is a very comfortable bed," she offered weakly.

"And you must have been tired," he added. She turned crimson. "From our long day of travel," he elaborated, straight-faced.

She shot a narrow-eyed look at him that was remarkably reminiscent of her friend Diana. "Yes," she agreed. "It was quite wearying."

Without warning, there was a frantic scrabbling of claws at the side of the bed, and Julian glanced over, startled—Cecil Lucifer Beelzebub was clutching at the sheet, dangling in midair. He must have been drawn by the sound of their voices, but was not quite big enough to make the leap from the floor to the bed, which was a somewhat lofty, elevated affair. Suppressing a sigh, Julian reached down with a single hand and scooped the creature up, depositing him on Emily's stomach.

"Cecil!" she cried joyfully, sitting up at once. While she was disappointingly careful to keep the sheet pressed to her chest, she did, at the very least, present Julian with a very nice view of the bare expanse of her back.

"Did you sleep well?" she cooed, tickling the hell-kitten under his chin.

"He did not," Julian said. "I heard him launching himself off the furniture in the wee hours of the morning."

Emily glanced over at him. "Couldn't you sleep?"

Julian was tempted to blame the kitten for his restlessness, just to see how she'd react (provoking her had proven to be strangely entertaining thus far), but he resisted the ignoble impulse.

"I never sleep through the night," he confessed. "My mind is too busy."

"That sounds dreadful," she said frankly, scooping Cecil Lucifer Beelzebub up in her arms to cradle him to her chest, an action that Julian was fairly certain would result in the loss of an eye if he himself attempted it. A moment later, however, any such uncharitable thoughts vanished, by virtue of the fact that this movement had caused the sheet to slip perilously low. Julian cast a firm, commanding sort of look at the cat, trying to mentally convince him to wiggle.

Cecil Lucifer Beelzebub merely began to purr.

"I'm used to it," he said, heaving an internal sigh of regret and returning his attention to the conversation at hand. "I've always been a fitful sleeper. My father used to—"

He broke off abruptly, surprised at the slip. He made a point of avoiding discussion of his father as much as was possible. He very rarely made such a mistake even with his closest friends—with Laverre, his manager, or Bridgeworth, his closest friend from Oxford. He supposed his head must be addled by the unexpected pleasures of last night's romp in the sheets, though he paused to be grateful that he'd never before had this reaction to bedsport.

Emily, he realized, was watching him carefully, even as she seemed to be trying to pretend she wasn't. He appreciated the act, unconvincing as it was—it allowed him to pretend not to notice her curiosity and steer the conversation past this bump.

"I used to wander the house a lot, as a boy," he said. "Once, when

I was thirteen, I snuck out and went for a ride just before dawn, and returned to find the stablehands all in a tizzy—they thought there was a horse thief."

"I can imagine," she said with a smile, even as she continued to gaze at him with thinly veiled curiosity.

She did not say anything else, however, and instead glanced past him toward the windows directly opposite the bed, through which faint sunlight streamed, sneaking through a gap in the dark blue curtains that obscured the French doors leading out to a small terrace. "What time is it?" she asked, reaching a hand up to cover a yawn.

"Early," he said, a quick glance at the bracket clock on the mantel above the fireplace confirming that it was not yet nine. Hours before he would normally be awake in town, in other words; if he'd had a late night at the theater, or at his club, or visiting whoever his female companion of the moment was, it was not unusual for him to sleep well past noon.

However, he *did* have a fair amount to do today, so it wouldn't hurt to get an early start. He'd want to have a meeting with Laverre, of course, to see how things at the Belfry stood after his absence, though that wouldn't be until much later in the day; no one would be at the theater at this hour, or any hour before noon. In the meantime, however, he'd no doubt there was a mountain of correspondence waiting for him in his study downstairs, and he wanted to take a look at whatever invitations had arrived while he was in the countryside.

The social Season was long over, meaning that the nonstop whirl of balls and musicales and dinner parties every single night had slowed considerably, but there were still members of the *ton* who lingered in town even when others had fled to the country, and Julian did not wish to waste any opportunities that might present themselves for parading his new wife about before polite society.

It would have been more convenient, of course, if they had married in the spring, with a full Season's worth of activities before them, everyone of importance in town, but perhaps this would work out for the best in the end. They could start slow, and by the time the next Season picked up in several months' time, he and Emily would be well settled into married life, a picture-perfect image of domestic bliss and harmony. Furthermore, in a few weeks, more members of polite society would be returning to town after their shooting parties in the country-side, which would offer plenty of opportunity for them to begin building their reputation as a besotted newlywed couple.

". . . have planned for today?" Emily asked, and Julian realized that he'd been so caught up in his thoughts that he'd not heard anything she said.

"I'm sorry?" he asked, shoving back the sheets and giving himself a stern mental admonishment to not be distracted when he noticed her gaze drop quickly to take in the amount of naked flesh on display.

"I asked," she repeated, "what you had planned for today, and if there was anything we might do together?"

"Oh," he said, feeling like a bit of an idiot. It had never occurred to him that she might wish to spend time together today, their very first day back in town—he'd thought she'd be busy getting to know her new home, visiting acquaintances she'd not seen in a few weeks, and generally . . . doing whatever it was that ladies did to pass their time, he supposed. He realized that he didn't really know, specifically, what that was. They always seemed to maintain frightfully busy social calendars, however, so he didn't expect Emily to have much difficulty in this regard.

"I'll need to attend to everything I've neglected in my absence," he explained, rising from the bed and sauntering across the room to where a dressing gown was always left for him, draped across the back of one of his chairs. He drew it on in an unhurried fashion, hoping that his blushing bride was enjoying the show. Whatever reputation she might have, Emily Turner—as he'd learned last night—was nonetheless a lady capable of enjoying the physical aspects of marriage, and this was a fact of which he intended to take full advantage at every possible moment.

"Surely you will want to familiarize yourself with the household, begin deciding what changes you wish to make?" he suggested. He turned toward her as he spoke, and did not think he was imagining the faint sagging of her posture at his words. He decided it was best to ignore this; ladies did sometimes prove to have mystifying emotional responses to the simplest of requests or observations, and he doubted Emily would be able to provide any sort of satisfactory explanation for her displeasure.

"Of course," she agreed, perfectly politely. "Will you be going to the theater this evening?"

"At some point this afternoon," he said, nodding. "I'll need to meet with my manager, find out what I've missed—and, of course, work out this situation with Miss Simmons." He sighed, running a hand over his face; in the pleasures of the previous evening, he'd nearly forgotten that headache. He lowered his hand to gaze speculatively at his wife. "In fact, it might behoove us for you to begin paying calls today."

"Why?" Emily asked slowly, drawing the word out slightly. "We've only just arrived in town—word of our marriage won't have spread yet. Heavens, I haven't even had new calling cards made—I can hardly go about presenting a card for Lady Emily Turner. Not when I am married."

"If Miss Simmons is truly not coming back, then word of her relationship with Delacre will soon spread around town like wildfire. We're fortunate that only a fraction of the *ton* is here at the moment, but it's still only a matter of time before gossip begins to spread—and the last thing I need is for the Belfry to get a reputation as the sort of place men like Delacre find women to join their harems."

"Does Lord Delacre have a *harem?*" Emily asked, looking shocked.

"No," he conceded, "but he's certainly known to entertain more than one mistress at a time, and I won't have word spreading that he picks them up there—which is why we'll want to immediately begin putting on a show of being a proper, staid married couple."

Emily frowned slightly. "Don't you think it likely that *our* marriage will produce its own fair share of scandal?" she asked. "After all, you're hardly considered to be the most marriageable of gentlemen, and until quite recently I was being rather obviously courted by another man. We might well shield Lord Delacre and Miss Simmons from gossip, but only with our own marriage, which I hardly thought was your aim." Her frown deepened. "Besides, I would think that the scandal of a young woman of good breeding marrying an actor and theater owner is significantly greater than that of an actress conducting some sort of liaison with a rogue like Lord Delacre—this can hardly be the first time that's happened, after all."

"What do you propose, then?" he asked, suppressing a surge of irritation; he was aware, on some level, that his irritation was directed at himself, for not having considered the concerns she had just raised, and did his best to keep any trace of his annoyance out of his voice, lest she think it was aimed at her. There was something so frightfully innocent about her, still—even now, as a married lady, joined forevermore to a man with a reputation as scandalous as his, she still seemed very young.

"Well, I thought I might wait a bit before attempting to fashion myself into the perfect society hostess," she said—she was Emily, so he would not have precisely described her tone as waspish, but it undoubtedly was not as sweetly patient as he'd grown accustomed to. "Perhaps I could accompany you to the theater this afternoon instead?"

Julian frowned. "I don't think that's terribly wise," he said, crossing his arms over his chest.

Emily blinked. "Why not?" she asked, tucking Cecil Lucifer Beelzebub more firmly against her breast, where the sheet—tragically—remained firmly stuck. "I thought it might be interesting to see it when a show isn't in progress—I've never been behind the scenes at a theater before."

"Of course you haven't," he said flatly. "Because a theater is no place for a lady."

Emily stared at him, silent for a moment. "But isn't your entire aim to prove that your theater *is* a place for a lady?" she asked after a beat. "How on earth do you expect to lure society ladies there if you won't even bring your own wife?"

Julian sighed. "Emily," he said, "what do you think you could do at the Belfry this afternoon that could possibly lure ladies of the *ton* there—sit and needlepoint and receive calls?"

Her face shuttered at his words, and he felt a pang of regret that he'd spoken so harshly. "I didn't mean—"

"I *thought*," she said, "that if we made it seem as though I were actively involved at the Belfry—taking an interest in the shows you put on, familiarizing myself with its operations, meeting your actors—then we could create the appearance that there was nothing untoward happening there." In her arms, Cecil Lucifer Beelzebub stirred, cracking open one green eye, and she glanced down, dropping a quick kiss on his fluffy head. "Besides," she added, "it's not as though I've never visited the Belfry before. You can hardly claim it's no place for a lady— not when I've already been there."

"Emily," Julian said, sighing again and crossing the room to sit on the bed next to her, "we've been back in town less than a day. I have a brewing scandal at the theater, and we've a marriage to sell to society. Let's begin by focusing on presenting the image of the perfectly happy and respectable married couple that people wish to see—because *that* is what will eventually draw them to the Belfry. No one wants to see a wife taking an interest in her husband's business—they just want to see her acting the way they expect a society wife to act." He saw her eyes spark at this, and added hastily, "I'm not saying it's right or fair, but it's the truth. You know it is." He leaned forward and pressed a quick kiss to her forehead. "Once more time has passed, you can come to the Belfry one evening—play the part of a proud wife, thrilled over a night out, as if going to the Belfry were no more noteworthy than attending a show at Drury Lane. But not yet. And in the meantime, surely you can . . ." He waved a hand vaguely. "Occupy yourself? I'll see to my business, you'll see to yours, and before you know it, things will be going just the way we planned."

Emily, it must be confessed, did not present exactly the picture of a besotted bride whose every anxiety had been chased away by the wisdom of her beloved husband, but he decided that a faintly frowning, not-verbally-protesting bride would do in a pinch.

This was all going, if not perfectly to plan, then certainly close enough.

Ten

"Married," Laverre said for at least the third time. Julian glanced up from the newspaper clipping he was reading—a review of the production of *Macbeth* that the Belfry had staged in his absence—to give his manager an impatient look.

"How many times do you need it repeated?" he asked curtly, not making any attempt to keep his tone pleasant. He and Laverre had worked together for the better part of a decade, and therefore, mercifully, felt little impulse to stand on niceties—not that Laverre was the sort of man to do so with just about anyone, truth be told.

"Well," the Frenchman said, leaning back in the chair he was seated in on the opposite side of Julian's desk, "I'm growing a bit concerned that there's something amiss with my hearing, you see, because I cannot possibly imagine a situation that would convince *you* of all people to take a wife." Laverre was a short, angular man several years older than Julian himself, and he was famously rather demanding when it came to the theater operations. It was strange to see him reclining casually in his chair, as if he hadn't a care in the world, and Julian immediately sensed a rat.

"Perhaps your imagination lacks scope, then," Julian said pleasantly, before redirecting his attention to the review. The reviewer for the

Evening Star apparently took issue with one of the musical numbers—Julian personally had thought the three witches' musical rendition of "Double, double, toil and trouble" was quite entertaining—but otherwise seemed pleased.

"Belfry." Laverre kicked a foot up onto the desk, which was the sort of thing that, had Julian attempted it in Laverre's office, he was fairly certain would have resulted in his own demise, for all that he was theoretically Laverre's employer, and not the other way around. "What is this about?"

Julian sighed, and let the newspaper clipping flutter through his fingertips back to the desk. "What do you think it's about? It's about convincing someone other than every dissolute gentleman in London to come to one of our shows."

"And you think that by virtue of you marrying some blond debutante, we'll suddenly be flooded with the society ladies who have stayed away for the past—oh, how long has it been?" Laverre tapped his chin thoughtfully, though Julian thought darkly that the man probably knew the tally down to the very hour. "Nine years?"

"I don't expect it to happen overnight," Julian said in clipped tones. "But it's a signal to society that I've left my days of freewheeling rakishness behind me—I've turned over a new leaf, if you will. Besides," he added, offering his manager a smug smile, "you underestimate Emily. She's not merely some empty-headed debutante."

"She paints beautiful watercolors?" Laverre suggested in bored tones. "She can play the pianoforte with uncommon skill? She can discuss the weather for ten minutes straight without launching herself off a balcony in boredom?"

"Yes," Julian said, "to all of the above. Emily is . . . perfect." He paused for a second, frowning; he sounded like a besotted fool, but that wasn't really what he meant. "She's the ideal wife," he clarified. "She's beautiful, from an old family with unimpeachable bloodlines, and she has a proven ability to be surrounded by scandal and somehow emerge smelling as fresh as a daisy."

"Then why on earth was she willing to marry you?" Laverre asked skeptically.

Julian sighed. "Her father's an idiot and got mixed up with Oswald Cartham."

Laverre's eyebrows shot toward his hairline—he might not mingle at the edges of the *ton*, as Julian did, but Cartham's name was widely known in London, and Laverre certainly knew men who had been unfortunate enough to find themselves entangled with him.

"Indeed," Julian said, rising to his feet. "Fortunately for Rowanbridge, I believe I can make sure that Cartham never so much as looks at him—or at Emily—ever again."

"Where are you going?" Laverre asked, sliding his foot off Julian's desk and straightening in his seat.

Julian gave him a grim smile. "To pay a visit to a gaming hell."

You could say what you liked about Oswald Cartham, Julian reflected half an hour later, but you could not deny that the man had an appreciation for dramatics. Cartham's gambling hell occupied prime real estate on St. James's Street, where Julian had been admitted by a threatening-looking doorman whose expression had darkened further when Julian had requested a meeting with his employer. A bit of blunt smoothed the way, as it so often did, and before too long Julian found himself seated opposite Cartham in an office that practically begged visitors to speculate about its decorating cost. There were two Old Masters on the gilt-covered wall, and everything from the candlesticks to the inkwell seemed to be made of gold.

It all fit perfectly with the impression Julian had always had of Cartham himself. He was a few years older than Julian, a minor relation of an aristocratic family who'd been born in America and had made his way back to his ancestral land as a young man. As Julian understood it, Cartham used his distant aristocratic connections to worm his way into every ballroom he possibly could, for no reason other than to round up potential customers for the gaming hell he had opened. The past couple of years since the end of the war with France had seen an explosion in business for gaming hells, and the ostentatious wealth on display in Cartham's office was a testament to the fact that business was indeed good. Very good.

But apparently, financial success had not been enough for Cartham. Which was why Julian was here.

"You know, Belfry, I wouldn't have thought you the type," Cartham said without so much as an opening pleasantry. "You've never given any indication you intended to wed, so I certainly wouldn't have expected you to steal a lady right from underneath my nose."

This was, more or less, the reception Julian had expected, so he was unfazed by this welcome. "I don't believe I stole her, Cartham," he said, reclining in his chair as if this conversation wasn't of much concern to him. "She is, after all, of age, with her own thoughts and opinions, and she was in no way coerced to accept my proposal."

Cartham waved a dismissive hand.

"She's a woman, and as far as I've observed over these past three years, she's a woman who does what she's told. It was clever of you to get her alone at Willingham's house party where you could get her all muddled, far away from her father and myself." Cartham's elbows were braced on his desk, his fingertips pressed together, his mouth a thin line. He had dark hair and seemed to have decided to grow an absurd mustache since the last time Julian had seen him. Everything about his countenance at the moment radiated irritation.

"Perhaps you didn't spend enough time actually speaking to her, then," Julian said, striving to keep his tone pleasant. "Because I can assure you, the Lady Emily that I know—Lady Julian, now," he added, with petty satisfaction, "has plenty of thoughts of her own. And she's intelligent enough to know that you never intended to marry her."

Cartham looked unrepentant. He wore a pair of gold-rimmed spectacles perched jauntily on his nose that Julian was almost certain were entirely for show, since he'd never seen him wear them before.

Julian waited.

"My intentions in regard to Lady Emily are none of your concern, Belfry."

And, in that moment, Julian was very, very glad that he had married Emily, so she would not have to spend a single minute more in this man's company.

"I haven't come here to argue with you, Cartham," Julian said. "I've come to see what Rowanbridge owes you, so that I can pay it in full—and whatever else will ensure that you never come within sniffing distance of my wife again." It still felt odd to utter the words *my wife*—he was not used to being in possession of one.

A crafty gleam came into Cartham's eyes, one that informed Julian in no uncertain terms that his bank account was about to take a very large hit. And, indeed, Cartham named a sum that caused Julian to spare more than one uncharitable thought for the Marquess of Rowanbridge—and to cast a suspicious glance at Cartham, wondering just how much he'd inflated whatever the true sum of Rowanbridge's debt was. Still, it was an amount that Julian's flush accounts could more than spare, and he resisted the urge to argue the point.

But this, he knew, would not be Cartham's full price.

"And?" he prompted.

Cartham's eyes widened innocently. "I can't imagine what you could be implying."

"I think you can," Julian said, unmoved. He leaned forward in his chair. "Because, Cartham, I'm no fool, and I asked a few questions around town before departing for Willingham's estate. Which is how I know that Lady Emily had at least one suitor in the past who was willing to shoulder Rowanbridge's debts, who was still warned off. So I dug a bit further, and imagine my surprise to learn that Rowanbridge had invested heavily in a smuggling operation during the war that went poorly—a few ships lost in a storm, as I understand it."

Julian watched Cartham carefully as he spoke, gauging his reaction. Cartham's expression was guarded, his fingers still pressed together, his gaze wary.

"Is that so?" Cartham said, straight-faced. "That's a nasty business to be wrapped up in, Belfry—almost treasonous, some might say."

"Some might," Julian agreed, leaning back once more and crossing his ankle over the opposite knee. "Which is why it would be terribly unfortunate if it ever came to light who it was who first got Rowanbridge involved in this operation."

Cartham went very still. "I'm certain I don't know what you mean."

Julian gave him a thin smile. "All right," he agreed. "That's fair enough. But please know that I've deep pockets—nearly as deep as yours, I'd guess—and it's simply astonishing what money will buy these days. Like damning letters that should have been burned, for example." He paused deliberately. "Hypothetically speaking."

Cartham's eyes narrowed behind those idiotic little spectacles.

"Of course," he said. "Was there something you wanted from me, Belfry?"

"Not at all," Julian said, almost—*almost*—starting to enjoy himself. "So long as you see fit to stay far away from my wife and her family, I don't think we need ever see one another again."

"What a shame," Cartham said in tones of exaggerated sarcasm. He shook his head. "The wench served her purpose, anyway—I've gentlemen from every family of the *ton* patronizing my—"

He did not get any further at that juncture because of the rather uncomfortable situation he found himself in—namely, with Julian's hand at his collar, pulling him halfway out of his seat.

"I'd advise you to think very carefully before you ever refer to Lady Julian in such terms again," Julian said quietly, never once breaking eye contact with Cartham, noting with petty satisfaction that his sudden movement had knocked the other man's spectacles askew. "Do we understand each other?"

Cartham gave him a murderous look.

"Get out, Belfry," he said, wrenching himself from Julian's grasp. He reached behind him to tug on a bellpull and a moment later the door of his office opened, presumably by a servant who had been waiting just outside for his employer's signal.

"Gladly," Julian said coolly, taking a step backward and shaking out his cuffs. "I'll have a bank draft sent over in the morning, and then I expect we need see no more of each other." He picked up his hat and gave Cartham a mocking sort of bow on the way out the door.

"You're a fool, Belfry," Cartham called after him. "Whatever your plan is—she seems like more trouble than she could possibly be worth."

"She's not," Julian tossed over his shoulder, not even bothering to turn, and realized as he made his way down the stairs and back out onto the street that, despite the amount of money Emily had cost him today—despite the fact that he'd been reduced to making primitive threats to a man he'd rather never speak to ever again—he still meant it.

Emily was worth it.

Or at least what she could do for him was.

Eleven

It was a bit strange, Emily reflected that same afternoon, to find oneself suddenly in command of a home.

Thinking logically about the matter, it was nothing more than she'd spent the better part of the past decade of her life preparing for—was that not the ultimate goal of every lady launched onto the marriage mart, after all? To marry an eligible man of means and find herself charged with the running of his household?

For Emily, however, the days when she had assumed herself to be imminently granted such a responsibility were long in the past. She'd had her first Season, of course, but then lost the next two, thanks to her brother. She and Jack had never been close—in the dark hours of the night when sleep eluded her, she could even admit to herself that she did not miss him, after his death—but if she could go back in time to that morning at dawn and implore him to shoot into the air, she would do so in a heartbeat. Instead, he'd killed his opponent—a gentleman who, as Emily understood it, had been the wronged party in their dispute, something to do with an insult to the man's wife—and been forced to flee to the Continent, where he'd later died under what her mother delicately referred to as "unsavory circumstances."

It had never seemed fair that Emily should be forced to spend the next two Seasons in seclusion in the countryside, first to wait for the scandal to die down, then to observe the proper mourning period. *She* hadn't done anything wrong, after all.

She had never given voice to this complaint, of course—she rarely gave voice to any of her complaints.

Ladies didn't complain. They simply got on with it.

But now, here she was, married to a husband of means at last, and suddenly with rather a lot more responsibility than she'd had a week earlier.

". . . menus for the week, just so that you can give your approval," Mrs. Larkspur was saying, and Emily realized with a guilty pang that at some point she had stopped listening to the housekeeper as they went from room to room. After Julian's departure this morning, his butler, Bramble, had handed Emily off into Mrs. Larkspur's capable hands, and they'd spent the past three-quarters of an hour on a thorough tour of the house, with Emily making mental notes as to which rooms needed new wall hangings, which chairs could be reupholstered. The house itself, as she had noted the day before, was respectable and well-appointed, but there was an unmistakable lack of a feminine touch in the decor that Emily intended to correct.

"Does that sound agreeable, my lady?" Mrs. Larkspur prompted gently. She was a kind-faced woman of middling years, who presumably could have found employment in any number of aristocratic households in town; Emily belatedly wondered what had prompted her to work for a dissolute theater owner instead.

"It sounds perfectly agreeable, Mrs. Larkspur," Emily replied, before adding, "How long have you worked for Lord Julian?"

Mrs. Larkspur smiled fondly. "Since soon after he bought this house, my lady," she said. "I used to work at Everly Priory, but the marchioness—I mean, I took it into my head that I'd prefer life in town, closer to my niece." She looked a bit flustered as she spoke.

"Everly Priory," Emily said slowly, frowning a bit. "Isn't that Lord Julian's childhood home?"

"Yes, my lady." Mrs. Larkspur nodded.

But this was not, Emily thought, what Mrs. Larkspur had originally been about to say. She had mentioned the marchioness—presumably Julian's mother—before abruptly catching herself.

It was odd.

Emily did not have the opportunity to reflect on it at the moment, however, because further conversation was forestalled by a polite, inquisitive *meow*.

Startled, Emily and Mrs. Larkspur turned in unison as a telltale paw emerged from underneath Emily's skirts.

"Cecil!" she cried, lifting her skirts enough to fish the kitten out and scoop him up in her arms. "Where did you come from?"

"*Meow*," he said cheerfully, purring. She leaned forward to press a kiss to the white stripe of fur on his nose.

"He's already been down in the kitchens this morning," Mrs. Larkspur said, a look of reluctant affection directed at the kitten. "I'm afraid the kitchen maids will spoil him dreadfully."

"No worse than he's already being spoiled," came a voice from behind them, and Emily turned to see her husband entering the dining room.

"Wife," he said, nodding at Emily. "Demon," he added cordially to Cecil, who raised one paw to lick by way of reply.

"Hello," Emily said, feeling strangely pleased to see him.

"Will you be dining at home, my lord?" Mrs. Larkspur asked.

"I will," Julian said, still giving Cecil a suspicious look.

"I'll let Cook know that you'll be joining her ladyship, then," Mrs. Larkspur said, beating a hasty retreat.

"Do you not normally dine at home?" Emily asked curiously, cuddling Cecil close to her chest.

"Not terribly often, no," Julian said, glancing up at her. "I suppose I shall make more of a habit of it, now."

"Don't feel you must on my account," Emily said a bit uncertainly. "I wouldn't want you to feel obligated to keep me company."

"We're married," Julian said, his mouth quirking up a bit in the corner. "I did think it likely we'd spend at least some time together, after all—particularly if we're not to see each other much during the day."

"Of course," Emily said, with a faint pang of disappointment. She'd rather been hoping that Julian had not envisioned every day unfolding as today had—she was terribly interested in seeing him at work, even as the practical voice inside her head that usually governed most of her behavior reminded her that the Belfry was hardly a place she would feel comfortable.

But still, she was curious. And for as long as she could remember, she'd never been permitted to be curious about much of anything.

Suppressing a sigh, she said brightly, "Would you care for some tea? I was about to have some sent to the library—I've not yet had the chance to explore in there."

"Something stronger, perhaps," he said dryly, but nonetheless offered her his arm as they exited the room and made their way downstairs to the library. Emily's parents' library had always been her father's domain—there were very few books of much interest to her within, and she was not permitted to linger there, anyway. Julian's library, she had noted on her tour with Mrs. Larkspur, was quite inviting—it was not terribly large, but there were several overstuffed armchairs scattered before the fireplace, as well as a window seat. The shelves were full of books with broken spines: such a sight always made Emily feel unaccountably cheerful.

Something in her expression must have conveyed some of her thoughts, because after Julian had rung for tea and crossed to the sideboard to busy himself with the decanter stored there, he said almost casually, "You must buy any books you wish to add to our collection."

Something within Emily warmed at these words. She'd always been faintly envious of Violet's library at the house she shared with Lord James, and felt a small thrill run through her at the thought that she, too, could have a room full of books to call her own.

Full of books that did not have to be approved by her mother, moreover. She'd have to ask Violet to suggest some thoroughly improper titles.

Emily regarded her husband thoughtfully as she deposited Cecil on the window seat; Julian had turned back to the sideboard after he'd spoken, so she could only see the straight line of his back, his hands working swiftly to unstopper the decanter and pour some of the liquid within into a tumbler.

He glanced over his shoulder once more and caught her gazing at him. "Would you like some?" he asked, raising the decanter slightly, a wicked glint in his eye.

"What ... what is it?" Emily asked. She should have said *no, thank you* immediately, of course, but she could not help but think that he was almost ...

Daring her.

"Brandy," he said, his gaze flicking up and down her body in rapid succession. "Very fine French brandy, in fact."

Emily lifted her chin. "Yes, please."

He raised a brow, then turned back to the sideboard, pouring a small measure of brandy into another tumbler. Wordlessly, he offered one to her, and she raised it to her lips before taking a healthy swallow.

Which she promptly spit out onto the closest surface at hand—which just so happened to be Julian's jacket.

"*Why*," Emily sputtered, coughing, "why would you drink that?"

Julian glanced down at the brandy dripping off his jacket, then at Emily, who was still coughing, and finally at the tumbler in his hand. He took a long sip before setting it down on the nearest side table and removing his jacket in businesslike fashion.

"I think a better question," he said, sparing a mournful glance for the soggy fabric in hand, "is why on earth *you* would waste it?"

"How was I supposed to know what it would taste like?" she said indignantly, placing her hands on her hips. She'd stopped coughing, and now regarded him with suspicion. "No one's ever seen fit to give me brandy before!"

"Which shows great wisdom on their part, if this is how you're going to treat it," Julian said darkly, tossing his jacket onto a nearby chair and loosening his cravat. He was now in his shirtsleeves and waistcoat, and Emily was possessed with a sudden memory of him loosening his cravat the night before, the patch of golden skin it had exposed.

She sat down in one of the armchairs before the fireplace, raised her tumbler to her nose, and sniffed.

"It even burns my *nose*," she said indignantly.

Julian gave her a half smile and perched on the arm of her chair, his tumbler back in hand.

"That's not generally how it's intended to be consumed." He took another sip of his brandy and tilted his head back slightly, savoring it, giving Emily the opportunity to cast an appreciative glance at the long line of his throat.

Emily looked down at her glass and took the tiniest possible sip. It burned her throat again, but less than it had with the first sip, and this time she was better able to appreciate the warmth that seemed to course through her body as she swallowed. "That's not so bad," she said cautiously, and Julian laughed outright at that.

"That bottle cost more than many men earn in a year," he said, shaking his head at her. "It's considerably better than *not bad*."

"To you, perhaps," Emily said. "I think I'd be just as happy with a glass of ratafia, if it came to that."

Julian grimaced.

"Ratafia is disgusting."

"No, it's not. It tastes delicious."

"It's too sweet."

"Says the man who drinks his tea sweeter than any lady I know," Emily said, feeling somewhat triumphant to have this knowledge to lord over him. Seeing that he had no ready reply to that, she added, "Besides, sweet things taste nice. I've never understood why gentlemen complain about ratafia. I suspect it's simply to look more manly."

"Oh?" he asked, drawing the word out slowly. "Do I need help in that regard?"

In that moment, Emily had the wild thought that it would perhaps have been better if she'd allowed other gentlemen to kiss her before her marriage. Oh, she would not have wanted to be ruined, of course—though at times, that had certainly seemed preferable to Mr. Cartham's company—but perhaps if she'd been a bit bolder, allowed gentlemen to take a few more liberties, she would not be so susceptible to Julian's charms now. She was three-and-twenty, after all; it seemed absurd that she should so easily fall prey to a seductive glance and a rakish lock of hair on her husband's forehead, and yet here she was, reaching up to brush it away without fully realizing what she was doing.

"If you're expecting me to compliment you," she said a bit breathlessly, "I hope you'll understand that I'm saving all my compliments for the ladies you wish me to impress."

Julian grinned as he leaned in closer.

"However shall my fragile ego recover?" he murmured, a moment before his mouth descended upon hers.

They kissed slowly, lazily, as if they'd all the time in the world, and it was some time later that they were interrupted by a knock at the door, which was then immediately opened by a maid bearing a tea service. Emily blushed scarlet to realize that, at some point in the proceedings, Julian's hand had come to rest on her breast, his other hand tangled in her hair.

The appearance of tea, however, put a halt to any such activities, and Emily hopped up so that she might pour for them, though Julian proceeded to pour so much brandy into his teacup that Emily questioned how accurate it was to even call the drink within *tea* any longer. Feeling a bit daring, she added the tiniest of splashes of brandy to her own cup before resuming her seat before the fireplace. It was only the middle of September, but it was a brisk, breezy sort of day, and flames flickered cheerfully in the grate.

"Speaking of ladies you wish to compliment," Julian said, having taken a seat—more appropriately, albeit with less immediate possibility of impolite behavior—in one of the armchairs opposite Emily. "Have you formed a plan of attack yet?"

"No," Emily said slowly, gazing down at the teacup in her hands, her eyes tracing the floral pattern on the saucer. "I've been rather occupied with learning the layout of the household today—tomorrow I thought to draw up a list of names of ladies I know to currently be in town, so that I might strategize as to whom I'll visit first." She tried to project some degree of enthusiasm into her voice, although, in truth, the prospect wasn't terribly appealing. She looked forward to visiting her friends, of course—Violet and Diana and Sophie, and select other ladies of their set with whom she'd enjoyed conversing over the years—but the idea of making polite conversation with some of her mother's more awful friends was . . . unappealing.

Still, it was no more than she'd agreed to when she accepted Julian's proposal, so she didn't wish to seem reluctant.

"I'll start with some of the easier ones—ladies who I don't think will treat me coolly, regardless of any gossip that might swirl surrounding our marriage—and then tackle some of the fussier ladies a bit later." She tried to keep any note of uncertainty out of her voice, hoping to give the impression that she'd thought carefully about this course of action before deciding upon it. It would take some getting used to, not having to look questioningly over her shoulder to see her parents' reaction before doing something. Julian was her husband, of course—legally, he could command her to do anything he wished—but he didn't seem like the domineering sort.

She was . . . lucky.

"Whatever you think is best," Julian said equably, sipping his brandy-laced tea. "I'll spend my days at the Belfry, making certain everything with the show is going well, you'll spend your days courting favor with society wives, and before we know it, we'll be the toast of the *ton*." His tone was one of smug satisfaction—that of a man who thought he had everything arranged perfectly to his liking.

It was not, Emily thought with another slight pang of disappointment, exactly to *her* liking, but it was still worlds better than the future she had imagined for herself a month ago. Who was she to complain?

A plaintive *meow* emerged from the window seat, and she glanced over her shoulder, having momentarily forgotten Cecil was there. "Hello, darling," she called. "Are you hungry?"

"I'm famished," Julian said. "Thank you for asking." He paused, mock-thoughtful. "Oh. Were you speaking to the cat? How charming."

"Cecil is a *baby*," Emily said protectively. Logically, Emily knew that Cecil was probably more than capable of fending for himself—any kitten who had been wily enough to make his way from whatever barn or alleyway he had previously called home into a warm bed at an inn clearly had finely honed survival instincts. And yet, she could not help worrying over him. She'd never had anything that was *hers* before—not like this. She had, in her own quiet way, taken care of her family—soothed her parents' moods and ruffled feathers, tried her hardest to ensure a peaceful home—but it wasn't the same. Cecil was her responsibility, hers to protect. Hers to love.

"Cecil Lucifer Beelzebub," Julian said, setting his teacup down and rising to his feet, "is a menace." He began to walk toward her.

"Did you have some sort of traumatizing childhood experience with cats?" Emily asked indignantly. "I can't think what else could explain this sort of antagonism."

"Can't you?" Julian asked. "Need I remind you of the fact that Cecil Lucifer Beelzebub spoiled our wedding night?"

Emily blushed. "We more than made up for it."

"Eventually," Julian said, looking pained. "And to answer your question, I adored cats as a boy. One of our barn cats had a litter of kittens the year I was eleven, and Robert, Frannie, and I were each allowed to name one."

"What was yours called?" Emily asked.

"Puck."

"Puck," Emily repeated slowly. "As in—"

"*A Midsummer Night's Dream*, yes," Julian said, waving an impatient hand.

Emily giggled. Julian sighed. "Yes, I know," he said, with the air of a man who had heard jokes along these lines many times before. "It's all very predictable."

"I must confess, I don't know many eleven-year-olds who are so taken with Shakespeare," Emily said, still giggling. "Did you dream even then of a life on the stage?"

"Have you ever *seen* that play?" Julian asked indignantly. "It's utter madness. Precisely the sort of thing that might appeal to a boy. My father—" He broke off abruptly, seemingly startled by the words that had come out of his mouth. Emily held her breath, not wishing to push, but so terribly curious nonetheless.

"There was a theater troupe that came to the neighboring village one summer," Julian said after a brief pause. "I went to see their rendition of *A Midsummer Night's Dream*—which was somewhat colorful, shall we say—and I became a bit obsessed." He was standing before her, gazing down at her from his considerable height as he spoke, and Emily found herself drawn to the force of his gaze, unable to look away. "I memorized several of the monologues and was known to recite them at the dinner table."

Emily could not help wondering what had happened to this boy— this boy whose family seemed like such a loving and welcoming one, so unlike her own; this boy who had adored the madness and humor of

A Midsummer Night's Dream. How had this boy become a man who had spent years not speaking to his own father? How had this boy become a man who thought that *Much Ado About Nothing* was a play that needed to be turned into serious philosophical fare?

How had this boy forgotten how to love the things he loved?

She knew she had to tread carefully here, so, a bit hesitantly, she asked, "Did your parents permit monologues at the dinner table?"

He was silent for a long enough moment that she thought he wasn't going to answer, before finally saying, "Yes. They . . . humored me. All three of us, really, but me in particular—I was always something of a troublemaker."

"I'm shocked," Emily murmured, straight-faced, and Julian grinned at her, quickly and fleetingly.

"I did it a bit deliberately, I suppose—my father and brother are both the upstanding, well-behaved sort, so I took some pleasure in provoking them, trying to get a reaction, to see what I could get away with. As many boys do, I expect."

The words sprang to her lips before she had time to consider their wisdom, and she asked, "Is that why you purchased the Belfry? To see how your father would react?"

The grin that had appeared on his face a moment before vanished, and he cut his glance away, gazing down into the contents of his teacup, the firelight casting dancing shadows upon his face. He looked surprisingly young, she thought, when the full force of that icy gaze wasn't evident—his eyelashes unfairly long against his cheeks, his brow slightly furrowed in thought, his mouth curving faintly down at the edges.

"Perhaps," he said simply, after a long moment of silence, glancing up again to meet her eyes. "I wanted to see how far I could push him—how much I could test him—before he became truly angry. And even then, he indulged me . . . for a while." A wry, bitter sort of smile twisted his lips. "Until he didn't." He paused for a moment. "I don't know if you've ever been told the full story—I don't know how accurate the *ton*'s gossip is in this regard—but my father tolerated the Belfry for several years. It was only when Frannie was making her debut that he lost patience and ordered me to sell it. Obviously, I refused."

"Do you . . . regret it?" she asked, knowing that she was pushing him, perhaps too far, but unable to stop herself, now that she was receiving this rare glimpse into his thoughts.

He sighed. "I regret any pain I've caused my mother," he said. "I regret not seeing Robert and Frannie as often as I'd wish to—I regret that my meetings with them have to be a bit furtive, that I can't simply come to a family dinner. But I don't regret the Belfry—I'm proud of what I've accomplished there. And if my father can't see that, if he's more concerned about scandal than about me, then—well, there's nothing I can do about that."

He sounded almost as if he were trying to convince himself, she thought suddenly, and she thought anew about his wish to make the Belfry respectable, proper, impressive, and wondered at once who, precisely, he was trying to impress.

He rose to his feet abruptly, setting down his teacup and advancing toward her. She reached up and placed her hand in his, allowing him to draw her to her feet. "I don't wish to discuss my family any longer," he murmured.

"Oh?" she said, feigning innocence. "Did you wish to discuss Shakespeare some more, instead?"

"No," he said, reaching out to run a hand lazily down her arm, causing gooseflesh to appear in the wake of his touch. "I'm more interested in continuing to address the matter of our aborted wedding night—we've some lost time to make up for, after all, do we not?"

Emily glanced out the window. "But—but it's the *afternoon*," she said uncertainly. Surely it wasn't proper to do such things during the daylight hours.

"All the better to see you, then," Julian murmured, his arms reaching around her to tug at the strings that held the neckline of her gown closed.

Right on cue, Cecil meowed.

"Not now, hell-beast," Julian murmured, lowering his head.

It was the last thing either of them said for quite some time.

Twelve

"*I do not think a newlywed should look so dissatisfied,*" Diana said a few weeks later. "Is Belfry neglecting you? Shall I challenge him to pistols at dawn?"

"You'll never get to see Jeremy at St. George's if you have to flee to the Continent, Diana," Violet reminded her.

"A good point, Violet, a good point," Diana conceded. "Shall I poison him instead?"

"I'd rather you didn't," Emily said calmly, applying jam to a scone with neat, precise strokes of her knife. "I'm afraid black makes me look somewhat sickly."

It was a Wednesday afternoon, and Emily had invited Violet and Diana to tea. It was a novel experience, being hostess to her friends— for years they had been in the habit of gathering at either Violet's or Diana's houses, where there were no overbearing mothers lurking nearby to eavesdrop. Now, however, Emily had a house of her own to which she could invite her friends. With her husband frequently out, she had little company.

"You have not answered my question," Diana said now, gazing at Emily shrewdly over the rim of her teacup. "What is the matter?"

"Nothing at all," Emily said hastily, having long experience with

Diana when she got that particular look in her eye. "Julian has been nothing but considerate and solicitous."

"Darling, he's a husband, not a footman," Diana said. "I rather thought that marriage to Belfry would lend itself to more exciting adjectives."

"It's difficult to find marriage that exciting," Emily said slowly, "when one is spending one's day in drawing rooms taking tea with the exact same ladies one has spent one's entire life taking tea with."

"You're not . . ." Violet trailed off, a look of dawning horror on her face. "*Sick of tea?*" She uttered the words in a hushed whisper, as though afraid to speak them into truth.

"No, I'm not sick of tea," Emily said a trifle impatiently, lifting her teacup to illustrate her point. "But I'm sick of taking tea with Lady Weatherstone, and Lady Warwick, and Lady Wight." These were just three of the society matrons Emily had paid calls upon that week—all of whom she'd known for years, thanks to their acquaintance with her mother, and none of whom was exactly scintillating company.

Diana wrinkled her nose. "I can't say I blame you—why on earth have you been spending time with them?"

Emily sighed. "It's all part of Julian's plan," she explained. "You will recall that he first invited you to the Belfry, Violet, because he was hoping to attract a more respectable clientele?" Seeing Violet's nod, she continued. "He's decided that, now that we are wed, the best way to lure ladies to the Belfry is for his oh-so-proper wife to form connections with various ladies of the *ton*."

"But why *those* ladies?" Diana pressed. "Why won't *we* suffice?"

Emily hesitated, not wishing to offend, but then realized who she was speaking to.

"You're a bit . . ." She paused, searching for the most diplomatic way to phrase this. "Spirited."

Violet, rather than taking offense, lifted a teacup in her direction in a sort of salute.

"That means we're *interesting*."

"It does," Emily agreed, because no one in their right mind could possibly argue on that point when it came to her friends. "But it also means that your attending a show at a theater with an unsavory reputation is more likely to be viewed as an eccentricity, rather than a sign that all the other ladies of the *ton* ought to follow suit."

"Fair enough," Violet conceded, slumping a bit in her seat. She frowned. "So that is all that Belfry is having you do—take tea with dull ladies every day whilst he abandons you to see to the business of running the theater?"

"Not *every* day," Emily said in the interest of fairness; she didn't wish to confirm Diana's fears that she was some sort of neglected wife. Indeed, she had the distinct impression that Julian was in fact spending more time at home now than he had done prior to his marriage—she had noted the looks of faint surprise on the faces of various servants when he returned home for dinner, something he must not have been in the habit of doing in his bachelor days. And she firmly refused to think how he might have passed his evenings then, too.

"But you've just married," Violet protested, frowning. "Shouldn't you still be so besotted with each other that you can barely tear yourselves apart for meals and bathing?" She spoke in the manner of someone with experience. Violet had had the good fortune to be in love with her husband when she married him, and their recent reconciliation had led to a second honeymoon of sorts.

Diana had said firmly, on more than one occasion recently, that she was afraid to visit Violet and Lord James's house on Curzon Street unannounced, lest she interrupt a scene that, as she put it, "would prove too traumatizing to ever scrub from memory." Considering that Diana herself was at present doing a terrible job of hiding the fact that she was sneaking off to her fiancé's house at every possible opportunity to engage in activities that were frowned upon outside the bonds of matrimony, Emily didn't really think she had room to complain, but ten years of friendship had taught her it was best not to argue with Diana on these matters.

"But ours was not a love match," Emily reminded Violet, taking a sip of tea. The servants had seemed a bit befuddled by her custom of taking a pot of tea and a tray of delicacies around the same time each afternoon—it was not a habit that was in fashion—but Emily had grown accustomed to it after years of the practice with Violet and Diana, and now she found herself growing peckish around four o'clock every afternoon. And how refreshing it was to simply eat as much as she wanted, without being conscious of her mother's eyes on her all the while. Emily had always been slender, but she had a voracious appetite, and her mother had seemed to find this a conspicuous moral failing in her only daughter.

Emily took a large bite from a blackberry tart, happily basking in the knowledge that her mother was nowhere near to comment.

"Even if it isn't a love match, you're *newlyweds*," Diana said, leering a bit. "My first marriage wasn't a love match, either, but I assure you that if Templeton had looked anything like Belfry does, I'd have ensured he never left the house." Emily frowned at her, which merely had the effect of causing Diana's mildly disturbing smile to widen.

"Diana, stop that, you'll put me off my food," Violet said, rolling her eyes.

At this seemingly innocuous statement, Diana's eyes widened in alarm.

"Don't tell me you're enceinte," she said bluntly, giving Violet a scrutinizing look. Violet was wearing a gown of green sarcenet with sleeves that ended just before her elbows, her dark hair in an elaborate knot atop her head, curls framing her face. She looked to be in good spirits, but otherwise appeared entirely her normal self.

"Good lord, why on earth would your mind go *there?*" Violet demanded, setting her teacup down with a clatter.

"Because you are recently reconciled with your husband, and you just mentioned feeling ill!" Diana said with all the shrewdness of a Bow Street Runner on a case.

"I said *you* were making me ill," Violet said in exasperation. "That's quite another thing entirely."

"If there's going to be a baby," Diana said, "I'll need time to prepare myself for the change."

"How would it affect *you*, Diana?" Emily asked. "Violet would be the one with a baby. Although," she added, smiling a bit, "I suppose it's possible that you and Lord Willingham could have need of a nursery sometime soon, too."

Diana's face paled.

"*We* are taking precautions," Diana said, shuddering a bit. "There's no guarantee, of course—we simply have to hope for the best."

"James and I did that, when we were first married," Violet said, nodding wisely. "We were so young—neither of us felt quite ready to be parents. We've been, er, less cautious, lately," she added, blushing a bit. "But I do not believe you need to be worried about a baby yet, Diana. I promise I'll let you know with ample time to emotionally prepare yourself, should that come to pass." Violet was admirably straight-faced as she spoke.

"Precautions," Emily repeated. "This is what you referred to, Violet, when you told me a man could—er—"

"Yes," Violet said, taking pity on her and not making her finish that sentence. "That really was a remarkably well-timed anatomy lesson I gave you at Elderwild."

"Well, I might've had a motive for asking," Emily mumbled, thinking of the repeated allusions to marriage that Julian had made over the course of the house party. Violet and Diana's faces broke into identical grins. "But don't you want a baby, Diana?" she asked, returning to their original discussion.

Diana shrugged. "Someday, I expect—after all, Jeremy has a title, and he'll need an heir. And a spare," she added, sighing heavily. "I wouldn't mind it so much if it didn't seem to take so terribly long—ladies are with child *forever*. And if I'm expected to do it at least twice—that's positively *years* of my life I'd be sacrificing. For a *baby*. Babies aren't even *interesting*." She brightened. "I do like children, though. Practical creatures. They tell you just what they're thinking. I think any offspring Jeremy and I produce will rub along nicely with me, once they're old enough to speak sensibly and less prone to alarming sounds and smells."

"What a beautiful picture of motherhood you present, Diana," Violet said. "Truly, it brings a tear to one's eye."

"I *like* babies," Emily added, smiling a bit. "You can send yours to me and I will rain affection upon them until they are old enough to be interesting to you, and then I'll send them home."

"Perfect," Diana said serenely. "In the meantime, however, I think I'll continue taking precautions. The last thing I want is to be ill on my wedding day."

"And how is the wedding planning going?" Emily asked, pouring another cup of tea for Violet, who could not be trusted to manage this task without half a cup's worth of tea ending up on the table. "Have you decided when the wedding will occur?"

"They're calling the banns for the first time on Sunday," Diana said, smiling smugly. "I must confess, the thought of Jeremy standing in St. George's, before all of the *ton*—or at least whichever ones are in town at the moment—is the happy image that lulls me to sleep most evenings." Her smile turned wicked. "Except for the occasions when he himself makes a concerted effort to lull me to sleep, instead."

"I wouldn't have thought you the sort to get terribly excited about a wedding," Emily said.

"Oh, I'm not," Diana said, waving a dismissive hand. "I'm considering not even purchasing a new dress, and just wearing one I already have. But it's *Jeremy* who makes it all so entertaining. I've already asked his tailor to send over the most appalling fabric samples he can find, for this waistcoat I've promised Jeremy I'd make him wear."

"Promised," Violet repeated skeptically.

"Threatened," Diana corrected cheerfully. "And I've grown fond of suggesting more and more outlandish ideas for the wedding, just to see what he'll agree to. Now that I've said yes, he's afraid to argue with me."

Violet and Emily let out incredulous snorts.

"About wedding matters, at least," Diana amended. "He seems perfectly content to quarrel about everything else, of course." Since quarreling was Diana and Lord Willingham's primary way of expressing affection, from all Emily could tell, this was reassuring to hear. "But in any case, we've settled on the sixth of November for the wedding. Invitations should be going out soon."

"Oh, I can hardly wait," Emily said, clasping her hands together. "I love weddings."

"And yet you yourself were content to be married in the morning room at Elderwild," Diana said mournfully. "Thus depriving us of what would have been a truly sensational scandal, if *Emily Turner* had married *Julian Belfry* in *London*, of all places."

"Are we *talking* like *this* now?" Violet asked. Diana flicked a crumb of scone at her.

"It was for the best," Emily said, thinking of her meeting with her parents a few weeks earlier. "Our marriage has already caused enough of an uproar—best not to court scandal by rubbing society's faces in it with a big wedding, I suppose. Especially given that I'm meant to be improving Julian's reputation, not further blackening it." She could not stop a slightly melancholy note from creeping into her voice as they returned to their original topic of conversation.

"What is it, dearest?" Violet asked, a concerned glint in her eye. An effect of Violet having so recently and happily reconciled with her own husband was a strong desire to see her friends equally happily settled. She had been successful in this endeavor with Diana—though Emily personally wasn't at all sure that Violet had had anything to do with that—and now seemed to have turned her attention to Emily. And Emily, while appreciative of the concern, was not certain she wanted it.

"Nothing," she said quickly, and then instantly regretted it, seeing both Diana's and Violet's gazes sharpen on her, clearly sensing that there was a story to be told here. This, Emily reflected, was the difficulty in having friends one had known for nearly half of one's life. Realizing that any attempt at evasion would be futile, she capitulated.

"It's just . . ." Emily started, trying to work out how to articulate precisely what she was feeling. "It's just that I suppose I thought being married to Julian Belfry, of all people, would be a bit more exciting?"

"I tend to think that the less exciting a marriage is, the better," Violet said with the wisdom of a woman who had spent a solid fortnight that summer coughing into a handkerchief, attempting to convince her husband that she was at death's door.

"In some ways, yes," Emily said, "but in others . . . I don't know. I've spent my entire life paying calls on ladies of the *ton* and discussing the weather and the latest society gossip. I've spent years on my very best behavior, afraid to put so much as a toe out of line for fear of it ruining all of my family's hopes. And now, I've married a man who was disinherited by his own father, who owns an infamously scandalous theater, who causes gossip whenever he puts in an appearance at any sort of society event . . . and yet, it doesn't feel terribly different. He expects me to be perfect, proper Emily, and go about much as I always have, courting the favor of women whom I find tedious at best. He won't even take me to the theater yet, because he wants to be sure that I'm presenting the image of a perfect society wife! So, really, what was the point of all of this, if I'm just to live the same life I've always lived?"

She broke off, breathing a bit quickly, and realized that both of her friends were staring at her, dumbstruck. She thought that that might have been the longest monologue she had ever spoken before them—while Emily did not hesitate to speak her mind when in Violet's and Diana's company, she was still not prone to speeches of that length or passion. But the past month, on top of the past six years of her life, seemed to have been some sort of breaking point for her, and now she could not keep back the sudden rush of feeling. Of frustration.

She was ready for her life to be something different, and had hoped that marriage to Julian would be the first step in making that happen.

It wasn't that she hadn't tried. Many evenings, when Julian returned home from the Belfry, they shared a cup of tea—or often, in Julian's case, brandy—in the library, and he had not been hesitant to discuss with her the many frustrations at the theater. He wasn't thrilled with the actress who had taken Miss Simmons's place, she knew, and he was worried that *Much Ado About Heaven* would not prove enough of a departure from the Belfry's usual fare to send the message he wished it to.

"I would be happy to come watch one of the rehearsals," Emily had ventured tentatively the week before, in the midst of one of these discussions. "If you'd like a lady's opinion on the matter."

Julian had surveyed her over the rim of his glass, and she'd tried to look casual, to ensure that none of her curiosity, her desperate wish to be a part of this aspect of his life, showed on her face.

"Emily," he said after a pause, "we need to ensure that everything about our marriage appears above reproach. You'll undoubtedly raise some eyebrows if you are seen popping in and out of the theater constantly."

"But," Emily said and then hesitated, weighing her words. She hated pressing—hated feeling that she was being a nuisance. "But I think I could help," she said a bit uncertainly. "If you are preparing for a show that aims to attract respectable ladies, then why not allow me to offer my opinion? Let me come watch a rehearsal—take me on a tour of the theater." She took a breath, realizing that she was speaking too fervently, her eagerness evident in her voice. "You married me because I am exactly the sort of lady you wish to attract to the Belfry. Why not allow me to help?"

"Because," he said firmly, taking a sip of his drink, "you will best be able to help me by courting the favor of society wives—not creeping around backstage where you're bound to see something that shocks you."

They had been interrupted then by the appearance of Bramble, announcing that Lord Penvale and Lady Templeton had arrived for dinner, but Emily could not help thinking, as she rose and prepared to greet her friends, that she was not, perhaps, as easily shocked as her husband thought.

"Emily," Diana said now, a touch gleefully, "are you saying that you want to cause a *scandal?*"

"No," Emily said, and Diana sagged a bit. "I don't think causing a scandal would be in my best interests. Julian married me to do quite the opposite."

"Well, he's hardly going to leave you if you don't perform up to standards," Violet pointed out. "You're his wife, not a member of staff. And I presume the marriage is consummated? In which case, you're in this together, so you needn't worry about not being useful to him anymore, because what on earth is he going to do, even if you aren't the perfectly behaved wife he thought he was marrying?"

"Find a mistress to take up with and never come home again," Emily said, giving voice to a thought that had lingered in the back of her mind ever since she and Julian had agreed to wed. She had made him promise not to lie to her, but she hadn't asked anything of him regarding fidelity. And yet, she could not help but feel a pang of sadness when she imagined such a thing—them spending their evenings apart, as well as their days.

Because the truth was, when he was at home, spending time with her, Emily *liked* being married to Julian. He listened to her in a way that no one other than Violet and Diana ever really had, with the entirety of his attention, and in such a way that she knew he was taking her thoughts and concerns seriously.

And then, in the evenings, he took her to bed—and, she'd learned, she very much liked that, too. She did not find this surprising, precisely—friendship with Violet and Diana had taught her that marital relations (or not-yet-marital relations, in Diana's case) could be just as enjoyable for ladies as they were for gentlemen, after all. And yet, Emily had always prided herself on her control, on the perfection of the appearance she presented to the world—in her looks, in her behavior, in her conversation. It was strange to realize how much she enjoyed these moments when she was not in control at all.

All that was to say: she didn't wish to irritate him enough to drive him to find a mistress. But she didn't wish to be excluded from his life, either.

She wasn't certain how to explain any of this to her friends, though—her friends, who had found the love matches that Emily had abandoned hope of long ago. Something in her voice, however, must have signaled some of her inner turmoil, because Diana's and Violet's eyes narrowed in identical looks of suspicion.

"Has Belfry indicated that he plans to take a mistress?" Diana asked, her tone deceptively casual. There was nothing in her demeanor to indicate that Julian's life might be in danger, but Emily had known Diana long enough to know that, depending on how she answered, he might be at risk.

"No," Emily said hastily, not particularly wishing to become a widow within a month of her marriage. "But we agreed to be honest," she added. "When we decided to wed, we agreed that there wouldn't be lies between us, no feigning a deeper feeling that didn't exist. It was one of the conditions I laid out before I accepted his proposal."

"But," Violet asked, uncharacteristically hesitant, "what if deeper feelings were to emerge?"

"They won't," Emily said firmly. "This is a marriage of convenience, nothing more."

"But darling, I thought you *liked* Belfry," Diana protested.

"I do," Emily said. "And because of that, I've no intention of ruining a perfectly pleasant marriage by mooning over a man who will never return the feeling."

"But you don't know—"

"Enough!" Emily said, setting down her teacup with a decisive *clink*. She very rarely assumed a stern, firm tone; it was so much easier to be pleasant, pliant, bending to the wishes of those around her—it was how she had kept the peace with her parents for years, after all. Where Diana liked to push against the boundaries of society, of what was expected of her, Emily was perfectly content to exist within its constraints. It was oftentimes possible to get what one wished with a smile and a polite word and a bit of cunning.

Never mind the fact that the single thing she had wished for more than anything else, which she had finally achieved—marriage to a man of her own choosing—had come about thanks to her tossing sweetness and propriety to the wind.

The rarity with which she adopted this tone made it particularly effective, and Diana and Violet subsided at once in their protests. Indeed, both were eyeing her with faint surprise—not that Emily could blame them.

She took a deep, steadying breath, and continued. "I'm perfectly happy with the arrangement Julian and I have come to for our marriage, and I think it will work out quite well between us. However," she added, then hesitated. "I don't wish to only be a society hostess for the rest of my life. I want to see him at work, I want to see the theater—it is what he has dedicated nearly a decade of his life to, after all. And it's so novel for a man of our class to actually have employment that I must confess I'm curious."

"Do you not think you could convince him?" Violet asked. "He doesn't seem like a terribly unreasonable man."

"He's stubborn where the Belfry is concerned," Emily said, sighing. "He can't be convinced to let me accompany him to a place that he thinks would—"

"Soil you?" Violet suggested.

"Exactly. Especially if I was not just there to visit—if I visited, as I wish to do, with the aim of helping him work out *how*, precisely, to make the Belfry more appealing to proper ladies."

"If he doesn't want you to visit behind the scenes," Diana said slowly, a speculative gleam in her eye, "what if you presented an alternative that was even worse?"

"What do you mean?" Emily asked with a faint pang of alarm. She'd been friends with Diana for long enough to know to proceed with extreme caution when she looked like this.

"Belfry is all in a tizzy about this actress fleeing town, isn't he?" Diana asked.

"Yes," Emily said. "How did you—"

"Belfry mentioned it when Penvale and I came to dinner, don't you recall?" Diana said. "Penvale asked him how things were at the theater, and Belfry turned properly brooding, said something about how he was less than pleased with the understudy preparing to take on Miss Simmons's role, and that he wished he could find someone more suited to the part."

"That's true," Emily said cautiously—she herself had had more than one conversation with Julian on the topic.

"What if," Diana said, a note of glee in her voice, "you suggested that *you* take on the role instead?"

Violet, who had just taken a large bite of scone, promptly choked, and the proceedings were momentarily interrupted by Diana reaching over to thump her heartily on the back. Once Violet was no longer in imminent danger of death, Emily was able to reply.

"You cannot be serious."

"Of course I'm not," Diana agreed.

"Because—I beg your pardon?" Emily asked, feeling somewhat lost.

"Of course I'm not serious," Diana explained patiently. "You, obviously, would never dream of appearing onstage—no lady of our class would, if she didn't wish her reputation to be irrevocably destroyed. Furthermore, darling Emily, I don't really think you'd be well suited to a career as an actress. No offense."

Emily couldn't understand why on earth she would possibly be offended by this, but didn't interrupt.

"But," Diana continued, "we don't need you to *actually* have delusions of treading the boards—we just need Belfry to *think* you have."

"Diana," Violet said, "Belfry's not a complete idiot. He won't believe for one moment that Emily actually wishes to appear onstage."

"But Emily's been acting quite out of character lately," Diana insisted. "Think about it—marrying a man without her parents' permission! A man with a scandalous reputation, no less. A man who's barely respectable! Does that sound like the Emily Turner we know and love?"

"No," Violet admitted slowly, still sounding uncertain.

Diana turned to pat Emily's arm. "I mean it in no way as an insult, darling," Diana hastened to reassure her. "I personally *adore* this new Emily. But you must admit, it's all been quite unexpected."

"I suppose," Emily agreed. "But—"

"Well, is it really such a leap, then, to convince Belfry that you've taken it into your head to try your hand at acting?"

"Yes," Emily said exasperated. "I really think it is. And besides—to what end?"

"Well," Diana said, a crafty light in her eyes, "if Belfry thinks that you have dreams of appearing onstage, then mightn't he look a little more kindly upon the notion of you simply accompanying him to the theater on occasion, by comparison?"

"You mean," Emily said, cottoning, "convince him to give me what I really want, by tricking him into thinking I want something much worse?"

"Precisely," Diana said, leaning back in her seat and looking pleased with herself.

Violet took a prim sip of her tea. "Has anyone else noticed that we spend an awful lot of time scheming of late?" she observed.

Diana and Emily said, "*Violet*," in unison.

"What?" Violet asked, raising her hands in defense. "It just seems—"

"We *do* seem to be scheming a lot lately," Emily interrupted. "Because you started the coughing and counterfeit doctors and lying in bed *pretending to be dying* in the first place."

"Oh," Violet said, at least having the grace to look a bit sheepish. "Well, I suppose that's not strictly inaccurate."

"I believe it's entirely accurate, you ninny," Diana said with an air of exasperated affection born of long friendship. "So if you can spend a fortnight putting fake bloodstains on handkerchiefs—"

"I did no such thing!" Violet protested, then paused, considering. "Though really, I should have done. It would have been much more convincing."

"My point is, I think Emily can pretend to have temporarily lost her mind for a single evening," Diana said dryly. "It's quite tame, by comparison."

"You think I'll be able to convince Julian of this in a single evening?" Emily asked skeptically.

"I do," Diana said cheerfully, "if you have reinforcements. And spirits." She leaned forward conspiratorially. "Don't you think it's time you had a dinner party?"

Thirteen

Hosting a dinner party in his own home, Julian thought, was surprisingly enjoyable. He'd never been in the habit of entertaining—as a bachelor, the logistics of hosting a dinner party had always seemed somewhat beyond him, and both Laverre and Bridgeworth, his closest friend from Oxford, were married, so it was easy enough to dine at their homes, to which he was frequently invited. The rest of his set—other friends from Oxford, acquaintances from the theater world—were either unmarried or had wives who wanted nothing to do with the scandalous Julian Belfry, so his evenings with them were passed in gentlemen's clubs and gaming hells and even less savory environs. Never at his home, across a table laid with gleaming china and polished silver, waiting for a soup course to be presented.

And yet, at the moment, that was precisely where he found himself.

Emily had suggested the idea of a dinner party several days earlier, noting that her friends were now returned to town and it would be nice to gather everyone together; furthermore, she had hinted significantly, it would be a perfect opportunity for him to introduce her to his friends, something he had rather shamefully failed to do so far. Julian had felt a bit sheepish about that, because truly, he should have done so—Bridgeworth and Jemma, his wife, would be entirely respectable company for Emily, and furthermore, he actually thought they would all get on quite well. But he'd been busy, and he wasn't accustomed to having a wife to care for, or about, and so he'd put it off. But tonight, both Bridgeworth and Jemma were coming, as were Audley and Violet, Willingham and Diana, Penvale, Laverre and his wife, Lucie, and—in what Julian strongly suspected was a bit of matchmaking, though Emily innocently protested otherwise—the Marquess of Weston and Lady Fitzwilliam Bridewell. West, being Audley's elder brother, did join their party on occasion, and Julian knew that Emily and her friends had befriended Lady Fitzwilliam that summer, but he still smelled a rat.

"If West and Lady Fitzwilliam wish to resume their romance," he'd said lazily as he perused the proposed guest list a few days earlier, "I think they're perfectly capable of managing it without your interference."

"Hmm," Emily had said, the noise implying a great degree of skepticism even if said skepticism was not expressed verbally. "*If* I were attempting to matchmake—and I will admit to doing no such thing; I think quite enough people's romantic lives have been interfered with among this set of late—I would feel compelled to note that I have yet to see any evidence that men are capable of working things out without a fair degree of outside assistance."

"I believe I managed my courtship and marriage without any interference from your meddling friends," he responded smugly. "I wasted no time in securing my prize."

Emily blinked at him. Twice. He had been married to her just— *just*—long enough to know that two blinks signaled danger.

"You make me sound like a fat pig to be won at the village fete," she said. This being Emily, there was no hint of anger or even irritation in her voice, but the moment she crossed her arms over her chest, he knew he was in trouble.

"Not at all," he amended hastily. "I merely meant that you were so clearly a desirable match that I did not hesitate for a second before I sprang into action."

"That is not quite how I recall matters unfolding," she said, her arms still crossed. Clearly he was not out of danger yet.

"And how, then, do you remember things?" he asked, setting down the list and rising from his spot in an armchair by the fire—they were ensconced in the library, enjoying after-dinner glasses of port and sherry—and beginning to slowly prowl toward her.

"If I recall correctly," she said, tapping her chin with a thoughtful finger, "you asked me to dance at a ball, then proceeded to mildly stalk me across several society events—"

"*Stalk!*"

"—before going out of your way to attend a country house party that I know perfectly well you never would have attended otherwise—"

"I *like* country house parties," he objected, nettled. "Blood sport and liberal amounts of brandy, what's not to like?"

"—before proceeding to suggest we *marry*, of all things, after having spent the better part of a fortnight attempting to convince me of all the ways that we might be of use to each other." She paused, registered his rakishly raised eyebrow, and added, "*Not* like that." His eyebrow rose even higher, and she conceded, "Well, not *only* like that."

"Are you quite done?" he asked.

"I believe so," she said with great dignity.

"All that monologue has illustrated," he said, bracing his hands on the arms of her chair and leaning down so that she could not look anywhere but directly into his eyes, "is that I was so taken with you that I proceeded to do everything in my power to woo you."

She snorted. "It hardly counts as wooing, Julian, when there's no feeling involved."

He registered, with a faint pang of surprise, that he didn't like to hear her dismiss their courtship in such terms. She was entirely correct, of course—the whole point of their marriage was that there was no feeling involved. And yet, as he had gazed at Emily, he'd realized that he *liked* being married to her. This in itself was somewhat startling, and so he'd quickly put the thought from his mind, instead bickering with her amiably and trying his very best not to consider the fact that it was not, perhaps, strictly accurate anymore to claim that no feeling at all existed between them.

He smiled over the memory now as he sat at his table, waiting for the cream-of-veal soup to be brought out. Emily had discussed the menu at length with him, before deciding to ignore his advice and settle upon exactly what she'd had in mind to start with. Julian, sensing that his role in these situations was merely to smile and nod agreeably, had done so with good humor. But the result of this was that he now knew precisely how much thought Emily had put into this dinner— how much she'd considered every last detail. It seemed an awful lot to worry about.

Darting a glance down the table at his wife, however, he was relieved to see that she didn't look worried at all. Indeed, she looked . . . luminous. This was, in and of itself, nothing out of the ordinary— Emily's aesthetic qualities were well established, both among the *ton* in general and, in greater detail, in Julian's own mind. Tonight she was wearing a gown of midnight-blue satin, the neckline lower than he'd seen her wear before. He'd told her, as soon as they'd arrived in town, to feel free to set up accounts at the modiste, the haberdasher, and anywhere else she might wish to give her custom; when she'd asked him hesitantly about pin money, he'd named a sum that had made her blink in astonishment.

"But that's merely an estimate," he'd told her. "You can of course spend more, if the need arises."

At these words, Emily, wide-eyed, had said, "You . . . you already paid off my father's debts—I hadn't expected this much in pin money."

"Your father's debts have nothing to do with you," Julian said coolly, thinking of the strongly worded letter he had sent to Rowanbridge the morning after his meeting with Cartham regarding the financial arrangements.

"You are my wife, and what is mine is yours," he added. "Besides, we made an agreement when we married—I can hardly have you wearing gowns three seasons out of date."

This had seemed to mollify her, and tonight she was wearing one of those new gowns. He didn't realize how accustomed he'd grown to seeing her wearing a style that was ever-so-slightly out of fashion until he saw her now, looking entirely à la mode. She looked grown-up. It was an odd turn of phrase to use, considering that she was his wife, and certainly not a girl, and in no way did he think of her as childlike. But her parents had, he realized in a rush, and so too had Cartham. To them, she was a girl incapable of knowing her own mind or making her own decisions, to be used as they saw fit.

But the version of Emily at the table this evening—she was a woman. And she knew it.

She was, at present, laughing at something Lady Fitzwilliam had said, and her entire face was alight. Julian found it impossible to tear his gaze away—which was why he did not miss the furtive hand she slipped beneath the table. Julian was quite certain that, were he interested in dropping to the floor like a madman and crawling around underneath his dining room table, he would see Cecil Lucifer Beelzebub happily holding court on Emily's lap. Julian, however—perhaps lulled by a couple of glasses of wine and not feeling quite up to a kitten-induced argument—decided against confirming this.

"You're mooning, Belfry," came Audley's amused voice from Julian's right, and he started, remembering that they were surrounded by friends and that any gawking he did would be in plain sight.

"I'm hardly *mooning*," he said shortly, shooting Audley a look—Julian generally liked the man, finding him thoughtful and serious in a way that most idiots of the *ton* were not, but he did have a tendency, now that his own marriage had been so happily reconciled, to look around with the gaze of the smugly besotted. "But only a fool could fail to appreciate how beautiful my wife looks this evening."

"Very good, Belfry," said Bridgeworth's wife, Jemma, who was seated on Audley's other side, and who never hesitated to interject herself into any conversation. When Julian had first met her, he'd thought her rather an odd match for his somewhat mild-mannered friend, but he supposed it was no stranger a match than his marriage to Emily.

"However," Jemma continued, "it is better to hold such compliments until the lady is nearer, so that she can pretend not to hear them but be secretly pleased nonetheless. I wish Bridgeworth would take note of this."

She had spoken a bit loudly, and her husband, several seats down the table, glanced over at the sound of his name. "Is there something wrong with my compliments, my love?" he called, interrupting whatever conversation he'd been having with Diana, who was seated next to him.

"You never *pay* me any compliments," Jemma said severely.

"I certainly do," Bridgeworth protested, his neck flushing a bit. He leaned forward in his chair with an embarrassed glance at those seated near him and said, a bit more quietly, "What do you think all those notes on your dressing table are?"

"Do you hear that, Jeremy?" Diana called down the table to her fiancé, who was sipping a glass of claret while Violet explained something to him with great eagerness; both turned at the sound of Diana's voice. "Love notes," she said, giving him a significant look. "On her dressing table. I hope you are taking notes on how to be a good husband."

"I do live in abject terror that you will decide to leave me," Willingham said lazily, not sounding remotely terrified. "Don't know if I can manage love letters, though, my precious diamond."

Diana shot him a look. "Do not call me that again—you'll put me off my food."

"Of course not, my radiant emerald," he agreed.

"Please stop speaking to me now," said his beloved, and she promptly turned back to Bridgeworth and Jemma, who were at the moment giving each other the sorts of lovesick looks down the table that Julian thought very likely to put him off *his* food.

"Are dinner parties always this chaotic?" he asked Audley, who looked faintly amused. "I don't frequent terribly polite circles these days, you understand, but it does seem as if the dinners I have attended in the past haven't borne quite such a strong resemblance to the kitten races the children in my village used to stage."

"How on earth do kittens race?" Audley asked, momentarily diverted.

"Without much semblance of order," Julian informed him.

"This is, unfortunately, what you've agreed to, by marrying Emily," said Audley, with the heavy sigh of a man already deep into his own sentence. He gazed at Violet. "Utter madness at every turn."

"*Speaking* of madness," Diana said brightly. "Belfry, did Emily tell you the positively *brilliant* idea she had?"

Diana gave him a dazzling smile. She was—there was no denying it—an extremely attractive woman; indeed, in his younger days, Julian thought, he likely would have wasted a fair amount of energy chasing after her. But when she smiled at him like this, with the full force of her attention, he found her—well—

Terrifying.

"No," he hazarded. "I don't believe she did."

He shot a glance down the table at his wife. Emily gave him a happy smile in return that did nothing to soothe the sense of foreboding that had suddenly gripped him as soon as Diana began speaking.

"*Well*," Diana said—she seemed to have a remarkable fondness for speaking in italics, Julian thought—"I recall you telling Penvale and me of the frustration you are currently experiencing, as regards the lead actress at your theater."

"Leave me out of this," Penvale said darkly from his spot midway down the table; he was seated next to Laverre, with whom he appeared to have hit it off quite well, and he'd interrupted his conversation to give his sister a wary look that spoke of years of experience with her scheming.

"Yes," Julian said with a bit of caution—something told him that he was not going to like wherever this conversation was leading. "It's been a bit of a headache."

"How terrible," Diana said with an exaggerated show of sympathy; beside Julian, Audley snorted, thus deepening Julian's sense of misgiving. "And yet, actually, how *wonderful*. Because, you see, we've been discussing it, and darling Emily has mentioned that she's always had a notion to try her hand at acting."

She presented this news cheerfully, as though there were nothing at all out of the ordinary about it, and indeed as if Julian were expected to fall to his knees in a fit of gratitude at any moment.

Instead, there was a decisive thump as, midway down the table, West set down his wineglass and turned to level that stern gaze of his upon Diana in such a way that implied he believed she'd taken leave of her senses; across from him, both of Laverre's eyebrows were approaching his hairline, and Jemma had turned to regard Emily the way one might regard a tiger that had initially been mistaken for a fuzzy kitten.

Julian had also turned to look at his wife, and she did not blush, or look shyly away, or engage in any of the habits he realized he'd grown accustomed to seeing in her, particularly in company. Instead, her eyes met his levelly, a look of polite curiosity upon her lovely face.

"You cannot be serious," he said.

"I've always been rather curious about the theater," Emily said, raising her wineglass to take a sip. "And I feel quite certain I could learn the lines—I've quite a good memory, you know."

"You would be ruined," he said. "You'd never be able to go anywhere near a polite drawing room ever again."

"Yes," she said, heaving a dramatic sigh. "And how *dreadful* that would be. Only think of all the discussions about the weather I'd miss out on—and, oh! The overcooked biscuits! However would I survive?"

There was appreciative laughter scattered around the table at this, but Julian did not so much as move a muscle, unwilling to break eye contact with whomever this creature was who had entered his dining room and replaced his perfectly sensible wife.

"You know nothing about acting," he said, feeling compelled to point out the obvious.

"But that won't matter much, once I'm onstage," she said, batting her eyelashes. "Everyone will be so distracted by the sight of *me*, a lady with a previously immaculate reputation, appearing onstage in a theater, that they won't notice a word I say. Only think of what it will do for your ticket sales! It will be a spectacle!"

"I don't want a spectacle," Julian said sharply. "I believe that was the point of this marriage." Something faltered for a brief moment in Emily's expression as he uttered these words—a bit of the confidence vanishing for a second, only to be replaced a moment later, as if it were a sheet that had slipped before being quickly yanked back into place. He felt a brief stab of regret at his words, but ignored it—he'd only spoken the truth, after all.

"And *I* thought you wanted to use my reputation to improve that of your theater," Emily responded coolly. "How am I possibly to do that, if I never set foot anywhere near it?"

"If you're curious about the Belfry, there are numerous ways you might be involved without resorting to *appearing onstage*," he enunciated very clearly, feeling as if he were conversing with a madwoman; she continued to lay out her argument as if there were nothing at all unusual in it, which made Julian, in turn, feel as though he might be losing *his* mind.

"Then you'll allow me to come with you to the Belfry? To watch a rehearsal, meet the actors . . . see if I've any suggestions about how you might make it more respectable?" Emily asked, brightening, and Julian instantly realized that he'd been played from the start.

"I didn't say—"

"If you wish me to be involved, but don't wish me to actually have a starring role in one of your shows, this seems like a nice compromise, don't you think?" She was doing that thing again that she did—blinking in innocent inquiry, as though she were being entirely reasonable and there was nothing out of the ordinary in her request. As though she had not just more or less threatened him with the destruction of her entire reputation—and his, by extension—only to back down from this threat to settle for what she *actually* wanted instead.

He saw all of this in an instant and, meeting her eyes once more, he saw something flicker in her gaze—some acknowledgment that she knew what she had just done, and she knew that *he* knew, too. And Julian, suddenly feeling a bit exhausted in the face of the concerted campaign he had just endured, simply said, "Fine. I'll take you to the Belfry."

"Lovely!" Emily said brightly, then promptly turned to Lady Fitzwilliam and resumed whatever conversation they'd been having five minutes ago.

Meanwhile, half the table was still staring at Julian, who felt as if he'd just weathered a typhoon.

"Welcome to married life, Belfry," Audley said, raising his glass to him. "I hope you're up to the challenge."

Julian could not help hoping the same.

Fourteen

"I really thought a hotbed of sin would look a bit more . . . well, sinful," Emily said two days later as she followed Julian through a non-descript door into the backstage area of the Belfry.

Her husband turned to offer her his arm, quirking an eyebrow at her as he did so. "You've been here before—has your memory faded that quickly?"

"No," Emily said, poking him in the side, "but I was only privy to the public areas of the theater that night—and Lord James did his best to hustle us to our box in record time. I only saw *two* couples engaged in illicit embraces before I was sequestered away, and I must confess it was a trifle disappointing."

"Jesus Christ," Julian muttered, but Emily was not finished yet.

"So I assumed the truly interesting things must happen behind the scenes," she continued cheerfully. She peered around eagerly, half hoping that a door would open to reveal an opium den hosting an orgy in progress.

"I hate to dash all of your wild hopes," Julian said dryly, "but you do understand that I've been making a rather concerted effort to make the Belfry into an upstanding establishment?"

"Yes," she said slowly. "But clearly it hasn't been *that* successful, if you still needed to marry me. So I remain hopeful that there will be scandal lurking around a dark corner."

"Debutantes need to get out of the house more," he said darkly, leading her down the hallway. "Clearly all that sheltered time in drawing rooms has a deleterious effect upon—er—"

"Moral fiber?" Emily suggested.

"Precisely," Julian said firmly.

Emily was, in truth, only half listening to anything he said, so busy was she taking in everything about her surroundings. While the public-facing portions of the Belfry were luxuriously appointed with wall hangings and carpets in shades of scarlet and emerald, backstage was considerably less elaborate. The walls were bare, the floors a plain and heavily scarred wood, and there were exposed wooden beams visible overhead. The corridor, while narrow, was at least well lit, which Emily couldn't help but think would be a comfort to any actresses or other female employees who might find themselves back here without any sort of escort.

Trying to take everything in, Emily was therefore several feet behind Julian when he rounded a corner and came to an abrupt halt. She barely avoided walking directly into the broad expanse of his back.

They were no longer in a narrow corridor, but in a cavernous chamber, with a ceiling that soared high above them, heavy wooden set pieces obscuring Emily's view of the stage itself and the seats beyond it. She lifted her head and saw overhead a number of ropes suspended from the exposed wooden beams, many of which were fastened to sandbags. She looked down again, then peered around Julian's shoulder, curious as to what had caught his attention.

Directly ahead, a young lady about her own age was standing in nothing but a chemise, her dark hair unbound and falling around her shoulders, a sheaf of papers in hand, arguing quite vociferously with the tall, auburn-haired gentleman standing a couple of feet before her. Even before Emily registered the words they were speaking, she noticed the tone—their voices tense and tight with anger—and she felt her shoulders stiffen in an innate response to arguing that she had learned over the long years of her childhood. But after a moment, she relaxed, belatedly realizing that the papers the actress was holding were a script, and that she and the actor—for that was who the man with her must surely be—were running lines.

"I wonder that you will still be talking, Signor Benedick," the actress was saying scornfully, "when your concept of the heavenly sphere so clearly misses the mark?"

"What, my dear Lady Disdain!" the actor replied, a teasing note evident in each word he spoke. "Are you yet living? Perhaps I would wish otherwise, if only to prove your misconceptions to be false."

"This is rubbish," the actress said, her shoulders slumping. She was no longer reading her lines, but speaking as herself.

"That's why I asked you to run lines with me again," the actor said, sighing; his brow furrowed as he looked down at his script.

"Dragged me out here, you mean," the actress said with a snort. "Half-dressed."

"I wasn't about to let you run home after that awful rehearsal," he said in frustration. "We've only another few weeks before the show opens, and—"

"And I certainly hope you'll manage to do better than that," Julian interrupted coolly; Emily glanced up at him in surprise, never having heard him sound quite like that before.

The actor and actress both started.

"Belfry," the actor greeted. "Just the man I was hoping to see."

"Oh?" Julian asked, turning slightly so that Emily was visible behind him. He offered her his arm, then took a few steps toward his actors. "Having trouble?"

The sight of Emily seemed to render the others momentarily speechless; Emily resisted the temptation to reach up and pat at her hair, a habit that she'd mostly managed to shed since her debut Season. She glanced down at her dress, which she had agonized over that morning— she hadn't wanted to seem too high in the instep, since she knew Julian did not like to pull rank at the Belfry, but she also didn't want to seem shabby. After all, the image she hoped to present to the world was that of the privileged wife of a wealthy and powerful man, who wasn't at all bothered by what he did for employment (or, indeed, the fact that he had any employment at all). She'd eventually settled on a high-necked gown with thin green and white stripes and lace at the collar, in no small part because her mother had once told her that vertical stripes made her look like a beanpole. Emily didn't particularly care if she looked like a beanpole—she thought the gown was quite fetching, and now there was no one to prevent her from wearing it.

"Lady Julian," the actress said, recovering quickest, and bobbing a quick curtsey. "Or so I presume?"

She shot an inquiring look at Julian that was considerably less deferential than the curtsey she'd just offered Emily.

"Apologies," Julian said lazily. "Emily, this is Julia Congreave and Andrew June. They're the leads in *Much Ado About Heaven*. June, Miss Congreave—this is my wife, Lady Julian."

"There's no need for the curtsey," Emily said, smiling at Miss Congreave, who was eyeing her with some curiosity. Emily supposed that Julian's sudden marriage must have been a source of considerable gossip at the theater, and wondered what Miss Congreave's impression of her would be. Whatever it was, Emily had little doubt that it would soon spread like wildfire among the other actors and stagehands—based on the few anecdotes Julian had shared of his work, she had the impression that the theater world was as bad as the *ton* when it came to gossip.

"I apologize for interrupting your rehearsal," she added, seeing that both Miss Congreave and Mr. June seemed somewhat taken aback by her presence. "I'm afraid I've been pestering my husband for a behind-the-scenes tour, and today was the day I finally wore him down." She risked a sideways glance at Julian, who had pressed his lips together tightly, no doubt to suppress the urge to correct her not-entirely-accurate summary of recent events. "I understand this show is a . . . new sort of comedy?"

"Theoretically," June muttered, more to himself than anyone else; Miss Congreave gave a rather dramatic sigh.

"It's a ridiculous, pompous bit of fluff," Miss Congreave said dismissively, not seeming remotely bothered by her company. "I've never disagreed with Belfry before, but he's bizarrely attached to this one, which June and I have to salvage somehow—"

"It's perfectly salvageable, thank you," Julian said, his tone curt. "I've watched your performances for the past two years, Julia, and I know how talented you are. The only problem at the moment is that you won't properly commit yourself to the script."

"I'd like to commit myself to tossing it out a window," Miss Congreave said. Emily had the fleeting thought that, in another life, Miss Congreave and Diana would have been great friends.

Julian sighed.

"Miss Congreave has some . . . concerns about the script," he explained to Emily.

"So I gather," she said solemnly, causing June to snort.

"However," Julian continued, ignoring this, "Miss Congreave is paid—quite handsomely, I should add—to show up and rehearse her lines every day, *not* to assume management of this theater, so she will be continuing to prepare for her role, now that her concerns have been noted."

Miss Congreave, Emily thought, did not look entirely satisfied, and Emily could not blame her—she had never found a man's assurances that a lady's concerns had been noted to be terribly soothing.

"Belfry," June said. "She's not entirely wrong, you know—if we could just do the original version of the play—"

"Anyone," Julian said firmly, "can put on *Much Ado About Nothing*—including this very theater, several times in the past. What we are doing will be new and different and unexpected."

"That's one way of putting it," June said under his breath. Julian seemed to decide to let the comment pass.

"Shall we continue with our tour?" he asked Emily, before either of his actors could raise any other objections.

"It was lovely to meet you," Emily said to Miss Congreave and Mr. June as she took Julian's arm and turned to walk backstage. She stopped in her tracks as they rounded a bit of scenery and found themselves in close proximity to a pair of stagehands who were decidedly *not* doing the work they were employed for.

Next to her, Julian muttered a curse under his breath.

"Not again," he said in the weary tones of a parent with a naughty toddler. "Woodrose! Kumar! Is the paint even dry on those trees yet?"

The entwined couple broke apart with a start, bearing identical guilty expressions; as they did so, Emily realized that what she had taken for two gentlemen were actually a man and a woman, but the woman was wearing breeches.

"It is dry, my lord," the man said defensively; he appeared to be about Julian's age and was quite handsome, with dark hair that was cut a shade long for fashion. "We wouldn't have—er—utilized it otherwise."

Julian's mouth twitched. "Very thoughtful of you, Kumar. Could you two perhaps see fit to actually do the work I am *paying* you for, and leave the other activities for when you're done?" He noticed the other stagehand gazing at Emily with unveiled curiosity, and he sighed. "Woodrose, Kumar, this is my wife, Lady Julian. Emily," he said, turning to her, "Miss Woodrose and Mr. Kumar are *supposedly* employed in set design—they're painting all the set pieces we'll be using in the show." Glancing around, Emily saw a half-finished depiction of an Italian villa as seen from a distance, with trees and elaborate gardens in the foreground.

"We were just catching our breath," Miss Woodrose said with a cheeky smile; she appeared to be a few years older than Emily, with curly brown hair pulled messily back from her face, and a scattering of freckles across her nose.

Julian snorted. "Didn't seem like you could possibly have been doing much breathing, under the circumstances."

Mr. Kumar blushed, which Emily thought was rather charming.

"I apologize, my lord. It won't happen again."

Julian made a skeptical noise.

"Considering this is the third time this week someone's found you under similar circumstances, I somehow doubt that." He waved a hand. "Just try not to get wet paint on anything, if you please. As you were."

Emily managed to wait until they were out of earshot before her questions bubbled over.

"Julian!" she said. "That was a *female stagehand!*"

"Indeed," Julian said, leading her around several more finished set pieces and nodding at a few other stagehands they passed before ducking through a doorway into another unadorned corridor. "Usually she hides it a bit better—it's known among the other stagehands and actors, of course, but we don't want any gentlemen giving her trouble on nights when there are shows, so she usually wears a cap, and always arrives and departs in a bulky jacket."

"However did you come to hire her?" Emily asked curiously as they walked down the empty hallway. Her mind was racing—it had never occurred to her that there were ways women might be employed at the Belfry beyond acting. The life of an actress had always seemed so scandalous, so entirely beyond the pale, that Emily had never given it much thought—but *this.* Working as a stagehand. The idea that a woman might choose this employment, rather than the life that was originally planned for her—in Miss Woodrose's case, likely that of a life in service . . . Emily was fascinated. Despite the fact that she and Miss Woodrose had presumably almost nothing in common, she could not help but feel an odd sort of kinship with the woman—in a way, she was almost envious of her.

Because Emily, for her part, was quite desperate for someone to see that she was capable of something beyond what was expected of her.

"She was originally a scullery maid in Laverre's household, and from what I gather, she was terrible at the work. Laverre's wife, Lucie, found her drawing on bits of discarded paper she found around the house, and thought she could be better employed here. So we hired her."

Emily looked up at him thoughtfully. "Were you not concerned about hiring a woman?"

"I was concerned the other lads would bother her, more than anything else," Julian said with a wry smile. "I told her we could take her on a trial basis, to see how it went—within a few days, one of the lads was offering her some unwanted attention, and she gave him a knee to the—a delicate area," he corrected himself hastily, casting a concerned glance at her, clearly worrying that this might have been too much for her innocent ears.

Emily gazed back at him, wide-eyed.

"Julian," she said utterly seriously, "can you teach *me* how to do that?"

His laugh was strangely rewarding.

By the time they at last arrived at Julian's office, Emily was practically vibrating with excitement—so much so, in fact, that she nearly walked right past the door in question, and had to be jerked somewhat abruptly to a halt by Julian's arm, which she was still clinging to.

"Here," he said, nodding to the nondescript door, upon which a small brass plaque bore his name. Not his title, not his role at the theater, simply JULIAN BELFRY.

"Laverre's office is next door," he said as he opened the door, nodding over his shoulder down the hall. "He's always popping in unannounced, so you'll no doubt see him in a moment—"

"Even better," Emily said cheerfully, sailing past her husband and into the room, where Mr. Laverre sat behind what was presumably Julian's desk, feet kicked up upon the surface, a speculative expression on his face. "Mr. Laverre, how lovely to see you."

Laverre hopped to his feet as soon as Emily entered the room and made rather a production of bowing over her hand—really, Frenchmen were *very* charming; it was a shame His Majesty's Army had spent so much time trying to kill them over the past twenty years. Emily personally thought that a number of English gentlemen of her acquaintance could learn something from their counterparts across the Channel.

"That's enough of that, Laverre," Julian said darkly, shutting the door behind him. "What are you doing here? I believe you do have your own desk, approximately twenty feet away?"

"But there aren't lovely wives in *my* office," Laverre said, giving Emily a smile. He was not a terribly tall man—about Emily's own height, in fact—but he was still a commanding presence when he spoke. Julian had told her a bit of Laverre's rather colorful personal history—he was the illegitimate son of a French nobleman and an opera dancer, and had appeared onstage himself in his youth. There was undoubtedly something compelling about him, as well as a comfort in his own skin that implied he was accustomed to being watched—even if, as Julian had explained, he'd spent the past decade behind the scenes, rather than center stage.

"Laverre, I have never seen you behave so charmingly in your entire life," Julian said, stepping forward to help Emily into a seat. "Are you feeling at all well?"

"Merely possessed with a feverish glee at the thought that you have finally met your match, *mon ami.*"

"He only speaks French when he's mocking me," Julian explained to Emily, who continued to watch this exchange with great interest. She'd gotten to see a bit of their repartee at dinner the other night, but there had been so many other people present that she'd not had much of a chance to pay attention. Julian was the son of one of the most respected aristocrats in England—the second son to a man who bore a title dating back generations—while Laverre was an illegitimate Frenchman raised in the demimonde. And yet, when the two men spoke, they interacted as equals—there was nothing in their manner to indicate their wildly different origins. Emily wondered if it had always been this way between them, or if Julian had become accustomed over time to this world that was so far from the one to which he'd been born.

Emily knew that she should be shocked by what she saw—by the actresses she'd met, women who lived outside the bounds of polite society; by this building, full of people who worked for a living, who spoke different languages, came from different places; by everything that was so utterly different from the rarefied environment in which she'd been raised, where everyone looked and spoke just exactly as she did, and where a lady was expected to be nothing but ornamental. Here, a woman could take up space, speak loudly, draw the eyes of a crowd—or, alternately, could slip into a role behind the scenes, quietly doing her work just as well as the men who surrounded her—and Emily found both prospects not shocking but . . . exhilarating.

She felt as though she'd been living in a cage for her entire life, and Julian had opened the door. There was an entire world beyond her mother's drawing room, waiting to be discovered.

The Belfry—well, the Belfry was only the beginning.

"Mr. Laverre," she said suddenly, interrupting whatever inane conversation the gentlemen were having, to which she had ceased paying any attention (a course of action that, according to Diana, was always the wisest). "What is it precisely that you do here at the Belfry?"

"I'm the manager," Laverre said, drawing himself up a bit.

"I understand that," Emily assured him. "I was under the impression managers are responsible for most everything that goes on at a theater?"

"That's correct," Laverre said, clearly pleased that she respected the importance of his position.

"Perhaps my question, then, should have been different," Emily said thoughtfully. "If you're responsible for almost everything that goes on—if the theater wouldn't run without you—then what, precisely, does Lord Julian do?"

"A very good question, my lady," Laverre said, nodding as Julian sputtered next to him, seeming about as discomposed as Emily had ever seen him. Laverre shot Julian a grin. "You should have married years ago."

"I'm beginning to think quite the opposite," Julian said darkly, then turned to Emily. "What is your concern here, precisely? I own the theater. I oversee the finances."

"Actually," Laverre put in helpfully at this juncture, "*I* oversee the finances. I merely send him the paperwork to look over after the fact."

"My original question still stands, then," Emily said thoughtfully. "Is it normal for owners to have an office at the theater?"

"I couldn't say," Julian said through gritted teeth, "only having ever owned the one theater."

At this juncture, Laverre offered, "Oftentimes the owner is some useless nobleman or other—"

"Present company excluded," Julian interjected.

"Did I say that?" Laverre asked thoughtfully, tapping his chin. "I don't believe I did." He shrugged. "In any case, normally Lord Chouchou—"

"You really are *very* French, aren't you?" Emily asked, diverted.

"He's putting it on for you," Julian said. "Normally, he sounds as English as I do."

"Do you see, my lady, the baseless accusations to which I am subjected every day?" Laverre asked mournfully, his accent becoming more pronounced. "In any case, those gentlemen do not normally have much to do with the day-to-day running of the establishment. But your husband and I have always operated as something of a team; the theater was in piss—I mean, in terrible shape when your husband bought it, young fool that he was, and he had to invest a fair amount of capital to get it operational."

"It was operational," Julian protested.

"All right," Laverre agreed. "But no one in their right mind would have wanted to spend more than ten minutes inside, unless they were foxed out of their minds."

"Which many of them were," Julian admitted. "We did extensive renovations, and then more a couple of years ago—when I was one-and-twenty, the fact that it vaguely resembled a brothel seemed charming and entertaining, but at some point I realized it was a bit . . ."

"Unseemly," Emily suggested.

"Precisely," Laverre said, nodding. "In any case, he was wise enough to know that he didn't know what he was doing pretty early on, which is when he hired me, and we've rubbed along together ever since. He's *supposedly* leaving more of the daily operations of the theater to me—"

"I am!" Julian objected.

"Theoretically," Laverre said, pressing his lips together. "But if you are so obsessed with making your society friends come to the Belfry— buy boxes, even—then perhaps you would do well to spend more time courting their favor, and less time actually here, when you know perfectly well that I have matters under control."

"I don't need to court their favor anymore," Julian said in the smug tones of a man who thought that he had worked things out perfectly to his satisfaction. "I have a wife to do that."

Emily's heart sank a bit at the reminder of where her value in their marriage lay. She could not linger on this feeling, however, because she was distracted by something Laverre had mentioned a moment before, an idea beginning to form in her mind.

"And yet your wife is here," Laverre was saying speculatively. "Instead of . . . doing whatever it is rich ladies like to do. Drinking tea?"

"They like to discuss whether so-and-so's ball was a terrible crush," Emily said conspiratorially.

"And that is . . . a bad thing?" Laverre asked.

"Oh, no," Emily said solemnly. "A terrible crush is all that any society hostess dreams of."

Laverre frowned. "It doesn't sound very comfortable."

"It's not," said Emily and Julian in unison, and Julian grinned at her, the flash of it warming her more thoroughly than an entire pot of tea on a winter day.

Emily then added, "And I'm here because *here* is vastly more interesting than any of those drawing rooms, having any of those conversations. I've sat in drawing rooms my entire life—I've never been backstage at a theater before."

"For good reason," Julian said darkly. "It's hardly appropriate."

Emily looked around the room. "Yes, I do see what you mean—all these . . . papers? And a desk? It does seem frightfully scandalous."

"Emily," Julian said with exasperation.

Emily knew she was pushing her luck, and quickly added, "Don't worry, I'll be in one of those drawing rooms making conversation tomorrow afternoon."

Julian's face softened a bit as he regarded her—she did not think of him as having a harsh face, precisely, but it was not a terribly warm one. He had a way of placing himself at something of a remove from whatever the situation was at hand—of playing the slightly bored observer, amused by his surroundings but not wholly *of* them. It was, in truth, part of what had first drawn her to him—she was used to men looking at her with great interest; Emily didn't like to think herself vain, but one could only hear one's beauty extolled a certain number of times before one started to believe it, at least a little bit. This interest had never lasted terribly long, of course—the circumstances of her father's debts and her pitiful dowry were sufficient to drive away many of her potential suitors (and whatever murmured explanations her father had offered alone with the gentlemen at the club or over a game of cards had been enough to scare off the rest). But Julian had been unusual—while he certainly gazed at her with frank appreciation, he'd never given the appearance of being awestruck.

Now, though, there was something softer, more concerned in his expression, though she thought he'd absolutely hate to be told that. So she tucked away the memory of that softening, even as the moment passed.

"I don't wish you to be miserable," he said, his voice low; out of the corner of her eye, Emily saw Laverre suddenly dedicating a great deal of attention to the ink blotter on the desk.

"I won't be," she said lightly, looking up at that unsettling blue gaze. "We had an arrangement, after all—and I can hardly convince anyone that I'm deliriously happy in my new marriage if the ladies of the *ton* never see me at all."

"Still," he said, sounding a bit doubtful, "I don't want you to associate with any ladies whom you truly dislike—any who may have been unkind to you, in the past."

"No one is ever unkind to me," Emily said entirely truthfully. "At least, not to my face."

"I don't doubt that," he said, a faint quirk at the corner of his mouth hinting at amusement. "It would be like kicking a baby bunny."

"Oh, thank you ever so much," Emily said, letting out a surprised laugh. "What a charming picture you paint of me. Do I have whiskers, then? Does my nose twitch?"

"It's the eyes," he said, that hint of a smile deepening a bit, lingering rather than vanishing. "You have the widest, most innocent eyes."

"I know," she said, sighing, her laughter fading. "It's why everyone thinks nothing of treating me like a child."

"I don't treat you like a child," he said, leaning toward her for a moment before seeming to remember Laverre's presence, which halted his progress.

"No," she admitted, her cheeks heating. "You certainly don't. But you also mustn't worry about me—I'm not being thrown to the wolves, I'm merely keeping up my end of the bargain." Realizing belatedly, however, that she might be about to toss away a rather fortuitous opportunity, she paused. She and Julian had promised each other honesty—but she had never promised not to take advantage of a bit of misplaced guilt on his part, to get what she truly wanted.

"But perhaps we could see our way to some sort of arrangement," she said slowly, and he arched an inquisitive eyebrow. "Perhaps, for every afternoon of social calls, or every dinner party, or every walk in Hyde Park with a lady I dislike, I might spend an afternoon here at the Belfry."

Julian sighed. "Emily—"

"No, listen," she said. "I'm not trying to interfere—I won't make a nuisance of myself, or get in the way, or do anything that might damage my reputation. But if your aim is to attract ladies to the theater, would it not be helpful to have an actual lady spending time behind the scenes, offering her opinion?" She reached out to rest a hand on his arm. "You are a man, Julian—"

"I'm so glad you've noticed," he said dryly.

"—and so you cannot possibly see things from a lady's perspective. But if I were to spend some time here—watch rehearsals, familiarize myself with the theater and how it worked—perhaps I might be able to offer you some suggestions that mightn't occur to you otherwise."

He regarded her for a long moment, a faint furrow between his brows.

"Please," she said, taking a step closer to him. "I want to be useful. And I want to try to be useful in a way other than the way I've always been before." She paused for a moment, allowing him to fully process her words. "I'll still go to tea—I'll be certain to let drop in conversation that I've been spending more time at the Belfry, in fact. But let me spend time here, too."

"All right," he said. "In fact, I've been pondering a few more cosmetic changes to the theater, just to give it a bit of a fresh appearance, and perhaps you could mention to these ladies that you helped guide this undertaking. Selected new cushions for the chairs in the boxes. That sort of thing. Then perhaps they'll be curious to come see the theater for themselves."

"Well—" Emily began, then hesitated. Did she dare? She took a breath. "You could *actually* let me guide this undertaking, in truth. Then it wouldn't be a lie. And it's certainly something I think I'm well capable of assisting you with."

He opened his mouth—then closed it. "You're right," he said, sounding faintly surprised. "I suppose that would make more sense."

"I am capable of making sense on occasion, I believe," she said, a bit more tartly than she intended.

He grinned.

"All right, Lady Julian," he said with good humor. "Your presence at my theater is officially welcomed. Within reason," he added hastily, but she didn't mind—anything was better than sitting in stuffy drawing rooms all day, not doing or seeing anything different.

She smiled then, a real smile, and before she quite realized what she was doing, she had flung her arms around his shoulders and was standing on her toes to press herself tightly to him. A moment later, she would have pulled away, but his arm snaked around her waist, keeping her close, the warmth and strength of it against her back surprisingly comforting.

"How touching," came Laverre's voice, not sounding terribly touched at all. "Please do remember my presence, though, before matters proceed any further."

"You're French," Julian shot over his shoulder, loosening his grip on Emily but still keeping his arm around her. "I thought your people went all in for such displays."

"If you want to win the approval of a Frenchman, you'll need to do more than give your wife a quick embrace," Laverre replied, a note of wicked amusement in his voice, and Emily, despite the warmth she could feel creeping into her cheeks, could not help herself:

She laughed.

Fifteen

Two days later, Emily returned home from a brisk trot in the park with Violet and Sophie to find her husband at home, much to her surprise. She glanced at the clock in the entrance hall as she handed her bonnet and gloves to Bramble, and noted that it was only half past three; she and her friends had gone out deliberately early that afternoon, hoping to avoid any of the fashionable set, as they strategized about Emily's Path to Propriety, as Violet had named their plan to see Emily restore her husband's good name.

As it turned out, they needn't have worried, even if they'd ventured out at the fashionable five o'clock hour—it was a brisk, blustery sort of day, the kind of afternoon that reminded one that autumn was tightening its grip as the October days grew shorter, with a weak sun only occasionally peeking out from behind the clouds. As a result, the park was fairly deserted, much of London having apparently decided to stay home with a pot of tea before a fire.

Emily herself had just such a reward in mind upon returning home, only to stop short in surprise when Bramble informed her that Lord Julian was at home, hours before Emily would normally have expected him. And, furthermore, that he was not alone.

"The Earl of Blackford," she repeated, feeling a further burst of surprise when the butler gave Julian's brother's courtesy title. "Where are they, then?"

"In his lordship's study, I believe," Bramble said, sounding very pleased with himself. Emily had, over the past few weeks, gotten the distinct impression that Bramble had been suffering in silence for these many years, serving as butler to an aristocrat who refused to behave as an aristocrat should. But now! O, joyous day! Not only had Julian married—a proper lady of the *ton*, no less—but he was receiving visits from his brother, first in line to a marquessate. Emily could practically see Bramble vibrating with unspoken pleasure.

Resisting the impulse to give him a congratulatory pat on the shoulder, she instead made her way down the hallway toward Julian's study, a room she had only visited once or twice so far. Julian had never seemed irritated by her presence there, but she had spent her childhood in faint terror of her father's study, and she was realizing that this was a difficult emotion to shake. Her father only ever called one of his children into his study to reprimand them, or to deliver bad news; Emily herself never did much to earn her father's ire, but she had vivid memories of shouting matches between her elder brother and her father echoing from behind the closed study door. It was also the spot where her parents had informed her that, for the first time, Mr. Cartham would be her escort for an upcoming ball.

Studies, in other words, were not Emily's favorite rooms.

Shaking aside these memories, she pushed the door open a few inches, peering inside. Julian was seated behind his desk, jacketless and cravatless, reclining in his chair, a tumbler of brandy in hand. Opposite him sat a gentleman of similar height and build with hair a few shades lighter than Julian's, slouched comfortably in his seat with one leg crossed over the other. Upon hearing the door open, both heads turned to look at her, and she realized that the earl had eyes of the same clear blue as both his younger siblings, though the effect in his face was somehow warmer and less rakishly dangerous than it was in her husband.

Both men rose, Julian coming from behind his desk to usher her into the room. "Emily, come meet my brother—Robert, this is Emily, my wife."

"I believe you and I danced together once, long ago," the earl said, offering a perfectly correct bow over her hand before straightening to give her a once-over that instantly made his resemblance to his brother stronger. "It must have been your first or second Season, you might not recall."

"I must confess that I'm surprised you do, then," Emily said, laughing a bit as Julian nudged back a chair with his toe, and she proceeded to sit down. She always tried to seat herself as quickly as possible upon entering a room, knowing that the gentlemen present could not sit until she did and always anxious not to be a bother to anyone. "I would not think a gentleman would recall a dance with a blushing debutante, years later."

"Hard not to remember the most beautiful debutante of her year," the earl said, smiling at her as he resumed his seat next to her, and Emily smiled back at him.

"You're just as charming as your brother is, when he wants to be," she said, dimpling at him.

"And quite a bit less dramatic, too," he said with a grin. "Are you certain you don't wish to file for an annulment and run off with me instead?"

"I'm right here," Julian said mildly, taking a sip of brandy.

Emily frowned thoughtfully. "It's a tempting prospect," she began.

"Directly across the desk," Julian added. "Three feet away. With perfectly functioning ears."

"But I must confess, I've had enough of carriage travel of late, and I fear we'd have to flee town to avoid the scandal," she concluded.

"Fair enough," the earl said, nodding solemnly. "We'll simply have to content ourselves with the knowledge of the happiness that could have been ours."

"You're even drinking my brandy," Julian put in. "I wouldn't have broken out the good stuff if I'd known you'd attempt to steal my wife out from under my nose the moment you arrived."

"In the interest of strict honesty, I believe it was technically the moment *I* arrived," Emily said primly, and the earl laughed out loud at that. "What is the reason for your visit today, my lord?"

"None of that," he said, waving a hand. "You must call me Robert, if you are to be my sister now."

"And I have already met your true sister. It's delightful to see you—I wasn't aware—" she added, but broke off hastily.

Robert, however, seemed to guess what she'd been about to say.

"You weren't aware that I saw very much of my brother?" he asked, quirking an eyebrow in another gesture eerily reminiscent of his younger brother.

"I was under the impression that Julian was somewhat distanced from his family," she said carefully. Frannie aside, of course.

Robert snorted. "It's our parents, specifically," he said, tossing a glance at Julian that Emily couldn't quite read, but which Julian could apparently decipher with little difficulty, since he offered an eloquent eye roll in return. "And when word started spreading that Julian had taken it into his head to marry, I had to come see it for myself."

"Word started spreading," Julian repeated, his eyes narrowing. "Word from whom? You were at Everly Priory, were you not?"

"I may have been," Robert said, would-be casual, rotating the cut-glass tumbler in his hand. "You know how gossip spreads."

"Gossip," Julian repeated.

"Gossip . . . or letters, perhaps," Robert said, which was apparently all the confirmation Julian needed.

"Frannie," he pronounced darkly.

"Come off it, Julian," Robert protested. "You didn't possibly think she would keep it from us."

"I suppose not," Julian muttered, taking a large sip of brandy before setting his glass down. "Did she even bother to wait until we'd left, or was she scribbling away whilst we were innocently enjoying an afternoon walk one day?"

"I believe she sent the letter the morning you left to return to town," Robert said, then added, "Don't be angry with her, she's done nothing wrong." There was a slight protective note in his voice when he spoke of his sister, whom Emily realized must be more than a decade his junior, and she liked him all the better for it.

"I'm not angry with her," Julian clarified. "More with myself, for not delivering the news myself. Is Mother in a tizzy? Did Father storm and rage?"

"No, and no," Robert said smugly, clearly delighted to be able to disabuse his younger brother of any preconceived notions he might have. "They actually seemed quite pleased."

"Oh," Julian said, deflating somewhat; Emily suppressed a wild desire to laugh. He looked like nothing so much as a boy who had been promised a treat and had found himself denied it.

"Did you *want* them to be upset?" Robert asked, giving voice to Emily's own question.

"No," Julian said. "Of course not."

"Ah," Robert said as if this explained quite a bit; seeing the inquisitive look Emily shot him, he added, "He wanted our father to be upset."

"Robert, for God's sake," Julian said, and Robert cracked a grin.

"Am I wrong?" he asked.

"Yes," Julian said shortly. "If I wanted to upset him, I'd hardly be—" He broke off abruptly, and Emily wished quite desperately that he'd finished that sentence. Any hope she might have had of provoking him to further speech on this topic, however, was forestalled by the sudden motion of Robert straightening in his seat.

"What the devil?" he yelped.

Startled, Emily turned to him; for a moment, she thought he might be having some sort of fit, and wondered if she should ring for help, but she soon realized the source of his distress: Cecil was dangling from Robert's shoulder, his claws dug deep into his jacket.

"Cecil, no!" Emily cried, rising at once and reaching forward to carefully extract the kitten from the earl's person. A fair amount of tugging was involved—Cecil seemed disinclined to let go of the secure grip he'd managed—but at last she had the disgruntled kitten in her hands, settled in her lap.

"I see you've met our new addition to the family," Julian said to Robert, sounding cheerful at the sight of someone else as the victim of Cecil's sharp claws. "If it were up to me, he'd be fending for himself on the streets right now, but Emily is tender-headed where he's concerned, so I'm afraid we're stuck with him."

"Er," Robert said, reaching up to rub at the shoulder that was so recently liberated from Cecil's clutches. "You mean tenderhearted, I expect?"

"That too," Julian said, unrepentant. Emily narrowed her eyes at him for a moment before returning her attentions to Cecil, who— apparently exhausted by all the excitement—had promptly turned two and a half circles in her lap before falling into a deep slumber. It gave her a curious warm feeling in her chest when he slept on her lap—she liked having someone to care for, she realized. Particularly in this house, where she spent so much of her time alone, Cecil had become more of a comfort to her than a two-pound ball of fluff fond of terrorizing her at midnight had any right to be.

"Is your shoulder all right?" she asked Robert, belatedly realizing she should perhaps show a modicum of concern when Cecil took to mauling people.

"It's fine," Robert assured her.

"If he was bleeding to death," Julian pronounced in ominous tones, "he wouldn't tell you. He's far too polite."

Robert raised an eyebrow. "I hardly think I'm likely to bleed to death from a cat scratch, Julian."

"You do not know that cat," Julian replied darkly.

"He's taken an irrational dislike to Cecil," Emily informed Robert, rubbing Cecil behind the ears with a finger and finding herself rewarded a moment later with the sound of a faint purr.

"He does tend to get a bit stubborn about things," Robert said to Emily in conspiratorial tones. "Consider the fact that he can't admit he regrets burning a bridge with our father, for example."

"Did you have any other reason for coming here today?" Julian asked his brother, irritation evident in his voice. "Now that you've ascertained for yourself that I am indeed wed, perhaps you might see yourself out?"

"Is he normally this grumpy these days?" Robert asked Emily in a stage whisper.

"Only when in the company of his siblings, from what I've observed," Emily said quite honestly.

"I can't imagine why they should provoke such a reaction," Julian said dryly.

"In any case," Robert said, rising to his feet, "I'll leave you now—I only came by to see proof with my own eyes of the marriage, and I have indeed seen it." He bowed gallantly to Emily, who smiled at him; Julian scowled. Robert hesitated, then added, "I believe Mother might force Father to return to town, now that you've married, and she'll no doubt wish to call."

"Of course," Julian said at once.

"Or," Robert said, his tone growing a trifle more uncertain, "she might wish you to come to dinner at the house."

There was a long moment of silence. "Unless Mother is planning to come to London without an escort, I don't see how that is likely to come about." Julian's voice was firm, unwavering.

Robert sighed, running a hand through his hair in a gesture that reminded Emily strongly of his brother. "Julian—"

"He made perfectly clear—on more than one occasion, might I add—that I was not welcome under his roof so long as I continued to operate the theater," Julian said quietly, in that moment not at all resembling the man Emily had thought she'd married. She was used to a slightly laughing note to his voice, some amused cadence lurking at the edge of whatever he said—but there was no hint of laughter in his tone now.

"He said that years ago," Robert said, clearly frustrated. He sounded, in fact, remarkably like Frances had when she had attempted to speak to her brother of their parents—specifically of their father. "Does it never occur to you that people are capable of changing their minds?"

"He's never said a word to me that would indicate that he's done so," Julian said stubbornly.

"Of course he hasn't," Robert said, obviously growing more exasperated by the moment. "Have you met the man? He wouldn't know how to admit he's made a mistake if his life depended on it—really, it's a miracle he and Mother remain so happy together, all things considered. But I thought that you—being, you understand, an adult yourself now—could perhaps see your way to making the first overture."

"I think not," Julian said, his tone leaving no room for disagreement. Robert clearly recognized this, because he merely sighed again before departing, at least managing to spare a last smile and bow for Emily.

Emily, who was now left alone in the room with a distinctly ruffled husband, and no clear idea of how to smooth his feathers.

The aforementioned husband, for his part, did not seem to expect anything of the sort from her, instead devoting a considerable amount of time to staring moodily into the amber liquid that remained in the glass before him. Emily had seen this look on a man before, and knew from careful observation that no good could come of interrupting Julian when he seemed hell-bent on working himself into a proper brooding sulk, but she did, as it happened, have practical matters to discuss with him—matters that, given the conversation she had just witnessed, could be viewed as extremely fortunately *or* extremely unfortunately timed. She just wasn't sure which yet.

"Er," she said, and he looked up, the lines of his face softening a bit as he focused on her. "I'll just be going to check with Mrs. Larkspur that everything is ready for this evening, then." The blank look he gave her confirmed what she suspected—that he had no memory whatsoever of the event that was shortly to occur. "When my parents come to dine?"

Julian muttered a rather foul curse, which seemed to slip out before he quite realized what he was saying. "Christ," he added, pressing his fingertips to his temples. "I'm sorry. Still not used to having a wife I need to watch my language around at all times."

"You don't need to watch your language around me," Emily said, a bit hesitant. "I don't mind if you swear sometimes. My ears won't spontaneously combust at the sound."

"No, no, I'm supposed to be reforming myself," Julian said wearily. "It just requires a bit more concentration than I feel capable of mustering at the moment."

"But," Emily said, rising from her seat—Cecil gave an indignant *meow* as she dislodged him—and slowly making her way around the desk, "what if I don't want you reformed?"

Something in her tone must have caught his attention, because when he looked up at her then, a bit of the weariness had gone from his face, and there was a gleam of definite interest in his eye.

"I believe I can leave certain things unreformed, wife," he murmured, reaching out a hand to grasp her by the wrist and tug her closer to him. She felt heat settle low in her belly at the warm, silken note to his voice when he called her *wife*, and she took several steps closer to him, until she was near enough to loop an arm around his neck and sink down onto his lap.

"Can you?" she asked lightly, tilting her head slightly as she leaned forward to kiss him. She felt wildly, wickedly bold as she did so—even after a few weeks of marriage, she was still usually very much the recipient of Julian's attentions, he very much the instigator. She was undeniably a willing, enthusiastic participant, but it felt daring to kiss him, rather than waiting to be kissed. To press her mouth to the bare skin of his throat, reveling in the slight hitch in his breathing. To gather her skirts in her hands and lift them, freeing her legs enough that she might turn herself on his lap, properly straddling him, pressing herself against where she could feel him beginning to respond.

"I—ah—" he said, his voice satisfyingly strangled, "don't wish to interrupt this interlude, but did you mention something about your parents?"

Emily sighed, pulling back from him slightly. "Oh. Right." Her hand was still pressed against his neck, underneath his collar, and she couldn't quite bring herself to remove it. "I believe I mentioned this last week, inviting them to dinner?" Julian looked at her blankly. "In the library, after dinner one evening?" Another blank look. "With the—er—brandy?"

At this, the blank look vanished, replaced by a wicked smile. It had been a rather memorable occasion the week before, when Julian had been so occupied in trying to pull Emily down onto his lap that he'd upended an entire glass of brandy onto his trousers.

Thus necessitating their immediate removal, of course.

So it was perhaps unsurprising that he didn't recall the conversation in question, given that it was undoubtedly not the most interesting part of the evening.

"I have fond memories of that night," Julian said, confirming her suspicions, "but I must confess I don't remember this particular portion of it."

"Well," Emily said, leaning back so she could look more directly into his eyes, "they're coming to dinner, tonight. Which means—"

"I'm not to go back to the Belfry to escape them," Julian said, his tone bored.

"Precisely," Emily said, then hesitated. She felt as though she were still feeling her way around this role of wife, unsure of when to press forward, when to relent. It was like wearing a new pair of shoes that she had yet to properly break in. "And . . . if you could be . . . nice?" she finished, wishing her voice sounded a bit more firm, a bit less hesitant, less questioning.

"I'm always nice," he said, that familiar gleam back in his eye as he slid the hand that was resting at her waist slowly up her torso. She swatted him away, sliding off his lap before she could become further distracted by creeping hands.

"Not *that* kind of nice," she said. "Just . . . make them like you. You're perfectly capable of doing that, when you wish to."

Julian watched her carefully as she spoke, in that unsettlingly focused way he had sometimes. It was always a bit disconcerting, to realize that this man who gave the impression, half the time, of not attending to much of anything that was being said, was in fact capable of watching her like a hawk.

"Why does it matter so much to you whether they like me?" he asked.

"I—what?" she asked, caught off guard by the question.

"Why," he repeated, coming to his feet, "does it matter? You knew when you married me that they were never going to be thrilled that you'd gone behind their backs to do so. Why are you trying to make amends now?"

"Because they're my parents," she said, feeling like a bit of an idiot, but unsure of any other way to explain it. "And I'm their only living child. It would be nice if we could all get along."

"You all 'got along' until quite recently," he said, crossing his arms over his chest. "It involved you doing whatever it was that they asked of you, regardless of the effect it had on you and your life. If that's their idea of getting along, then I would think you might be perfectly glad to be a bit less cozy with them."

"Julian," Emily said, trying not to inject a note of pleading into her voice. "Please."

He sighed. "I'll be nice," he said shortly, "so long as *they* are nice to you."

"Thank you," Emily said simply, and turned to leave the room, reflecting as she went that that promise was not, perhaps, as reassuring as she might have wished.

It was, Julian thought, something of a miracle that they made it all the way to dessert before things went to hell.

Of course, it hadn't precisely been an enjoyable evening up to that point—it was impossible to properly enjoy oneself in the company of a man whose sense of humor seemed to be almost entirely nonexistent, and a lady who looked as though she were at risk of bursting into tears at any moment—but Emily, bless her, had put all those years she'd spent on the marriage mart to good use, keeping up a steady stream of conversation that, under different circumstances, Julian would have been inclined to admire. And so they'd rubbed along well enough, with Emily doing much of the heavy lifting, until dessert.

"This has been a very nice dinner, Lord Julian," the marchioness said a bit stiffly. She'd never been precisely warm toward him, but he really thought it a bit unfair that she'd been more friendly when she'd thought he was a disreputable scoundrel sniffing around her unmarried daughter's skirts than now, when he had actually married said daughter—and rescued her family from dire financial straits, too. "You must give my compliments to your cook."

"I will," Julian said, nodding, running a finger around the rim of his wineglass, which was still half-full. "I think she's been pleased to have an excuse to cook proper meals at last, now that I'm wed. I was in the habit of eating many of my meals out, in my bachelor days."

"I hope Emily has been taking a firm hand, then," the marchioness said, looking at her daughter, who at the moment was still absorbed in eating her pear tart. Julian enjoyed watching Emily eat, since sometimes, if she didn't realize he was watching, she would forget herself and consume with such clear joy that it was almost transfixing. He had begun watching her more carefully in general, he realized, in search of these moments. She had been so long in the habit of monitoring her speech, her demeanor, everything about her that was visible to the eye, that it was eminently satisfying to catch a moment when she let down her guard and reacted with unfeigned, undiluted glee to something.

Too late, however, Julian realized that Lady Rowanbridge was watching Emily, too—and she did not appear to appreciate what she saw.

"Emily," she said, keeping a rather terrifying smile fixed upon her face, "you will not wish to eat so much dessert that you cannot contribute to the conversation. You are the hostess this evening, after all—you must know all that that entails."

Julian took a breath, trying to keep his annoyance at bay.

"Emily," he said definitively, "has been keeping our conversation afloat for the whole evening. I think you might allow her a few moments to enjoy the food that she agonized over, the menu that she perfected with the cook."

Lady Rowanbridge looked at him then.

"You will not understand, Lord Julian, not knowing Emily so well as I do, that occasionally, if one is not watching her carefully, her behavior . . . well, it slips a bit."

Julian let out an incredulous laugh that he didn't even attempt to suppress.

"Emily is the most well-mannered lady I've ever met—in fact, I believe she is well-known among the *ton* for her proper behavior. It was, after all, your salvation for many years." He uttered these last words quietly, but they landed with weight in the silence of the room. "I do not think, therefore, that she is in need of any instruction from *you* on how to behave—particularly when it is no longer your place to offer it."

Across the table, Emily set down her fork, her shoulders slumping slightly, and Julian felt a brief pang of guilt, which was washed away as soon as Emily's father opened his mouth.

"Now, Belfry, there's no cause to speak to my wife like that," Rowanbridge said, barely sparing a glance for the wife in question.

"You are sitting at my table," Julian said calmly, "eating my food and drinking my wine, and you can afford to go home and do more of the same in your own house thanks to my generosity. I do not, therefore, think it too much to ask that you treat your daughter with at least a modicum of respect whilst you are under my roof."

"Julian," Emily said, her tone sharper than he'd ever heard from her. "That's enough." She turned a placating gaze upon her parents, looking at each of them in turn. "Papa, Mama, let's not spoil the evening. Mama, I've the sherry you like so much waiting in the drawing room, if you'd like to—"

"That will not be necessary, Emily," the marchioness said, rising. "I believe I feel a headache coming on, and it is best that we return home. Thank you for your . . . hospitality," she added, pausing for just long enough before the final word to make it clear that she didn't really mean it.

Emily was rising as well, words of protest forming on her lips, but the marquess and marchioness were already making their way toward the double doors at the end of the dining room, calling for their coats. By the time they were gone—with handshakes and hand kisses and all the other niceties that polite society required, regardless of how impolite an occasion might have been—Julian was beginning to feel rather cheerful at having been rid of undesired guests a couple of hours earlier than expected.

All of his cheer evaporated, however, when Bramble had bowed the Rowanbridges out and a footman had closed the front door and Julian turned back to face his wife, who looked stricken.

"I believe I'll go to bed" was all she said, however, and she proceeded to turn and make her way up the stairs.

"Emily," Julian called after her, exasperated, but she did not turn, merely continuing her steady progress up, skirts clutched in one hand. Muttering a curse, Julian took off after her, his long legs—unencumbered by layers of petticoats and skirts—eating up the distance between them, and he passed her before she reached the landing. "Listen," he began, but Emily brushed past him and set off down the hall, Julian close on her heels.

This was new territory for him, he reflected as he said her name once again, still eliciting no response. He and Emily hadn't had a proper argument yet—in truth, though he was now embarrassed to admit it, he didn't think he'd really thought her capable of this. The loud silence. The rigid line of her back. The quick, purposeful footsteps.

She drew to a halt at her bedroom door and Julian darted forward to open it for her; for a moment, he thought she was going to refuse to pass through while he was holding the door, but she seemed to realize how absurd (and self-defeating) that would be, so she entered the room, coming to a halt before the fireplace and whirling around to face him, crossing her arms over her chest.

For his part, Julian closed the door behind him and approached her carefully, as one might approach an unfamiliar dog.

"Emily," he said yet again, still not quite certain what the next words out of his mouth were going to be, but as it happened, it didn't matter, because she seemed to have found her voice.

"Why couldn't you have just let it go?" she asked quietly.

Julian drew to a halt beside a high-backed armchair and reached out to rest his forearm upon it, allowing the chair to bear a bit of his weight.

"Is that how you expect to spend every family dinner for the rest of your life, then? Ignoring your mother's attempts to put you down, to make you small?"

"She wasn't trying to make me small," Emily burst out, her voice faltering a bit on the last word. "That's just how she is sometimes—you know our marriage is still very new, and it must be quite an adjustment for her, not having me at home anymore."

"Home to order about," Julian said flatly. "Home to use as she saw fit. Like a beautiful vase she wanted to display just so."

"She is my *mother*," Emily said, real heat in her voice now. "It might be easy for you to turn your back on your family—a family that, from what I've seen so far, I'd have given anything to be a part of as a girl— but for some of us, it's a bit more difficult."

"Easy," Julian repeated. "You think I find it easy, having to see my brother in secret, when my father's not in town?" He pushed himself upright and took a slow step toward her, then another. "Do you think I found it easy, sitting in the very back of the church at Frannie's wedding, then skipping the wedding breakfast altogether so I wouldn't cause a scene?"

"And yet your brother was here today, all but telling you that your father has had a change of heart, but you refused to listen! To even consider seeing him!"

"My relationship with my father is my own concern, not yours," Julian said, each word coming out as chipped and cold as ice. "It's nothing you need worry about."

Her face went pale at that, and Julian instantly wished—what? Did he wish the words unsaid? It was more that he wished the entire evening undone; nothing had gone right today, from the moment Robert showed up on his doorstep, demanding to know what this talk was of a wife.

"Of course," Emily said calmly, her face resuming a bit of color. "I'm sorry—I don't know what I was thinking. This marriage is based on an arrangement between us that, I believe, we both understood perfectly well, and I seem to have forgotten myself."

Julian gazed at her a long moment, wishing to tell her that she was wrong, that she hadn't forgotten herself at all, that he felt it too, this uncomfortable desire to be more to each other than they had agreed to be—but something at the back of his mind, some voice that lurked there, warned him to be cautious. Take the escape she was offering.

"It's nothing to apologize for," he said, his voice sounding stiffer to his own ears than it had ever done in his life. "I—I became too emotional. I should have left you to deal with your parents as you see fit. It's none of my concern, after all."

"Right," she said faintly. "None of your concern." She shook her head a bit, as if to clear it, and then said, "Goodness, it must be getting late," despite the fact that it was barely past nine. She gave a large, patently false yawn. "I'm afraid I'm quite tired tonight—perhaps I'll just go to bed."

Alone, was the unvoiced but clearly understood addendum to that sentence.

"Of course," Julian said politely, inclining his head, and then—for lack of anything else to do—turned and left the room, angry with himself for the small pang caused by the realization that he'd have to sleep by himself. Theirs was not a love match, after all—why on earth had she been sleeping in his bed to begin with? She had apologized for forgetting herself, but clearly he had done so, too, if he was now sulking at the prospect of sleeping alone, as any man of his class might reasonably expect to do.

However, as he walked into his own bedchamber, preparing to spend the night alone for the first time since he'd been married, he couldn't help but think: For a marriage of convenience, this—their fight, the emotions that had been stirred up, everything about the entire bloody evening—wasn't feeling terribly convenient at all.

Sixteen

Emily didn't like to think herself a coward, but the undeniable fact was that it was proving to take a bit of time to work herself up to these afternoon calls. It wasn't that they had gone terribly, precisely—she, like any sensible person, had started with the ones that she had known would be well received, which had really just given her an excuse to pay calls on all of her friends. Violet and Diana had both been the recipients of her visits, of course, as had Sophie, who had seemed terribly glad of the company. Sophie had been widowed a few years earlier, and though her husband (and the remnants of her sizable dowry) had left her well-provided for, she did seem a bit lonely at times, tucked away in her large house near Hyde Park.

From there, Emily had moved down the list of ladies she had befriended during her various Seasons, most of them married now and therefore not subject to the whims of easily scandalized mamas. These had, for the most part, been fairly enjoyable, too—none of them would outright snub her, no matter how scandalous her marriage.

From that point, however, things had gotten a bit trickier. There were a fair number of ladies whom Emily was not at all certain would be receptive to a call from a lady who had impulsively married a man who dabbled in the *theater*, of all things—particularly one with a reputation like the Belfry's—but she was obligated to try.

And so she did.

And this was how she found herself smiling over too-hard lemon biscuits in the drawing room of Baroness Northbridge, trying very hard to rid herself of the impression that she was not at all welcome there. The baroness was a thin woman in her late thirties, Emily guessed, with dark hair and eyes and an angular face that would have been lovely under ordinary circumstances, though at the moment it was slightly marred by the hard, scrutinizing look in her eyes.

"Tell me, Lady Emily," Lady Northbridge said, then quickly corrected herself. "I mean, Lady Julian. I apologize."

"Not at all," Emily said, smiling sweetly, though she thought that it was nearly impossible to believe that such a slip was accidental after the third time it happened in as many minutes.

"It's just so difficult to adjust to your change of circumstances," Lady Northbridge said in confidential tones, as if Emily herself had not even noticed that she had gotten married and moved into a new home, with a new name. "It all seems rather . . . sudden."

This raised a warning flag in Emily's mind, carrying as it did its delicate implication of scandal. She would have to proceed carefully.

"It wasn't terribly sudden, actually," she said, setting down her biscuit with some relief. "Lord Julian and I became acquainted during this year's Season, you see, and met at a number of events, before we were able to spend more time together at Lord Willingham's house party."

"Which *part* of the Season?" Lady Northbridge asked like a dog with a scent.

"The . . . latter part," Emily hedged.

"Around which month?"

"One of the summer months," Emily said vaguely, which was not untrue, since she had, in fact, first visited the Belfry in July. She did not care to give Lady Northbridge any precise details.

"And how convenient it was that you and Lord Julian both attended the same house party," Lady Northbridge continued, her tone implying that the likelihood of this being a coincidence ranked similarly to the likelihood of the Duke of Wellington and Napoleon enjoying a cozy meal together. "And without your dear mama to chaperone!"

"I was chaperoned by the Dowager Marchioness of Willingham," Emily said serenely, glad to at least have this card to play. "I'm certain you don't wish to imply that her ladyship is anything less than suitable as a protector of a young woman's virtue?"

"No, of course not," Lady Northbridge said hastily, paling at the very notion of ending up on the dowager marchioness's bad side. "I merely meant that you and Lord Julian must have had the opportunity for many . . . walks."

This, Emily thought with some exasperation, was why the *ton* was so maddening. Walks! The way Lady Northbridge said the word, it sounded like a visit to a brothel.

"We enjoyed the opportunity to become better acquainted," she said carefully, "in the company of our friends—who were, of course, the ones to first introduce us."

"How delightful," Lady Northbridge said, her gaze on Emily still as sharp as a razor. "I'm sure you did."

Emily could feel herself growing more irritated by the moment, but did as she always did: took a deep breath, and smiled. It was a habit she had honed from years of practice. Then, as she was searching her mind for something—anything—to possibly change the subject to, her gaze landed on the clock. And, miracle of miracles, fifteen minutes had elapsed. She'd always thought the rule that calls should only last a quarter of an hour was ridiculous—and she, Violet, and Diana had, of course, completely ignored it among themselves, visiting one another for far longer than society deemed polite—but, in this moment, Emily thought it must be the best rule the *ton* had ever come up with.

"Well, Lady Northbridge," she said, working her face into an expression of mournful regret, "I'm afraid I must be going. I was having such a lovely time that I quite lost track of the hour."

"Of course," Lady Northbridge agreed, rising with Emily. A slightly crafty expression crossed her face. "You will be certain to give the marquess my best, will you not?"

"The marquess," Emily repeated.

"The Marquess of Eastvale? Your husband's father?" Lady Northbridge gave a trill of laughter that was one of the more horrifying sounds Emily had ever heard. "You do know which family you married into, do you not, Lady Em—Lady Julian?"

"Naturally," Emily said, smiling as though this were indeed a hilarious joke. "However, I do not believe my husband and his father have spoken recently, given the marquess's absence from town."

"Of course," Lady Northbridge said. "But I know they must be close—closer than appearances would make it seem, at least. Given all the efforts the marquess has taken over the years, of course. On Lord Julian's behalf?"

"I beg your pardon?" Emily asked, frowning.

"My dear!" Lady Northbridge said, tittering. "You must know how well the marquess speaks of his son to various society hostesses."

"Oh," Emily said, thinking quickly. "Yes, of course."

"Why, I doubt Lord Julian would still be invited anywhere at all if it were not for his father," Lady Northbridge continued, seeming not to notice Emily's confusion. Emily wasn't certain whether that was because she'd hidden it well, or because Lady Northbridge so enjoyed the sound of her own voice that Emily could have clutched her chest in shock and collapsed upon the drawing room floor without the baroness paying the slightest bit of attention. "The marquess has made it perfectly clear, of course, that anyone who snubs Lord Julian will regret it most heartily—and no one wants to offend a man as well-connected as Lord Eastvale, of course."

This last bit was pronounced with just enough resentment to inform Emily that this was why her visit had been accepted today, despite Lady Northbridge's clear disapproval of her marriage. It was fear of offending Lord Eastvale that kept the doors of society open to her—and to Julian. Emily was surprised she had never heard whispers of this before, but in truth she hadn't known very much about Julian before she'd met him. She knew the name, of course, knew vaguely of the story of his theater, had heard rumors that he'd been disinherited by his father, but not much beyond that.

And yet, if Lady Northbridge was to be believed, it was because of his father that Julian had not been completely ostracized by polite society.

Her mind was racing, her thoughts tangled into a knot, but to Lady Northbridge she merely said, "The marquess is very protective of his family, I believe."

Which was, apparently, nothing more than the truth.

The real question was: how was she going to tell Julian?

In the short term, as it turned out, she didn't have to tell him at all. Julian had planned an evening out with Penvale that night—knowing

Penvale as she did, Emily was quite certain that there would be a high-stakes card game on the agenda, and idly hoped that Julian would manage to escape without losing the deed to the house. But this meant that Emily was in bed asleep by the time Julian returned home that night. This was, in and of itself, not necessarily a bad thing—things between them had been slightly strained after their argument of the night before, and Emily was perfectly content to have an excuse to avoid any further dispute with her husband.

The next morning, Julian was abed late, and Emily departed for an appointment at the modiste before he made his way downstairs; by the time she returned home, he was gone—off to the Belfry, Bramble informed her.

Emily, however, decided that she was not going to let a bit of lingering awkwardness from their argument put her off from her desire to spend more time at the theater, so a couple of hours later she ordered the carriage brought round, and set off for the Belfry with one stop along the way.

"This is all rather thrilling," Sophie said, peering out the carriage window half an hour later as they drew to a halt. "I must confess, nothing half so interesting ever used to happen to me before I met you and Violet and Diana."

"Violet and Diana do have a way of making interesting things happen," Emily agreed, reaching up to adjust her bonnet. She was wearing a new gown of white satin, with a new blue spencer to match the embroidered blue vines on the gown's skirts, and as she prepared to alight from the carriage at the theater her dashing husband owned, she was feeling very far removed from the prim and virginal Emily Turner who had begun the Season last spring in her usual gowns of pale pink and a polite smile fixed upon her face.

"It's not just Violet and Diana," Sophie said as the door opened and she prepared to step out. "Last I checked, you've made the most interesting match of the year, done so without even asking your parents' permission, and are currently on your way to visit an establishment where no proper lady should dare tread. You're perfectly interesting in your own right, Emily Belfry."

She then took the proffered hand of the footman and stepped down from the carriage, leaving a slightly flabbergasted Emily in her wake.

It wasn't that Emily thought herself dull—it was simply that she had always considered Diana and Violet to be more interesting than her. They were louder, more outspoken, less concerned about always saying and doing the right thing. And yet, Sophie's words rang in her head.

She was interesting.

"Are you sure you're not concerned about being seen in such a place?" Emily asked as she alighted from the carriage, repeating the query she'd asked upon collecting Sophie at her home. It had been something of an impulsive decision to stop and invite Sophie on the way to the Belfry, but Emily knew that Violet had already—very reluctantly—agreed to have tea with her mother that afternoon, and Diana and Lord Willingham were meeting with the rector at St. George's to discuss their impending nuptials. Sophie, however, had been at home when Emily stopped by, and had professed herself delighted to accompany her.

"I know you're widowed," Emily added, "but if you don't wish to risk your reputation—"

"As a matter of fact, I'm feeling perilously unconcerned with my reputation of late," Sophie said lightly, twining her arm through Emily's as they made their way up the steps past the graceful columns at the building's entrance. Unlike on her previous visits with Julian, Emily had chosen to enter through the front doors instead of the stage door; she was curious to see the entrance hall of the theater in the light of day, without a crowd of dissolute gentlemen obscuring her view.

"I rather hope," Sophie continued, "that if I'm just a little bit *more* unconcerned, a certain insufferable gentleman will grow irritated enough to do something about it."

Emily frowned, Sophie's words drawing her back from her contemplation of her surroundings. "Are you talking about West?"

"I can neither confirm nor deny that supposition," Sophie said airily as they walked through the doors, which was really all the answer Emily needed. She knew that Sophie and Lord James's brother had something of a history—they had been courting years earlier, before West had been involved in the curricle race that had killed Lord Willingham's brother, and grievously injured himself in the process. Emily did not know what had happened thereafter, only that Sophie had somehow ended up married—in rather hurried fashion—to Lord Fitzwilliam Bridewell, an old friend of West's who had himself been killed on the Continent a few years ago, leaving Sophie a very young widow. Just this past summer, Sophie had been involved in a brief affair with Lord Willingham, one that had ended with relative haste without any bad feeling on either side, a liaison that Emily had always found somewhat surprising, since they did not seem particularly well-suited. She could not help but wonder if there might have been motives that she was not privy to.

It was all very curious. And, while Emily might be polite enough not to press, she was not so unobservant as to have failed to note more than one lingering glance, on the part of both West *and* Sophie, when each thought the other wasn't watching.

There was no opportunity to continue this line of discussion, however, since Sophie had drawn them to an abrupt halt in the foyer of the theater. "It doesn't look very scandalous by the cold light of day, does it?" she asked, craning her head back to take in the chandelier suspended from the soaring ceiling above them, its candles extinguished.

Emily turned in a slow circle. The first time she had visited the Belfry with her friends, she had been surprised by how luxuriously appointed it was—she didn't know what, precisely, she had been expecting, but given the theater's reputation as something almost akin to a gentlemen's club—albeit one where they could bring their mistresses—she'd thought it would look a bit seedier. Instead, she'd been met with the sight of thick carpets and silk damask paper hangings on the walls, and now, knowing the money Julian had poured into renovations, she could see what care had gone into so many of the details. Something within her clenched as she took all of it in. She might find Julian's fixation on the status her connections and reputation could bring him a bit ridiculous, but he had poured years of his life—and, from the looks of it, a not-insignificant portion of his inheritance—into this place. She wanted him to achieve his goals.

"No," she said, in belated reply to Sophie's query. "I don't think I'd realized how . . . elegant it is, I suppose."

"It is, rather," Sophie agreed. "More elegant than you'd expect, given its reputation," she added, echoing Emily's own thoughts.

"That," said Emily firmly, linking her arm through Sophie's once again and preparing to plunge deeper into the theater, "is why we are here."

They found Julian not in his office, but in the wings of the stage, deep in conversation with a woman, paying no heed to the stagehands wheeling several pieces of completed scenery past or the sounds of the orchestra rehearsing in the pit. As they drew nearer, Emily registered the dark mane of curls and realized the woman in question was Miss Congreave, the understudy for Miss Simmons. And, judging by the way her arms were crossed over her chest, whatever she was discussing with Julian was not making her terribly happy.

"No," Julian said flatly, not having noticed Emily's approach. He was wearing a shirt and waistcoat, but his jacket was nowhere in sight, and his sleeves were rolled up to the elbow, leaving his forearms bare. Emily paused, her gaze snagging on that expanse of bare skin for a moment—who would have possibly thought forearms, of all things, could be seductive? She continued her perusal, noting with appreciation that his cravat was loosened enough to show a bit of his throat. By the time her gaze made it up to his eyes, she realized that Julian had noted her presence and was watching her with some amusement. She blushed, realizing that she had essentially been ogling him, and, glancing sideways, saw that Sophie was biting her lip, apparently to prevent laughter as well.

"Julian," she said, deciding that the best course of action—as it so often was—was to pretend that nothing out of the ordinary had happened at all. "There you are." She approached him a bit hesitantly, given their argument of two nights before, and saw a faint trace of her own wariness reflected in his gaze, which actually reassured her a bit.

"Emily," he said, reaching out for her hand to draw her closer. Glancing over her shoulder and registering Sophie's presence, he inclined his head. "Lady Fitzwilliam, welcome to the Belfry."

"It's much more impressive than I was expecting," Sophie said frankly, and Julian laughed.

"I don't know whether that was a compliment or an insult."

"A compliment," Sophie said, grinning at him. "Men are so quick to take offense, it would be such a nice change if you didn't."

"Very well," Julian agreed, and Emily had to press her lips together to prevent herself from smiling. Despite their quarrel, it was very difficult to not like him when he was determined to be charming.

"What brings you ladies here today?" he added, before seeming to belatedly recall that he wasn't alone. He turned back to Miss Congreave, who was watching this scene curiously, and offered her an apologetic smile. "I'm sorry—Miss Congreave, I believe you remember my wife, Lady Julian?"

"Of course," Miss Congreave said slowly, looking at Emily with no less interest than she had displayed on their first meeting. This look had grown familiar to Emily by virtue of the fact that everyone at the theater had greeted her with some version of it upon first making her acquaintance. She supposed they must all be intrigued to meet the lady who had convinced Julian Belfry, eternal bachelor, to hop to the altar, though she felt like publicly announcing that she, not he, had been the one to require a bit of convincing.

"This is my friend Lady Fitzwilliam Bridewell," Emily said, gesturing to Sophie, who smiled at Miss Congreave.

"Miss Congreave, you appeared at the Adelphi last year, did you not?" Sophie asked, and Miss Congreave nodded, smiling at the question.

"I did. Did you have the opportunity to attend one of my performances?"

Sophie shook her head. "I'm afraid not—I heard all about you from friends, though," she added. "I gather you were quite spectacular."

"She was," Julian confirmed. "Why do you think I poached her for the Belfry?"

"That is Lord Julian's habit these days," Miss Congreave said, rolling her eyes. "If he hears of any actor or actress having a modicum of success anywhere else, he is desperate to have them performing on his stage instead."

"Because we are going to have the finest theater in London," Julian said mildly, in the tones of a man who had explained this many times over. "We'll need the finest talent, if we're to do that."

"And yet you *do* have the finest talent, writing a play that I know would be a smash hit—"

"A smash hit that no gentleman will wish to watch," Julian interrupted, and Emily could tell by his tone that this was the subject about which they had been arguing when she arrived—and, furthermore, that it was not the first time they had had this argument.

"What is the play in question?" Emily asked, curious.

Miss Congreave turned to her at once, her face lighting up with enthusiasm. "It's a comedy, my lady—a burletta written by a young playwright who lacks experience, but who shows great promise. It would feature entirely women—"

"Which no gentleman is going to come to buy tickets for," Julian interrupted.

Sophie laughed incredulously. "I'm sorry, Belfry, but I was under the impression that there was nothing gentlemen liked more than watching a whole bevy of attractive women prance around the stage together."

Julian rolled his eyes. "It wouldn't be *that* sort of show. It's a comedy—a satire of aristocratic ladies."

"That sounds rather entertaining," Emily said, her interest piqued.

"I think it is, my lady," Miss Congreave assured her. "Lord Julian himself laughed out loud whilst reading the script."

"But it's not the sort of show gentlemen will want to see," Julian insisted, seeming to grow more frustrated by the moment. "I've been running this theater for nearly a decade. I've worked out which shows will drive a man to buy tickets, and which ones won't."

"But," Emily said slowly, an idea having suddenly taken hold in her mind at his words, "what if gentlemen weren't who you were trying to sell the tickets to?"

Three confused expressions met her eyes.

"What if," Emily continued, "instead of trying to attract gentlemen, you tried to lure their wives here instead?"

"That *is* what I'm trying to do," Julian said impatiently. "Have you not understood anything we've discussed? I want to make the Belfry a place gentlemen will feel comfortable bringing their wives, and to do that—"

"No, no, you misunderstand me," Emily interrupted. She *never* interrupted, but her mind was racing now, this thought that had suddenly taken hold seeming less and less insane by the moment. "I don't mean that you should attract wives who want to be escorted by their husbands—what if you made this show something aimed at ladies, and ladies alone?"

A slow smile began to creep across Sophie's face. "Take the traditional notion of the Belfry—a theater for gentlemen and their mistresses, but nowhere a real lady would dare set foot—and turn it on its head?"

"Precisely," said Emily. "If there was a show directed squarely at them—depicting *their* world—"

"But it is not a flattering portrait," Miss Congreave warned. "It's a satire of proper society ladies. They might take offense."

"Oh, I'm certain some of them would," Emily said, nodding. "But if we can get them talking about it—convince enough of them that they wish to see it, if only so they'll know what everyone else is discussing—well, gossip can really do all of our work for us."

"And then they'll be so offended that they'll never set foot in the Belfry ever again," Julian said flatly. "Which would serve my purposes . . . how, exactly?"

"But it would make you the talk of the town," Emily protested. "Don't you see—people would entirely change their opinion about what the Belfry is, and who it's for."

"Because they'd be convinced that it was nothing to be taken seriously," Julian continued, crossing his arms over his chest; Emily could see him digging his heels in, and she wanted to shriek with frustration.

But Emily Turner never shrieked. She never raised her voice.

Previously, she would have let the matter drop. But not this time—for she was not Emily Turner anymore. She was Emily Belfry. And this time, she would convince him—somehow. But just not yet.

So instead of protesting further, she merely smiled and said sweetly, "We'll see about that, husband."

Seventeen

*It was much later that evening that Emily finally had the opportu-*nity to raise the subject of Julian's father with him. She had thought to find a moment at the theater for a private word, but with Sophie nearby, and a constant litany of demands on Julian's time—from a disgruntled supporting actress to a pair of stagehands who nearly came to fisticuffs over some sort of accident involving sandbags—she had no opportunity to speak to him alone.

Then Laverre had invited them to dine with him at home that evening, and they had offered him a lift in their carriage. This, Emily had no complaint about—she had been curious to see where Laverre lived, which turned out to be a quiet street in Bloomsbury, just off of Russell Square. They were met at the door by Laverre's two sons, who promptly roped the gentlemen into admiring the card tower they'd spent the better part of the afternoon constructing, leaving Emily with Laverre's wife, Lucie, and her toddler daughter.

Emily liked Lucie, whom she'd had the opportunity to converse with at her dinner party. Lucie had led an interesting life, the daughter of a viscount who had granted freedom to her mother, born into slavery. Lucie herself had lived in Jamaica before traveling to England with her father upon her mother's death. Emily, who had never ventured even so far as Wales, could not imagine crossing an ocean.

"I assure you, it's not an experience I'm eager to repeat, either," Lucie had said, a smile crinkling the corners of her eyes. She was a beautiful woman, small and compact in build, with dark, thick curls, light brown skin, and rosy cheeks. "And I can't tell you how much I hated it here when I first arrived—it was so dark and gloomy, and all of my father's relatives didn't know what to do with me. But my father settled a large enough dowry upon me that the family got over their hesitation quickly enough." She rolled her eyes, her expression softening a bit when it landed on her husband, who was currently crouched on the floor on the opposite side of the drawing room, his younger son dangling halfway off his back, listening solemnly to something his elder son was saying.

"Did people . . ." Emily began, then trailed off, blushing, realizing her question was a bit forward. Lucie looked at her inquisitively.

"Did people—well, did they think Mr. Laverre was after your fortune, when you married?" Emily blushed at the impertinent nature of the question. "I only ask because, given the difference in your circumstances—"

"I'm sure some people whispered," Lucie said, "but I learned long ago not to worry overmuch about what people whispered about me— particularly not people who judged me for the color of my skin, who only considered me worth their time because of my fortune." She gave Emily a long look. "Is that something you find yourself struggling with, my lady—ignoring gossip?"

Emily sighed.

"*I* wouldn't be so bothered, but I know it upsets Julian." Her gaze landed on the man in question, who had flung himself down on the floor alongside Laverre without hesitation, seemingly engrossed in the conversation at hand.

Glancing at her companion, Emily saw that Lucie's gaze had followed her own, a faint frown playing at her lips.

"I've known Belfry for more than five years now," she said after a moment. "He's a decent man, for all he used to pretend otherwise. He . . . well, he loves his family. When his sister married that earl, he paid all the bills at the modiste." She glanced at Emily, then looked back toward the men before she spoke again. "He sends his mother flowers for her birthday. He's even brought his brother here to dine with us. And—" Here she broke off, looking at Emily once more, considering. Emily thought she might be taking her measure. "And he used to send an invitation to his father before the premiere of every single show, offering him a seat in his box on opening night."

Emily swallowed around a sudden lump in her throat, watching Julian nod solemnly at something one of the boys was telling him. "And the marquess never came."

"And the marquess never came," Lucie confirmed. "Eventually, I think Belfry stopped sending the invitations. But I can't help but wonder—" She broke off yet again, and Emily looked over at her, watched her lips press into a firm line.

"You can't help but wonder . . ." Emily prompted.

"I can't help but wonder," Lucie said after a moment, "if all of this—his marriage to you, this ridiculous-sounding new play, his entire fixation on respectability—is simply another way of extending that invitation."

And Emily, looking back at her husband, found herself wondering the same.

That conversation echoed through her mind now, hours later,

in the warm glow of her bedroom as she stood before the fireplace, wrapped in a dressing gown, staring at the flames. The evening had grown chilly and she was grateful for the sudden warmth at her back as Julian approached her; she'd been so lost in her thoughts that she hadn't even heard the connecting door open, but she could feel him behind her now, only inches away, and after a second the weight of his hand settled on her shoulder.

"Penny for your thoughts."

She turned, dislodging his hand from her shoulder in the process; he let it fall to his side. As she had done, he had changed clothes, and now wore just a pair of loose-fitting breeches and a banyan, his bare chest visible. This was a mildly distracting sight, as ever—Emily did not quite know how to grow used to the fact that she could be surprised at every turn by a half-naked man, particularly one who looked as good with his clothes off as Julian did. The desire she felt when she looked at him still felt almost wrong somehow, despite the fact that she knew how much he enjoyed it, that it stoked his own desire in turn.

"I had an interesting conversation with Lady Northbridge yesterday," she said, reflecting that this might well be a sentence no one had ever had cause to utter before. "Whilst paying an afternoon call."

Julian arched a brow, a similar thought writ plainly on his face. "Oh?"

Emily took a deep breath. "She mentioned something about your father."

The effect was instant: the raised brow lowered, the slight smile that played about his lips vanished, the lazy, seductive heat that had lingered in his eyes as he gazed at her cooled. Emily had not really expected any other sort of reaction, but she still didn't enjoy watching it happen.

"What about my father?" he asked calmly, crossing his arms over his chest. He was watching her very carefully now, as if she were a wild animal whose behavior he could not quite predict.

"Were you aware that he has been putting in a good word for you for years?" Emily asked bluntly. "Among polite society, I mean?"

Julian frowned. "No, he hasn't."

"He has," she insisted. "Lady Northbridge mentioned it today—all but implied that the marquess was the only reason you were still invited anywhere."

Julian's jaw tightened. "Well, Lady Northbridge must be mistaken. If my father can't bring himself to so much as walk down the same street as the Belfry, I don't think he's terribly likely to bestir himself on my behalf." Tension was evident in the lines of his body, practically radiating off of him, and Emily hated that she had been the cause. Carefully, she reached out a hand and placed it on his arm.

"Perhaps your father," she began, "does not know how to tell you in words that he still cares for you."

Julian shook his head. "Don't be absurd," he said shortly. "If this is true—which is a very big *if*, I would remind you—he's no doubt only done it to ensure that my mother and sister don't suffer snubs from these ladies. It's nothing to do with me."

Emily stiffened slightly at his dismissive words. "I apologize if I misread the situation, then," she said tersely, and Julian frowned.

"Emily," he said, frustration evident in his voice. "I don't wish to quarrel with you. Why do our parents keep working their way into our marriage?"

"Because," Emily said simply, "you don't simply marry a person. You marry their family, too, even if you'd rather have nothing to do with them," she added, thinking of her own parents. "I can't simply dismiss my parents, despite everything, for the same reason I can't simply ignore the possibility that your father wishes to reconcile with you." She could feel her heart pounding as she spoke, fearful that she had overstepped, spoken too boldly, gone too far. She was not accustomed to speaking her mind, to pressing someone on a matter they clearly didn't wish to debate any further.

Julian watched her for a long moment, then uncrossed his arms and reached out to loop his thumb and forefinger around one of her wrists, raising her hand between them.

A hand that, she belatedly realized, was trembling.

She hated this, hated the fact that her own body betrayed her discomfort, that she could do nothing to control it. She felt heat creeping up her neck—she was trying to be an adult, to have a proper conversation with her husband, and here she was, blushing and shaking like a schoolgirl.

"Are you frightened of me?" he asked her softly, allowing her hand to drop back to her side and making no further move to touch her.

She shook her head at once. "No," she said emphatically, and something in his expression eased slightly—her answer mattered to him, more than she had realized. "I—" She took a deep breath. "My parents never encouraged me to speak my mind. I still find it . . . difficult, I suppose, to do so."

He reached out a hand, then hesitated, uncertain, and she took a step toward him instead, reaching her own hand out to take his.

"You don't need to worry about that around me," he said, and she felt a slight surge of irritation.

"Except you dismiss me whenever I try to discuss your father," she said evenly. "So I believe I *do* need worry about that, if this is how you will reply every time I broach the subject."

He frowned, and she braced herself for a quarrel. She didn't think she had it in her to weather another argument, particularly so soon after their last one.

"You're right," he said, and her eyes shot to his in surprise; her feelings must have shown on her face, because a small smile curved at the corners of his mouth as he gazed at her. "It *is* possible for a husband to utter those words, you know."

A surprised laugh escaped her mouth, and his own smile widened a bit. He lifted her hand to his mouth and pressed a soft kiss there. "I apologize. My father is a . . . touchy subject, for me."

"You don't say," she said tartly, and it was his turn to laugh.

"Can I make it up to you?" he asked, his hand reaching out to fiddle with the ties of her dressing gown.

"I don't think we've finished our conversation," she said, even as she felt the garment loosen. He reached out to tug her closer to him.

"Must we finish it now?" he asked, sliding his hand into the heavy fall of her hair, pulling it back to expose her neck. "When there are so many other, more interesting things we could discuss?"

It was difficult for her to think when he was doing this—as he no doubt intended. This thought strengthened her resolve so that, even as he lowered his head to place a lingering kiss on her neck and she felt warmth coursing through her, she found the presence of mind to speak at least somewhat intelligently.

"So, that's it then?"

"Mmm?" he asked against her skin, and a shiver coursed through her. She could feel her resolve weakening by the moment. Her legs seemed to have a mind of their own and they took a step closer to him, close enough now that her breasts brushed his chest, only the fabric of her nightgown separating their skin. He took this opportunity to push her dressing gown off her shoulders entirely, and she felt it pool at her feet.

Realizing that the situation would shortly progress to a point at which she would no longer be capable of intelligent speech, Emily reached a hand up to his chest, causing him to pause.

"Something wrong?" he drawled slowly, lifting his head.

"I think we should send your father an invitation to the opening night of *Much Ado About Heaven*," she said, pleased that she'd gotten all the words out in the correct order.

"He won't come," he said shortly. "I've—I know he won't come."

"Just because he didn't come once—"

"It wasn't once," he said, straightening, the lazily seductive expression vanishing from his face. His hand was still at her waist, the fabric of her nightgown bunched in his fist. "I invited him to the Belfry at least a dozen times. I'm not such a fool that I'm going to continue sending an invitation to a man who doesn't wish for one."

"But," she said slowly, "isn't the whole point of this show that it will change how people see the theater? Wouldn't this be a perfect time to try again?"

Julian sighed, raking one hand through his hair. "Some people, yes. But not him."

"What's the point of even doing the show, then, if you're not willing to invite your father?" She frowned, feeling her frustration growing. "If you're so certain he won't even enjoy it, then why not simply do as you please? Stage one of your bawdy musicals. Or," she added, a thought occurring to her, "why not stage the comedy Miss Congreave mentioned? The one about society ladies? It sounded most entertaining, to hear her describe it."

"It would," he said dryly, with a slight twist to his mouth that Emily didn't understand. "The fact that Miss Congreave neglected to mention to you is that she wrote it."

Emily's jaw dropped.

"Miss Congreave is a playwright?"

"She seems to have ambitions, yes," Julian said in exasperation. "Which would be all well and good, if they didn't interfere with the job I actually hired her to do, which is to *be an actress*."

"But Julian!" Emily exclaimed, stepping out of his grasp. She began to pace, her mind racing, all thoughts of any amorous activities instantly having vanished. Julian sighed, then flung himself into one of the armchairs before the fire, reclining lazily with one leg draped over an arm of the chair.

"This is perfect," she said, turning to face him. "Don't you see? The fact that it's a play about women, *for* women, *written* by a woman—it practically sells itself."

"To *whom?*" Julian asked incredulously. "Not to any gentlemen I know."

"But you already have quite enough of those, don't you see?" Emily asked eagerly. She didn't understand why he couldn't see the brilliance of this plan—he made so many of his decisions at the Belfry with such clear-eyed intelligence, and yet he seemed to have lost that ability of late. First, *Much Ado About Heaven*—about which Emily privately continued to have doubts—and now this.

Perhaps, she thought suddenly, it was time to turn to more underhanded means.

"I don't want every drawing room in London to be full of ladies discussing how appalled and insulted they are—" Julian was saying, but Emily stopped listening. She reached out her foot to kick at his leg dangling over one arm of the chair, bringing it back down before him, his foot landing on the floor with a thud.

Julian broke off mid-sentence. "What—" He cleared his throat as he gazed up at her, and Emily realized that, lit as she was by the firelight behind her, her nightgown must be somewhat sheer at the moment. "What are you doing?"

"I am employing my feminine wiles," she said—a bit primly, it was true, but she negated this by sliding down onto his lap and straddling him without further hesitation. "Is it working?" she asked, gazing down at him; she liked this angle, raised up slightly on her knees, as she'd never before had the advantage of height over him.

"See for yourself," he murmured, reaching out both hands to seize her firmly by the waist and pull her down on top of him; she wiggled slightly, and he groaned.

"So," she said, her breath coming a little more quickly as his hands began a path up her torso, "as you can see, ladies, in fact, *do* have ways of exerting power over their husbands—"

"Mmm," he murmured, one hand at her breast, leaning forward to place a kiss to her jawline. His other hand busied itself with the hem of her nightgown, tugging it upward.

"—so really, all you need to do is appeal to the ladies and they shall quickly take—" She broke off as he pulled her nightgown over her head, something within her going molten at the look in his eyes as he gazed at her, at the bare skin on display. His hand curved back around her waist, pulling her down for a long, heated kiss.

"You were saying?" he murmured against her mouth when they broke apart for air at last.

Emily inhaled deeply, her heart pounding in her chest, all of the sensation in her body seeming to have fled south and taken up residence in one particular spot between her legs.

"I—I don't recall," she said breathlessly.

"Excellent," he said, lowering his head to her breast.

"But I will!" she said as firmly as she could manage, and could not help but experience a moment's satisfaction when he let out a resigned sigh. This conversation was one she was determined to continue, even if she had become sidetracked for the moment.

But really, she thought, as his mouth touched her skin and one of his hands began a slow, deliberate path down her body, under the circumstances, who could blame her?

Eighteen

The next afternoon, instead of heading to the theater, Julian took himself to his club.

It was not, in the past, an establishment he had frequented. He had never been ostracized, exactly—indeed, in something of a miracle, his membership had never been revoked—but he generally didn't like to risk running into his father.

It was undeniably a good place to go if one wanted to run into acquaintances by happenstance, and so over the course of this year's Season, he'd taken pains to visit more often, as he slowly tried to work his way back into this world. It was here, in fact, that he had happened to share a drink with Penvale one evening, which had led to his invitation to dinner at Penvale's sister's house, his entire involvement in the Audleys' marital woes, and—ultimately—that fateful meeting with Emily.

Emily, who, at the moment, was occupying many of his thoughts.

Too many.

"Women," he muttered aloud, only belatedly remembering that he wasn't alone. He was slumped in a chair in the morning room at White's, a glass of brandy in hand, Bridgeworth sitting in the chair opposite, looking annoyingly composed as he sipped his own drink. He'd been here when Julian arrived and hailed him, and they'd made friendly enough conversation for a quarter hour before Julian lapsed into a moody silence.

"Ah," said Bridgeworth, setting down his glass. "I wondered if that was what had you so despondent."

"I'm not *despondent*," Julian said, appalled; Christ, had things really sunk so low that he was being described in the same terms used to describe widows and invalids? "I'm merely . . . contemplating the virtues of celibacy."

Bridgeworth snorted. "I wasn't aware you knew that word."

"I'll admit it's not one I've been overly familiar with," Julian said, "but I'm beginning to consider its advantages."

"Marriage, Belfry, is the greatest gift a man can ever receive," Bridgeworth began, and Julian briefly contemplated flinging himself out a window. "All one has to do is remember one simple fact."

"Oh?" Julian asked, now considering the curtains and whether it would be possible to strangle Bridgeworth with them.

"Your wife is always right," Bridgeworth said simply, then leaned back in his seat, smiling cheerfully as though he had just imparted some great wisdom.

Julian stared at him incredulously. "You cannot be serious. *That* is your advice?"

"It is," Bridgeworth said calmly, picking up his glass. "I've found it serves me admirably—you've seen how well Jemma and I get on."

"The last time I was at your house for dinner, she threatened to disembowel you with a toasting fork if you didn't agree to accompany her to some dreadful poetry recitation," Julian said.

"Ah, an excellent case for study," Bridgeworth said, still wearing that infuriatingly smug smile that every happily married man of Julian's acquaintance seemed to find necessary to adopt during these sorts of conversations. "She did indeed threaten me with grave physical harm, which I neatly avoided by simply agreeing to attend."

Julian stared at his friend.

"Bridgeworth," he said, feeling a trifle alarmed, "this sounds like a hostage situation."

"Oh, it is," Bridgeworth said while smiling, not sounding at all bothered by this characterization of his marriage. "But all marriage is, old chap, so you're best off accepting that and proceeding accordingly."

"I don't think this is the sort of advice I was looking for," Julian said.

"You weren't looking for any advice at all," Bridgeworth reminded him. "You were content to stare broodingly into your drink and mutter about women without discussing any of the specifics of your female-shaped problem—not a very productive line of attack, but whatever you think is best, I suppose."

"It's the theater," Julian said, more to get Bridgeworth to shut up than anything else. "Emily and I have . . . differences of opinion, shall we say, about what the best path forward for the Belfry is."

"Ah," Bridgeworth said, as if he understood things much more clearly now—which it was entirely possible that he did, given the length of their friendship. He was one of the few of Julian's Oxford friends who hadn't abandoned him over the years; it wasn't that he had been cast out of his social circle, but as his friends aged and took their places in society—some by inheriting their titles; some by joining the army or the clergy; some by marrying—they seemed to find less room for him. It was vastly amusing to have a friend who'd made himself the talk of London when one was five-and-twenty; it was somewhat less so when one was approaching thirty and beginning to haunt the assembly rooms at Almack's on Wednesday nights, in search of a bride.

"What's her idea, then?" Bridgeworth asked curiously.

"One of the actresses fancies herself a playwright, and she's written a script for a show entirely starring women," Julian explained. "It's a satire of the *ton*—bound to be utterly offensive to any lady who watches it. Men might find it amusing, but no gentleman is going to want to come to the theater to watch a show full of women standing around talking, instead of removing their clothing."

"Is it any good?" Bridgeworth asked, taking another sip from his drink.

"It is," Julian admitted reluctantly, feeling a bit guilty over his dismissive characterization of Miss Congreave. She didn't just *fancy* herself a playwright—in fact, if that script was anything to judge by, she was a damned good one. "It's very good, actually."

"And Emily thinks you should stage it?"

"Emily hasn't even read the script yet, but she's taken this idea into her head that we could pitch it directly to the ladies of polite society—bypass the men entirely. She thinks gossip about it would spread and draw a crowd solely out of curiosity."

"She might be right," Bridgeworth said, raising an eyebrow.

"I know," Julian said heavily. "But our reputation would never recover—it would be the only thing we were known for. I don't want to change the nature of the scandals the Belfry is known for; I want us to be seen as a theater on par with the patent theaters, with the finest theatrical fare and the best talent. That would show—"

He broke off abruptly, slightly rattled; his tongue had gotten away from him, and he'd found words spilling out of his mouth that he hadn't intended to speak aloud to anyone—words that he hadn't fully admitted to himself.

Bridgeworth was watching him very carefully now, his gaze sharp. Julian had known the man long enough to know that the sleepy look he gave the world at times was nothing more than an act, but it was still disconcerting to be reminded of this fact.

"If you think that you are proving something to . . . anyone," Bridgeworth said, speaking carefully now, "by running your theater in such a way that any joy you find in the endeavor is robbed from you, I wonder if you might wish to reconsider."

"I run my theater the way I please," Julian said tersely. "I think of myself, and my actors, and every man and woman in my employ, and try to make decisions that will best suit them. No one else comes into the equation."

"Not even your wife?" Bridgeworth asked slyly, and Julian mentally cursed, knowing he had walked right into that one.

"Emily and I had an understanding when we decided to wed," he said. "We knew that we could each be of use to the other, and she understands that fact perfectly well." As soon as the words were out of his mouth, he paused to consider them. They *had* had an understanding—one which did not include Emily being involved at the theater in any meaningful way, beyond putting in an appearance at a show on occasion.

So why was she there? Because she had asked, of course—but that begged the question: why had he acquiesced? She had been determined, to be sure, but Julian had overseen the running of a business for nearly a decade. He knew how to say no.

Except to her.

He voiced none of these unsettling thoughts to Bridgeworth, however; instead, he merely added, "We are experiencing a—a difference of opinion, at the moment, but she'll come to see things from my point of view soon enough."

"Is it worth it?" Bridgeworth asked abruptly, leaning forward to rest his elbows on his knees. "Living your life like this? Trying to turn yourself into something you're not?"

"I'm not doing anything of the sort," Julian said, feeling his hackles rising, trying not to let his temper get the better of him. "I'm merely trying to make a success of something I've dedicated almost ten years of my life to."

"It's *already* a success," Bridgeworth said, exasperated. "You sell out shows routinely. Most men I know frequent the Belfry on a regular basis."

"But not—"

"But not their wives, I know," Bridgeworth said, waving a hand. "And yet I believe *your* wife has suggested a plan that, were I to judge, would result in many of those wives flocking to your doors."

"And then never returning again."

"Most of them, undoubtedly not," Bridgeworth agreed. "But some would. And furthermore, who the hell cares? You're making money hand over fist. Why are you so fixated on changing course?"

"Because I'm going to bloody well show the *ton* what I can do," Julian said tersely.

"The *ton*, or your father?" Bridgeworth said the words calmly, without emotion in his voice, but Julian felt each one like a physical blow.

"My father has nothing to do with this," Julian said quietly.

"I think he has everything to do with this," Bridgeworth said flatly. "Belfry, I've known you for nearly fifteen years—if you think you can fool me, you're mad."

Julian pushed his chair back, all at once fed up with everything to do with this conversation. "For the sake of that fifteen-year friendship, I won't tell you to bugger off, which I badly wish to do at the moment," he said. "But I'm going home."

"Consider what I've said," Bridgeworth called, as Julian began to walk away. "And think about who you're really doing this for—and at what cost."

Bridgeworth's words echoed in Julian's mind the entire walk home. He'd taken his curricle when he set out that afternoon, but had sent his groom home without him, preferring a bit of exercise and fresh air to clear his head. It was not a terribly great distance back to Duke Street, however, and Julian found that by the time he arrived home, he'd not managed to make much progress with the mire of his thoughts.

Upon his return, he noted the ostentatious carriage parked in the street, and realized that, given the hour, Emily must be entertaining afternoon callers. He briefly considered continuing on his way, but decided that if he was going to ask her to play nicely with these ladies, the least he could do was put in an appearance, a show of support.

Bracing himself for an awful lot of chatter about so-and-so's new hat, he walked up the steps, a footman opening the door as he did so. He handed off his hat and gloves to Bramble and winced at the sound of a shrill giggle emanating from the drawing room. He set off down the hall, pausing to listen in the doorway for a moment.

" . . . my duty to repay your call, of course," came a voice that sounded vaguely familiar—no doubt a lady he'd been introduced to at some point in the past, the memory quickly wiped from his brain owing to its insignificance.

"That was very kind of you, Lady Cunninge," Emily said, and the name dimly registered with Julian, who was certain that he had indeed met this lady before. There was nothing in Emily's tone that should have given him cause for alarm, and yet he felt a chill course through him nonetheless, for no reason that he could fully discern.

"After your dear mama's many years of loyal friendship, it was the least I could do." The speaker—Lady Cunninge—heaved a dramatic sigh. "It no doubt must pain her to see her daughter in such circumstances, but I suppose she had no choice but to accept the matter as settled, when you snuck off the way you did."

"I do not believe that is entirely correct, ma'am," Emily said, and her tone was still perfectly polite. Julian paused for a moment, fully appreciating the skill that she had—something he had always been aware of, of course, but which he had perhaps not acknowledged as being as impressive as it was. Half the reason he had married her was for this ability of hers—to be polite above all else, to smile sweetly no matter what was said to her, to somehow keep herself above the fray, golden and lovely and untouched.

And yet, in this instant, he hated it—hated that she should be forced to make use of this skill, to speak politely to a lady who clearly bore her no goodwill.

"I was fortunate enough to be able to accompany my dearest friends to a house party, in the company of a chaperone of such impeccable reputation that I need not even ask if you are questioning her suitability."

Julian bit back a grin at this—indeed, no one would dare question anything about the Dowager Marchioness of Willingham, for fear of being on the receiving end of her famously fierce tongue, but he himself had grave doubts about her suitability as a chaperone. Not, of course, that he was complaining.

"Lord Julian and I realized our mutual regard whilst at Lord Willingham's house party," Emily continued, "and simply could not wait another moment to be wed, now that our feelings were known. I'm afraid there is nothing more interesting to the tale than that, my lady."

"Of course," Lady Cunninge cooed. "And Lord Julian must have been most curious to marry his new bride, to see what, precisely, all that time spent in Mr. Cartham's company added up to."

Anger pushed Julian into motion, his feet moving seemingly of their own accord, his hand wrenching open the drawing room door. He felt curiously out of control, as though he were not truly the master of his own behavior—and he didn't like the sensation one bit. But that didn't matter. What mattered was that this harpy had just insulted his wife, in his home, and he'd be damned if he was going to let this woman sit here drinking his tea and eating his food a moment longer.

"Julian," Emily said, looking up at him, startled, upon his entrance. Lady Cunninge also looked startled, and Julian didn't think he was imagining the expression of worry that flashed across her face. She was just the type to insult a lady to her face in private but then immediately fret the moment it seemed likely that anyone else had heard her do so.

"There you are," he said, would-be casual, pasting an expression of lazy good humor upon his face. He wasn't certain it had fooled Emily, but that didn't bother him overmuch—she, after all, was not the one he was trying to fool at the moment.

"What are you doing home?" she asked, still looking surprised to see him.

"I was having a chat with Bridgeworth at my club, and then realized I'd really rather be at home. With you," he added, as if anyone could have failed to take his meaning. He'd reached Emily's chair by this point, and leaned down to press a kiss to the top of her head. Miraculously, Lady Cunninge did not reach for her smelling salts.

"Lady Cunninge has come to call," Emily said, gesturing to where the lady in question still sat, teacup in hand, watching this display with avid curiosity.

"So I heard," Julian said, turning to give the lady a sweeping look that he usually reserved for business acquaintances who were trying to fleece him out of his money. "I happened to catch a bit of your conversation as I was on my way into the room."

Lady Cunninge paled.

Julian offered her a thin smile.

"Did you?" Emily asked serenely. "Then perhaps you'll excuse me for a moment, my love, as I say what I was about to say to Lady Cunninge before you interrupted us."

"But of course, my darling," he said gallantly, not budging from her side.

"I think I really must be going," Lady Cunninge began, setting her teacup down hastily—clearly, bullying a newlywed was one thing, but confronting said newlywed and her wildly indignant husband was another thing entirely, and not a task that she quite felt up to.

"Yes, I'm sure you must," Emily said, and this time there was a note of steel in her voice. "But before you leave, Lady Cunninge, please allow me to assure you that I shall never inconvenience you with my presence ever again. And please *also* rest assured that if you ever take pains to try to smear my good name among the *ton*, I shall be more than happy to see to it that your husband's various mistresses all come calling. At once."

"I don't have the faintest idea—"

"Oh, I believe you do," Emily said placidly. "And if you think that I am bluffing, I assure you that this is *vastly* kinder than whatever my husband would dream up as retribution in such a scenario, so really you might consider me quite merciful." She rose to her feet. "Not, of course, that I ever expect any of this to ever be a problem, since I do not anticipate that you would ever deliberately attempt to ruin my reputation for sport." She flashed a sickening smile over her shoulder at Julian. "And you don't either, do you, my dearest?"

Julian shook his head solemnly, suddenly gripped by the mad desire to laugh. "I do not, my hedgehog."

Emily pressed her lips firmly together—Julian was nearly certain that she too was now trying not to laugh—before turning back to Lady Cunninge. "I hope you have a lovely afternoon," she said cheerfully, bobbing an extremely shallow curtsey. Lady Cunninge managed her own attempt at a curtsey before she was ushered from the room.

No sooner had the door closed behind her than Emily rounded on Julian.

"'*My hedgehog*'?" she asked him incredulously.

Julian held up his hands in defense. "Not my best work."

"Couldn't you have taken a leaf out of Lord Willingham's book and called me your magnificent ruby, or something along those lines?"

"I'm not good at improvising!" he said defensively.

"*You are an actor.*"

"Actors have scripts!"

"Oh, for heaven's sake." She crossed her arms over her chest and flopped rather dramatically back down onto the settee she had been occupying—Julian thought it might have been one of the least graceful things he had ever seen her do. Rather more slowly, he sat down next to her.

"Emily," he said, "was that scene indicative of how the other ladies you've paid calls on have been treating you?"

She turned her head to look directly at him. "Not all," she said.

"But some?"

"But some," she confirmed.

261

"Christ," he said, rubbing his hands over his face, feeling angry—at the miserable women who had treated her this way, and also, perhaps even more so, at himself. "Please don't accept a call from anyone who was rude to you the first time."

Emily threw her hands up in the air.

"What do you expect me to do, then? You're the one who is so insistent that we make ourselves the model of propriety so that society will accept us. These are the people we need to win over. All the more reasonable ones, like Violet and Diana and their husbands, already care too little for *ton* gossip to worry about us; it's the ones like Lady Cunninge that will prove trickier, and I don't see how you expect me to convince them that you're not a scandalous reprobate if I don't meet them socially."

Julian rubbed his forehead.

"We'll do without them, then," he said tersely. "I don't want you having to make polite conversation over tea buns with women like that one. You deserve better than that."

She deserved, he felt in a moment of utter self-loathing, better than a husband who would put her in that situation in the first place.

"I don't need *you* to be the person deciding what I can bear and what I can't," she said pointedly. "One of the things I've always liked about you is that you don't treat me like a child—that you let me make my own choices, that you trust me to know my own mind. I'm perfectly capable of defending myself, as I believe you just saw—I'm only feeling a bit put out that I haven't been doing so for years, whenever some lady in the retiring room at some ball or another made a sly comment about Mr. Cartham's escort, about my lack of dowry, about my brother's scandal."

"You cared about your family," he said quietly, reaching out a hand to touch her knee through her skirts. "For better and for worse."

"I still *do* care about them," she said, clearly frustrated. "That's the trouble. It's not just about you wanting me to try to curry favor with these women—it's that many of them are friends with Mama, and I don't wish to insult them or embarrass her."

"What has she ever done, Emily, to be worthy of such concern?" he asked, beginning to feel frustration to match her own.

"She is my *mother,*" she stressed. "She doesn't have to do anything else. I love her, even if I don't like her very often. I can't just cut my family out neatly, like a bit of mold on cheese, even if you've done so."

"We weren't discussing my family," he said, drawing back from her, stiffening his shoulders.

"You never wish to," she said, still looking at him, her blue eyes wide and guileless, "and yet who are you fooling, Julian? Your father is the real reason I've been having miserable cups of tea and exchanging veiled insults for the past month. He's the only reason you're so fixated on gaining society's approval again—you want *his* approval."

"And if I did, would that be so bad?" he asked.

"Yes," she said simply. "If you're trying to turn yourself into someone you aren't, merely to please him. I've spent much of my life doing that—half the reason I married you was because it was so entirely unlike what the Emily I'd become would do. It was something for me alone, something I had control over. And yet here I am, watching you do the same thing I've done for so long, and it makes me miserable to witness it."

By this point, Julian was barely even listening, his mind was so hung up on one word: *miserable.*

He was making her miserable.

Brilliant job, Belfry, he congratulated himself. *You've married the loveliest, most sweet-tempered lady you could possibly hope to find, and she's sitting beside you close to tears.*

Abruptly, he stood.

"What are you doing?" she asked, blinking up at him, confusion writ plain on every inch of her face.

"I'm going—out," he said, sounding like a complete and utter idiot, of course.

"But," she said, then fell silent. "But we were talking," she said, and if it was possible for Julian to feel like more of an ass than he already did, then he did so in that moment.

"I can't talk to you right now," he said, his tone blunt, realizing that he was dangerously close to allowing something approaching real emotion into his own voice, too. None of this was going according to plan—they'd had an arrangement, they'd had terms that they both clearly understood, and yet at some point things had become muddled. Here he was, acting like a damned fool, all because—what? Because his wife had looked a bit crestfallen?

Because she'd seen through him and realized what he truly wanted?

Nothing about this marriage was feeling terribly convenient—not the wide-eyed, tearful wife whose emotions he was suddenly dangerously concerned about; not the rush of feelings inside his own chest that felt as though they were pressing against his ribs, filling him to bursting. And not the fact that, five minutes earlier, he would have gladly thrown away everything he'd thought he'd wanted, if it meant Emily would never have to sit in a drawing room and be cunningly insulted ever again.

None of this was right, and he didn't know how to make it so.

"Don't wait up for me," he said, and then he fled.

Nineteen

It would be considerably more tolerable to be making a mess of his marriage if he also didn't feel like he was making a mess of his theater, Julian thought.

A few days later, he was seated in the auditorium at the Belfry, his eyes fixed on the stage, watching the rehearsal underway. It was the climactic scene, one in which Beatrice and Benedick each attempted to adopt some measure of the other's faith, as a grand romantic gesture. It should have been emotional, exciting. But it was leaving Julian entirely cold.

"There you are."

He turned his head as Laverre dropped into the seat next to him, his own eyes fixed on the stage as the dramatics continued apace. "I haven't seen you watch a rehearsal in a while," Laverre said after a minute or so had passed, his tone neutral.

"I haven't been this worried about a production in quite a while," Julian said frankly. Were it anyone else, he wouldn't have admitted this so readily, but he'd learned long ago that there was little point in trying to fool Laverre on matters such as this—the man had a keen ability to see through whatever act Julian attempted.

Laverre watched the scene unfolding onstage for a long moment, his mouth quirked slightly to one side the way it did when he was deep in thought. "She's not as good as Miss Simmons," he said at last. "But she's perfectly suitable. It will be fine."

"I don't want fine," Julian said shortly. "I want brilliant."

Laverre glanced at him and gave an eloquent, extremely French eye roll. "I know. You've mentioned it a time or two, the past few months." He paused, gazing at Julian for a long moment.

"Just say it," Julian said impatiently; Laverre occasionally had an irritating penchant for dramatic pauses that Julian did not feel like humoring.

"You need to step back," Laverre said shortly. "You're not acting rationally—first, you were obsessed with luring June away from Drury Lane this season, which you managed quite successfully. Then came this whole business with Miss Simmons—she's a brilliant actress, but we've a perfectly competent understudy, and you refuse to acknowledge that fact."

"It's not just the show," Julian said, his eyes fixed on the stage once more, where June and Miss Congreave had started the scene over again, the orchestra once more beginning to play the music that would accompany their words. "I don't want my name mixed up in any scandal that Delacre and Miss Simmons might cause. The last thing I need is to be the source of further gossip."

"Belfry, you've been the source of gossip for years, and you've never seemed to care two pence about it, until recently."

"Because—" Julian began, but Laverre cut him off.

"I understand perfectly well that you wish to compete with the patent theaters, to ensure that every pompous ass in London knows that you didn't make a mistake in your investment all those years ago. And you can tell yourself that it's not your father you wish to prove something to, but I won't believe you."

Julian opened his mouth to object and then closed it again, his mind occupied with Laverre's words.

"You're beginning to sound like Emily," he said peevishly.

"Interesting you should mention her," Laverre said slowly, a smug note to his voice that did not bode well. "Because, if you want my opinion, it's only once you met her that you truly became fixated on this."

"That's not true," Julian said automatically. "I've been trying—"

"To improve our reputation for the better part of a year, yes," Laverre said impatiently. "And yet I've never seen you so single-mindedly focused on it as you have been these past three months."

Since he met Emily.

Because that was the reason he had married her.

So of course he was bloody focused on it, he thought with some irritation. If he'd gone to the extreme of getting married—of leg-shackling himself to a woman for the rest of his life—then he'd damned well better get what he hoped to from this marriage. He had to. Because if he abandoned his goal now—

He stilled.

If he abandoned his goal—this obsession with the Belfry's reputation—if he no longer cared about impressing anyone . . .

Well, then he might have to admit that maybe, just maybe, there had been more to his motivation for marrying Emily than convenience alone.

That he wanted more from her than a marriage based on a passionless arrangement.

He sat motionless in his seat as this realization washed over him, eyes on the stage but not taking in a single detail of the drama unfolding before him, until, after a moment, out of the corner of his eye, he became aware of a stagehand hovering nearby.

"Yes?" he asked, trying to keep any sharpness out of his tone.

"My lord," the stagehand said quickly, "there's a visitor here to see you."

"We're in the middle of a rehearsal," Julian said, as if he were actually watching the rehearsal any longer. "Can't it wait?"

"I think you'll wish to see this visitor now, sir," the stagehand said uncertainly, before leaning forward and adding, "It's Miss Simmons."

"Do you think the yellow paisley or the orange stripes will look more atrocious?" Diana asked, scrutinizing each fabric sample in turn as though the very safety of the kingdom depended on it.

"The yellow paisley," Violet said definitively, after a long moment of staring at each one in turn. "Jeremy's hair is so blond. He will look horrid in the yellow—like an overgrown daffodil."

"Emily?" Diana asked, turning to her; Emily, who had only been halfway attending to any of their conversation, started guiltily, then added—because this was generally, though not always, a safe response—"I agree with Violet."

Diana turned back to look at the fabric samples laid out before her. "Yes," she said thoughtfully. "I do believe you are correct." She chuckled a bit ghoulishly. "He's going to look simply *awful*."

"Diana," Violet said carefully. "You do realize it is going to be his wedding day, too? Would you not have Jeremy enjoy the experience, rather than have half the guests staring at him in horror, wondering if he's temporarily lost his eyesight?"

"No," Diana said cheerfully. "That, in fact, sounds like the perfect wedding day to me."

"You'll be the one who has to look at it, not him," Emily pointed out, attempting to appeal to Diana's practical side. "So aren't you in actuality punishing yourself?"

"Oh, I assure you, the sight of him in this waistcoat will be anything but a punishment," Diana said, clutching the fabric samples to her impressive bosom with an expression of starry-eyed glee upon her face. "It will, in fact, be a miracle if I can make it through the entire ceremony without bursting into hysterical laughter—but then, I suppose that was always going to be the case," she added practically, and Emily couldn't argue with this; Diana wasn't really the teary, sentimental sort, even when it came to her own nuptials.

They were sitting in the solarium at Diana's house—which would remain her house for only a little bit longer and would soon be occupied by her late husband's nephew, the current Viscount Templeton. Part of her extensive wardrobe, in fact, had already been relocated to Lord Willingham's house in Fitzroy Square, though Diana herself would not take up residence there until the wedding night.

They were due to visit Lord Willingham there in a little under an hour, in fact; Diana wanted to go room by room, noting down the changes she wished to make—Lord Willingham had apparently given her more or less free rein, since, as Diana put it, "gentlemen wouldn't know how to decorate a house if their very lives depended on it"—and had enlisted Violet and Emily as accomplices. For now, however, they were sitting in the solarium, drinking cups of tea and watching Diana scrutinize fabric samples with an unholy amount of glee.

Emily thought, not for the first time, that Lord Willingham really ought to be applauded for his courage—it was not just anyone who could face marriage to Diana.

"The yellow will certainly be the *most* horrifying," Diana said, casting aside the samples and sinking elegantly back down onto her settee. "I'll send that one off to his tailor at once."

"That poor man," Emily murmured, sipping at her tea, and Diana shot a grin at her as she lifted her own teacup.

"Speaking of poor men," she said, lowering it a moment later, "how is *your* husband, Emily?"

Emily worked to keep her usual, carefully neutral expression upon her face.

"Perfectly well, I believe," she said calmly. "He is at the Belfry this afternoon, watching a rehearsal."

"Hmm," Diana said, still watching her closely. "He continues to spend an awful lot of time there, then?"

"He does own it," Emily pointed out. "I should think it rather strange if he didn't."

"On the contrary," Diana said. "I believe it would be far less strange if he put up the financial investment and then left everything else to his manager—that's how I understand these sorts of arrangements normally work. And yet Belfry seems peculiarly invested in the workings of his theater."

"You know that he has ambitions for it," Emily said, lowering her teacup. "I personally find it rather refreshing to find a gentleman of his background who is not content to merely rest on his family fortune and while away his days at the card tables, or at the horse races." She blinked, realizing that might sound like a more pointed barb than she had intended. "I do not refer to Lord Willingham or Lord James, of course."

Violet waved a dismissive hand. "I'm sure James would agree with you—have you never heard him moan about the gentlemen he used to meet with at Tattersall's, when he was still running his father's stables?

Utterly tedious—with minds only for horseflesh and nothing else, he used to say." She reached over to touch Emily's arm gently. "I think it admirable that Belfry should care so much about his theater."

"So long as it does not come at the cost of caring about *you*," Diana said pointedly. "You are quite recently married. I do not like that he should be away from home so often."

"We do not have that sort of marriage," Emily reminded her, gazing into her teacup and feeling unaccountably glum as she uttered the words, which were, after all, nothing more or less than the truth. She looked up to see Violet and Diana both staring at her, wearing identical incredulous expressions.

"What?" she asked, a bit defensively.

"Emily," Violet said, adopting what Emily recognized at once as her Attempting To Reason With Someone Unreasonable tone, and which she felt somewhat resentful at having to be on the receiving end of, for once. It was a bit galling to be condescended to by someone who had just a few months earlier been pretending to have an inconsistently symptomatic mortal illness.

"Are either of you actually *enjoying* your arrangement, at the moment?"

Emily frowned.

"What do you mean?"

"Well," Violet said slowly, "do you think you would be happier in your marriage if, instead of attempting to craft yourself into the perfect model of respectability that will earn the approval of all of the same ladies you've been trying to impress your entire life, you instead just did as you pleased and enjoyed yourself and your dashing husband?"

"It's not a matter of what makes me happy," Emily said. "We had an agreement, and I won't go back on my end of the bargain. We aren't like you and Lord James, or Diana and Lord Willingham."

"Do mine ears detect the sound of my own name?" came the voice of the very man in question. Lord Willingham entered the room, offering the ladies a rather exaggerated courtly bow and a roguish grin.

"What are you doing here?" Diana asked, standing to greet him.

"Standing, my cherished ruby?" he asked her, feigning astonishment, even as he snaked an arm around her waist to pull her close. "Are you feeling at all well?"

"A lot better than you'll be feeling in approximately ten seconds if you don't stop comparing me to gemstones," she said, smiling sweetly at her fiancé.

"To answer your question, my treasured opal," he said, dropping his arm from her waist and neatly avoiding a kick to his shins as he darted nimbly to the side, "I was out and about, and decided to pop in to see if I could provide my escort as you make your way to my humble home." He flashed them a charming smile—it was no surprise, Emily thought, that he had been so infamous a rake prior to meeting his match in Diana. "So you would not have to face the ordeal of travel through the dangerous London streets alone," he added helpfully, with the air of a man who clearly expected them to fall at his feet in paroxysms of gratitude at any moment.

"Why are you *really* here?" Diana asked, unmoved by this display of gallantry.

Lord Willingham sighed. "I was walking down the street and saw Lady Wheezle coming from the opposite direction, so naturally I sought shelter." He adopted a mournful, vaguely harried expression. "In the warm and welcoming arms of my beloved, of course."

His beloved was, in fact, sitting once more on a chaise, regarding him as though she suspected him of recently having committed a crime. A touching scene, indeed, Emily thought, though she could not help but note that Diana seemed to be biting her cheek as if to prevent a smile.

"Sit down and do stop talking," she said instead. "Emily was in the middle of telling us something when you interrupted, and she'll never finish if you keep distracting us."

"Your wish is my command, my adorable sapphire," Lord Willingham said with what Emily personally considered to be alarming disregard for his physical well-being. He sank down next to Diana on the chaise and rested an arm along its back, his hand lazily beginning to play with a curl at her neck that had escaped her coiffure.

"Yes," Emily said a bit more uncertainly now, not at all sure that she wished to continue this discussion in Lord Willingham's hearing. It wasn't that he made her nervous, exactly—she had known him for years, after all—just that they didn't have terribly much in common. Except for the fact that they both adored Diana—which, Emily reflected, was really more than enough. Before she could work out what to say next, however, she heard the distinct sound of her own husband's voice echoing down the hallway, growing louder with each moment.

"Does every man in London think it necessary to visit my house this afternoon?" Diana asked peevishly, before shooting an apologetic look at her betrothed.

"Don't start fussing over my feelings now," Lord Willingham said. "I might expire from shock."

A moment later, Julian appeared in the doorway of the sunroom, Diana's long-suffering butler hovering anxiously behind him.

"Lord Julian Belfry," Wright squawked over Julian's shoulder as Julian walked into the room.

"Yes, Wright, thank you," Diana said. "I do believe that is self-evident. Belfry, sit down before you cause poor Wright to take to his bed," she added.

Julian, for his part, ignored Diana entirely—and Diana was not a terribly easy person to ignore—and instead looked at Emily.

"Emily, I need to speak to you," he said.

"All right," she said, rising. "Let me just collect my—"

"No, it will only take a moment," he said, shaking his head. "There's no need to alter your plans for the afternoon. If I could just speak to you privately for a moment or two."

"Of course," she said, frowning, conscious of three very curious gazes watching this exchange. She swept past him through the doorway that led from the solarium into one of Diana's drawing rooms, shutting the door firmly on her friends' intrigued faces.

"Is something wrong?" she asked, turning to him. He looked . . . odd. She couldn't quite put her finger on what was amiss, and yet he was not at all himself. It was unsettling. There was something unsettled about *him*, in fact—some strange, indescribable energy hovering about his lean form that she didn't think she'd ever seen in him before.

"Yes," he said, running a distracted hand through his hair. "No—I don't know."

"Of course," she said politely. "That clears things right up."

He cracked a grin at that. "Sorry. I'm all at sixes and sevens." He walked toward her, reaching out to grip her hand. "Miss Simmons showed up at rehearsal."

Emily frowned. "Miss Simmons, who was last seen fleeing into a rosy dawn in the company of Lord Delacre?"

"The very one."

"Did she . . . have second thoughts?"

"Something like that," he said grimly, and Emily's frown deepened, not understanding his tone.

"What is the matter?" she asked, perplexed. "Isn't this good news? Now you can stop worrying about the production so much."

"Emily . . ." He took a deep breath. "She came back because my father went to fetch her."

"What?" she asked, his words not fully registering.

"My father. Followed her halfway across England." The words came out as short, clipped sentences, like chips of ice broken off a large block. "Apparently by the time he arrived, she'd already realized her mistake—Delacre is a right bastard, after all, and Miss Simmons is no idiot, so it didn't take her long to realize she'd cast her lot in with the wrong man, but she had no money, no way to escape him."

"She's very young—barely twenty, I believe?" Emily said softly, feeling a pang of sadness for the lonely, fearful days she must have experienced before Lord Eastvale appeared. And feeling admiration, too, for a girl who was bold enough to chase happiness, even if it ended up not amounting to anything. That was who she wanted to be, too. Someone who chased her own happiness, no matter the risk.

"Oh, I know," Julian said. "I don't blame her. Well," he amended, "I do blame her—she did run off on me, in the middle of rehearsals for a show that's going to be the biggest role of her entire career." He shook his head in exasperation. "But Delacre is a blackguard; she's hardly the first woman to be taken in by a charming smile."

"And calves," Emily said thoughtfully.

"Emily," he said sternly, then paused, a slight frown wrinkling his brow. "As in, his legs? Or baby cows?"

"His legs," she clarified. "I could not speak to his livestock holdings." She sighed. "I do not like the man at all, but I was recently advised to carefully consider a gentleman's calves, and I could not help but notice that he has very nice ones."

"I thought the fairer sex was supposed to be above such earthly concerns," he said, his mouth twitching a bit at the corners. "More interested in a communion of souls."

"I don't see why a communion of souls can't also involve nicely muscled calves," she said primly, then added, trying to call upon a bit of the inner boldness she'd been cultivating of late, "Yours are very nice, Julian."

"Emily Turner," he said mock indignantly.

"Belfry," she reminded him.

"Emily Belfry, have you been *ogling* me?" He put his hands on his hips, and Emily, all in a rush, had a flash of recollection of the feeling of having her own hips gripped firmly by those very hands, in the darkness of their bedroom, nothing but the sound of their own breaths between them.

"It's rather difficult not to," she said, perfectly honestly—he was many things, including at times incredibly frustrating, but he was undeniably an extremely handsome man.

"I know the feeling," he murmured, his intent gaze causing a blush to rise to her cheeks.

"But that is rather beside the point," she squeaked, taking a hasty step backward and glancing at the door leading to the solarium, where she knew their friends would be eagerly waiting to interrogate her. "You were saying that your father has convinced Miss Simmons to return?"

"Yes," he said on a sigh, his gaze losing its molten heat, his expression suddenly businesslike. "It's Frannie's fault, of course—that blasted letter she sent that Robert mentioned. She must have explained the entire situation, not merely our marriage, and apparently my father took it upon himself to intervene." There was a strange note in his voice that Emily wasn't entirely able to interpret; it wasn't quite bitter, nor was it angry, but it wasn't happy, either. It almost sounded . . . regretful.

"Julian," she said hesitantly, wondering if she was badly putting her foot in it, but determined to try anyway, "don't you think that this is further proof of what your brother was telling you? That your father wants to make amends?"

She wasn't certain what response she expected from him—men could be so maddeningly difficult to predict, she was learning—but it wasn't what came: a brief pause, a raised eyebrow, and . . .

"Perhaps."

"Are you . . . agreeing with me?" she asked, taken aback.

"You say that like it's a bad thing," he said, looking amused.

"I just didn't realize it was possible for a man to realize that his wife had made a reasonable point and concede it promptly, without dragging it out into a dramatic ordeal."

"That," he said darkly, "is because your friends set terrible examples."

"That—" She said indignantly, then paused to consider. "—is actually fair."

"In any case," he said, crossing his arms over his chest, "I will concede that you might have a point."

"What do you intend to do about it, then?" she asked, the wheels of her mind already turning.

"I don't know," he said frankly, his blue eyes serious, the line of his jaw tight—she could practically see the tension and uncertainty radiating off of him, and, entirely on impulse, she reached out a hand to clutch his.

"You know your parents have returned to town, don't you?" she asked quietly; she had heard the news that very afternoon from the Dowager Marchioness of Willingham, whom she'd encountered at the circulating library, and who was always a reliable source of gossip.

He gave a jerky nod. "Robert told me."

"What if we invited them to dinner?" she said, trying to make the words casual, not lace any of her desperate hope into her voice as she spoke. "We can invite my parents too. And our closest friends—it can be a party."

He gazed at her for a long moment, rubbing the back of her hand in a slow, soothing motion.

Finally, he said, "All right. Why not? If it's a disaster, well—at least we'll have a story to laugh about later."

"Shall we plan it for the week that *Much Ado About Heaven* opens?" she suggested. "It could be a celebration of sorts." As she spoke, her mind was racing, an additional possibility in mind. Did she dare voice it to Julian?—no, not yet, she decided.

"If you wish," he said, not sounding as though he particularly cared, which she supposed, on the whole, was better than outright disapproval. He reached his hand up to tuck an errant lock of hair behind her ear; she had not bothered to curl it today, knowing she would only be seeing her friends, having no one to impress. No one to satisfy, other than herself.

And Julian, of course, who did not appear to give a fig about whether she took the time to crimp her hair into ringlets that framed her face as her mother had always insisted, despite Emily's suspicions that it made her look insipid.

"My hair doesn't curl very well, you know," she blurted, the words out of her mouth before she even realized what she was saying. Her cheeks heated—he didn't care. Why would she tell him such a thing?

"Your hair is perfect," he murmured, leaning forward to press a soft kiss to her cheek in the spot that the unruly lock of hair had been brushing against a moment earlier.

"My mother always insisted that I curl it," she continued, her mouth apparently having decided that, now that she'd started this idiotic line of conversation, she might as well see it through to its conclusion. "But I don't like it curled—I hate the way it flaps around my face."

Julian drew back a bit to look down at her, frowning slightly. "Then don't curl it."

She opened her mouth—and then shut it again.

Then don't curl it.

It sounded so ridiculously simple when he put it that way, when of course it was anything but.

Of course she couldn't simply stop curling her hair—not when it was the style, and when being the perfectly proper, stylish wife that Julian desired was so terribly important.

But she couldn't say that to him, of course—couldn't let him see the way this agreement, one she had made so willingly, had come to feel like a weight on her shoulders, so similar to the weight she had carried there for so many years before this.

She smiled up at him, but something of her thoughts must have shown on her face, because a faint line appeared between his brows. "Emily, I don't give a damn what you do with your hair—I personally rather like being able to kiss you without having to risk getting my eye poked, but it doesn't really matter what I like. What matters is what *you* like."

Emily felt rooted to the spot, unable to formulate any sort of intelligent response. *What matters is what you like.* She didn't think anyone had ever uttered those words to her before—they had been more than she had ever dared hope to hear, in fact. All that had ever mattered had been what other people liked, what other people wanted.

Never her.

And now, this man—her *husband,* a man she had pledged her love and fealty to for the rest of her life, no matter their motivations for the match—this beautiful man was standing here, telling her that what she wanted was what mattered.

So she kissed him.

It was, from the moment her lips first touched his, a heated, impolite sort of kiss. Emily didn't think that she'd ever considered kissing in terms of politeness until this moment, but this one was unquestionably impolite. This was her mouth opening under his, her tongue tangling with his, his hand at her waist and sliding lower, a moan catching in her throat.

It was a moment—or perhaps an hour—later when Emily dimly registered the sound of the door opening behind them.

"*Diana,*" came Violet's exasperated voice, and Emily broke away from Julian with a startled gasp, turning as she did so.

"I knew it," Diana said smugly, standing in the doorway with the air of a governess who'd just caught her charges attempting to abscond with an apple tart. "I knew you weren't to be trusted alone in a room together!"

"Diana," Emily protested, her cheeks warming. "We're *married.*"

"You're as bad as Violet and Audley!" Diana said, pressing a dramatic hand to her heart. "Everywhere I turn, lewd behavior is afoot."

"How very right you are, Lady Templeton," Julian said with a bow

280

so correct that it was impossible not to view it with some suspicion. "Now, if you will excuse me, I should very much like to kiss my wife in the privacy of my carriage." He turned to Emily and offered her his arm. "Shall we?"

And Emily, as she blushingly took the proffered arm, could not help but relish with some satisfaction the incredulous laugh Diana let out as they departed.

Twenty

It was opening night, and Julian wasn't nervous.

It was odd, he thought, as he stood in his box, Emily on his arm, surrounded by their friends. He was not a nervous man by nature, but there was usually a pang of adrenaline each time a new show opened. Tonight, however, he felt strangely calm—now that Miss Simmons had returned, relieving Miss Congreave of her duties as leading lady, rehearsals had gone considerably more smoothly, and he found himself anticipating the evening's show with an odd sense of contentment that he could not help wondering about. Was it Emily's presence on his arm that led to this feeling? Was he now a husband who found the weight of a wife's hand tucked into the crook of his elbow the very peak of happiness?

How ... domestic.

Emily, of course, looked radiant—she was wearing an evening gown of gold silk a shade or two darker than her hair, which was smoothed back from her face and piled high atop her head. He was reminded of the night he'd first met her, in this very box—she had been so lovely that night, wrapped in a demure gown, her hair carefully curled, her manners impeccable, her posture impossibly straight.

By contrast, tonight she seemed far more relaxed, though he did notice her darting an occasional glance over her shoulder. One arm rested lightly on the empty seat next to her as she reclined, and he watched her give a curt shake of her head when Violet made to take it. Julian frowned, but before he could open his mouth to ask Emily about it, she turned to answer some unheard query from Willingham, and Julian's own attention was distracted by the sight of the faint strip of bare skin between where her gloves ended and her sleeve began.

When he reached out a hand to trace a pattern on that patch of skin, she did not stiffen or pull away, but merely shot him a coy glance from beneath her lashes. While the gown she wore was hardly daring compared to many others he'd seen that evening, it was rather risqué by Emily's usual standards, and he could not stop his gaze from lingering on the swell of her breasts above the golden silk. As if sensing his thoughts—or perhaps just noticing the direction of his gaze—her mouth curved into a small, satisfied smile that was not at all reminiscent of the Emily Turner he'd met three months earlier.

This bit of contemplation was unceremoniously interrupted, however, when, on his other side, Penvale leaned over and said, "Stop leering."

He gave Penvale his best withering stare.

"I believe I'm allowed to leer at my own wife, if I please."

Penvale, the bastard, merely grinned. "Not when you're in public, if you please. Besides, I thought the entire point here was to make this theater more respectable? It will hardly be good for your reputation for you to be seen ravishing a gently reared lady in your brightly lit box."

Penvale was right about one thing: they were certainly in plain view. An enormous chandelier blazed overhead, illuminating both the audience and the stage. He had already noticed more than one curious glance in their direction. Now that the summer season had ended and Drury Lane and Covent Garden were fully operational once more,

Julian had worried—as he always did—that the more well-heeled of his clientele would abandon the Belfry for more elevated entertainments, but he was pleased to see a full house with plenty of gentlemen he recognized. And, as usual, very few ladies that he did. As ever, the gentlemen of the *ton* had viewed an evening out at the Belfry as a chance to take their mistresses out on the town without any concern about running into their wives—or anyone else's wife, for that matter. It was this very reputation that Julian was seeking so desperately to change, but gazing around this evening at the cheerful, chattering crowd, he felt the enormity of this challenge—and, all at once, experienced a moment of uncharacteristic doubt.

Because the fact was, Laverre was right: ticket sales were steady, and they continued to draw crowds to their shows. Was Julian attempting something that would ultimately ruin everything that had made the theater so successful?

He was so rattled by these doubts that he was scarcely aware of anything happening around him, and so had a feeling that it was not the first time Penvale had said his name when he paired it with a sharp poke in the side.

"Christ—what?" he asked with an irritated glance at his friend, but Penvale's head was turned, and so, Julian realized, was Emily's.

Standing in the entrance to the box was his father.

As always, the Marquess of Eastvale was impeccably turned out—his hair was combed neatly back from his face, streaks of silver at the temples; his snowy cravat was knotted tightly at his throat, keeping his chin up, his jaw tight; he wore evening kit of black and white, no color visible even in his waistcoat, but its severity suited him, emphasized that this was one of the most powerful men in the kingdom.

And he was currently staring directly at Julian.

"Father," Julian said, rising from his seat; he reached a hand down to assist Emily, then tucked her arm within the crook of his elbow as they crossed the box toward the marquess. "I did not expect to see you here tonight."

It was the understatement of the year, of course; Julian had not expected to see his father within the walls of the Belfry—well, ever, but it was only now, seeing him here, that he realized how badly he had wished for this. And what a perfect night for him to attend; after all, the entire reason Julian had been so interested in *Much Ado About Heaven* was because it was, he thought, a new take on comedy—something more thoughtful, more serious.

It was, in fact, just exactly the sort of thing to show his father—to prove to him that whatever preconceptions he had about the sort of show the Belfry staged were wrong.

"Given the invitation from your wife, I thought you might expect to see me?" the marquess said, sounding a bit stiff, the slightest hint of a questioning note in his voice. Julian glanced down at Emily, a telltale guilty flush warming her cheeks. She watched him, unapologetic.

"I thought it was high time I saw one of these shows that I hear so much gossip about," his father added. Despite the slightly stilted nature of his father's speech, Julian didn't think he intended to be disapproving—rather, he thought his father was uncomfortable, unsure of how to behave.

Well, that made two of them.

"And how could I resist the opportunity to meet said lovely wife?" his father added, smiling at Emily, who met his smile with one of her own. "Lady Julian, it is a pleasure to make your acquaintance."

"You must call me Emily, my lord," she said, extending her hand. "Lady Julian sounds so fussy."

Julian's father's smile widened. "I'm simply pleased that there *is* a Lady Julian—my wife and I had begun to wonder if Julian would ever marry." Julian was unable to resist an eye roll at that—he was, after all, only thirty, and was hardly in his dotage, but he saw a twinkle in his father's eye, and realized he was . . . *joking* with him.

It had been so long since he'd been on the receiving end of one of his father's rare jokes.

"I'm glad I was able to assuage your fears," Emily said to the marquess with a cheeky smile. "Would you like to sit with us? I believe the show is to begin any moment, and I've saved an extra seat." Julian now understood her strange dance with Violet minutes before.

The marquess's glance flitted back to Julian, an unspoken question contained therein. Was he welcome?

Julian gave a short nod. "Please, join us."

And so the marquess did.

It was strange, Julian thought, to see his father in this space that he had worked so hard to build. Strange to see him watch actors on his stage, to smile at jokes, to even chuckle on occasion.

During intermission, the marquess mingled easily with the rest of their guests—with Bridgeworth and Jemma, with the Audleys, with Willingham and Lady Templeton and Penvale. West had shown up late, with Lady Fitzwilliam on his arm.

And then they were seated once more, the show having resumed, and before Julian knew it the curtain was falling and the crowd was applauding and Julian was gripped with a horrible, sinking feeling:

The show wasn't that good.

Oh, it wasn't terrible—nothing that would embarrass him around town, nothing so awful that spectators would be tempted to walk out. But still, what had seemed so lofty to him when he first read the script—the rejection of comedy for comedy's sake, the *message* the play sought to convey—all suddenly seemed rather . . .

Well, pompous.

Beside him, Emily was biting her lip as she politely applauded, and he didn't need her to voice her thoughts to know that she agreed with him. Could probably have told him this would be the outcome, if he'd been willing to listen.

She did not say anything, however, but took his hand tightly in hers.

It was comforting—more comforting than it had any right to be.

Just then, his father leaned past Emily, extending his hand, which Julian reached out to shake.

"Well?" Julian asked casually, as if he wasn't terribly bothered by what his father had thought of the show, as if his opinion carried no weight at all.

"It was amusing," the marquess said, something slightly dubious in his tone. "I'm not certain I entirely understood all the bits about religion, to tell the truth—a bit intellectual for me, I suppose," he added, shaking his head. "The comedic bits were quite enjoyable, though, more in line with what I was expecting." He cast an apologetic glance at Emily before adding, "I must say, though, Julian, considering how many gentlemen come to these shows, I'd expected it to be a bit more—well—" He cleared his throat. "*Bawdy*." He gave his son an inquisitive look. "Perhaps there's another production you might recommend, if I'm to be properly shocked?"

Emily let out a giggle at that, and his father actually *winked* at her. Winked!

Julian, for his part, felt as though he were having some sort of otherworldly experience, in which everyone around him looked and sounded like themselves, but didn't behave remotely as they were supposed to.

Something of Julian's shock must have shown on his face, because his father leaned a bit closer, smiled at him, and said, "I suppose I shall simply have to come to another one."

Some strange mood had overtaken her husband after his father's departure, but Emily had little time to linger on it in the aftermath of the show. They were surrounded by friends, and then by a steady stream of acquaintances who popped into the box to say a word or two to Julian.

These were gentlemen acquaintances, of course—some in the company of their mistresses, some merely in a crowd of friends—and while she caught the occasional surprised glance when her presence (and that of Diana and Violet and Sophie, too) was registered, no one made any sort of a fuss. She supposed word would spread, however, that Lady Julian Belfry was in the habit of attending her husband's shows—which was, of course, exactly what Julian wanted.

She was fulfilling her end of the bargain.

So she smiled politely and made pleasant conversation until at last she was alone with Julian in their carriage, rattling home along the cobblestones, the carriage lanterns creating a warm, cozy glow within.

"Your father came," she said quietly, thinking there was no point in beating around the bush—she knew he must have had difficulty focusing on anything else for the rest of the evening, and she couldn't blame him.

"Yes," he said and lapsed into silence. His handsome face was unsmiling—not stern, precisely, but thoughtful, the sharp angles of his cheekbones creating shadows on his face in the dim light of the carriage. For a moment, Emily didn't think he was going to say anything else, and she was just beginning to wonder indignantly why she should be forced to pry every single confession out of this man, but then he spoke again.

"He enjoyed the play."

"Of course he did," Emily said, feeling a strange rush of pride, despite the fact that she was perfectly well aware that there was little about Julian that she could take credit for. But he was *hers*, she thought in a sudden fierce rush—hers to be proud of, hers to comfort when comfort was needed.

Hers to . . . love.

Of course.

Because of course she loved him—how could she not? But, more important, how could she ensure that he did not know, did not ever discover her secret? Because, after all, in a marriage of convenience, love would be the most inconvenient surprise of all.

Julian was regarding her with something akin to amusement, his mouth quirked slightly up at the sides, and for a moment she worried something of her thoughts must have shown on her face, but then he said, "You say that as if it's no surprise."

"You put on good plays, Julian," she said, reaching out a hand to gently touch his knee.

He raised an eyebrow at her. "Did *you* enjoy the show?"

"I . . . appreciated its ambitions," she said diplomatically, though what she *really* wanted to say was that she was rather in agreement with the marquess; she would have enjoyed one of the Belfry's bawdy shows significantly more.

He leaned forward, bracing his elbows on his knees. "You didn't like it, and I want you to say it."

Emily felt a touch indignant. "I didn't say that!"

"I know," he said, that slight quirk to his mouth threatening to turn into a full-fledged smile. "Which is why I want you to. Say something impolite. Tell the truth, even if it's rude." He gazed at her in that maddening way, everything from his tone to that superior arch of his eyebrow akin to a taunt.

"Fine," she said, crossing her arms over her chest. "The show wasn't my favorite."

"And?" he prompted.

"And," she said, taking a deep breath, "I thought it was a bit . . . pretentious." She was surprised how liberating she found it to express an unguarded opinion.

He reached out to take her hand, his thumb stroking across her palm, the feeling like a flicker of flame even through the fabric of her glove.

"I don't think comedies need to—to be *about* anything important, to be worthy of merit," she said, the words coming out in a rush. She felt a bit giddy, and glanced up at his face with a momentary pang of anxiety, wondering if she'd gone too far.

But he was smiling at her.

"I agree," he said simply.

"You do?" she faltered, then deflated. "Oh. Because your father didn't like it."

"No," he said, shaking his head as he tightened his grip on her hand. "Because I sat there and watched the same performance you did, and spent the entire time wishing my father had come to any other show. This isn't the sort of production I want to put on. My father reminded

291

me of that, yes—but I already knew it." He shook his head. "I should have listened to you long ago. The Belfry makes a sizable profit each year—why should I change anything about what I'm doing?"

"But I thought you wanted the approval of the *ton*," Emily said slowly, unable to understand the sinking feeling in the pit of her stomach. Wasn't this precisely what she'd wanted him to realize for weeks?

"Ah, again you were right all along," he said. His smile widened a bit, making him look entirely unlike the rakish, seductive Julian Belfry she'd first met on a night like this one, at the same theater they'd just departed, three months earlier. "I only wanted the approval of one particular member of the *ton*."

"Your father," she said softly.

"My father," he agreed. His face, which had brightened and grown more animated as he spoke, darkened again slightly at whatever he saw in her expression.

"What is it?" he asked. "I thought you'd be pleased. No more tedious litany of afternoon calls. You can simply be yourself—be Emily."

Be Emily.

But who, precisely, was that? She had spent so much of her life crafting a perfect version of herself—one who always spoke and acted a certain way, because that was how she was expected to speak and act.

And who was she to be now, if he no longer needed her to be the Emily he'd first met?

Did he have any use for her at all?

To him, of course, she said none of this. Instead, she did what she did so well, what she had always done: she pasted a bright, cheerful smile upon her face, and took great pains to ensure that not a single one of the thoughts currently swirling around in her mind was evident in her voice.

"This is such wonderful news," she said, still smiling. "We shall have to celebrate when we get home—drinks in the library, perhaps?"

"Are you all right?" he asked, frowning at her, and a momentary flash of panic gripped her. No, no, no. He mustn't see through her smile—her uncertainty.

"Of course," she said, waving him off.

He continued to regard her for a long, thoughtful moment.

"Yes," he said. "Let's have drinks. And then I'll take you upstairs and show you my *favorite* way to celebrate good news."

So they did, and he did. And Emily enjoyed every moment of it, as he must have known she would. But long after he had fallen asleep, she lay awake, curled up beside him in the enormous expanse of their bed, wondering how on earth she was going to bear life with a husband she'd accidentally fallen in love with—and who would shortly realize that he no longer needed her at all.

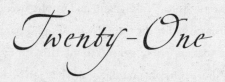

Twenty-One

"You look appalling," Diana said three nights later as they gathered in Emily's drawing room before dinner.

"Diana," Violet hissed, glancing around to make sure no one had heard her. "What on earth is the matter with you? Were you raised by wolves?"

"More or less," Diana said, unrepentant, continuing to fix Emily with a suspicious stare. "What is the matter with *you*, Emily, is the real question. Did you sleep at all last night? You've dark circles under your eyes, darling, this is most unsettling."

"She's a newlywed, Diana," Violet reminded her. "Perhaps sleeping is not her first priority."

"Violet Audley, there is no cause to be lewd," Diana said sternly, which had the effect of reducing Violet to indignant sputters, considering who was admonishing her. Emily rather suspected that this had been Diana's entire aim, since she wasted little time in redirecting her attention toward Emily herself.

"You hardly look like a woman who's enjoyed a healthy romp between the sheets," she said bluntly. "You look positively ill. Whatever is wrong?"

"Nothing," Emily said, but even to her own ears it was a pathetically unconvincing attempt at a protest. She sighed, then cast a quick glance around the room. Julian was deep in discussion with Bridgeworth and West, while Penvale and Bridgeworth's wife, Jemma, seemed to have hit it off. Lord James, Lord Willingham, and Sophie were chatting with evident enthusiasm before the mantel, while Emily's parents and Julian's seemed to be making polite conversation. This Emily watched with some trepidation, before abandoning it as a bad job—she couldn't hear what they were saying, and if her parents were saying something awful about her to Julian's parents, there wasn't anything she could do about it.

All of this meant, however, that Violet, Emily, and Diana did indeed have a brief moment of privacy in which to speak.

"Julian has mended things with his father," she said quietly, so quietly that her friends leaned closer to hear her.

"But that is a good thing, is it not?" Violet asked, her brow wrinkling in confusion.

"It is," Emily assured her, hating every single thought inside her head, thoughts which suddenly felt so petty and mean and selfish. "And their reconciliation seems to have made Julian realize that he does not need to be so fixated on propriety."

"Which is also a good thing?" Diana suggested.

"It is!" Emily agreed hastily.

"But . . . ?" Diana prompted.

"But nothing," Emily said, trying desperately to project an air of cheerful goodwill that she knew would not fool her friends for a second. "I'm delighted that he's come to this realization." She adopted a breezy, casual tone. "Of course, it means that the terms we agreed to upon marrying no longer really apply, and that he doesn't necessarily require a wife who will gain him the approbation of society, but that's all right. I always knew that we might not need to spend much time together, once our aims had been achieved. He's welcome to seek pleasure elsewhere, now that we needn't try so hard to appear the perfect society couple."

She hoped her voice hadn't cracked anywhere during that little speech, but she couldn't say for certain. She was suddenly feeling rather warm, she realized; her cheeks felt dreadfully hot, and she wished she had something to fan herself with.

"Emily," Violet said slowly, reaching out to grip Emily by the elbows and turn her so that her back was to the rest of the room, "have you discussed this with Belfry?"

"No," Emily said, continuing in that dreadful tone of feigned breeziness that even to her own ears sounded quite horrible. "There's nothing to discuss, of course."

Was there something wrong with her vision? Why were things suddenly looking blurry?

"Here," Diana said quietly, pressing a handkerchief into Emily's hand. She was about to protest that she needed no such thing, when all at once she realized that by blinking she had caused the tears that were blurring her gaze to spill over and splash down her cheeks.

Quickly, she pressed the handkerchief to her face, not daring a glance over her shoulder to see if anyone had noticed.

"All right," Violet said, her tone suddenly firm and businesslike. "Emily, I don't wish to upset you further—watching you cry is rather like watching a baby deer wander about looking for its mother—"

"*Excuse me?*" Emily began indignantly; she was sufficiently indignant, in fact, that her vision cleared, the film of tears receding, for which she supposed she should be grateful, at least.

Violet, however, ignored her interruption. "—but you do realize that you're in love with Belfry, don't you?"

"Of *course* I do," Emily hissed, beginning to get truly angry now. Did everyone think she was a complete idiot? "How could I possibly have failed to realize that, given that I am weeping in mixed company?"

"All right, all right," Violet said a bit defensively. "But you've never admitted as much, and I thought it possible you hadn't made that connection yet."

"I most certainly have," Emily said, still nettled, "but it doesn't matter, because I can't ever tell him! This wasn't our bargain! We had a perfectly reasonable agreement, and I've gone and ruined it by *falling in love*."

"You're starting to sound like me," Diana said cheerfully. "I promise you, Jeremy has only made me cry once—love isn't all bad."

"Do you not think it possible that Belfry might be in love with you, too?" Violet asked Emily. "I've seen the way he looks at you—and when the two of you are speaking together, you seem terribly—well..." She trailed off, clearly searching for the most appropriate word.

"Married?" Diana suggested.

"Precisely," Violet said.

"He's merely playing the role of dutiful husband," Emily said, but even as she uttered the words, she wasn't certain of their truth. *Was* that merely what he was doing? His behavior toward her publicly could certainly be explained away in such a fashion, but what about when they were alone? Whiling away an evening in the library before the fire, or in the peaceful sanctity of their bed at night? There was no one around to witness Julian's performance of a doting husband, and yet it was no less convincing than it was when they were around others.

The way he spoke with her, the way he listened to her, the way he kissed her—and more . . . it was all very like how he might behave if theirs was a love match. If he loved her.

"Are you certain?" Violet asked gently.

And all at once, she wasn't. She wasn't certain of anything. She felt as if the ground were shifting beneath her feet, and she had nothing to hold on to. It had all been so terrible and wonderful to realize that she loved her husband, this man she had married for entirely practical reasons, but to now have even the faintest hope that he loved her too, when it was nothing more than that—a hope, something that might not prove to be true after all. . . .

Well, it was too much to bear.

She had to know the truth.

She needed to ask him.

But unfortunately, she was in the middle of a drawing room full of people, including her parents—and while she might, in a moment of uncharacteristic recklessness, be willing to tell her husband she loved him before their dearest friends, she was entirely unwilling to share that moment with her parents. Her parents who, had they been left to their own devices, would still be allowing Mr. Cartham to squire her about town.

"No," she said to Violet, in response to her question. "I'm not certain at all."

But she intended to find out. Perhaps she could ask Julian for a word—all at once, the thought of sitting through the evening ahead with this conversation looming over her was too much to bear—and with this thought in mind, she took a couple of hesitant steps in his direction—

Before tripping over something small, furry, and currently yowling.

"Cecil!" she exclaimed, scooping the kitten up into her arms. "How did you get in here?" When last she had seen him, he'd been curled up on a bed of cushions before the fireplace in her bedroom, and yet here he was. "Did I step on you?" she asked, cradling him close to her chest; at this gesture, he stopped his wailing and commenced purring instead.

"That cat is positively diabolical," Diana said in admiring tones, watching Emily drop a kiss onto Cecil's nose. "Emily, I'm surprised you haven't yet crafted him a litter to carry him about the house, merely to ensure he doesn't get trodden upon."

"I don't think he would sit still in one," Emily said entirely seriously, taking comfort in the feeling of Cecil's purrs vibrating against her chest. "Besides—"

"*Emily.*"

She glanced up, startled, to see her mother crossing the room toward her. Belatedly, Emily realized that her mother was not aware of Cecil's existence, he having been left to doze in the carriage when she and Julian had called to inform her parents of their marriage.

"What are you doing with that creature?" her mother asked, coming to a halt beside her and staring down at Cecil's face with some distaste; behind her, Emily could see Julian's parents craning their necks to try to see what had caught Lady Rowanbridge's attention, their expressions puzzled.

"He's mine," Emily said, cradling Cecil protectively; he plainly did not like being squeezed, and let out a plaintive *meow* of protest. Emily loosened her grip on him as her mother continued to stare at her as though she'd taken leave of her senses. "I found him in an inn Julian and I stayed at on our return journey to London," she explained. "No one could account for him, so Julian and I decided to adopt him."

This was, admittedly, a bit of a stretch, given Julian's lack of enthusiasm, but just then, the man in question appeared at her side, his clear blue gaze inquiring.

"Is everything all right?" he asked politely.

"Mama was just—" Emily began, before being immediately interrupted.

"I was trying to determine how on earth Emily came to be in possession of this flea-ridden creature," her mother said, positively bristling with indignation. Her mother despised cats, and so Emily had never been allowed one before; on one memorable occasion, Violet had helped her hide a litter of kittens from her mother for an entire month before she'd been caught out and forced to give the kittens in question away to various friends.

"I don't believe Cecil has fleas, my lady," Julian said, still with utter politeness. "In fact, considering his humble origins, I find it remarkable what fine fettle he is in—Emily has taken good care of him."

For a moment, Emily was rendered speechless; Violet appeared to be trying not to laugh, while Diana wore an expression of supremely knowing smugness. Julian had called him *Cecil*, not *Cecil Lucifer Beelzebub*. He had *defended* him. And, much as she might hold out hope for an eventual change of heart toward Cecil on Julian's part, Emily did not for one second believe that Julian's defense of Cecil had been done out of any great affection for their feline companion.

He had done it for her.

Emily reflected that she must be growing older, if the starry-eyed fantasies of her girlhood involving handsome knights on horseback had instead come to this: standing speechless with a lump in her throat because her husband had spoken kindly of a small kitten whose appearance could only—with extreme charity—be described as unkempt.

"Lord Julian, you might wish to take a firmer hand with Emily," her mother said, her gaze fixed on Emily. Emily once would have been cowed by that stern look in her mother's eye—Mama was never one to raise her voice, but Emily was always so eager to please that the merest suggestion of her mother's displeasure had always been sufficient to send her scrambling to mend whatever she'd done to incur that disapproval.

But no longer.

"Mama, it's a kitten—there's no need to cause a scene," Emily said, straightening; Cecil, with his usual impeccable sense of timing, chose that moment to launch himself out of her arms in some sort of demented bid for freedom. Julian, without missing a beat, caught Cecil with one hand, tucking him under his arm with a sure grip.

"*I* am not the one parading an oversize rat around in polite company," her mother said, looking positively horrified, and Emily all at once found she had had quite enough. She had spent most of her life trying to please her mother—had sacrificed Season after Season to doing as her parents wished, doing her part to preserve the family reputation—but *this*, an insult to Cecil, was simply too much.

"He is not a rat, Mama," she said, lifting her chin and meeting her mother's gaze dead-on. "He is a kitten, and he is *my* kitten, and we are in *my* home, so I will do as I see fit, and I will not have you lecturing me about it."

"I was hardly—"

"You were," Emily said calmly, marveling at the clear, steady tone of her voice. For so long, in the rare moments she allowed herself to imagine speaking her mind to her mother, she'd worried that she'd become emotional, that her voice would waver, that she wouldn't find the right words. And yet, now that the time had come, she had no difficulty in saying her piece.

"Mama, I love you, but I am not yours to command anymore—and I am not Julian's, either. Cecil is *my* kitten, and if I wish to place him in the centerpiece on the dining room table so that we all might admire his adorable little paws, I'll do just that." She paused, considering. "Though I will grant you that I do not believe his paws to be the cleanest portion of his anatomy, so perhaps it would be better if he were not in such close proximity to the food."

"Emily." Julian's voice was amused, and she snuck a glance at him out of the corner of her eye, pleased to see the smile curving his lips.

Her mother, meanwhile, gave every indication of preparing for a display of wounded offense.

"I was merely trying to ensure that you knew how to act a proper hostess—a proper wife," her mother said.

"I already know how to do that, Mama," Emily said, striving to keep exasperation from entering her voice. "I lived with you for twenty-three years; I spent six Seasons under your wing. But I am married now," she added, her tone growing firmer, "and I am perfectly capable of taking care of myself. I'm sorry that you disapprove of my marriage, but I—" Here she faltered, took a breath, then plunged on. "I'm very happy, and if you cannot see fit to accept that, then I've no interest in inviting you to my home again anytime soon."

"What is wrong, Mary?" came her father's voice now, close at hand; Emily had been so focused on her mother that she had not even noticed his approach.

Emily's mother paused for a long moment before answering, her gaze on Emily unwavering.

"Nothing," she said after a moment, her voice softer than usual. "It is just—I am feeling unwell, all of a sudden." Emily held her breath, willing herself not to feel disappointed when her parents left early, her mind already on the seating arrangement at dinner, how she would move guests around in the wake of their absence. "But I think it is passing," her mother said after another moment, and Emily exhaled slowly, Julian's hand suddenly at her waist, a warm, comforting weight.

"Perhaps we should return to our discussion with Lord and Lady Eastvale," Lady Rowanbridge added—a bit stiffly, it was true, but Emily was not inclined to complain as she watched her parents cross the room to where Julian's parents still stood. Her mother's spine was stiff, irritation writ clearly into the lines of her body—but she was still here. She had stayed.

"Emily, I could positively weep with joy," Diana said, glee evident in her voice. "You were brilliant."

"You were," Julian murmured in her ear, sending warmth coursing through her, but then he was placing Cecil back in her arms with a dark look, muttering about bloodshed, and there were guests to be spoken with, a dinner to preside over, and little time at all for Emily to reflect on the wonderful and terrible fact of how desperately she loved her husband—and how desperately she wanted him to love her, too.

Twenty-Two

"I should have known it would storm on my wedding day," Diana grumbled a few days later, though Emily found it difficult to take her complaints seriously, given that she was suppressing a smile with great effort. "I suppose this is some sort of omen, and Jeremy and I shall end up murdering each other before the year is out," Diana continued, before adding philosophically, "Perhaps we should wager on who will end up killing whom."

"Diana," Violet said, affection and exasperation evident in equal measure in her tone, "do you think you could perhaps wait until after the wedding before you start contemplating killing Jeremy?"

"If you insist," Diana said with a shrug, in the tone of someone humoring an unreasonable request but not willing to argue the point. She surveyed herself in the mirror in her bedroom—shortly to be her bedroom no longer; this was, Emily realized, the last time she and Violet would ever visit Diana at this house, where she'd lived for the five years since her marriage to her first husband. Diana was wearing a gown of green silk embroidered with white flowers, lace at her sleeves, a bonnet nowhere in sight.

"Where are my flowers?" Diana asked, turning away from the mirror to face Emily and Violet, who were alone in the room with her. Diana's ill-tempered lady's maid had departed a few minutes earlier.

"Downstairs," Violet said, smiling, and forbearing to point out that this was the second time she'd answered this question. For all of Diana's bravado, she was still nervous. It was odd to think of Diana as being nervous about anything, much less a wedding—even her *own* wedding. She certainly had not displayed any sign of nerves at her first wedding, Emily recalled, despite the fact that she'd been a girl of merely eighteen.

There was a tap at the door, and Penvale poked his head into the room. "Are you ready?" he asked his sister, his gaze softening as he regarded Diana in her wedding finery. "The carriage is downstairs, and Jeremy and Audley are already at St. George's. It would be cruel to force anyone to stare at Jeremy in that waistcoat for a moment longer than necessary."

"What I *believe* you mean," Diana said briskly, "is that it would be cruel to deny *me* the sight of him in that waistcoat for a moment longer than necessary." She crossed the room to her brother, Violet and Emily trailing in her wake, and took his proffered arm.

"Diana," Penvale said, resisting her attempt to tug her out the door.

"What?" she asked impatiently. "Waistcoats await us, Penvale! The most horrifying waistcoat known to mankind, in fact!"

"You look beautiful," he said simply, leaning down to press a quick kiss to her cheek, and Emily felt an unexpected rush of tears spring to her eyes.

"I love you, Penvale, but if we don't leave this room in five seconds, these two"—Diana jerked a thumb over her shoulder—"will turn into watering pots, and I refuse to tolerate that."

And with this heartfelt exchange of sibling affection, they were off.

"It really is appalling," Emily whispered to Julian as she took her seat next to him in a pew at St. George's, her eyes on Willingham as she spoke.

Julian spared a glance for the groom—the most noticeable thing about his appearance, as Emily had noted, was the truly awful waistcoat he was wearing. It was a yellow paisley pattern and was, quite honestly, the single ugliest article of clothing Julian had ever seen in his life. Furthermore, it did nothing so much as highlight the fact that Willingham was looking rather more pale than usual.

"However much money Lady Templeton spent having that made, it was too much," he said in an undertone.

"I feel certain Diana would disagree with you," Emily said with a smile that lit up her whole face. She looked lovely today—she always looked lovely, he supposed, but she was positively glowing, clad in a demure gown of butter yellow that was a far cry from the garish hue that Willingham was sporting. Her hair was pulled back neatly from her face, a flowered bonnet firmly in place, and her eyes were shining as she gazed up at the waiting groom.

Wait. Were they shining, or were they *glistening*?

"Are you crying?" he demanded.

"Of course not," she said, her voice giving a telltale waver. "I may have shed a tear or two before we left Diana's house, but I'm quite done now." Her lip trembled as she continued to look determinedly ahead.

"If it's the waistcoat that's making you weep, I can't say I blame you," he said, and was rewarded with an unsteady smile. Those smiles of hers had at some point become something precious to him— something to be earned, something worth the effort to win.

"It's not the waistcoat," she said, her voice unsteady. "Or, rather, it's not the waistcoat *itself*—it's what it *represents*."

"Bad taste?" he suggested.

"Love!" she said indignantly, then glanced sideways, caught sight of his teasing grin, and elbowed him gently. "Don't be unsentimental and practical today of all days, Julian. My dearest friend—who swore she'd never marry again—is about to walk down the aisle toward a man wearing the ugliest waistcoat ever made, just because he loves her. This is a lovely day."

Further comment on his part was forestalled by the appearance of the bride on the arm of her brother, and as the wedding guests rose to watch her proceed down the aisle, Julian glanced forward at her waiting groom—and froze.

Willingham was standing at the front of the church, clad in that hideous waistcoat, wearing an expression that made it perfectly clear that he considered himself to be the luckiest man in all of England. His attention was focused entirely on Diana as she walked down the aisle toward him—somehow without laughing or recoiling in horror at the sight that awaited her—and in that moment it was perfectly obvious that Willingham would have worn that waistcoat every day for the rest of his life, if that was the cost of marrying Diana.

And all at once Julian had the most startling thought: he would wear that waistcoat, too.

If Emily came to him and demanded it, he'd put the bloody thing on—complaining all the while, naturally—and parade around before her until she collapsed into laughter.

He loved making her smile, making her laugh.

He loved *her*.

And what was truly galling was that it had taken a waistcoat that was an offense to God and man alike to make him realize it.

"Jesus," he muttered under his breath, suppressing a wild desire to laugh.

"Julian!" Emily hissed. "We are in *church*!"

"Of course we are," he murmured, casting a dark look upward, waiting to be struck down by lightning at any moment. Of course he would be in a bloody *church*, of all places, surrounded by a good portion of the *ton*—including, several rows away, his parents and brother, with whom he'd made gloriously unstilted conversation while waiting for Emily to arrive—when he realized that he was in love with his wife.

And now he had to wait to tell her.

Emily wasn't certain whether it was the wedding or the champagne that had made her bold, but she was undoubtedly not feeling entirely like herself at the moment.

Diana and Jeremy's wedding breakfast—hosted at Violet and Lord James's house on Curzon Street—was a long, festive affair stretching well into the afternoon. The newlyweds at last departed for Lord Willingham's house in Fitzroy Square amid a chorus of well-wishes, though the last words anyone heard Diana call out the carriage door were, "If you don't stop carrying on so much, I'll cancel this evening's ball." No one took her threat terribly seriously, given that Diana had already extracted a promise from her new husband that he would wear his waistcoat to that evening's festivities as well.

The rest of the party broke up at that point, with people scattering for their various homes for the chance to rest for a few hours before presenting themselves in their evening finery. Emily and Julian lingered for some time—she found herself deep in conversation with Julian's mother, who had welcomed her into the family with the joy that only a mother who had long since despaired of her rakehell of a son ever marrying could muster.

"Emily," Julian said, appearing at her shoulder as she was listening to the marchioness explain why Julian had been such a particularly fussy baby. "Are you ready to go home?"

"Hardly," she said, barely sparing her husband a glance. "Your mother was just explaining to me how you were prone to promptly vomiting back up whatever food you were given as an infant."

Lady Eastvale smiled mistily. "He made up for it by being such a darling baby, of course. Those chubby cheeks!" She reached up to pinch one of the cheeks in question, despite the fact that her son was nearly a foot taller than she and glowering threateningly.

"Julian," Emily said earnestly, "perhaps this explains your particular bond with darling Cecil. He does have that same unseemly habit, you know."

Julian's glower deepened. "I will thank you to never compare me to that mangy ball of fluff ever again."

Emily, however, was unfazed by his malignment of Cecil after his defense the other night.

"Mother, I am going to steal Emily away now," he said, stooping to kiss Lady Eastvale on the cheek; out of the corner of her eye, Emily saw Lord Eastvale several feet away, watching this casual moment between his wife and son. She glanced down and bit her lip to prevent a smile.

Several minutes later, she and Julian were alone in their carriage, rattling across the London streets the short distance from Violet's house to their own, a comfortable silence between them.

Or, rather, it *should* have been a comfortable silence. And it would have been, if Julian had not spent the past couple of minutes staring at her with an unreadable expression upon his face.

"What is it?" Emily burst out at last, taken aback by her own boldness. Emily Turner never would have demanded a reply from a gentleman in such a fashion—but Emily Turner and Emily Belfry, she had learned, were two different people.

She found that she vastly preferred the latter.

Julian raised an eyebrow. "Is something the matter?"

"*You* are," she said bluntly. "You're making me nervous."

"Am I?" he asked, brow still raised, wearing an arch expression that Emily should not have found half so attractive as she did.

"Now you're doing it on purpose," she said grumpily, crossing her arms. "I do hate when people attempt to disconcert me for sport."

Julian frowned. "I wasn't doing any such thing."

"Then *why* were you looking at me?" she asked huffily, beginning to find the entire conversation tiresome, and wondering if perhaps drinking champagne at noon was not, in fact, the wisest course of action.

"I was *trying* to work out how to tell you something," Julian said, frustration evident in his voice.

"Well, just come out with it then," she said impatiently. Dimly, she realized how little care she was taking with her tone; her desire to project nothing but sweetness and demure grace was entirely absent, and she didn't mind one bit.

"Fine," he bit out. "I love you."

A brief silence fell.

"Oh, this is too unfair!" Emily wailed, lifting her hands to her mouth to stifle a wild desire to laugh.

"I beg your pardon?" Julian asked, nonplussed.

"*I* was going to tell *you* that I loved you, and I've been trying to work out the best way to do so for *days*, and now you've beaten me to it!" she said, unable to suppress her giggles.

"I—what?" Julian asked, lifting a hand to rub at his forehead in a way that made Emily giggle harder. She hiccupped loudly, and then dissolved into laughter once more; Julian began to regard her with something approaching alarm.

"I love you," she repeated. "I know that wasn't our bargain," she said, her eyes locking with his. "I know that ours was intended to be a marriage of convenience, that love wasn't part of the deal, that we were—we were simply to be of use to each other, to be friends and nothing more, nothing deeper, but I *love* you and I don't know when it started but now I can't imagine *not* loving you, and I don't even want to, because you're my—my favorite person! And I was going to tell *you* first!"

She fell silent, trying to control her rapid breathing, feeling her heart pounding in her chest.

"Emily," Julian said, and then paused—and in that pause, Emily, who normally had no problem holding her tongue, who was never one for ceaseless babbling, rushed in.

"I know that you don't *need* me anymore, for our original agreement, but—"

"Emily," Julian interrupted, sounding half-amused, half-frustrated. "Will you let me speak?"

Emily clamped her lips shut and gave him a pointed look. One side of his mouth quirked up, causing one single dimple to appear in his cheek, and her traitorous heart nearly exploded at the sight. Dimples were dangerous things.

Or perhaps it was just Julian who was dangerous.

"Have you noticed," he said, his tone almost conversational, "that you've never actually been that convenient to me?"

"Excuse me?" she asked stiffly, shrinking back into her seat; Julian reached out a hand to grasp hers, however, his grip comfortingly tight.

"Lurking around the theater. Insulting ladies you were supposed to impress. Being quite determined to be nothing at all like the Emily I thought you were when I met you," he said, holding up his fingers one by one. "This has never really gone according to plan."

She opened her mouth, then shut it again, not certain what response she could offer.

"But," Julian continued, before she could make any attempt at a reply, "have you also not noticed that I don't care?"

"What do you mean?" she asked.

"I don't care about impressing insufferable ladies who would insult you. I don't mind having you haunting the Belfry—I rather *like* it, in fact, because it gives me an excuse to see you, and seeing you is the best part of any day."

"It is?" she asked, her heart now pounding so rapidly in her chest that she felt as though it were going to launch itself out of her body entirely—which, aside from being anatomically impossible, sounded like a frightfully messy business, too.

"And," he continued, that piercing blue gaze pinning her in place, making it impossible to glance anywhere else, "I like the Emily you are ever so much more than the Emily I met. I like when you speak your mind. I like when you argue with me. I like when you are bold. And even if I didn't like all of that, it wouldn't matter one damned bit, because *you* like it. And that, Emily, is all that matters to me.

"I love you," he said, more softly this time. "The evening you walked into my box at the Belfry was the best evening of my entire life." He reached out his free arm to wrap around her waist, pulling her out of her seat and unceremoniously onto his lap before she quite realized what had happened. "I would wear a bloody yellow waistcoat for you, even, if you asked it of me."

"Don't make promises you don't intend to keep," she said breathlessly, her eyes locked onto his, trying desperately not to allow the tears that were filling her eyes to spill.

"I won't," he murmured, lowering his head to hers. It was perhaps a minute or several centuries later when he lifted his head from hers. "But just to be clear—I didn't actually promise to wear a yellow waistcoat. You do understand that?"

"Not yet, at least," she said cheerfully, pulling his head back down to hers, and smiled against his mouth as she felt his answering grin.

Twenty-Three

"*My head is still aching,*" *Emily said ruefully on Thursday morning* of the following week as she stepped down from the carriage in front of the Belfry. *Morning,* truth be told, might have been a stretch—she was fairly certain she'd heard the bells of St. Martin's tolling the noon hour just a minute ago—but now wasn't the time to quibble over details.

"I'm not surprised," Julian said, sounding amused as he handed her down and shut the carriage door behind her. "How many glasses of sherry did you have?"

"Two," Emily said with great dignity, trying not to squint in the sunlight. In actuality, it had been three. The previous evening had been a festive one, with the wine flowing liberally at a dinner party hosted by Violet and Lord James, and it had been well past midnight before they'd arrived home, whereupon they'd retired to their bedroom and proceeded to not get very much sleep at all.

Today, however, Julian had risen in the late morning, and had bundled a protesting Emily out of bed, downstairs to breakfast, and into the carriage before she quite knew what had happened. It was an unseasonably beautiful late-autumn day, the sky a perfectly crisp blue, a few wispy white clouds scuttling overhead on a faint breeze. Emily shivered and was glad she'd at least had the good sense to put on her spencer—it was a new one in a rich shade of green wool that she thought looked quite fetching on her—before allowing herself to be hauled from her perfectly warm home. Not that she felt particularly fetching at the moment, truth be told—her hair had been hastily braided into a knot at the nape of her neck, but strands of it were already coming loose around her face, no doubt completing the picture of a lady who was feeling decidedly rumpled.

"We're at . . . the Belfry," she said, stating the obvious as she blinked up at the building before her.

"We are," Julian agreed cheerfully, looking maddeningly unaffected by the previous evening's excesses. She was quite certain he'd had a good deal more to drink than she had, but he looked as fresh as a daisy, his cheeks slightly flushed in the cool wind, that rakish lock of hair doing all sorts of rakish flopping on his forehead. It all seemed distinctly unfair to her—but then, as Diana would say, such was the life of a woman.

"Is there a reason we are here at the Belfry and not at home in bed?" Emily asked, striving to keep her voice pleasant. The past week had passed in a blissful blur—it would be a shame to ruin it with a sleep-deprivation-caused argument with her husband.

"Tempting as that does sound," Julian agreed, keeping her hand tightly gripped in his as he led her up the steps, "I have something to show you."

He proceeded to lead her into the theater and through its hallways, Emily struggling to remain patient despite her curiosity. Eventually they drew to a halt before Julian's office door.

Emily looked at him inquiringly. "You do realize I've been here before, don't you?"

Julian, however, merely looked smug, the infuriating man. "Do you need your eyes checked, wife? Perhaps you might take a second glance at the door."

Narrowing her eyes at him, Emily did as instructed—and then went still. Perhaps she *did* need spectacles—she wasn't sure how she hadn't noticed it before. There, on the nondescript wooden door before her, was the plaque with Julian's name—and then, directly below it, one that read EMILY BELFRY.

There was nothing so terribly remarkable about it, a simple brass plaque with her name printed plainly, and yet Emily felt a strange emotion course through her at the sight, her name there on the door beneath her husband's, a signifier that, in this world so different from the one she had been born to, she had a place where she was welcome—where she belonged.

"Julian," she said, her eyes still fixed on the plaque before her, but before she could continue, he interrupted.

"Let's look inside, shall we?" he asked, opening the door and then stepping back to allow her to pass through before him. Stepping into the office, it was impossible not to notice that the furniture had been moved; whereas previously Julian's desk had dominated the back wall, that space was now lined with bookshelves, Julian's desk having been moved to the left wall instead.

And against the right wall was another desk.

Her desk.

There was a soft *click* as the door shut behind them, and Emily took a few steps into the room, reaching a hand out to run along the wood of the desk that would be hers. It was empty at the moment, barring a pen and inkwell, and—she stopped.

A script.

She took another step closer, reaching down to pick up the first page.

The Talk of the Ton.

She whirled around, and Julian was there, behind her.

"You were right," he said simply. "It's a good idea. Let's roast the *ton*, and make them all come here to watch it—most of the ladies who come out of curiosity won't return, but some . . . perhaps some will. And in any case, the ones that won't return aren't the ones we need to be worried about, anyway."

He stepped forward to take the piece of paper from her unresisting hand and place it back on the desk.

"I know who you think I saw you as, when we agreed to wed—I know you think I married you because you were perfect and well-behaved and had already proven that you could emerge unscathed from even the muckiest of scandals. But Emily, there is no other prim and proper debutante in all of London I would have even considered marrying for a second—from the moment I met you, I could not stop thinking about you. The parts of you that always fascinated me the most—well, they weren't the parts of you that paint lovely watercolors or make polite drawing room conversation. It's the Emily who speaks her mind, who meddles at the theater, who tells her parents and her husband exactly what she thinks—that's the Emily I fell in love with. Glimpses of that Emily were the reason I married you in the first place. And I'd like to spend the rest of our lives making sure you never again doubt that I want you for who you truly are."

Emily could feel a tear tracing a path down her cheek, and made no move to brush it away; instead, she reached a hand up to cover the hand of his that now cupped her face.

"I don't think you'll regret this, Julian—I think the play will be brilliant, and you'll be the talk of the town."

"For better or for worse," he agreed, his mouth quirking to one side in that way that she adored. "But so long as you're there on opening night, I don't much care who else is."

"I do love you," she said, hooking an arm up around his neck and standing on her toes to press a kiss to his lips. Pulling back a moment later, she added, "I never would have imagined a desk could be so romantic."

"Even more romantic than a waistcoat?" he asked, a bit of smugness evident in his voice. In fairness, she supposed he'd earned it.

"I don't know if I'd go that far," she replied, mock-thoughtful.

"I would," he said, resting a hand at her waist, pulling her slightly closer. "In fact, I think I'd be perfectly happy to never discuss waistcoats with you ever again." He pressed a gentle kiss to her jaw. "Out of an abundance of caution, you understand."

"Julian?" she said, a bit breathless.

"Mmm?" His mouth was occupied with the spot where her jawline met her neck, his hand trailing from her cheek along her throat and then lower, lower.

"I love you," she said. "But I'd really prefer we didn't speak anymore at the moment, if you must know."

"Something else in mind?" he murmured against her mouth.

"How sturdy do you think this desk is?" she asked, her heartbeat already accelerating as he began to walk her backward.

"Shall we find out?" he asked and Emily nodded, her mouth rather occupied at the moment.

And as they had cause to learn—on that morning, and on many other occasions to come—her desk was very sturdy indeed.

Author's Note

The very earliest idea for Emily and Julian's story came to me several years ago, while I was still writing an early draft of my debut novel, *To Have and to Hoax*. I had the good fortune at this time to happen to read a fascinating book: *The Secret Rooms* by Catherine Bailey, which I cannot recommend highly enough if you enjoy really gripping narrative nonfiction.

It's about Belvoir Castle, the ancestral home of the Duke of Rutland, and it uncovers some rather unseemly family history—parts of it read like fiction; it's truly that interesting. What caught my attention in this book, however, was the story of Lady Diana Manners, the daughter of the eighth Duke of Rutland (officially, at least; she was actually a product of one of her mother's affairs). Diana was famous across the country for her beauty, and during the First World War, her mother— desperate to keep her son, John, the heir to the dukedom, safely away from the front lines—took advantage of the fact that an American millionaire named George Gordon Moore both was obsessed with Diana *and* wielded peculiar influence over his close friend Sir John French, who was commander in chief of the British troops in France.

Essentially, Diana was ordered to encourage Moore's attentions so that he might intercede on her family's behalf with Sir John and ensure that Diana's brother stayed out of the trenches. The entire arrangement was quite sordid—Bailey interprets some of Diana's mother's letters as going so far as to encourage her daughter to actually seduce Moore—but I am happy to report that Diana eventually went on to become a nurse in the war, against her mother's wishes, and then marry a man her mother didn't approve of (Duff Cooper, who went on to become a rather famous diplomat). She also had a successful career onstage as an actress.

This bit of Diana Manners's personal history stuck with me; I remember thinking what great material for a romance novel it would make. And then it occurred to me that *I* was writing a romance novel (albeit one set one hundred years earlier than Diana lived) and, furthermore, that I had already written a secondary character, Lady Emily Turner, whose personal history I was at that very moment trying to sort out. The character of Mr. Cartham was directly inspired by George Gordon Moore (both were Americans, very wealthy, and looked down upon by members of the British upper class) and while I've written Emily's arrangement with Cartham to be rather less seedy than Diana's with Moore, the former was absolutely inspired by the latter. Diana's later career as an actress was also what inspired me to have Emily matched with an actor. I knew I could not have her appear onstage, given that this would have resulted in her being cast out of polite society, so I decided to create a character who was an actor, but who also had an aristocratic pedigree that would make it more likely that Emily and her friends would cross paths with him. Thus, the groundwork for her romance with Julian Belfry was laid, years before I would actually come to write their story.

I'd also be remiss not to note that I've taken a few liberties with history when it comes to the world of Regency theater. The patent theaters that Julian references a few times in this book, about which I never go into much detail, are the Theatre Royal Covent Garden, and the Theatre Royal Drury Lane, the two London theaters that had royal patents, which licensed them to perform spoken drama. (The patent system that placed these strict limitations on theaters was established under the Licensing Act of 1737 and would eventually be abolished, but not until 1843.) In *To Have and to Hoax*, I refer to Julian having obtained a royal patent to perform spoken drama during the summer months, when the patent theaters were closed—this was a loophole that *did* exist, but the Haymarket was the only theater in London that had the limited summer patent. (And if the Belfry *had* obtained such a patent, it would have had "Theatre Royal" tagged onto its name—which, frankly, seemed like a bit of a mouthful, so I cheerfully dispensed with this.) In any case, the Belfry's lack of a patent for most of the year is the reason that, in this book, they intersperse their production of *Macbeth* with musical numbers (employing a trick many theaters employed to get around the limitations of the patent system, whereby spoken words were accompanied by music), which would be employed in *Much Ado About Heaven* and *The Talk of the Ton* as well.

If you're curious to learn more about the history of theaters in Britain—both during the Regency and before and after—then I highly recommend *The Time Traveller's Guide to British Theatre* by Aleks Sierz and Lia Ghilardi, which was extremely helpful as I attempted to decide, as ever, precisely how closely I wished to adhere to historical fact, and how much history I wanted to sacrifice for the sake of good fiction.

Acknowledgments

I heard a lot about the difficulties of writing a second book, but personally found writing this, my third, to be the biggest creative challenge of my life. I wrote the entirety of this book during a global pandemic, and it was such a struggle to give Emily and Julian—two characters I love wholeheartedly, and have dreamed of writing a book about for years—the fun, joyful story they deserved. My gratitude to the following people is honestly limitless:

My agent, Taylor Haggerty, who fielded a series of increasingly hysterical emails from me over the course of the summer and fall of 2020, and who was a calm, cheerful, comforting voice of reason when I needed it the most.

My editor, Kaitlin Olson, who had such a smart, clear-eyed vision for this book, and who helped steer me in the right direction when I really needed it.

Everyone at Root Literary and at Atria, including (but not remotely limited to) Jasmine Brown, Jade Hui, Katelyn Phillips, Megan

Rudloff, Sherry Wasserman, and Polly Watson, as well as the lovely overseas editors who have brought my books to readers around the world.

Sarah Hogle, who was the first person other than my agent and editor to read this book, and who offered really thoughtful feedback, in addition to being an all-around excellent friend and sounding board for all my ideas (and complaints!). I'll forever be grateful for the twist of debut day fate that led us to each other.

The many, many writers who have been so generous and supportive of my work—they are too numerous to name, but at various times in the past year, I've been particularly grateful for the enthusiasm and kindness of Manda Collins, Evie Dunmore, Emily Henry, Kaitlyn Hill, India Holton, Natalie Jenner, Susan Lee, Rachel McMillan, and Hannah Orenstein.

The readers, reviewers, bloggers, booksellers, and librarians who make up the online book community, who are so critical in getting the word out about books they love.

And, finally, my family, friends, former coworkers, and entire Chapel Hill community, who listened to me complain about this book an unreasonable amount, helped me celebrate not one but *two* pandemic book launches in the most fun, safe way possible, and supported me when I decided to move to Maine on a total whim in the middle of a pandemic. This book is about Emily being brave and choosing a life of her own making—thank you so much for loving and supporting me as I've tried to do the same.

About the Author

MARTHA WATERS is the author of *To Have and to Hoax* and *To Love and to Loathe*. She was born and raised in sunny South Florida and is a graduate of the University of North Carolina at Chapel Hill. She lives in coastal Maine, where she works as a children's librarian by day, and loves sundresses, gin cocktails, and traveling.

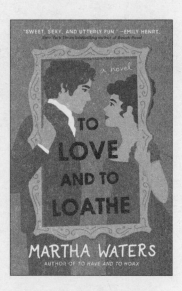